A SCANDALOUS MAN

About the Author

Gavin Esler was born in 1953 in Glasgow. He began his career in print journalism on the Belfast Telegraph. He then joined the BBC as their Northern Ireland correspondent. After a short stint on Newsnight he was made Washington correspondent in 1989 and Chief North America correspondent a year later. In 1997 he became the anchor for BBC News 24 reporting from all over the world. He returned to Newsnight in 2003.

Visit www.AuthorTracker.co.uk for exclusive updates on Gavin Esler.

D1638757

GAVIN ESLER

A Scandalous Man

HARPER

Harper
An imprint of HarperCollins*Publishers*
77–85 Fulham Palace Road,
Hammersmith, London W6 8JB

www.harpercollins.co.uk

This paperback edition

1

First published in Great Britain by
HarperCollins*Publishers* 2008

Copyright © Gavin Esler 2008

Gavin Esler asserts the moral right to
be identified as the author of this work

A catalogue record for this book
is available from the British Library

ISBN: 978 000 7280919

All
repr
in
phot

This b
way of tr
circulat
bindin
wi

Mixed Sources
Product group from well-managed
forests and other controlled sources
www.fsc.org Cert no. SW-COC-1806
© 1996 Forest Stewardship Council

FSC is a non-profit international organisation established to promote the
responsible management of the world's forests. Products carrying the FSC
label are independently certified to assure consumers that they come
from forests that are managed to meet the social, economic and
ecological needs of present and future generations.

Find out more about HarperCollins and the environment at
www.harpercollins.co.uk/green

This book is dedicated to my friends from Iran, Turkey and the Arab world, India and Pakistan, whose friendship and love inspires me.

Acknowledgements

I would like to thank a number of people for their help. Two have been outstanding. My agent Toby Eady was from the start utterly enthusiastic about the idea of a political novel. At every stage he urged me on. It would not have been written without him. And my editor at HarperCollins, Susan Watt, showed similar enthusiasm from the very beginning and – I'm delighted to say – is an editor who actually edits. I'd also like to acknowledge the Scott report as a source for some of the information on Iraq, and Alan Clark's diaries for offering a flavour of Westminster in the Thatcher years. Others who have helped me would best stay in the shadows, but they know who they are, and I have thanked them individually for their help. The errors are mine, and I have taken considerable liberties with – among other things – the way trains run on the London Underground.

Too long a sacrifice
Can make a stone of the heart.
Oh, when may it suffice?

Easter, 1916. W. B. YEATS

Birds make great sky circles of their freedom.
How do they learn it?
They fall,
And falling, they're given wings.

Rumi, PERSIAN POET, *13th Century*

London, Spring 2005

Father was murdered today. Or it might have been yesterday. He might even have tried to kill himself. No one can say for certain, and that is typical of father, slippery and devious to the end. The television news said he is not dead yet, or not quite. He was found in a pool of blood on the floor of his cottage, clinging to life. My first thought was that I hoped he survived long enough to suffer.

I heard the news late because I had my mobile phone switched off all day, working, and because I had a row with my client. This never happens. I am too polite for that kind of thing, but he was an up-himself New York corporate lawyer for a private equity firm that was trying to buy up half of eastern Europe, and I was helping them. I'm not particularly proud of it, but there you are. Not many people in London speak fluent Czech, and they paid me five times my normal fee for a bit of translation and a bit of interpreting, and probably would have paid me twenty times if I'd had the nerve to ask. The New York lawyer and I finished going through the paperwork enabling his company to buy a sizeable slice of the Czech economy which he told me he intended to 'remodel'. He signed the contract as I spoke to his opposite number in

Prague confirming the deal. At the same time he talked to his office in Manhattan. I could hear him gloating.

'Get Karl and the boys down from Frankfurt,' he told New York. 'Pink slip everything that breathes and flatten everything that doesn't. Terminate all contracts. We need everybody out of all sites and everything levelled with immediate effect. We need this turned by the end of the year.'

I was at the other end of the room but could still hear him yakking. He told me to give him the thumbs up the moment I had confirmation the contract was signed in Prague. When I did so, he told New York, 'It's done,' and then put the phone down. He was beaming, as if he had just had sex. Maybe at that point he needed someone to boast to and I was the only one in the room. Whatever the reason he turned to me and said that in that one instant, in that one stroke of a pen, his company had made more than seven hundred million dollars. He personally had pocketed around thirteen million, and was going to find a club and what he called some 'broadminded women' to celebrate with. I ran off at the mouth.

'You're celebrating putting thousands of Czech workers out of a job?'

He looked as if I had just hit him, then he laughed and started putting his papers into his attaché case.

'Interpret this, Harry: Welcome to globalization. Welcome to the world where you make dust or you eat dust. Welcome to the twenty-first century.'

Then he handed me my cheque with all the good grace of a client stuffing money into the bra of a lap dancer.

'Your interpreting fee. A thousand. Don't spend it all at once.'

I wanted to hit him. He waved a finger at me.

'You wanna know why people like you don't like Americans, Harry? Because we're so goddamn successful in every field of human endeavour.'

That angered me even more. It had nothing to do with his nationality. It had everything to do with his behaviour.

'I do like Americans,' I protested. 'Most of them. But some of you don't travel so well. The ones who have no values except what you can pay for. People like you.'

'Well, fuck you too, Harry,' he called out with another laugh as he stepped out of the door. 'When people say they don't care about money it's usually because they don't have any. G'bye now. I'll be thinking of you.'

When I cooled down, I went home and switched on the TV news, only because I wanted to hear if Blair had finally got round to calling the General Election. And he had. But there was also a big surprise. Father's picture suddenly appeared on the screen as he crawled towards his footnote in history.

'A reminder of today's top stories: the Prime Minister, Tony Blair, has given the go ahead for a General Election to be held on May 5th. He's bidding to win an unprecedented third term for Labour, an achievement which would match that of Mrs Thatcher ... And one other piece of political news this hour: the former Conservative Cabinet Minister Robin Burnett – credited with being one of the chief architects of Thatcherism – has been found close to death at his home in Gloucestershire. Police refused to confirm local speculation that Mr Burnett had been attacked and stabbed. For more on this we can go over to our political editor Tom Agnew at Westminster. Tom.'

An affable looking man in glasses standing in Downing Street started to speak. He was talking about my father. He appeared to know him better than I did.

'... Robin Burnett, nicknamed by the tabloids "Big-Brain Burnett", was one of the intellectual fathers of modern Conservatism. A formidably clever economist, he was once tipped to succeed Mrs Thatcher as Prime Minister until the scandal which toppled him caused devastation at the heart of the Conservative party. It still rankles even today ...'

Then there was an interruption. The man in glasses held his earpiece with his index finger.

'And I am just hearing that the Vice President of the United States, David Hickox, who is on an official visit to Europe and who met Robin Burnett in London earlier this week, is about to pay tribute to his friend. Let's go live to the Élysée Palace ...'

They cut to pictures of Vice President Hickox, a thickset man with the build of an American footballer, standing next to a bemused French President Jacques Chirac.

'Let me just say that Robin Burnett is a friend of freedom, a friend of the United States and a good friend of mine,' Hickox was saying. *'He understood the need for Britain and the United States to stand shoulder to shoulder in a difficult and dangerous world. The Robin Burnett I have known for years is a brave man and a fighter – and I pray that he'll pull through. My thoughts are with him and his family at this time.'*

Then the Vice President put an arm round President Chirac and they walked inside. The affable reporter started to speak again.

'Publicly neither the Labour party nor the Conservatives are saying much about Robin Burnett, but privately Labour cannot believe their luck. On the day Tony Blair has called a General Election, here we have a reminder of all the sleaze once associated with the Conservative party and attached to the scandal involving Robin Burnett.'

He paused for a second to deliver his punchline.

'In politics, of course, as in stand-up comedy, timing is everything. Now back to the studio.'

Oh, god, I thought. It's starting again. All over again. And there is nothing I can do to stop it. I closed my eyes and took a deep breath. Could this day possibly get worse? Another deep breath. Perhaps I should introduce myself properly. My name is Harry Burnett. I am a full-time translator and part-time interpreter. Despite what the New York lawyer said, I do a lot of work for American clients, most of whom I like, and I only very rarely lose my temper. I am also the estranged son of the former British Cabinet minister Robin Burnett. And he is a scandalous man.

London, 1982

ROBIN BURNETT'S STORY

The first time I saw the woman who was to change my life was in 1982. I had no idea who she was, but I had an instinct that she meant trouble. At the time I could not imagine how much trouble. Let me set the scene for you. It must have been early in 1982, because it was shortly after the Argentine junta had sent their troops to invade the Falkland Islands. I was preoccupied. Happy. Busy. Successful. Duties. There was a profound air of crisis within the British government, but it brought out the best in everyone, especially the Lady. She knew the old wisdom that the Chinese written script for the word 'Crisis' contains the characters for 'Opportunity' as well as 'Danger', and so did I. Up until the moment the Argies invaded, I was convinced we were going to lose the next election. It had to come by the spring of 1984 at the latest. Unemployment was very high. Not our fault, of course, but people thought it was. Cyclical factors. World downturn. They blamed us. In fact they hated us. I was spat at in the street at a housing project in Bristol. One of the other ministers, Henry Charlwood, had red paint thrown over him in Glasgow. Another, Michael Armstrong, was sprayed with slurry at a market in Leicester. Our economic policies needed more time to work, much more time – as I kept telling everybody and anybody who would listen. Thankfully, the Lady was one of those who did listen.

'Prime Minister, you cannot turn around a pessimistic, unionized, programmed-to-fail economy like Britain in less than a decade.'

'We do not have a decade, Robin,' she reminded me. She actually looked at her watch as if the seconds were ticking away towards the next General Election and the end of her time in Downing Street. 'We have five years. Four, actually. I intend to go to the country next year. So we have about twelve months remaining.'

'It's not enough.'

'It might have to be enough,' she whipped back at me.

We were in her room at the Commons, having tea. She had a whiff of perfume about her. Powder blue suit. Handbag. In real life she was smaller than most people will ever understand if they only ever saw her on television, where she seemed a huge figure. And in reality she was also much more feminine than she appeared on TV. Her femininity tended to bring out the masculine in a man. You were aware of her physical fragility, which was impossible to reconcile with her mental strength. It made some men go a bit wobbly. Mitterrand had a soft spot for her. He said she had the mouth of Marilyn Monroe and the eyes of Caligula. One of the few things in life Mitterrand ever got right.

'If you go to the country next year, then you almost certainly will lose, Prime Minister,' I told her. 'I am sorry to say it, but you will. We need as long as possible.'

The Lady looked at me coldly. Caligula. She knew they were plotting against her, within the party, but the word 'lose' was not in her active vocabulary. I changed the subject.

'And also, Prime Minister, as I keep reminding people in Cabinet, *we* do not fix the economy. It fixes itself. We in government can only help by getting out of the way as much as possible. Benign neglect. It works for houseplants, and it certainly works for the economy. The more you fuss around, the worse it gets. The houseplants wilt and die from too much fussing. Just let it be. You cannot buck the market.'

The Lady looked at me quizzically, turning her head to the side, that way she did which always reminded me of a small bird.

'Say that again, Robin.'

'You cannot buck the market, Prime Minister.'

'Thank you, Robin. For speaking honestly, as always. So many don't, you know.'

Oh, yes, I knew. The trades unions were behaving like donkeys – mules – desperate to bring us down as they had Callaghan in '79. The only thing that stopped them taking action was their terror that we would call their bluff. I wanted them to try it, so we could announce an election on one simple question: who rules Britain? Them or us? The democratic parliament that you elected? Or a bunch of union leaders that you did not? I wanted to hit them in the face with it. The unions circled, waiting for their chance, snapping and barking, but not daring to bite. I repeatedly told the Lady that if she insisted on holding a General Election in 1983, the only way she could win would be to engineer a crisis.

'A crisis?' she said, the way Oscar Wilde's Lady Bracknell said 'a handbag?' 'Did you say a crisis, Robin?'

I gulped.

'Take on the unions, Prime Minister. Make it Them or Us. Take on the despots.'

She smiled. Marilyn Monroe. Then she shook her head. The miners had destroyed Heath. The public sector workers had destroyed Callaghan. She did not feel strong enough to risk being destroyed in '83, though I thought she might be destroyed anyway, and it was better to go down fighting. And then! And then! Hallelujah! Along came a better class of despot, from the other side of the world. Thank god for General Galtieri! A central casting villain! A proto-fascist South American in a bad uniform, with the air of a man who could strut even when sitting down! Just what we needed. What luck!

When Galtieri sent his Argentine conscript troops to the Falklands, I confess that most British people, including me, could not have pinpointed the godforsaken islands on a map. Peter Carrington, decent man, resigned as Foreign Secretary. Someone had to carry the can. It could not be her, of course. We were agreed on that. So it had to be him. The truth is, we had all ballsed it up. We had a British submarine lurking off the coast of the Falklands for a while and then removed it in the name of 'constructive dialogue'. Not only that, we *told* everybody we had removed it, including the Argentine military dictatorship. I don't recall the word 'dialogue' being much used in the Lady's presence thereafter. It also taught us a lesson about dictators, Saddam Hussein and the like. You can show them the brink, but they never pay attention until they fall over it. The Lady knew this was her crisis. Her moment in history. Winning was never the most important thing to her. It was the only thing.

'It's a carrot and a stick policy with Galtieri,' she told Cabinet the Thursday following the invasion, slapping her tiny right hand on the table. 'He can get his troops out immediately, or we will destroy him.'

There was much bemusement around the room. People looked at their hands, or at their papers, not at the Lady and certainly not at each other. Every single person present around that Cabinet table wondered if she would fail, including her. Every single person present wondered who would succeed her, if she did fail. Including her.

'Why is that a carrot and stick policy, Prime Minister?' one of the plotters, one of the Wets, emboldened by the Lady's perceived weakness, dared to ask. It was Michael Armstrong, then at the Home Office. A Shit.

'What's the carrot?'

The Lady glared at him.

'The carrot, Michael, is that we won't use the stick.'

The Cabinet went silent. Michael Armstrong looked as if he had swallowed his tongue. He was booted up to the Lords by the end of the year. The Lady went into a frenzy of hyper-activity, spurred on by the mutterings about whether she was up to the job. One or two backbenchers privately talked about her being Neville Chamberlain in a frock. I nailed them for it.

'I am sure the Prime Minister will respond to your comments,' I told Gowing and Mattings, two spivs of the old sort I caught lunching in Victoria. Double breasted blue pinstripe suits and oily hair. Sharks in shark's clothing. Friends of Armstrong. 'If you care to mention your misgivings to the Lady personally, she will most definitely respond. And I am sure the Chief Whip could arrange a meeting. Perhaps you could bring Michael Armstrong along to lend his support?'

Gowing and Mattings looked as if I had shot them. Which of course I had. And then ... It is difficult to keep a straight face, recalling the moment, but one must never underestimate two things about politicians: their cowardice and their stupidity. Gowing and Mattings thought they would blacken me by spreading word of what I had said. What a lark! First they told Armstrong, and then some of the worst elements of the 1922 Committee. In total confidence, of course – which meant it leaked to the press in time for the next morning's papers. The idea was to make me look bad. The idiots! From being that ami-able old academic buffer Robin Burnett who loves his econom-ics charts, his Laffer's Curve and his lectures on the difference between Tax Take and Tax Rate, I suddenly became Mac the Knife. The Enforcer. It got out into the *Telegraph* and the *Mail*. The *Mail* called me 'Bovver Boy Burnett', and I was metamor-phosed into 'the Lady's hard man', according to the *Guardian*. Their cartoonist drew me as a skinhead with bovver boots! Ooooh, how that hurt! Ha! Let's just say there was no more talk of Neville Chamberlain in a frock after that. Only of Winston Churchill. The Empire Strikes Back. The steel fist. The

Iron Lady. I loved it. And, more importantly, so did She! What times we had! The Lady's energy was infectious. It was as if I was taking a major policy decision once an hour, like Old Faithful, erupting with ideas around the clock, changing the country, gush, gush, gush, as the Lady started to change the world.

Once a week or so I was summoned to Downing Street for a late night whisky and soda. One night, after the Royal Navy Task Force had set sail but before there had been any significant engagement in the war, she told me I was to be despatched to Washington. As her special envoy. Washington?

'Good,' I said, puzzled. I hadn't a clue. I smiled with enthusiasm.

'Robin, you have a safe pair of hands,' the Lady explained. Geoffrey was there. And Bernard. And the Defence Secretary, who quipped that I was to use my safe pair of hands to milk the teats of the American administration for everything they'd got. Everyone laughed. I pretended to laugh along with them.

'The Task Force is to liberate the Falklands from the Argies,' Bernard said, 'and you are to liberate the Reagan administration from the peculiar belief that they should not upset General Galtieri.'

'He's their son-of-a-bitch in Latin America,' Geoffrey chimed in. 'They love him because he hates Communists.'

'So did Hitler,' I said. 'And look where that got us.'

'Precisely,' the Lady agreed.

The Reaganauts were going to do their bit for us whether they wanted to or not.

'The entire fate of the government depends upon y*our* success,' the Lady told me, a little redundantly. 'You have contacts and friendships in Washington. Use them. Get them on-side, Robin.'

'There are competing baronies in Washington, Prime Minister,' I told her. 'You can usually only appeal to one baron by alienating another, but I'll do my best.'

'You bring me solutions,' the Lady said. 'Others just bring me problems.'

She poured me another whisky.

'And you'll need a bit of extra nourishment,' she winked, handing me the glass. Marilyn Monroe.

There was to be an open part of the trip and a covert part. The open part was that I was scheduled to meet the Council of Economic Advisers and talk to the Reagan administration about oil prices, the tension in the Gulf, and our joint commitment to bear down on inflation. Everybody was terrified of the Iranians. The Gulf states and the Saudis had puffed up a two-bit Iraqi thug called Saddam Hussein by telling him that he was the bulwark for the Sunni Arabs against the Persian Shia menace. Some 'bulwark'. Saddam decided that his place in history was assured. Iraq invaded Iran in September 1980, much to everyone's satisfaction.

'It's just a pity that in this war both sides cannot lose,' Jack Heriot told me, in a preparation meeting for my Washington trip. Heriot was number two at the Foreign Office. He used to be a diplomat. He was my age, my status. My rival. He offered me a briefing when he heard of my mission, and I accepted gratefully. We sized each other up, and I confess I liked him instantly, despite the rivalry. I could also see that we would need each other, when the time to replace the Lady finally came around.

'You will want to talk to the Americans about the Falklands, but they will want to talk to you about the Gulf,' he told me. 'It is their obsession. Dual containment.'

I had never heard the phrase before.

'What?'

'Dual containment,' Jack Heriot repeated. 'That's what the Americans call it. One load of evil bastards in Iran, and another load of evil bastards in Iraq. Killing each other, big time. Does anyone have a problem with that? I don't think so.'

12

'And our role is?'

Heriot smiled. He was already beginning to put on weight and his belly was tight in his dark blue suit.

'Publicly, we call on both sides for a ceasefire, for restraint and mediation, and hard work towards peace. Privately, we keep it going for as long as possible.'

'How?'

'By backing the loser. Currently, Iraq.'

Ah, the sophistication of the diplomatic mind.

'Divide and conquer?'

'If you like. More like the historic British policy of never letting any one rival get too strong. Remember Part One politics at university? *We have no permanent friends, no permanent enemies, only permanent interests.*'

'Thanks for the seminar, Jack.'

'Don't mention it. You'll find it useful leverage with the Reaganauts.'

Oh, will I?

Yes, I did. And yes, we really would come to need each other, Jack Heriot and I. We were called 'The Likely Lads' by the newspapers at the time. One of us, they deemed, would 'go all the way'. The Fleet Street wisdom was that if the Lady fell because of her economic policies then I would carry the can and Heriot would succeed as Prime Minister. But if – by some miracle – what they were now calling 'Thatcherism' did work, then I would be the natural successor, especially if the Falklands war was taken to mean our foreign policy was way off track. I knew that being tipped as a future leader carries with it the kiss of death, but I was flattered. Strange, isn't it? You see disaster ahead, but you take the road anyway. Maybe you even accelerate. It was like that in private matters too. Sex and love? Be careful? No. Full speed ahead, over the cliff.

The covert part of my trip to Washington was that I was to see the US Navy Secretary, Don Hall, an old friend from rowing days in Oxford. I had asked Don to fix up an informal meeting with David Hickox, who was then the Director of Central Intelligence. Hickox was on the way up. Some people said he could make it to Vice President. Or even President. And I needed him on-side. But here was our problem. Jeanne Kirkpatrick, the US Ambassador to the United Nations, was causing trouble. She said the United States should remain neutral in what she called a 'post-colonial dispute' between the United Kingdom and Argentina over '*las Malvinas*'.

Personally I was happy if Sad, Mad, Bad Jeanne remained neutral, or was even openly hostile to us. Having a demented old trout arguing against you in Washington does your cause no end of good. But the FCO and Jack Heriot in particular seemed unnerved by her opposition, and there were also intelligence issues. What were we going to get from the Americans? Communications Intelligence? Signals Intelligence? Eavesdropping on the Argies? Access to information from American human sources in Buenos Aires? Or perhaps, bugger all. What would Hickox be prepared to do? We did not know. It was up to me to find out.

In preparation for the trip I had to visit the US embassy in Grosvenor Square for a courtesy call with the ambassador. It was pleasant enough. Political bottom-sniffing. Coffee and chat and then I left. Half an hour, tops. So there I was, walking out of the embassy, looking for my official car, when I glimpsed a woman walking in. She was – she is – very beautiful. Striking. I had no idea who she was, but I remember thinking of the English folksong, 'The First Time Ever I Saw Your Face'. It was just a glance, but no woman had ever looked at me like that before. It was the look that a hungry lioness gives a passing zebra. Raw hunger. I was the prey. I glanced back but the moment had passed. She was walking briskly into the US embassy. I remember even now, after all these years, the shape of her body, her hips, the bounce of her hair. I remember thinking that she walked as if she were wearing expensive lingerie. She radiated a secret and exotic sexiness which made me think of the whisper of lace and silk on tanned skin. I climbed into the ministerial Jaguar and returned to the Treasury, humming the tune of 'The First Time Ever I Saw Your Face' and feeling vaguely ridiculous. Love at first sight – like a belief in socialism – is wonderful at age fourteen but absolutely stupid after the age of, let's say, forty. I shook my head to clear it of all memories of her, and determined to forget I had ever seen her.

The embassy had booked me my usual hotel in Washington, but my old friend Don Hall offered to put me up for a weekend at his place in Middleburg, Virginia, prior to my official meetings at Treasury and State. He said he would gather together a few 'like minded souls' – which meant the Brit-loving community of Washington, members of the Senate Armed Services committee that I might need to sweet-talk, and, I was relieved to hear, Hickox himself, who – Don said – was keen to meet me.

'He said you are one of us,' Don Hall laughed.

'An American?' I replied, puzzled.

'No,' Don corrected me. 'A neo-con.'

I thought I had misheard or misunderstood. I had never heard the phrase before.

'A what?'

'A neo-conservative. He's done his research. Don always does his research. He says you are a true believer in free markets and in rolling back communism rather than just acquiescing. I told him he was goddamn right.'

Neo-con? What a strange phrase. I thought no more about it. There wasn't time. Maybe I should have ensured I had received an intelligence briefing about David Hickox in as much detail as he had received one about me, but there wasn't time for that either. By the time I did get briefed about Hickox, it was too late. I had already made my deal with the devil.

On the plane to Washington, I tried to plan how the meetings should go, but other thoughts crept into my mind unbidden. The exotic looking woman that I had seen walking into the embassy, even though I did not know her name or anything about her. Why could I not get her out of my head? I did an inventory of my life. I had two perfect, photogenic children. I had a hugely intelligent wife with her own career. Elizabeth taught at the LSE. I had hundreds of contacts in politics, in the press, all over Washington, at Oxford, in the American universities and the think tanks. I might make it to Prime Minister, and if I didn't I could always switch to Wall Street or the City and make a fortune. And yet … And yet.

I did not need this woman I had glimpsed walking into the embassy – absolutely not. I would probably never see her again. But I wanted her, and I could not explain why. I had read a survey around this time in which a thousand people were asked what they would do if the Russians fired nuclear missiles towards us and we were all about to be obliterated. We had ten minutes to live. Ten minutes to decide what to do. Most of the people surveyed said they would have sex with anyone reasonably attractive in the vicinity. All inhibitions disappeared. You had to laugh at this notion. End of the World Sex, they called it in the survey. What a wonderful thought. Was that what was happening to me? End of the World Sex? The world was about to change for me inexorably and forever. Everything speeded up.

Much later in our relationship she gave me something which explained it all better than I could explain it to myself. It was a book of Sufi poetry. Every culture has its Romeo and Juliet love story. For the Sufis it is the story of Leila (or Layla) and her beloved, a man nicknamed Majnun. Like all Romeo and Juliet stories it ends in desperate and permanent separation. Happy love affairs are tedious literature. Nothing cheers us up more than reading about other people's personal lives going catastrophically wrong. In this case, Layla dies (of course) Majnun chooses to lie on her grave and fade away until the dust of their bodies finally unites them in death though they were always separated in life.

In the Sufi poem a headstone was put on the grave and it reads:

Two lovers lie in this one tomb
United forever in death's dark womb.
Faithful in separation, true in love:
May one tent house them in heaven above.

My plane landed at Dulles International Airport and I had work to do. The entire fate of the British government lay in my hands – apparently. And yet all modern politics is an exercise in compartmentalization, or – if you prefer – organized hypocrisy. I was a hypocrite, even to myself. I did not have long to wait for the compartments to fall apart.

Oh, yes, may one tent house them, Layla and Majnun, faithful in separation, true in love.

London, Spring 2005

HARRY BURNETT'S STORY

Harry Burnett finally got around to switching on his mobile phone after he had watched the news bulletin.

Amanda's text read:

'Someone tried to kill father. Or poss. suicide. No way 2 know 4 certain. Am in Tetbury. Police here 2. Facts not clear. Huge mess. Call me asap. Love A xx.'

He dialled her number.

'Aitch! Thank god!'

'Tell me.'

'Where have you been? I've been desperately …'

'Working. Sorry. Phone's been off. Just found out … Shitty, shitty day, already. Tell me.'

'The police called. A couple of hours ago. His cleaner found him lying on the carpet first thing this morning, fully clothed. Suit. Shirt. Tie. Pills of all sorts scattered by his side and an empty whisky bottle. Wrists slashed and a kitchen knife by his side. I came straight over. I'm at his cottage now.' She stopped gabbling and took a deep breath. 'Aitch, they are not sure whether it's suicide or maybe murder done up to look like suicide.'

'I heard,' he said.

'Attempted suicide. Attempted murder,' she corrected herself and started gabbling again. 'He's at the hospital in Gloucester having his stomach pumped and a blood transfusion. I can't see him until later and nobody can tell me what his chances are. The police wanted me here at the house in case they have questions, but I'm like, well, maybe I don't have any answers.'

'What are they doing?'

'Mooching. It's as if they think they ought to be looking for something, but haven't a clue what it might be. It's terrible, Aitch! Terrible, I …'

'Who would want to kill him now? Twenty years ago, maybe you could understand it. He had enemies. But now?'

'No idea,' she replied. 'The police are saying – you know – Inspector Morse-type bullshit – "keeping an open mind". "Exploring all avenues." But bottles of pills? Whisky and knife wounds? And they're pumping his guts for a drugs over-dose? So what does it sound like to you, Aitch? A mistake? He wasn't the mistake type. Or the cry-for-help type.'

'He wasn't the suicide type either,' Harry said.

'What is the suicide type?'

'I don't know – but not him. He'd have done it years ago if he had any shame, but he didn't because he hasn't. It doesn't make any sense.'

'How would you know?' Amanda shot back. 'You are hardly the expert on what makes sense. Or on our father's character, for that matter.'

Harry wondered what percentage of telephone calls with his sister ended in a row. He guessed at fifty-fifty.

'Maybe,' he conceded. 'But all I ever remember was Mr Stand-On-Your-Own-Two-Feet, Rugged Individualism, every day is full of opportunities, seize it while you can blah, blah.'

'I don't see …'

'He'd never top himself, Amanda. Never.'

'People change, Aitch. You have.'

He let it pass. *People change.* His father used to say that all the time, as if he could actually talk in italics. *People change.*

19

It was one of his favourite parables. Father loved his parables. Harry had seen the clip on TV.

'It's a flip-flop,' some smirking BBC television interviewer was hectoring Robin Burnett when he was Chief Secretary to the Treasury.

'Certainly, it's a change in direction,' Robin agreed smoothly.

'A change in direction?' the interviewer repeated, his voice dripping with scorn. 'This government has just done a complete economic U-turn and ...'

'John Maynard Keynes,' Robin Burnett interrupted, 'was once asked why he had changed his mind about some aspect of economic policy. And do you know his reply?'

The interviewer opened his mouth like a goldfish.

'Well, do you?' Robin Burnett persisted.

'I ...'

'No?'

Robin Burnett was on top form, intimidatory, like a pike about to swallow the goldfish. He leaned towards the interviewer and wagged his finger.

'Keynes would thunder, "*When the facts change, I change my mind.*" And then he would say, "*and what do you do, sir?*" So, what do you do, Mr Day?'

And Robin Burnett laughed. The interviewer was crushed. Harry thought it was funny that his father would quote Keynes at all, given his views on Keynesian economics, but there you are. The TV viewers would laugh too.

'Painkillers,' Amanda was saying.

'What?'

'Painkillers. What he swallowed. Co-proxamol. Is that a name of a painkiller? And paracetamol. And some other –ol. Oh, yes, alcohol. I knew there were three –ols. Whisky. The police said it was *The Oban*. That would be father. Nothing but a good malt.'

'That saves us identifying the body,' Harry suggested. 'If he had a bottle of *The Oban* beside him, it was him all right.'

'Harry!'

She only ever called him 'Harry' like that when she was upset. 'How can you talk like that when ...'

He wanted to avoid tears.

'I mean, Amanda, just as you suggested, if he did try to commit suicide, there would be a good malt whisky involved in the story somewhere,' Harry replied emolliently. 'That's all.'

'Anyway, Aitch,' Amanda recovered, 'the police are wandering around in white suits. Forensic officers, they call them. And then there's something else. They asked me to check out father's house in London.'

Harry blinked.

'He hasn't got a house in London.'

'Exactly what I told them. Just the cottage in Tetbury, I said. So then this police officer says, very suspicious now, "Oh, really, Miss Burnett?" And he does something with his eyebrows while he's saying it, like he regards me as a total tosspot. And then this other one asks how often father visits his flat in Hampstead.'

'His flat in Hampstead?' Harry echoed.

'Yes,' Amanda went on. 'They showed me papers scattered all around the floor where they found him, photographs of this mansion block and utility bills with a Hampstead address and the name Robin Burnett on them. The police need to check it out. Today, they said. And they want one of us – which means you, Aitch – to go along. I'll stay here for a bit and then go to the hospital. One of us should be at the hospital in case he ...'

'Dies,' he said brusquely.

'Recovers,' she corrected him. 'In which case, I'll call you. And if he dies, then I'll also call you. You go check out the Hampstead place, yes?'

'Yes,' Harry agreed.

She gave him the details.

'And you?'

'I want to get out of here before the TV crews arrive. It's already on the radio. *"Disgraced Thatcher minister gravely ill."* Something ghastly like that.'

Oh, god. Harry's heart sank. *Disgraced Thatcher minister.* His father's life and career reduced to a headline. *That headline.* The nightmare really was starting again.

'Funny thing,' Amanda said, 'after the card he sent me last week.'

'The card?' Harry felt numb. He knew he was sounding like an echo.

'I kept it. Here, in my bag.'

He could hear her rustle around.

'Pretty picture. Birds in clouds and blue sky. Inside a few lines of Persian poetry about birds having to fall before they can fly, for "in falling they're given wings". Sweet. Let me read the message ... "I hope that one day you and Harry will understand everything."'

'Understand everything?' Harry repeated, twisting his face.

'"... because to understand all is to forgive all."'

'Yeah,' Harry scoffed. 'Well, what I understand is ...'

She interrupted.

'"... and that because you were only children at the time, you could not possibly understand, so you can not forgive." More stuff like that, and then there's a bit at the end when he asks if I would be prepared to listen to him if he told me the whole story. The words "whole story" were underlined. He said the time was right.'

'His time, maybe,' Harry said. 'My time was right years ago. Did you reply?'

'Yes.'

'What did you say?'

'I said, fine. I called him and he sounded pleased. We were going to meet. Then he asked if you would come along. I said there was no point in asking you. Your mind was made up.'

She sounded thoughtful.

'Correct,' he answered. 'My mind is made up.'

'But maybe you have a point, Aitch. It doesn't make sense to write something like that and then try to kill himself, does it? Perhaps someone tried to make it look like suicide ...'

Harry scoffed.

'Nothing about him ever entirely made sense. More importantly, how much do you think it's worth, this place in Hampstead? A million? Two?'

'Harry!'

'I mean, *Hampstead*.'

'Harry! You should not talk like that and you should not even think like that. Instead you should visit him in hospital and ... and ... forgive him. It's not too late to change things.'

She hung up.

'But it is too late,' Harry said aloud. 'Too late for me, anyway.'

He swore quietly under his breath. The previous week Harry had also received a card from his father, though he had not bothered to mention it to his sister. It contained a similar invitation to meet and hear the 'whole story'. Harry's card had a different poem on the front, a few lines of Yeats' poetry about 'too long a sacrifice' making 'a stone of the heart'. Did his father know that he was working on a translation of Yeats into Czech? How?

Maybe it was a lucky guess. Maybe Amanda told him. Either way, Harry had put the card into his shredder, without replying. *Too long a sacrifice makes a stone of the heart.*

'Oh, when may it suffice,' he muttered to himself as he walked into the bathroom to take a shower, to wash himself clean of his impure thoughts. '*Disgraced Thatcher Minister*,' he said out loud, 'gravely ill.'

Pimlico, London, 1987

Almost twenty years earlier, Harry was just eight years old, and the scandal involving his father had just broken in the newspapers. Harry was standing in the hallway of the family house in Pimlico, chewing at the sleeve of his grey and blue school uniform. Saliva stained the jacket cuff. He listened, a small, cornered animal. Nothing. But he knew they were out there. Waiting. They were always waiting. Packs of them. He wanted to find a burrow and bury himself under the warm earth. His father called them 'the Wolves of the Forest'.

'But without the morality or solidarity of the wolf pack,' his father would thunder.

Harry could see their yellow eyes glowing with hunger. He knew that to the wolves he himself was just a small piece of meat. A snack. His father was the main meal. But that fact did not make Harry any more comfortable. Saliva foamed on Harry's cuff. He closed his eyes and swayed from side to side. In his mind he could see them now, waiting and watching and filming, howling with their notebooks and microphones pointing towards him, leaning back on their haunches on the pavement outside the house, licking their chops and ready to snap as he and his father emerged. Harry's knees knocked rhythmically. He gripped his canvas school bag. His name was printed in red block capitals. Underneath he had written in big black inky letters: *'Her name is Rio!!!'* And: *'Duran Duran!!!!'* And: *'Atomic!!!! Blondie!!!'*

The wetness of saliva was on his wrist. His mouth tasted of wool. A sudden noise outside made him twitch. The pack was getting restless, scratching, snarling, biting on the doorstep. Suddenly one knocked at the door, and another rang the bell. Harry wondered what primitive instinct, what ordering of wolf society enabled them to decide who would do the knocking and who would do the ringing, and when. He tried to figure out if there were rules. He made notes in his diary, scientific observations of times and intrusions over the past week since the siege began. It started at seven in the morning, never before. It continued until nine at night, never later.

'Too late for their deadlines after that,' his father explained, when Harry told him about his observations, though Harry did not know what a deadline was.

'And of course the pubs are still open. The watering holes for the wolves, Harry.'

'But what do we do?' Harry's older sister, Amanda, asked. 'How can we just make them go away?'

'We do nothing,' their father advised. 'They can't get in. And when we go out, we will do it quickly. Walk straight to the car, look ahead, not to the side, and hold my hand. Say absolutely nothing. Ignore them. They'll leave us when they realize there is nothing for them here. Nothing.'

Harry's eyes widened with fear. *Ignore them?*

'Remember the Three Little Pigs?' his father suggested. 'The wolves can huff and puff but they can never blow the house down. We are safe here. Completely safe.'

Safe, Harry thought. He had learned at school that safety and shelter were the two most basic human needs, ahead of food and love and comfort. Harry dreamed of safety. His burrow. His castle. He had read about the Persians surrounded by the forces of Genghiz Khan, the Seljuk hosts at Byzantium,

English castles under siege in the Wars of the Roses and Italian cities besieged in the interminable wars of the Middle Ages. He marvelled at tales of attackers using catapults to throw plague victims or diseased animals inside the walls, the earliest form of biological warfare. The doorbell rang again. It had a particular urgency, as if a catapulted plague victim had thudded into the hallway.

'*What new hell is this*?' his father bellowed from up the staircase, and then called down in a softer voice. 'Just ignore it, Harry. Believe me, they really are a lot less comfortable out there than we are in here.'

So Harry ignored it, with all the success of the Persians ignoring the Mongol hordes. He hopped from foot to foot in alarm.

'Wait there,' his father called down again. 'I'll get Amanda. We'll go to the car together in about ten minutes and I'll drop you off at school. Then I have a meeting with the Lady.'

Harry waited by the mirror. He knew who the Lady was. It was the Prime Minister. She was his father's boss, which was good. He always called her 'the Lady'. And the Lady was not pleased with his father, suddenly. Which was bad. Not pleased at all. And then Harry heard the claws on the flap of the letter box. A pair of eyes scanned across the hall. They were not yellow, as Harry had expected, but blue, cornflower blue. The brightest blue Harry had ever seen, like those on a husky-type dog that had once jumped up on him in Holland Park. He stared back at the cornflower blue eyes, transfixed. There was a voice where he almost expected a bark.

'Here,' the voice said. Mellifluous. What his mother would call 'well spoken'. Then, more loudly: 'Over here.'

Harry looked at the eyes in the flap. Said nothing.

'Hello, young fellow-me-lad. How are you?'

Nothing.

'I'm Stephen Lovelace.'

Nothing. Then Stephen Lovelace named the newspaper he represented. It wasn't any of the newspapers they had delivered

26

in the mornings. Harry decided it must be one of the smaller ones. His father said the Lady called the smaller ones, 'Comics for Grown-Ups'. He thought that was very funny.

'You must be Harry,' the voice said.

Yes, Harry thought. I must be Harry. Still he said nothing.

'You're big for an eight year old.'

Harry was puzzled now. He most definitely was NOT big for an eight year old.

It irritated him. This pair of bright blue eyes in his letter box were connected to a mouth which knew things about him – his age – and yet which was saying things about him which were obviously not true. Why would he do that, this Stephen Lovelace person? The eyes in the letter box reminded him of something. He frowned. Not a wolf, after all. Not even the bright blue eyes of the husky-type dog in the park. No, it was the hypnotizing stare of the snake, Ka, in the cartoon of *Jungle Book*. Harry felt woozy.

'Listen, Harry,' Stephen Lovelace said, eyes whirling. 'My paper wants to do all right by you and the family, put your dad's side of the story. So can you tell your dad we just want to hear his side, that's all. He can name his price. You got that?'

Harry nodded.

'Want to repeat that?' Stephen Lovelace said, his eyes swirling in the letter box. 'Your dad's side of the story ...'

'His side of the story.'

'... and name his price.'

'Name his price.'

'You're a clever boy, young fellow-me-lad.'

This irritated Harry even more. How would the eyes in the letter box know that? Did this Stephen Lovelace spy on him at school? Perhaps people who worked in newspapers, especially the small ones that the Lady and his father called the comics for grown-ups, perhaps these people knew everything about you. Ooooooh! That made Harry feel strange. Did they spy on him when he did something bad, like picking his nose? Or farting? Without warning, the letter box shut. The eyes of Ka disappeared. His father came down the stairs with Amanda in tow, her schoolbag hanging from her shoulders.

'Right,' his father said. 'Time to … to … what's that on the floor?'

They looked down at a pool of liquid spreading out under Harry's shoes on the parquet flooring.

'It's wee,' Amanda said, half in amazement, half in triumph. 'Harry's peed himself!'

Harry thought he saw steam rising from the pool of liquid by his feet, though he might have imagined it. He burst into tears, not because of what he had done, not because his crotch and trousers were wet and uncomfortable, sticking to his legs, not even because his sister was joyous in his humiliation, but at the thought that the bright blue eyes-in-the-letterbox called Stephen Lovelace might have seen him do it, and that he would write about it in his newspaper, the small one, the one the Lady called a comic for grown-ups. And he knew something else. He knew he would remember those eyes. Forever.

London, Spring 2005

As soon as Amanda rang off, Harry Burnett called the Metropolitan Police on the number his sister had given him. To his surprise, someone answered almost immediately.

'Hello, my name is Harry Burnett and ...'

'You are Robin Burnett's son, Harry Burnett?' the voice interrupted.

'Yes.'

The last time Harry had called the Metropolitan Police was six months before. He had been mugged in a park near Fulham Broadway. The muggers had stolen his iPOD and run off towards the Peabody Estate, a housing estate so rough it had become almost a no-go area. That time, the police telephone rang for forty-five minutes without any police officer managing to answer it. That time, Harry had given up. This time was different. Instant access. Suddenly, he realized, he was Somebody. Or the Son of Somebody.

'Yes. I'm Harry Burnett,' he confirmed. 'My sister said you were interested in meeting me at my father's flat in Hampstead?'

The detective said yes, he was indeed very interested to meet Robin Burnett's son at his father's flat in Hampstead.

'Can I check the address with you?' Harry said.

'Why?'

'Because I've never been there. Until a few moments ago I didn't even know my father owned a flat in London.'

'Oh?' The officer sounded genuinely puzzled. 'And – um – why is that?'

'Because ... because I have not talked to my father in years.'

'Oh.'

The policeman confirmed the address and they fixed a time. Harry checked his watch and decided to head to the flat immediately. He walked towards Fulham Broadway Underground Station marvelling at how his father's name opened doors for him, and how even the affable TV reporter had known about his father's most precious political gift, right from the very beginning, of perfect timing.

The beginning was 1979. Harry thought of 1979 as Year Zero. A lot of things happened in Year Zero, including Harry, who – in tribute to his father's impeccable timing – was born on the same day that Mrs Thatcher was elected Prime Minister.

'The Lady will just love it,' Robin Burnett told Harry's mother, Elizabeth, when he suggested they schedule her Caesarean section for polling day. 'The Lady just *loves* the idea of traditional families. The more babies the better.'

'Oh, good,' Elizabeth responded. 'Obviously I am pleased to go through with surgeon-assisted childbirth on a day that best suits the future Prime Minister.'

Robin Burnett did not respond to sarcasm. Perhaps he did not even hear it. Besides, he and the Lady were busy with other matters. She celebrated her historic election victory, that May of 1979, and immediately offered Harry's father a place in her government. Harry, meanwhile, was throwing up in hospital. It took the doctors twenty days of head-scratching to figure out what was wrong and then to operate and put it right. It meant, coincidentally, that when nowadays the TV networks show library pictures of Mrs Thatcher's election victory they are also showing TV footage of the day of Harry's birth. He had seen it so often, it was as if he had witnessed it first hand.

In the TV library pictures from May 1979 the Lady is always radiant, twin-sets, pearls, handbags, surrounded by pale-faced, earnest-looking men wearing bad spectacles. Flag-waving crowds cheer the first woman Prime Minister of the United Kingdom of Great Britain and Northern Ireland.

Hurrah! Hurrah!

She smiles quizzically, cocking her head to the side, trying not to look too pleased with herself, but Harry can tell that she is very, very pleased with herself. She has a helmet of blonde hair which manages to be stiff and wavy at the same time. Then she quotes the words of St Francis of Assisi, as if speaking to a class of particularly slow-witted children.

'Where there is hatred, let me sow love. Where there is doubt, faith. Where there is despair, hope. Where there is darkness, light. Where there is sadness, joy.'

Every time he saw the TV clips, Harry thought: that was Mrs Thatcher, wasn't it? Love. Faith. Hope. Light. Oh, yes, and joy. Mustn't forget the joy.

Rejoice. Rejoice.

As they went through the divorce, Harry's mother told him that during those first twenty days of his life, Robin Burnett visited the hospital just three times, and never for more than fifteen minutes. She kept score. She said she 'counted him in, and counted him out.'

'The hospital was the best place for you,' Robin Burnett defended himself.

Harry was by this time eight years old. The scandal had broken and their father sat him on the sofa in the large drawing room of their house in Pimlico. Amanda was by his side. She must have been ten. It was a time for explanations.

31

'Besides, I had other duties.'

Harry was bewildered.

'What other duties?'

'Well,' Robin Burnett nodded sagely, 'duties to the country as a whole.'

It sounded big stuff to an eight year old. *Other duties. To the country as a whole.* Fifty-seven million British people were depending on his father, not counting Harry, Amanda and their mother.

'Harry, you must understand that on the day you were born I absolutely had to be in Gloucester.' Robin Burnett explained that he had been elected that day as a Gloucestershire MP as part of the 1979 Thatcher landslide. 'And then I had to go to Number Ten because the Lady summoned me to brief her. And that meant I must ...'

When Harry thought back, he remembered that his father 'must' go off to Washington or Bonn or Paris or Brussels. He always 'had to' do his paperwork, what he called 'my boxes'. Harry recalled some words from Lessing: *'Kein Mensch muss muessen,'* which translated literally as 'no man must "must".' Nobody has to do anything. Except his father.

'Why were you not there in the hospital when I was born?' Harry demanded. 'When I was sick?'

'These were different times,' Robin Burnett explained. 'Men left childbirth to women. The best you could do was stand outside and pace up and down and smoke cigarettes. It was a different world.'

Robin Burnett made 1979 sound like some far off period in medieval history. Perhaps, Harry had come to realize, it was. In 1979, Year Zero of our current predicament, people worried about things as peculiar to us now as the Black Death or the Turks at the Gates of Vienna. In 1979, the Cold War would last forever. The Soviet Union would invade Germany. There were nervous TV dramas about a nuclear war followed by a nuclear winter. Nobody had heard of Global Warming.

The Big Scare was precisely the opposite, a nuclear Ice Age. In February 1979, the Shah of Iran, Reza Pahlavi, was overthrown. Militant Islamists hijacked the Iranian Revolution and seized the American embassy, holding diplomats and their families hostage for more than a year. Soviet troops invaded Afghanistan. British trades unions were out of control. Inflation. Unemployment. Strikes.

This strange alignment of the planets brought us Mrs Thatcher, Ronald Reagan, the collapse of the Soviet Union, the end of Soviet Communism, the rise of the Taleban and al Qaeda, and – eventually – the whole mess we're in now, everything from 9/11 and the London and Bali bombings to the so-called War on Terror and several wars with Iraq. And of course, the Masters of Our Current Predicament, George W. Bush and Tony Blair.

Harry sat down in the Underground train on his way to Hampstead. Suddenly half a dozen teenagers jumped in behind him. They were wearing hoodies or baseball caps and eating foul-smelling hamburgers and chips, shouting at each other with their mouths open, sitting with their feet in unlaced trainers on the seats. One of them had a boom-box and cranked it up. Hip-hop. Another scratched something on the glass of the train window with a bottle opener. Harry looked away. It was the Art of London Zen. What was happening was not really happening. If you did not look at it, it did not exist. A couple of stops later, the teenagers finished eating their burgers and chips. They rolled the wrappers into balls and threw them at each other, then headed and kicked them around the floor. They wiped the grease from their hands on the seats. Two of them started doing pull-ups on the commuter loops hanging from the roof of the train. Harry and the other passengers stared out the window at the Tube blackness. He wanted to scream at the teenagers to sit down. For god's sake, behave. But he said nothing. There had been half a dozen stabbings on the Northern Line since the beginning of the year. One of the victims had been cut open from his ear to his chest and then photographed on the attackers' mobile phones as he lay bleeding on the floor.

'Happy Stabbing, yeah?' one of the attackers had yelled at the other people in the carriage, then they started slapping people and photographing that too.

Harry stepped out quickly at Hampstead, leaving the gang of teenagers in the carriage behind him. Relieved. Feral beasts. There was a newsagent's stall with two billboards. One said: *'Iraq War "In Good Faith" – Blair.'* The other: *'Election Called for May 5.'*

Harry asked the newsagent for directions to his father's apartment block.

'Hampstead Tower Mansions?'

Blank look.

'Heath View Road? Do you know it?'

The man was fat and balding, with a comb-over of greasy brown hair. He grunted and continued sorting his papers. The grunt could have been a yes, or a no, or a fuck-you.

'You know it?' Harry tried again. This time the grunt was definitely a fuck-you.

'You wanna know somefink get one a'these.'

The man nodded his greasy hair towards a stack of London A to Z guides, then turned away. Harry bought an A to Z, cursing under his breath. He handed over a ten pound note. The change was returned slowly and without a word. Harry looked at the newsagent's flabby, white, unshaven jowls.

'Somefink else I can do for you?' the newsagent snapped.

'Yes,' Harry said. 'You could die.'

He took the map and walked out. The newsagent mumbled curses of his own. Harry searched for the address and began walking towards the heath. The apartment was part of a red-brick Victorian mansion block facing south. It sat squat like a fort. He climbed the steps to the front door and into an entrance hall lined with polished brass panels and tinted mirrors. The jade-coloured marble floor was spotless. The concierge was formal, black tail-coat and white shirt. It was like stepping back into the London of Charles Dickens.

'Good evening, sir. How may I help you?' Harry cleared his throat.

'My name is Harry Burnett. I ...'

'Ah yes,' the concierge interrupted. He beamed. 'I've been waiting for you, Mr Burnett. I'm due to go off duty, but I wanted to help in any way that I can. I am so sorry about what has happened to your father.'

The concierge proffered a hand and they shook formally.

'Sorry?'

'Yes, ever so sorry, sir.'

Harry blinked and then savoured the moment. He could not remember ever meeting anyone sorry about his father before.

'Thank you,' he murmured.

'How is he?'

'Still alive is all I know,' Harry responded.

'A bad business.'

'Yes, indeed.'

'I'm Sidney Pearl, chief concierge here at Hampstead Tower Mansions. Anything I can do for you, just ask. Anything.'

'I'd like to look around the flat while I wait for the police, if I may.'

'Of course.'

He gave Harry the keys.

'Thank you, Mr Pearl.'

'Sidney, please.'

'Thank you, Sidney. Please call me Harry. The police are on their way...' He checked his watch. 'They should be here any minute.'

'I shouldn't bet on it,' Sidney responded. 'Always late in my experience. Last time I called them to report a spot of vandalism, they arrived two days late. Do you want to go up now – or perhaps have a cup of tea? I've just made myself a pot.'

Tea sounded a good idea.

Harry wanted to hear more from the only living human being he had ever directly encountered who showed respect for Robin Burnett. The concierge nodded towards the leather armchairs in the hallway as he disappeared into his private kitchen.

'Please, make yourself at home.'

Sidney emerged a few minutes later, smiling, with cups and a plate of bourbon biscuits.

'The burglar alarm in the flat is off,' he said, placing the tray in front of Harry. 'I turn it off for the cleaners. I will re-set it when you leave. Your father was very particular about his security. I'm pleased to say he trusted me. *Trusts* me. He called this his "Place of Safety". I like to think of it like that. A haven, if you will.'

Harry waited for an explanation. There wasn't one. Sidney picked up his own tea-cup and smiled again.

'You knew him well?'

Sidney shrugged.

'For many years I have had the pleasure of knowing your father in my professional capacity. We are neighbours, so to say. My wife and I have a flat in the basement here. Very handy, it is. Otherwise we would certainly never be able to afford Hampstead, prices being what they are. Your father was – is – a great man, Harry. I hope you don't mind me saying so. I am sure he will pull through.'

'Thank you again,' Harry responded, now somewhat embarrassed. 'Why do you think he called this his "Place of Safety"?'

Sidney Pearl looked thoughtful.

'I am not sure that I could answer that, except to say that many of our owners put a lot of store in their privacy. And who can blame them? We have television people here, business people, politicians. Celebrities, so to say. These kind of people have no privacy nowadays, do they?' Sidney nodded at the window, 'Not out there, in that world. It's a fishbowl. Always someone trying to sneak a picture or ask an impertinent question. I sometimes think there is no such thing as privacy any more for anyone who seeks to serve the public. But in here in the Mansions, well, it's different, isn't it? Safe. And after… well, you know … after it all blew up around your father, I suppose that a lot of things happened that made him … cautious.'

'Yes,' Harry agreed. 'A lot of things did happen.'

'They hunted him, sir.' Sidney Pearl sounded aggrieved. 'They hunted him like it was a sport.'

'Fox-hunting and politician-hunting,' Harry replied. 'Traditional British blood sports. Ought to be banned.'

They agreed it was an awful business. Harry sipped his black tea and sucked a bourbon biscuit. Sidney Pearl put his own cup to the side and busied himself with a ledger on the desk.

'May I ask you something, Sidney?'

'Of course. Anything at all.'

'You said my father was a great man. Why was that exactly?'

Sidney Pearl looked surprised, as if the answer was so obvious it did not bear repeating.

'Well, he changed this country, didn't he? He – and others like him – got us back to work, got the unions off our backs, made us feel it wasn't all hopeless.'

Now it was Harry who looked surprised.

'Oh, you're too young to remember, a young man like you.'

Harry agreed.

'I was born in 1979. On the day Mrs Thatcher became Prime Minister. My sister jokes that I am one of Thatcher's Children and that if I'd been a girl my father would have called me Maggie.'

37

'Were you born that day? Were you indeed?' Sidney beamed. 'Well then, until the moment you arrived among us this country couldn't do anything right. Our cars were rubbish. I had a British Leyland. Montego it was. Named after a Bay in Jamaica. Very fancy. Only it leaked oil in my driveway and wouldn't start in the winter. Chap next door had Japanese – a Honda. We laughed at him at first, but it didn't leak anything, ever, and started every morning without trouble. Nowadays the Japanese have a car industry and we don't. Tells you something, doesn't it? People were always on strike. The buses, the trains, the council workers. Your father helped turn it all around. On top of that he is a gent, a real gent. Invited me and the family to the House of Commons. Several times, it was. A big man always has time for the little people, if you get my meaning. The cleaners, the gardeners. Your father always had a kind word or two. He has character, Harry. And character is destiny, isn't that what they say?'

Harry finished his biscuits in silence. The man Sidney Pearl had just described was a complete stranger to him.

'Why don't you go up to the flat,' Sidney said. 'I'll send the police on, when they arrive. If they ever do turn up. You can't be certain, can you, with any of the public services nowadays? You get what you pay for.'

Harry thought for a moment and then did as he was told. He wanted to look around the home of a person of character. A big man. A great man. And he wanted to see what a Place of Safety might look like.

The elevator was retro. It had criss-crossed metal doors, glass panels, 1920s art deco in style, but it moved up the shaft to the top floor silently, with twenty-first century efficiency. The doors opened on a marble-white corridor which Harry noticed smelled of disinfectant. The hallway was lit by gleaming chandeliers. The carpet was rich, thick and blue. Everything seemed very clean, especially compared to the grime of the Tube.

'A Conservative party carpet,' Harry muttered jovially. 'Rich, thick and blue.'

He had the sensation that he was bouncing on a trampoline, jumping in the air like a child on Christmas day, as he approached the apartment door.

'My inheritance,' he whispered.

There were two locks. Harry twisted the keys and eventually managed to get the door open. A yellowish glow from the sun was falling on the windows. They faced out towards the heath. Harry took a deep breath and walked quickly around. It was bigger than he had imagined. Three bedrooms, two bathrooms, three reception rooms, a hall and an enormous modern kitchen, granite and sherry-coloured wood with German appliances. Harry stood for a moment gazing in wonderment. He did not know much about property prices, but the apartment would be worth at least two million pounds, probably more. Three million. Hampstead prices. And it did not look like anything his father would ever buy.

Besides, how could he afford it? Robin Burnett had not earned anything, as far as Harry knew, since the scandal broke. He had resigned immediately from the government and quit as an MP. He had no job. He had written no memoirs. There was no deal with the press. No income. Despite the offers from the newspapers, from Stephen Lovelace and the others – or perhaps because of them – Harry's father had defiantly refused to write his side of the story. No kiss, no tell, for almost twenty years. Or at least, not by him. The only quote Robin Burnett was known to have given on the scandal was typically opaque. He was challenged by a TV crew on the doorstep of his Pimlico house as he left it for the last time.

'Those who speak, do not know,' he said. 'Those who know, do not speak.'

'What do you mean by that, Mr Burnett?' the interviewer shouted.

'*Res ipsa loquitur,*' was all they got by way of explanation. *The thing speaks for itself.* As far as Harry knew, that was his father's last public statement to anyone about anything, and typical of his father, it was in Latin.

Immediately in front of Harry in the apartment there was a striking antique mirror, full length, with pitch pine surrounds. Harry had seen a mirror like that before. In another hallway.

In another life, during his childhood in the house in Pimlico. As he stared at it, the memories shaking his bones, the telephone rang. He followed the noise and found the phone in the main room of the apartment, on a table next to a baby grand piano.

'It's Sidney Pearl, Harry. The police have just called. They say they do not think they can make it today. Can you believe it? Two shootings of teenagers in South London. Bad traffic. The election being called. Some kind of security alert. Bomb scare. Every excuse in the book except that the dog ate their homework. They wondered would it be convenient to call at the flat tomorrow morning, and meet you then?'

'Of course, of course,' Harry responded, wondering why London had become such a city of private wealth and public inadequacy. 'Give me their number and I'll ...'

'I'll call them back if you wish. Save you the trouble. They were suggesting around ten tomorrow morning?'

Harry felt relief. Someone was looking out for him, for the first time in years. A place of safety.

'Yes, Sidney, around ten. And Sidney ...'

'Yes?'

He hesitated.

'Thank you for being so kind.'

'Don't mention it. It's all part of the service. The least I could do for Robin Burnett's family.'

Harry put the phone down, relieved. If the police were not racing across London to meet him, then presumably they did not think Harry himself had anything important to say about

40

whatever had happened to his father. Good. They were right about that, at least. Harry took his shoes and socks off. He walked barefoot through the apartment, taking a quick mental inventory of his inheritance. Walnut dining table. Nice. Three thousand pounds. Plus eight chairs. Five thousand? Baby grand piano. Very nice. Ten thousand? Twenty thousand? He wasn't sure. He touched the keys. Beautiful tone. Modern flatscreen TV and DVD player. Leather sofa and chairs. Shiny table tops. The master bedroom overlooked the heath. Another bedroom set up as a study. Harry looked out and noticed a bench at the side of the heath facing towards him. A young woman with spiky hair was sitting on the bench, gazing towards the apartment, lost in thought. There was something – he could not think of the right word – cheeky, perhaps, or defiant – about the way that she looked up towards him. Harry pressed his face to the glass.

Suddenly, as if alarmed, the woman snatched at a rucksack on the bench beside her and turned away, moving quickly out of sight behind the trees towards the heath ponds. Harry stepped back, puzzled. He had caught her doing something wrong, this strange spiky woman. She was guilty, though he could not guess the crime. How odd. Harry returned to the main room and spotted a tray of malt whiskies, six or seven good ones. *Oban, Bowmore. Glen Moray. Macallan.* Plus a couple in the distinctive green-labelled bottles of the Scotch Whisky Society. At last. Signs of his father in residence. Gin. Vodka. A crystal ice bucket. Beside the tray of liquor, a big black and white photograph in a silver frame caught his eye. He snatched it up. It was of the father he remembered, taken in his prime about twenty years ago. Big shouldered, athletic build, tall, with a shock of black hair. Wearing a dinner jacket. But it was his father's companion who really startled Harry. She was strikingly beautiful. She was younger, in her early thirties. She had thick dark hair, tied in a chignon, and she was bedecked in a glittering ball-gown, her eyes brimful of intelligence. And there was something else. The woman and his father were laughing. The photographer had caught them at precisely the moment their eyes engaged. There was no doubting the expressions on their faces. Harry looked again at the face of the woman, and at his father. Then he called his sister.

'Leila Rajar?' Amanda's voice rose to high pitch.

'Yes.'

'You are sure it's her?'

'Absolutely. Yes. It's Leila Rajar.'

'But how could he be with Leila Rajar?'

Harry did not know.

'The American TV news woman?'

There was only one Leila Rajar.

'Yes, the American TV news woman. I'm holding the picture in my hand right now,' Harry insisted. 'This is either Leila Rajar or it's her body double.'

'But how can you be sure, Aitch?'

Harry grew exasperated.

'How can I be sure of anything?'

Harry watched Leila Rajar read the news most nights on satellite TV. Leila Rajar had just been signed up by CBS News for a contract reported to be worth $22 million a year, making her the best-paid newsreader in history.

'How can I be sure I am talking to you? It's her, Amanda. She's got darker hair in the photo than she has now, and she must have been about thirty when it was taken. She'd be fifty-something now. But it's her all right. And she is heart-stoppingly beautiful.'

'What about him?'

'He looks as he did in those photographs from after the Falklands War, when he was promoted to Chief Secretary to the Treasury. The cat that got the cream. Except for one thing.'

'What one thing?'

42

Harry looked at the picture and tried to sum it up.

'He is glowing.'

'Glowing?' Amanda scoffed. 'Aitch, have you been drinking?'

'Not yet.'

'Then what do you mean by ...'

'I have never seen him look so ... happy. Amanda, she is in love with him, and he is quite definitely in love with her. It's as if there is something warming them both from within.'

Harry took a deep breath. Until he said the words, it had never occurred to him that his father might love anyone other than himself.

'What?' She sounded shocked.

'Love, Amanda. It makes him look ... younger.'

'Younger?'

'And nicer.'

She raised her voice. 'Nicer?'

'Vulnerable.'

There was a long pause.

'But Leila Rajar!' Amanda broke in eventually. 'How would he know Leila Rajar?'

Harry shrugged.

'All I'm doing is looking at one moment between two people captured at one two-fiftieth of a second twenty years ago in black and white.'

'Exactly my point, and ...'

'It's enough. Really it is. They love each other.'

Amanda went silent.

'Fuck,' she said.

Middleburg, Virginia, 1982

ROBIN BURNETT'S STORY

Middleburg is fox-hunting country. It's about thirty miles from Washington in the rolling Virginia hills, but it's a different world. The day I arrived was a Friday. The *Washington Post* that day reported that the murder rate in the District of Columbia was going to hit 500 deaths in a year – in a city of 600,000 people. Fifteen times the murder rate in Northern Ireland, where we thought we had a problem big enough to send in troops. Some of the liberal commentators in the US were blaming the socially divisive policies of the Reagan administration. They criticized the President for designating tomato ketchup as a vegetable in school meals as a cost-saving device. How any of this was linked to the murder rate, I never understood, except that it was the usual liberal media elite sociological mumbo-jumbo, where you began with tomato ketchup and ended with blood on the streets, and it was always the government's fault. The Reaganauts blamed individual human wickedness for the crime rate, though that did not entirely explain why more people were more wicked under Reagan either. It looked to me like simple market forces. Drug dealers were competing for customers and eliminating their rivals. As the cocaine market matured, things would settle down. Supply, demand. Gunfire to settle market share, the emergence of a monopoly supplier. Peace on the streets. Eventually.

Anyway, the next day, the Saturday, the British embassy driver picked me up at my hotel and whisked me away from the war zone that Washington had become to spend the weekend at Don Hall's stud farm on the outskirts of Middleburg. We drove through a huge white arch inscribed with the words 'Hall Estate'. The driveway must be about a mile long, cutting through deep-green fields with white picket fences in between.

We stood around at a lunchtime barbecue in Don's capacious 'yard' – an enormous area between the house and the main barn – surrounded by horses grazing peacefully, a bucolic picture of pastureland and all-American contentment, a different planet to the street battles down the road in Washington.

When I first saw him, the Director of Central Intelligence, David Hickox, was squirting mustard from a yellow plastic bottle on to his hotdog. He was talking with his mouth full to Don Hall. I joined the half dozen others who were listening. Introductions were made.

'So, Robin, it looks like you have the Chileans on-side in the Falklands,' Hickox said, tearing at the bun and meat and nodding in my direction.

He was a surprisingly big man, more than six feet tall, I'd guess all of 250 pounds, but with no fat on him. Don had told me he was a former college football star who never quite made it professionally as a result of injuries.

'We do?' I replied.

'You do. And I believe you know you do. The Argies certainly know it. They think you have British special forces operating out of Chile right now. SAS and SBS.'

David Hickox was right about that. The Argies were right. The government of Chile hated the Argentine junta more than we did. They were being very helpful. In secret.

'Most of South America wants those arrogant Argie bastards to lose,' Don Hall said.

'And who can blame them?' I responded, insistently. 'They *will* lose. Now is a good time to be with the eventual winners.'

'And we will help you in any way we can,' Hickox said, looking at me directly.

That was a big admission. It made me think that for me this was already mission accomplished.

'I am very pleased, Director. Thank you. The Prime Minister will be very grateful.'

'I know she will,' Hickox said, and then he paused, wiping a slick of bright yellow mustard and grease from his lips with the back of his hands. 'So let me say it clear. We will be helpful in any way we can – consistent with our national interests and the directives of the President.'

I swigged at my beer. It was a reasonable caveat. Don Hall had already made it plain that anything the Royal Navy wanted from the US Navy would be forthcoming. There would be no problems at sea. It was all coming together.

'And I know we both agree that maintaining a strong trans-Atlantic relationship is absolutely consistent with your national interests,' I insisted. 'And ours.'

Hickox tore at the remains of his hotdog.

'So is maintaining the sanctity of the Monroe Doctrine,' he said.

The Monroe Doctrine was a 150-year-old piece of convenient US strategic high-flown self-interest much loved by Jeanne Kirkpatrick and a few of the others. It stated that the United States would not tolerate outsiders interfering in Latin America – except, of course, if that outsider were to be the United States itself. I thought Hickox was teasing me.

'Speaking personally,' I replied, 'I think we can agree that, once this war with the Argies is over, the biggest question facing both of us as allies will not involve this hemisphere at all. It will be how to stand up to the Soviets in Europe, Afghanistan and elsewhere, and how to roll them back.'

Hickox reached for more food, accepting a hamburger.

'I like the way you're talking,' he said. 'Go on.'

'The Prime Minister has instructed me to say that it is in British interests to accept a new generation of US mid-range nuclear weapons on our soil. We are well aware what is on offer, and we are sure our abilities to persuade other European countries of the need for Cruise and Pershing will ultimately outweigh any interests your government might have with the undemocratic military junta which temporarily runs Argentina.'

Hickox smiled.

'You Brits,' was all he said, and then slapped me on the back with a thump that made my teeth rattle. 'You Brits.'

As I was trying to recover, suddenly Hickox put his hamburger on the table and fell to the ground on his front. It was one of the strangest things I had ever seen and I was completely unprepared for it. David Hickox, Director of Central Intelligence, began doing a series of one-arm push-ups on the dirt, counting out loud as he did so.

'One ... two ... three...'

A small crowd gathered to cheer him on. I recognized the smiling faces of the deputy defence secretary, the head of the National Security Agency, and the under-secretary of state at the State Department. Don Hall pointed out a couple of generals and admirals in the mix, and the Commandant of the Marine Corps. No women. A few of the wives had gathered near the house, well away from the show by the barn, but this was a gathering of men. We were all clapping rhythmically, as Hickox pumped on his right arm. I quickly understood it was some kind of party piece.

'Twelve ... thirteen ... fourteen ...'

Each push-up pumped on his right arm. He held the left arm crooked behind his back.

Don Hall walked towards me.

'Twenty one ... two ... three ...'

'Did you upset him ...?' Don began.

'I didn't upset him,' I protested.

47

'Twenty eight … nine …'

'Well, then, he really likes you if he's giving this kinda performance. David Hickox only does his push-up thing when he wants to distract attention or celebrate. It works well with the Washington press corps, and other simple life forms.'

Hickox stood up, red in the face. He had managed thirty one-armed push-ups, which would have defeated most men half his age. I doubt if I could have managed a single one, even though I considered myself fit. The crowd cheered and slapped him on the back.

Hickox abandoned his half-eaten hamburger and instead went to grab ribs from the barbecue and another beer. When he had gone, Don Hall whispered to me, 'Works every time.'

'What? That?' I said in disbelief. 'But it's just a circus act.'

'And Washington is a circus, Robin. The biggest of big tops. You know the President says that being in the White House is just like showbiz? You have a helluva opening, you coast a little, and then you have a helluva close. It's all showbiz. Acting. Something you might need to think about if you get the top job. You'll make a great Prime Minister.' He dropped his voice. 'Though I'm not sure Hickox would make such a great president.'

I looked at him for a reason, but Don Hall just shrugged. I did not know what to say, so I just smiled, puffed up by the compliment he had paid to me. I could see that Hickox was still being congratulated as he fed himself pork ribs, licking the barbecue sauce from his fingers.

'You know our boys really want to see how you do it,' Don Hall changed the subject. 'Hickox especially.'

'How we do what?'

'Force projection. If you can get your Task Force to re-take a bunch of rocks in the South Atlantic, thousands of miles from home, it proves at least one navy in NATO works.'

I laughed.

'So, despite Jeanne Kirkpatrick, there are some people on this side of the Atlantic who do want us to win?'

Don laughed too, and then went off to attend to the chicken.

'Go talk some more to Hickox,' he called over his shoulder. 'He'll be playing horseshoes behind the barn. He's the one you want to use your famous British charm on. Now you've got started.'

Hickox was throwing horseshoes and cursing like a Marine every time he missed.

'Here, British boy, take a turn.'

My first horseshoe missed the pole by a foot. Hickox hooted.

'You do that to make me feel good?'

'Absolutely. I usually get it right first time. I just wanted to see you do some more push-ups.'

My second attempt missed by a foot the other side.

'Triangulation,' I said.

'Eh?'

'Like artillery.'

The third horseshoe rang around the pole. Beginner's luck.

'Bullseye!' Hickox yelled and then thumped me on the back again. If I had false teeth, the force of the blow would have knocked them out. I coughed and tried to smile.

'Tell me something, Director…'

'David. Or you can call me Wild Bill, like the press here do. It helps with the image if the Soviets think I am borderline crazy.'

After witnessing the push-ups, it wasn't just the Soviets who thought he was borderline crazy, but I knew better than to show it. Besides, Hickox had his own charm, which I was slowly warming to. There was – how should I say it? – an honesty about his ruthlessness which I found refreshing. In Britain, it is necessary to hide such things.

'Tell me, David, just straight here between us, you do know how important retaking the Falklands is to the British government?'

He nodded, then picked up the horseshoes and began throwing again.

'An existential crisis,' he muttered. 'You lose the war, you're gone. You win the war, you're back, big time. Maybe for another ten years. We want you to win the war.'

'Good,' I said. 'I hoped you would say that. Then given the seriousness of the matter, we will, as I suggested to you a moment ago, be grateful for anything – anything – you or other US agencies come across which would be of interest. Very grateful.'

He said nothing. Threw a horseshoe. Missed. He collected the horseshoes and came back and stood in front of me.

'I'm all ears,' he said.

'Beyond what I said about the Soviet Union, what is it that keeps you awake at night?'

Without missing a beat Hickox spoke softly, just one word. 'Iran.'

He pronounced it 'Eye-ran'. Jack Heriot had been right.

'So,' I said, riding a surge of thankfulness. 'So, is there anything we can do about Iran that would help you sleep more easily?'

Hickox threw another horseshoe then stood up straight and looked at me.

'Matter of fact, Robin,' he said, putting a big arm round my shoulder, 'I do believe there is.'

Now it really was Mission Accomplished, I told myself. Hickox squeezed me tightly. I could smell the barbecue sauce on his fingers. We both grinned.

London, 1982

The trip to Washington was judged a success. Even better, it really was a success. Reality matched perception, which in British politics is quite unusual. The Lady went out of her way to praise me. She had heard from the Ministry of Defence that naval and intelligence cooperation had never been better. No complaints. GCHQ were delighted with assistance they had received from the US National Security Agency, their electronic eavesdropping and signals intelligence people, and the RAF were pleased with something from the National Reconnaissance Office. I never found out what all this was about, and I didn't ask. I didn't need to know. All I needed to know was that it was a triumph and that, apparently, was put down to me.

'We were sure you were the right man for the job, Robin,' the Lady told me, clapping her hands together in pleasure late one night over the customary whisky and soda at Number Ten. By this time the Marines had landed on the Falklands and were yomping to victory. The Gurkhas had also landed. Argentine conscripts were falling over themselves to surrender. It had been put about that the Gurkhas liked to cut the ears off the bodies of those they killed. We denied this story at every opportunity. There is nothing which promotes an outrageous story more effectively than a firm government denial.

Of course, there had also been setbacks. *HMS Sheffield*. The terrible damage caused by the Exocet missiles supplied to the Argentines by our good friends, the French. But from that point onwards there was no doubt about the final result, no doubt the Argentine junta would collapse, and no doubt either that the Lady would call an election and we'd be back in power for another five years. Ten, I thought. Fifteen, as it turned out. I called David Hickox to thank him.

'Congratulations,' he said. 'I hear it's gone real well.'

'Yes. But it would not have gone so well without your personal help. Thank you. I owe you.'

'Indeed you do. The Lady gonna go for an election?'

'Next spring,' I replied. 'Most likely. And we will win. Thank you for that, too.'

Hickox laughed.

'You think we wouldn't bale you out? And let Labour back in? Jeez, Robin, no way.'

Hickox was correct, of course. The Labour party was in one of its self-destructive phases, hijacked by the Impossibilist Left, the ones who preferred keeping their ideological purity to getting elected. They wanted to abandon nuclear weapons. The Falklands victory and their own catalogue of stupidity meant they'd be unelectable for years.

'We'll talk,' Hickox said.

'I'll look forward to it.'

Well, well. An accidental Argentinian tango had taken us from defeat to victory in a few easy steps. Almost at the very end of the conflict, a few days after British troops had finally re-taken Port Stanley, I was invited to a Foreign Office drinks party. It was not officially a celebration. That would have been premature and a bit un-British. But the Foreign Office mandarins – with their usual ability to sniff political careers the way dogs sniff each other's bottoms – had decided – sniff, sniff – that I might – sniff, sniff – make Foreign Secretary one day. My ascent had taken me ahead of Jack Heriot, and he was graceful enough to admit it.

'Well done, Robin,' a card from Heriot read. '*Primus inter pares.*'

First among equals, the usual description of the Prime Minister.

Looking back on it, I think that the FCO party was the moment when I was at the very top of my game. My reputation at the Treasury was high. The civil servants there understood what we were doing to liberate the economy. And now at the MoD and the Foreign Office they had begun to treat me with something close to respect. Three of the top four ministries in HMG had something good to say about me. The Lady noticed. The Americans noticed. Everybody noticed.

I made sure my press secretary gave a couple of briefings – off-the-record, of course – outlining the key role I had played with the Reagan administration, without giving away too many details. When the press asked me to confirm my role I was shocked – *shocked* – that anyone had leaked such a sensitive matter. I thundered that one should never comment on matters affecting national security. *Loose lips sink ships.* What fun! My conceit and arrogance expanded to fill the available space. I was asked to help draft the manifesto for the 1983 election. I was asked to prepare my plans for selling off state-run industries. I was asked to address party gatherings all over the country. I was applauded in Cardiff and Perth, in Manchester and Leeds. I was offered a top speaking slot at the autumn party conference. I was on *Newsnight* so often, one of the presenters joked I made more appearances on BBC television than he did. I think that all of this helps explain – though it does not excuse – what happened when I met Leila again, and this time learned her name. I thought I could do no wrong. Or if I did, that no one would ever find out.

There was to be no escape, for either of us.

The Foreign Office drinks party was in the Locarno Suite. It's one of the greatest function rooms in Whitehall, a magnificent old-fashioned barn big enough to stage an opera, or from which to govern an Empire. Some of the performances in the Locarno Suite have been truly operatic. I entered with a peculiar feeling of nervousness, without knowing why. People were falling over each other to talk to me. That old cliché about power being an aphrodisiac, perhaps. More accurately, a pheromone.

'Hello, Robin ... oh, Robin, it's you ... Mr Burnett good to see you ... Robin, how delightful ...'

Within minutes of entering the Locarno Suite I was surrounded by lobby reporters. They were looking for some kind of high-grade gossip, an insight into what would happen next, now that the war was more or less won. What might monetarism and trade union reform mean in practice, now that the Lady's administration was not just an historical blip? It was taken for granted that we would win the next election, just as a few months before it had been taken for granted that we would lose. Conventional Wisdom is about as reliable as the hemlines of women's skirts for predicting the political future. Some of the brighter ones in the Locarno Suite wanted to know whether the cost of re-taking the Falklands might blow public spending and the economy off course. I said it had blown our politics back on course.

'You do things because they are right,' I boomed at them. 'Not because they are cheap. Defending British citizens and British interests against a proto-fascist Argentinian dictatorship was the right thing to do. We will pay for it. But we will do so proudly, because that is the nature of this country.'

There was a lot of harrumphing at this.

'Despite what now looks like the certainty of the Falklands victory you have to admit that immediately before it, the government was never less popular,' a blue-stocking type from *The Times* insisted. She dripped frustration of all kinds. One of the soft lefties from the BBC chimed in.

'If you win, you have to thank Galtieri. It will be a khaki election, not an endorsement of your economic policies.'

'Not true,' I replied. 'Everyone understands that we won a difficult war after being attacked. Explaining how we are turning the economy around takes more time. But government is a package. It is everything that we stand for, not a few separate bits and pieces, not a la carte. And we are very clear about it.'

'So you admit you have failed to communicate to the voters how you are managing the economy?' *The Times* bluestocking shot back at me.

'Well, I have obviously failed to communicate it to *The Times*,' I said. 'Though I daresay I have communicated it successfully to your proprietor.'

I could feel her intake of breath. *The Times* hacks were all shit scared of Rupert Murdoch. We were quite respectful of him too.

'Please understand me. British governments do NOT manage the economy, though some are deluded enough to think they do. Governments set a few broad conditions and then the economy manages itself. Invisible hands. And while we expect British sailors to manage Exocets, I think the rest of us can manage to turn around the opinion polls.'

There was laughter at this.

'The unions will never submit to the kind of reforms you are demanding,' a stout, balding fellow from the *Guardian* told me. He was swallowing copious amounts of cheap Foreign Office claret, as if desperate to get his share. When he spoke I started to imagine that his tongue was too big for his mouth, like a claret-swilling frog. I remember it was stained purple. I had a glass of red in my hand but looking at him I could not bear to drink from it and put it down on a table. I was desperate for a decent whisky.

'It'll be back to Ted Heath and the three-day week with the miners,' the woman from *The Times* agreed.

'Winter of Discontent will be like a sideshow,' another said.

'Challenges ahead,' was all I said. 'You are all correctly noting that there are definitely big challenges ahead.'

I was growing tired of the sparring, but at that moment Leila entered the Locarno Suite. Heads turned, including mine and – as I could see – that of the Deputy Foreign Secretary Jack Heriot. Leila had the grace of a ballet dancer. Her dress whispered on her body. I swallowed hard.

'Let me introduce the CBS News correspondent in London.' An American diplomat, Peter Doberman, steered her into the room. 'Jack Heriot, Her Majesty's Deputy Secretary of State for Foreign and Commonwealth Affairs, please welcome Leila Rajar.'

'I do believe we have met once before,' Heriot said smoothly, shaking her hand and looking into her eyes. 'Perhaps at one of the news conferences here during the conflict?'

'I do believe we have,' Leila responded, her voice measured and firm. 'I've been here a few months – since the start of the Falklands crisis. And it's certainly a pleasure to see you again, Mr Deputy Secretary.'

Mr Deputy Secretary. Oh, how Heriot loved that.

'The pleasure is mine, Ms Rajar,' he beamed. Creep. I walked towards them.

'We are always ready to improve on the Special Relationship,' Heriot was saying with a smile that contained within it a leer.

You are too old for her, Jack, I remember thinking. But she is not too young for you.

Leila's eyes flickered towards me. I could see that she thought Heriot was being a creep as well. I smiled inwardly at her good judgement.

'Let me also introduce –' the American diplomat began, nodding towards me, but Leila interrupted him.

'Oh, I know who this is, Peter,' she said, turning her smile towards me. 'Professor Burnett, you wowed us all at the Kennedy School summer lectures a few years ago.'

Did I?

'Robin did what?' Jack Heriot said in disbelief. 'He … wowed you?'

'Oh, yes, he wowed everybody. It was the Kennedy School of Government in Harvard. Do you remember, Professor Burnett?'

'Yes,' I answered. I remembered Harvard. But I did not remember her. 'I was ...'

Leila interrupted.

'... a visiting lecturer in – I'd guess – summer of 1978 or thereabouts. During the worst of the Carter Days, and just after the worst for you folks here in Britain too. Strikes. Oil shocks. Stag-flation. I remember you gave a lecture as part of the supply-side economics forum called Defeating Defeatism – how to beat inflation and other ills of the modern economy. Something like that.'

'You remember it?' I beamed inwardly.

'Remember it? I still have the notes,' she laughed, and the laughter danced in my heart. 'I was with the *New York Times*, writing a piece about world economic prospects. I was scheduled for an interview with John Kenneth Galbraith. While I was waiting for the great man I thought I'd catch this new Brit performer who offered entirely the opposite view to that of Galbraith ...'

'I think the word you are looking for is "professor", rather than performer,' Heriot said unhelpfully. 'Though "performer" probably works for Robin too.'

'Performer, professor, whatever ...' she laughed again, but refused to be deflected. 'Anyway, there was this new Brit who was saying the impossible, that inflation could be tamed, the unions could be controlled, and the Soviet Union could be outspent into economic disaster if we only had the wit, nerve and optimism to do it.'

I blushed.

'I may have said all that, but I didn't exactly invent it. Hayek and Friedman ... '

'Whoever invented it, it came across as so ... so very American,' she added slyly. 'Optimistic. Positive. Problem

57

solving. Not the kind of pessimism we associate with the British.'

'One out of three isn't so bad,' Jack Heriot said.

'One out of three?' Peter Doberman the American diplomat asked.

'Bearing down on inflation,' Heriot explained. 'At least we are doing that. The rest of Robin's crystal ball seems a bit fuzzy. The Soviet Union will be with us for many years to come. And what's worse, so will the unions …'

I wanted to kick Heriot in the balls, crystal or otherwise.

'You see, that's the difference between the two sides of the Atlantic,' Leila Rajar suggested, as if Heriot had just proved her point. 'Typically, you guys always see the glass half empty. We always see it half full. That's why I thought Professor Burnett was more like an American. He believed things were possible, which is maybe why he's Chief Secretary to the Treasury now, and why he was such a big hit on his recent visit to Washington.'

Briefly she laid a hand on my arm as she talked about me. No more than half a second, but it contained a jolt of pleasure that I wanted to repeat. I could sense her perfume. Her eyes washed over me. Silk and lace on tanned skin. I was lost, but I did not yet know how completely.

'They say that you, single-handedly, got the Reagan administration on-side,' she smiled at me. 'That you wowed Hickox and the neo-cons, and that they all love you. They say that you are "One of Us".'

'Then they say wrong,' I replied firmly. 'I have many friends in the Reagan administration and I can tell you that your President is a proud defender of democracy against military dictatorship. He needed no prompting from me. Supporting Argentina was never a realistic option.'

She laughed.

'You say that with a straight face?'

Not any more. I burst out laughing too. She got to me with her wit, as well as with her beauty.

58

'Let me just repeat the wisdom of Winston Churchill,' I said. 'That the American people always do the right thing – usually after having exhausted every conceivable alternative.'

Doberman and Heriot began arguing cheerfully about European pessimism and American optimism. It was standard diplomatic party talk, and a silence fell between me and Leila. I drank in her beauty. Her eyes were big and dark brown, her hair long and thick. I felt a strange apprehension strike me. I wanted her, but I did not want to be at that party any more, not in the Locarno Suite, not with any of these people. It was almost my last attempt at sanity, before what was to become the madness of falling in love with her. It was as if I was to make a last attempt to break free, before Leila overwhelmed me.

'Very nice meeting you, Ms Rajar.' I put out my hand suddenly, to shake farewell. Her hand felt small and soft in mine and the touch of her fingers moved me again like an electric charge. 'I'd better circulate a bit.'

I tried to read her expression, hoping it might be one of disappointment. I don't think many men said goodbye to Leila Rajar, but if she was surprised then she did not show it. She merely smiled. It was a diplomatic cocktail party kind of smile, with no meaning or warmth.

'Very nice to meet you too,' she said. 'I hope our paths cross again.'

'I hope so.'

'Well, if you are not prepared to admit to your secret diplomacy – which is not so much a secret anyway thanks to some well-orchestrated leaks – then perhaps you could give me an interview about the future health of the British economy?' she suggested cheekily.

I nodded.

'It would be a pleasure, Miss Rajar. Call my office and arrange it. Tell them I have definitely agreed to it.'

And we parted. My heart was thumping. I was nervous, and I was almost never nervous. I felt my hands tremble and my legs go weak as I moved towards the door through the journalists who launched another fusillade about the economy. Remorseless. Relentless. Feed the beasts. Feed the beasts.

My heart was beating curiously and I wanted to get away, far, far away. I answered questions for a few more minutes. I told the woman from *The Times* that it was not simply up to the government to manage the unions, it was up to employers.

'Like *The Times*?' she suggested mischievously. Clearly mentioning Rupert Murdoch had hit a chord with her.

'Fleet Street is home to some of the worst abominations in British industry,' I told her. 'Over-manning. Restrictive practices. Buying off trouble rather than confronting it. One of these days some proprietor will have the courage to take on the print unions. Perhaps it will be your proprietor. We in government admire Mr Murdoch's robust leadership.'

'Take on the unions with government support?'

'With enthusiastic government support. Perhaps you should mention that to Mr Murdoch, if the opportunity arises. Or perhaps I will.'

She could not have mistaken what I was suggesting. As I left I looked back to see Leila smiling at some remark from Jack Heriot. I closed the door and ran down the stairs. When I reached King Charles Street I sucked in the cool night air, and hurried off to my desk at the Treasury for the therapy of some late night work on the monetary supply figures. They never failed to calm me down.

Leila fixed up a meeting almost immediately. I was impressed, though I should have guessed that she would not wait. She called my office after a day or so, although it took another forty-eight hours for a slot to be found in my diary. Since Leila worked for CBS News at the time, it would have been reasonable to assume she might want a television interview. Reasonable, but wrong. She asked for an off-the-record chat. I felt a shiver of pleasure. I suggested lunch. Lunch is the best meal in London. It can have the air of business. It can be innocent. Dinner or breakfast with a woman as strikingly pretty as Leila carried an entirely different connotation. And yet I'd bet that more careers and more love affairs are made or broken over lunch than any other meal or meeting. My staff booked a quiet sushi place in St James's, and I walked over through the park. They have private booths in the sushi place. I go there when I want to plot something. It occurs to me now that perhaps I was plotting my own downfall.

'Tell me about the Lady,' Leila whispered, almost immediately as she sat down opposite me. She touched me gently on the arm as she spoke. Again it was for less than a second, the merest brush of her hand, but I felt my body stir. 'She's such a superstar now in the United States. You must tell me everything.'

'Everything?' I laughed. 'That would be a breach of the Official Secrets Act.'

'Oooh,' she giggled, 'how exciting.'

'Then perhaps I will tell you everything,' I replied. 'After all, you're a journalist. I can obviously trust you. It will go no further.'

When she laughed she threw back her head and I watched her dark brown hair fall on her shoulders. My life until that point had been full of rational choices and decisions, some hard and some easy, but falling in love with Leila was not like that. It was not a choice or a decision. It was as involuntary as breathing, and I sometimes think that perhaps it was as necessary. I had always thought there was a rational world, which was where I lived, a world of graphs and statistics and economic theories, of university departments and Treasury meetings. There was also an irrational world, which I despised – a world of horoscopes and beliefs, of hatreds based on race or bigotry or religion. Falling in love with Leila made me realize there was also something else. I called it a meta-rational world, a world which was beyond explanation, but which also, somehow, made sense even if I could not say exactly why.

That was Leila. Meta-rational. I looked at her, straight in the eyes. It was a long time before either of us blinked. I handed her the sushi menu and for the briefest of moments our hands touched, and I thought again of silk and lace. We ordered. I chose the set sushi menu because it did not involve any thought. I didn't care what I ate. In the years with her that followed, I was rarely hungry for food. I was hungry for her, and it showed.

And so that very first day I did tell her about the Lady. Not everything, of course. No real secrets. I am loyal and discreet. But I did tell her a lot about the mechanics of how government worked, about how the Lady was so very meticulous, so very neat, how she had her own dresser whom she relied upon, how she really responded to men in uniform, how – there is no other word for it – she flirted with those she liked, and demolished those she did not. Leila listened and played with her food, pushing a stray hair behind her ear and sometimes cocking her head to the side as she lifted a tuna roll or a slice of sashimi. I had a sudden desire to touch her cheek gently with my fingers. The thought made me gasp.

'Do you mind if I take notes?'

Do you mind if I make love to you, I thought.

'This is off the record.'

'Yes, but ... deep background? Who knows, I may one day write a book about all this.'

'So might I,' I joked. 'I keep a diary and one day it might keep me. Go ahead. Take notes if you wish.' She had a frank way of holding my gaze that I have never seen in a woman before or since. 'Curiously, I trust you,' I said slowly. I thought I was about to die. After a minute or so getting out a suitable pen and notebook, she plugged the silence.

'You clearly think the Lady is wonderful.'

'Yes, I do.'

'I have heard she is also bossy, intolerant of dissent, that she doesn't listen to her Cabinet and ...'

I stopped her.

'But that is precisely why she is so wonderful. These are compliments.'

'It is a compliment to say she's bossy and won't listen?'

I sighed.

'The British Cabinet is full of people who think they should be Prime Minister. They all think they are in with a chance to succeed her, eventually. In the meantime, most of them do what they are told. Some of them – like Michael Armstrong – in their hearts despise her because she has the capacity for greatness, whereas they do not and they know it. She is intolerant of dissent. But she loves argument. That's not the same thing. She listens and she argues back, then she takes a decision and you fall in line or you get out. In government you need to be bossy when you're right. That's why she fired Armstrong.'

'And what if you're wrong?'

'She's not wrong.'

'But what if you are?'

'Then to be bossy in pursuit of error is the classic political tragedy. Read Macbeth. Or Caesar. Or Lear.'

'I have. And I have also acted in Macbeth.'

'Let me guess which part.'

Leila laughed again. I watched her hair fall on her shoulders and her tiny teeth flash white. God, how I wanted her. Waiting was the most delicious pain.

'Don't change the subject. They say that she listens to you?'

'Sometimes. Mostly. Yes, I think so. That's why she is so rarely wrong.'

I laughed at my own arrogance, though I knew Leila was impressed. Then I changed the subject.

'Now Miss Leila Rajar, I have a number of questions for you.'

'Oh,' she said, putting her hand to her breast in mock shock. 'You do? Questions for me? On deep background?'

'Yes. I am a great friend of the United States of America but I have watched American TV news and I do not think that anything an obscure finance minister in the government of the United Kingdom has to say will be of any interest to your viewers. Neither do you, otherwise you would want an on-camera interview rather than a very pleasant lunch.'

She looked down at her food and picked at a piece of salmon.

'Hmmm. Let's suppose you are correct,' she admitted. 'But let me also admit that what you say is of great interest to me personally.'

'Why?'

She put down her fork and put her hands together on the table.

'Because *you* are of great interest to me, Robin. Ever since Harvard. I like the way you think. I ... I want to get inside your head.'

I should have been less surprised had she slapped me across the face. There was that look from her again. The look of a hungry lioness. I was uncharacteristically lost for something to say.

'I ... well ... are you flirting with me, by any chance?'

'Of course. You are ... you have something against flirting during the hours of daylight?'

I took a deep breath. Lace and silk and the touch of her hand.

'You realize that if we ever get together no one will ever get us apart?' I blurted out. Leila said nothing. She stared at me, slightly taken aback.

'That might not be so good for your career,' she said.

'Or yours,' I replied. She coughed. We both looked away.

'Perhaps we should have some coffee,' I suggested. 'In my case a very large espresso. I have to meet some spending ministers this afternoon and apply a vice to their ambitions. Or their testicles. Which are mostly the same things.'

We sat in silence until the coffee arrived. By the end of the lunch I had discovered a number of things about Leila Rajar.

She had a PhD in international relations from Georgetown and a first degree in economics from Pepperdine in California – facts that she kept hidden from the viewers of CBS News.

'American viewers like pretty,' she said. 'But they get suspicious of smart. Especially smart women. I don't play dumb, but I don't emphasize any of my qualifications either. It's survival.'

I also found out where the name Rajar came from.

'It's Persian,' she said. 'Iranian, though I prefer the word "Persian" since it pre-dates the religious gangsters who are now destroying my country. It's really spelled Qajar, but some-how it was botched when it was trans-literated from Farsi when my father fled to LA.'

'Fled?'

'When I was seven, I guess. The Shah's secret police, SAVAK, had it in for him. I grew up in Los Angeles – Los Iran-geles as they call it. There are so many Iranian exiles in LA. The rest of the Qajars have been forced out by the Islamic Revolution. They are scattered around France, England and the US.'

'Why were they forced out?'

'Why do you think?'

'Stupid question,' I admitted.

'Politics,' she answered anyway. 'Just like under the Shah only worse.'

'What kind of politics?'

'The only type that matter in Iran. Dirty politics. Violent politics. In which people lose everything their family has had for hundreds of years, and sometimes lose their lives.'

'*Animal Farm*,' I said.

'Excuse me?'

'*Animal Farm*. George Orwell. The Pigs overthrow the Humans in a farmyard revolution but by the end of the book the Pigs behave exactly as the Humans do, or worse. Orwell thought all politics was like that. He's wrong. But Khomeini and his followers are certainly in the mould, persecuting the same people that the Shah persecuted.'

'*Animal Farm* then,' she agreed. 'Pigs, certainly.'

Another silence fell over the table.

'I really should go,' she began.

'Can I see you again?' I blurted out. 'Despite the potential dangers to our careers?'

Her eyes washed over me. There was a delay of a few seconds. Excruciating. Yes or no?

'Yes,' she said, and then she stood up and kissed me gently with her full lips on my cheek. It was the most sexual thing that had ever happened to me in my life. Just a kiss, but hotter and more passionate than any kind of sex. I felt the blood pound in my neck and face as if during an orgasm.

'Of course,' she said hoarsely. 'Call me.'

Then she was gone. I called her a few hours later.

'This is me playing hard to get,' I said. I could hear her giggling. 'I really do want to see you again.'

'Good,' she responded. 'Because I really do want to see you again too.'

It took a couple of days for us to fix a date because I was – as I told her – busy with the spending review. It meant I had to call in ministers from various departments to tell them why they could not have any money. The newspapers called the process the Star Chamber, after the medieval torture.

'That's illogical,' Michael Armstrong's replacement as Home Secretary, Lewis Jones, challenged me on the cuts I was forcing him to make. In the political pecking order he was senior to me. But the Lady had offered me his job, and I had turned it down because I wanted to complete my work at the Treasury. Plus, I did not want the Home Office. Who'd want to be responsible for law and order? Kiss of death to any political career. I had Lewis Jones' budget in my hand and I squeezed hard. He squealed.

'You want more effective policing, more spending on new prisons, and yet you want to give me less money overall ...'

'Correct, Lewis. I do.'

He looked astonished.

'You want more for less?'

'Yes.'

'It's ...'

I stared at him the way you do at something on your shoe. Lewis Jones was a fool, but clever enough to realize I thought he was one. He carried some weight among the backbenchers in the 1922 Committee. I had made an enemy, and I didn't care. I chose my enemies carefully. He harrumphed.

'... it's illogical.'

'Illogical?' I replied.

'It doesn't add up.'

'I'll tell you what doesn't add up, Lewis.' I pointed my finger at him like a stick. 'What doesn't add up is the idea that a Conservative Home Secretary cannot shake up the worst bureaucracy in Britain, which you happen to be presiding over, Lewis, without spraying more money on it like petrol on a fire. I can think of at least three different ways of dividing up the Home Office to make it less unwieldy and far more efficient. If you would like me to outline in Cabinet my plans to reduce your department from underneath you, then I will gladly do so, Lewis, but you might find it more convenient to come up with your own savings.'

He was reeling from this verbal assault. I could see it in his face.

'Three little words, Lewis: cut the fat.'

Before my second date with Leila, I wanted to do some research. I got the senior Treasury press officer to do it for me.

It turned out that 'Qajar' was not just a Persian name like Smith or Jones, it was the dynastic name of the Persian royal family before the Pahlavi dynasty. If there was ever to be a restoration of the Iranian monarchy, it might not be a Pahlavi after all. It might be a Qajar. Leila's father did indeed have to leave Tehran, but mostly because he was a potential rival to the Pahlavis and had demanded democratic reforms. The Shah had refused to take his advice and thought he was potentially a traitor, hence the attentions of SAVAK, the secret police. I called Leila again.

'Good morning, princess.'

'What?'

'I checked you out. You are a princess.'

'No,' she said. Can people blush on the telephone? I think she blushed. 'Not really.'

'So, I'm more or less clear of the Star Chamber. Can we meet?'

'Yes.'

I paused, but only for a second or two.

'Listen, Leila, I very much want to see you. But we must be careful. If I am seen with you, it will get into the papers. There is no way round it.'

Without missing a beat she said, 'There is, if you come to my apartment.'

And so there it was. My fate was settled. Our fate was settled. Fate, Destiny, Providence, or something like it. I sensed again that it would end in disaster, but I did not care. I embraced the possibility of catastrophe with both hands. I did it with both eyes open, and I hugged my fate like an old friend. A few months later, Leila confided in me that at first she thought it was just a bit of fun.

'Alone, in Britain, an attractive, powerful Englishman,' she said. 'What's not to like? I wanted a little adventure.'

'And then?' I said.

I remember she looked at me with her wet eyes.

'And then, I fell in love, which was a terrible personal and professional mistake. A catastrophic error of judgement.'

I loved her from the first moment I saw her, and I told her so. She giggled.

'Don't be silly. There's no such thing as love at first sight.'

I was not being silly. It was the truth. I remember it now so well because after that moment, the truth and I became strangers.

Hampstead, London, Spring 2005

HARRY BURNETT'S STORY

It was now dark, but something drew Harry Burnett back to the study of his father's Hampstead apartment. Perhaps it was the memory of the defiant girl looking up from the bench on the heath below. He checked the bench again but this time it was empty. He returned to the kitchen, fetched water from the tap in a crystal pitcher and poured a couple of fingers of Glen Moray into a whisky tumbler. He splashed a drop of water on top.

'Just a wee splash to open the nose,' he said in a mock Scottish accent. 'As *faither* would say.'

He stared at the picture of his father with Leila Rajar again, then switched on the television. His father's suicide attempt was the last headline on a specially extended edition of the *Ten O'Clock News*. The top story was, of course, the beginning of the General Election campaign with polling day set for 5th May 2005.

'5 – 5 – 5,' Harry said. 'Very auspicious. Probably. In China, or somewhere.'

Historic, the journalists said, repeatedly. They loved adjectives, Harry thought, so everybody knew what to think. The news presenter – historic, historic – explained that the parties were preparing to launch their campaigns for this – historic – battle of historic ideas. He tried to make it sound exciting, which was a bit of a stretch since everyone knew that Blair would win. The Tories were in the same mess they had been since the Lady left office. That was the great thing about the Conservatives, Harry thought. They hated each other more than they hated anyone else. To a Tory, Labour was just the Opposition. The real Enemy was always on their own side. It was half an hour into the extended bulletin and two whiskies later before they got to his father, a political footnote to the main news of the day.

'Now to a story – and a man – the Conservatives would rather forget. Robin Burnett. He's credited with being one of the great brains behind Thatcherism in the late seventies and eighties, and he has been found close to death in mysterious circumstances at his home in Gloucestershire. Empty pill bottles and a knife were discovered by his side, and it is known that his wrists were cut. Police sources are saying that it may have been a suicide attempt, but foul play has not been ruled out. Here's our political correspondent, Sheena Hayworth.'

Harry let the whisky trickle over his tongue. The report that followed looked and sounded like his father's obituary.

It began with the tribute from the American Vice President David Hickox and the commentary noting that Robin Burnett had 'helped put the word Special back into the Special Relationship with the United States.' There followed more familiar TV clips from the past, threaded together with interviews with his father's contemporaries.

'Robin Burnett was talented,' Jack Heriot, the former Prime Minister and Cabinet contemporary of Burnett was saying. Heriot was now a puffy-faced elder-statesman in a grey pinstripe suit. *'No doubt about it. Brilliant, even. Mrs Thatcher certainly thought so. Driven. Charismatic. But he had a fatal flaw.'*

'Which was?'

The puffy face broke into a grin.

'He always wanted to be the centre of attention. If Robin Burnett were invited to a wedding, he wanted to be the bride.

If it was a funeral, he wanted to be the corpse. What happened to Robin was a classical tragedy. His fatal flaw was pride. Arrogance. He thought he could get away with it. And he very nearly did.'

The voice-over continued.

'That barbed tribute from one of his contemporaries. But when we asked the current Conservative leader Michael Howard to give his reaction today, it was not forthcoming.'

There were pictures of Howard smiling vacantly in a crowd of Tory supporters in some south of England market town, ignoring shouted questions.

'What do you think of Robin Burnett's apparent suicide attempt, Mr Howard?'

Grin, grin. Shake, shake.

'Are you worried it reminds voters how the party lost its way under Mrs Thatcher?'

Grin, grin. Shake, shake.

'About the Sleaze Factor?'

The Art of Political Zen. For Michael Howard, if he pretended it wasn't really happening, then it wasn't really happening. But it was happening. More voice-over.

'A Conservative party spokeswoman said Michael Howard was too busy focusing on the current election campaign to be bothered by what she called "a figure from the distant past." The spokeswoman then read out a single-line tribute.'

The TV report cut to a picture of a young Tory woman in a blue suit reading in a dull voice from a piece of paper. She must have been about Harry's age, too young to remember who his father really was.

'Our sympathies go out to the Burnett family at this difficult time. We intend to respect their right to privacy.'

That was it. She folded the paper and walked away. The voice-over picked up again.

'Twenty words – just twenty words in tribute to one of the intellectual fathers of the modern Conservative party. All this

shows that Burnett's mixed legacy is not forgotten, though some wish that it were. The Conservatives are desperate to distance themselves from everything the Burnett scandal symbolized. Political amnesia – you might say – is today's ailment of choice.'

The report then cut to old footage of Harry's father brushing back luxuriant black hair with his left hand, grinning broadly as if at a great joke and pounding the rostrum at a party rally. Harry noted the date. It was less than a month before he was born. A strap across the pictures said April 1979. His father was speaking.

'Our mission is to get government off the backs of the British people.' The deep baritone was resonant with conviction, almost as if he were in the room. It made Harry shiver. On the TV screen his father pointed at the audience, as if at each person individually. It was a clever trick.

'To the people of Britain I say this. We intend to turn you loose – you – and you – and you – each and every one of you – to do what you can do for yourselves and for your families and for your country. Our mission is to take the dead hand of government out of your pockets, out of your wallets, off your backs – to lift the burden of the state from the British people and to set the people free!'

The audience took up the refrain.

'Set the people free! Set the British people free!'

Harry sipped the whisky. He knew what was coming, and he felt for the TV remote control. There were more shots of Robin Burnett, this time canvassing in his Gloucestershire constituency. He was thin and angular, handsome in a way, with a glow of certainty about himself and his message. The commentator was saying something about Burnett's personal closeness to Mrs Thatcher, to the Americans, his charisma, his intellectual background as an economist.

'Some tipped Robin Burnett as a future Prime Minister. But that all fell apart in the late eighties in a scandal which seemed to symbolize the rottenness and arrogance at the core of ...'

A newspaper picture of a young woman appeared. She was wearing a striped bikini and high heels.

'... *a woman called Carla Carter who* ...'

The woman's backside was stuck out towards the camera, and she looked over her shoulder while her tongue licked her red lips. Her hair was big and wavy. Harry hit the off button. He did not need to hear any more. Ever. He drained the whisky and decided to try another.

'And why not?' he said aloud to his father's image in the photograph with Leila Rajar. 'Funny, isn't it? If they had got a sniff of you and the delicious Leila, that would have perked up the obituary, yes? That would have given them a very different kind of scandal. I wonder how much I'd get for this picture now, eh?'

The alcohol was doing its work. His hand felt for the *Macallan*.

'And while we are on the subject of totty, should we invite the delish Leila to your funeral? Or your hospital bed? Does she even know you are close to death? Maybe someone should tell her? Maybe it should be me?'

Harry picked up the whisky glass and began to mooch around the rooms one more time. He was drawn back to the study. On the desk under the window facing the heath there was a silver grey Sony Vaio laptop computer connected to a laser printer and to a broadband router. Harry switched on the printer but it required a password. He switched it off again. He had never considered his father might be surrounded by so many modern gadgets, but then he supposed that he hadn't really considered his father much at all. The bookshelves bore a number of biographies and political books, many of them by former colleagues, some with friendly inscriptions.

'*To Robin. In memory of better days. Nigel.*'

'*To Robin, the man who made it all possible! Best wishes, Margaret.*'

'To Robin. The man who got out at the right time!!! Pity the rest of us!!! Norman.'

'The Bastards!!! Don't let them grind you down!!! Best, always, J.H.'

Harry found a ready-made pizza in the freezer and stuck it in the oven. He tried to imagine his father eating a frozen pizza, but that was impossible. A lot of what he was seeing simply did not add up. While he waited for the pizza to cook he freshened up the whisky and searched through his father's DVD collection. Old Bogart movies. *Brief Encounter. Reservoir Dogs. Pulp Fiction. Blue Velvet*, the complete edition of *Twin Peaks*, and *Mulholland Drive. The Player.*

'Tarantino and David Lynch? Robert Altman? Jesus. Pizza? Plus Leila Rajar? Who knew, eh, dad? Who knew?'

Harry ate the pizza, more confused about his father than ever before. He lay back on the sofa in the main room, determined to get raging drunk. He turned the volume down on the television and fell asleep where he lay. It was a deep, undisturbed, whisky sleep.

When Harry woke, it was with a start. It was hours later, his tongue was furred and his mouth tasted of sour alcohol. The middle of the night. Harry tried to check his watch but his eyes were sleepy.

Something about the room felt strange, like a chill. He shivered. He sensed someone watching him and shook himself awake. Then he caught sight of a blur. It was a woman. A young woman with a small rucksack and spiky brown hair. Harry shook himself again as the woman broke into a run and burst through the room towards the front door. She was carrying the Sony Vaio laptop from the study under her arm plus papers and files and the silver-framed photograph of his father with Leila Rajar. Harry sat upright, startled, and then leaped after her. The young woman ran as Harry stumbled. It was as if he were trapped in a pot of thick oil, unable to move, while she ran from the room like a faun leaving behind a whiff of her scent, a perfume without a name, flicked open the front door and was gone. Harry broke into a run, then paused to make sure he had the front door key so he would not lock himself out. He swore at his slowness as he burst into the hallway and raced down the blue carpet, following the tease of her scent. He ran towards the elevators, but they were silent. Nothing moved. The emergency stairs, he decided. She must have used the emergency stairs. But where were they? Where was the fire escape? Where was the sign?

He ran to the other end of the hall, his bare feet pounding on the trampoline of a carpet. The fire escape was marked and he pulled at the door. He could make out the sound of footsteps below and ran after them, the balls of his bare feet thumping on the concrete of the fire stairs. He hit the jade coloured floor of the main entrance hall as the front door clicked shut. The young woman was running down the hill towards the heath. The faun had escaped into the woodland. Gone. Barefoot in the dark Harry had no chance of catching her. He stood panting in the hallway and checked his watch. It was three o'clock in the morning.

'Jesus,' he hissed under his breath. He wondered why he had not heard the girl breaking in, but then immediately understood. She had used keys. She had crept past him, and had almost managed to leave without rousing him. She knew exactly where she was going. She had been there before. Harry pressed the elevator button and returned to the apartment. He checked the front door. As he had guessed, there was no sign of forced entry. He went from room to room trying to decide what had gone missing. His own wallet was lying undisturbed on the table. But the computer was definitely gone. And the photograph of his father with Leila. Some papers. Nothing else, he decided. He thought about calling the police immediately, then he hesitated. Finally he decided to leave it until daybreak. The girl was long gone. There was nothing the police could do for him, except give him a long, sleepless night. After a while he wondered whether he had dreamed about the burglary, whether it had really happened.

He rubbed his face in his hands and then tried to decide whether the real dream was the love he had seen in his father's eyes for someone called Leila Rajar, in a photograph which had now disappeared, and which, as far as the rest of the world was concerned, had never existed.

The two Metropolitan Police detectives finally arrived at the Hampstead apartment at eleven in the morning, an hour late, or a day late, depending on how you calculated it. Sidney Pearl told them to go up to the flat, and he then called Harry to warn him they were on their way.

'The traffic,' one of the detectives apologized, as he shook Harry's hand and stepped through the door of the apartment. 'Plus the election. And we had a terror alert. And then a couple of shootings in south London. Busy day yesterday, all in all.'

The detective was a few years older than Harry, in his early thirties, white, fleshy, rubicund. He introduced himself as Detective Constable Steven Harpenden.

'Even this morning, took us an hour to get five miles from Scotland Yard. We were going to blue light it, but thought we'd sit through it. Nothing works in London except the traffic lights.'

'And us,' his colleague interrupted. 'We work, yes?'

Harry looked at the second detective. He was around 40, black, skin the colour of milky coffee, slim, in a well cut brown suit.

'Detective Sergeant Donald Sylvester,' he said, shaking hands. 'We talked on the telephone yesterday. I'm so very sorry we're a day late.'

'Not a problem,' Harry said. 'I was here anyway. I just thought what with it being an attempted murder inquiry, you'd be here last night.'

DS Sylvester eyed him closely.

'Who told you it's an attempted murder inquiry?'

'I just thought …'

'Most likely attempted suicide,' Harpenden interrupted. 'That's what we're hearing from Gloucester. No signs of breaking and entry. No signs of a struggle. No evidence to the contrary. But we're keeping an open mind, know what I mean?'

Harry said nothing. The whisky and the early wake-up call from the spiky-haired girl had got to him. He wasn't sure exactly when it was that he decided not to trust the detectives. It was simply a matter of instinct. He would tell them as little as possible. A line of Seamus Heaney poetry kept buzzing in Harry's head.

'*Whatever you say,*' Heaney wrote, '*say nothing.*'

He was not going to mention the girl, the laptop or the photograph with Leila Rajar. Say nothing.

'Shall we – um – get on, then, Mr Burnett?' Detective Sergeant Sylvester said, still looking him over as if he sensed that Harry was about to lie to him.

'Of course. How can I help?'

'Maybe just answer a few questions and let us poke around a bit?'

'Of course,' Harry repeated. 'But I don't understand what we're all doing here exactly.' Harry turned to Donald Sylvester. 'I mean, if it's not attempted murder, then is there a crime? And if there's no crime, why is there an investigation?'

'Well, we – um,' Sylvester hesitated. 'Like Steve said, we don't think there's a crime, but we have to tick all the boxes.'

Harry smiled.

'So you're not going to charge my father with wasting police time if he lives?'

'Just a precaution really, sir,' Sylvester began to explain. 'Bearing in mind your father's – um – high visibility. We need to be seen to cover the ground. Your father attracted ... a lot of attention ... some of it – um – undesirable.'

'But you really don't think that someone tried to ...'

His voice trailed away as he gestured round the apartment with his hand.

'Did you know of anyone with a grudge against your father?'

'No.'

'Did you know of anyone who would want to harm your father?'

'No.'

'Did you know of any threats to your father of any kind?'

'No.'

'Do you know of any reason why he would kill himself?'

Harry shook his head.

'And do you think he is capable of committing suicide?'

'I have no idea what he might be capable of,' Harry said. 'He was a stranger to me, as I told you on the phone. Was there a suicide note?'

Sylvester looked back at him.

'No. Or at least, no one has found one. Did you find anything here?'

'No.'

The detective was just over six feet tall but Harry was even taller. They stared at each other.

'What are the police in Gloucestershire saying?'

'Things point to a – um – self-induced drugs overdose and self-inflicted wrist wounds,' Sylvester said flatly. 'The cuts were at the correct angle for self-harm. Was your father left or right handed?'

That caused Harry to pause.

'Right handed,' he replied. 'I think.'

Sylvester nodded.

'You don't sound so sure.'

'I haven't seen him in years.'

Detective Sergeant Sylvester couldn't read the emotions in Harry's eyes, but he knew what he was not seeing. Grief.

'Are you in the politics business yourself then, Mr Burnett?' Harpenden wondered.

'Politics? No,' Harry protested and then grinned. 'Well, not really.'

'Not really?'

'I work as a volunteer for my constituency Labour party in Fulham, if you consider that the politics business. We have a local joke: Are you a member of an organized political party? No, mate. I'm Labour, me.'

Sylvester smiled, surprised.

'So you're not – um – Conservative like your …?'

He did not have to complete the sentence. And Harry did not have to reply. He wondered whether the detective's occasional stammer gave him a second to think.

'I am the opposite of my father in many things,' Harry responded eventually. 'I am pleased to say.'

'But it's not your job, politics?' Harpenden repeated, as if asking the same question in different ways might produce a different answer.

'No,' Harry said firmly. 'Just a hobby. On the grounds that if I don't help elect the people I want to run the country, some other person will. By profession I'm a translator.'

'An – um – interpreter?'

'No, well, I do a little interpreting but mostly I'm a self-employed translator.'

'It's all languages, isn't it?' Harpenden said.

'Yes, but an interpreter lives for the moment, switching between languages. A translator works with books or documents. That's my line. They are different skills.'

'You speak lots of languages?'

'Some better than others. French and German. Also Czech, which is what pays the bills right now. And I'm learning Arabic in evening classes.'

'Very handy, sir. Could – um – come in useful. Given the way the world is going we might all be speaking Arabic before long.'

Harry shook his head.

'Nobody cares about French and German any more. It's Chinese, Arabic and Farsi – Persian – that's what people need.'

The detectives began to move from room to room, businesslike, picking up things, opening drawers. Harry followed.

'You are welcome to do this – but what exactly are you looking for?'

'We'll know it when we see it,' Sylvester explained lamely. 'Maybe something, maybe nothing. Anything – um – out of the ordinary.'

Like a picture of my father with an American TV newsreader, stolen by a woman in the night? Harry thought. He played a couple of chords on the piano.

'What would be "out of the ordinary" in this kind of situation?'

Detective Sergeant Sylvester ignored the question.

'Please don't touch things for now. Make me happy.'

Harry stepped back from the piano.

'Of course. Except I stayed here overnight so I must have touched a lot of things already. Sorry.'

'He – um – live here mostly, then, your father? Or down in the West country?'

'Tetbury,' Harry responded. 'Not here. It doesn't look much like anyone lives here, does it? Too clean. But there's no point in asking me. Like I said, I never saw him. And I didn't even know this place existed until yesterday. I haven't really seen him since ... not since it happened. You know, the scandal.'

The detectives looked at him. Sylvester nodded.

'Yes,' he sympathized. 'The scandal. I saw the TV last night. And your mother?'

'She … died a few years ago. She killed herself, though in her case it was with help from Mr Smirnoff. A bottle of vodka a day by the end. Cirrhosis.'

Sylvester said, 'I'm very sorry.'

The apartment suddenly felt oppressive.

'Did you blame your … um … father for what happened to your mother?'

'Of course. It was his fault.'

'And for what happened to you?'

'Yes,' Harry replied coolly. 'He behaved like a complete shit. Although in front of the children he would say that as "S-H-one-T", as if we couldn't spell.'

'Did you hate your father?' Sylvester said suddenly.

'I didn't kill him, if that's what you mean.'

'He's not dead yet. Did you hate him?'

'I didn't try to kill him. And I didn't hate him either. Not any more. He was irrelevant to me. A stranger. He was not in my thoughts and not in my life.'

Harpenden suddenly said, 'Where were you two nights ago between the hours of six p.m. and midnight?'

Harry thought for a moment.

'I was at my Arabic class in west Acton until approximately ten o'clock and then I went to the pub with two other students. And then I came home, around midnight.'

'Alone?'

'Sadly, yes.'

'But you have witnesses in this Arabic class?'

'Of course. I haven't been out of London in weeks, and I have never been to my father's cottage in Tetbury. I couldn't even find it.'

The atmosphere suddenly changed. The two detectives started to move around again, picking things up and looking at them.

'Still, it's a nice gaff all right,' Harpenden said brightly, looking at the bookshelves. 'Good taste, your father.'

Beyond the political biographies in the study, the book-shelves in the main room were full of expensive picture books, Ansel Adams and Andrew Wyeth, celebrations of Rembrandt, Goya and Matisse, books on Islamic art, Persian culture, and several on the Moors in Spain.

'In most things, yes,' Harry replied.

'Most things?' Sylvester wondered.

'Not in women,' Harry responded.

'Ah,' Harpenden responded, perking up. 'I believe there is a technical term for having bad taste in women, Mr Burnett. It is called "being a man". What was it exactly with your father that went so wrong, sir?'

Harry took a deep breath. He recited the history of the scandal as if ordering a list of vegetables from the greengrocer.

'When I was eight years old, a woman sold her story to the *News of the World* saying that she and my father were lovers. She was half his age and a lingerie model, so there were plenty of pictures of her in her knickers for the papers to print. It ruined my father's reputation. And his marriage. Oh, yes, and his political career. And – what else? His family. And his life. And probably a few other things too, but I can't remember it all. He became a pariah. Went off to Gloucestershire and spent most of the last twenty years growing organic vegetables and fruit which made him a small income, or so I believe ...'

Harry's voice trailed off.

'Not a great – um – move then, sir, all in all,' Sylvester said with a wan smile. 'The lingerie model.'

'No, not really,' Harry agreed.

'He should have just denied it,' Harpenden suggested cheerfully.

'He did.'

'Oh.'

'Then they published pictures of them together. Tapes. Video tapes. The woman ... well, you get the picture.'

'Oh,' Harpenden volunteered. 'Bummer.'

Sylvester said, 'And you and he ...?'

Harry bristled.

'I really find it difficult to talk about this.'

'No, no,' Sylvester apologized. 'You don't have to ...'

'I am not used to talking about it,' Harry said. 'I tell people my parents are dead, which stops the questions. And they are dead. Both of them. I have not seen nor talked to my father since he walked out. Or was thrown out by my mother.'

'Didn't you want to? See him, I mean?'

'No. He wanted to see me, and tried from time to time.'

'Recently?'

Harry shrugged.

'He sent me a card a week or so ago saying we should meet, but I didn't reply. One of his parables was that when he was fourteen years old he thought his own father was the stupidest man in the world, but by the time he got to twenty-one, he was amazed how much the old boy had picked up in just seven years. He tried to tell me that maybe it would be the same with him and me, but I got to twenty-one and he was nothing to me at all. He died years ago, when he walked out. *Too long a sacrifice makes a stone of the heart.*'

Sylvester looked at him.

'William Butler Yeats,' Harry explained. 'I'm helping with a new Czech translation of Yeats, and also I'm translating Milan Kundera short stories into English. Very difficult, actually, Kundera.'

Harpenden and Sylvester nodded as if they were interested, then moved away again. Harry followed the detectives as they nosed about the unfamiliar rooms. There were several paintings in the sitting room, Victorian scenes of Venice, the Rialto, the Bridge of Sighs.

'I never knew my father either,' Sylvester said suddenly, shuffling through an address book by the telephone. Harry was surprised.

'You didn't?'

'No. He went back to Grenada before I was born. My mother said that she *did* know him, and that was enough for both of us.'

'Families, eh?' Harpenden laughed.

'Of course, you'll inherit this place,' Detective Sergeant Sylvester said, 'in the event that your father dies.'

'Presumably, yes,' Harry shrugged. 'Me and my sister. Though if you are suggesting I tried to kill him for it, then, well, firstly I didn't, and secondly I didn't even know this place existed, but I am happy to keep repeating what I have just told you again and again until we all get very, very bored.'

He glared at Sylvester defiantly.

'I don't think that will be – um – necessary,' Detective Sergeant Sylvester replied. 'But thank you for your patience.'

Ten minutes later the detectives said they were done.

'Nothing of interest as far as I can see. If we need to come back, we'll – um – let you know.'

'Any objections to me staying here?'

'None, Mr Burnett. It's yours to do what you wish as far as we're concerned. I hope your father pulls through.'

'Thanks. Before you go, can I ask you something?'

Sylvester grimaced a little but tried to look happy.

'Of course.'

'If it really was a suicide attempt, why do you keep asking me all these questions?'

Sylvester shrugged.

'Nothing personal, sir. Strictly business. But this is political, right? Number Ten's taking an interest, so is the American embassy. It means I can tell my gaffer we went through all the hoops.'

Harry stared at him. Harpenden broke the silence.

'Y'know, they were saying on the radio that he could have been prime minister.'

'Yes, they do say that.' Harry smiled grimly. 'Maybe we are all lucky that he wasn't.'

'Oh, I dunno,' Harpenden said again. 'There are worse things than what your father did. I mean, a lingerie model? What man wouldn't be tempted? Nobody died, did they? At least he never sent us into Iraq with no hope of getting out.'

'You could be right,' Harry agreed awkwardly.

'Thanks for your time, Mr Burnett.'

'Thank you.'

'If you think of anything ...'

'Yes of course.'

'You have our numbers.'

'Yes. And you have mine.'

The detectives left. Harry shut the door and leaned against it. There were worse things than what his father had done, he repeated. A lingerie model. What man wouldn't be tempted? Nobody died. He looked back into the apartment and at the big mirror in the pitch pine frame that he remembered from his childhood home in Pimlico. And as he looked at it, he stepped back into the place he had once called home.

Pimlico, London, 1987

It was the day the scandal broke in 1987. Harry was in the hallway of the family house in Pimlico, chewing the cuffs of his blazer, looking at his reflection in the big mirror with the pitch pine surrounds. He could hear his father and mother arguing in the breakfast room. A newspaper was thrown. A door was slammed. More doors were slammed. There was coming and going. His father switched the radio on so he could listen to the Today programme. His mother switched the radio off so she did not have to listen to the Today programme.

'Elizabeth, please!'

'How could you, Robin? How could you?'

'Elizabeth, I ...'

'But how could you! Did you never once think of me or the children? Just *once* think of someone other than yourself? Ever?'

His father's silence was the loudest silence Harry had ever heard. He pushed his maths book into his school bag. He tried to screw up his courage. He wanted to walk into the breakfast room and tell them to be quiet, but he did not dare. Amanda was at the top of the stairs wide-eyed. She was near to tears as she clumped down and stood next to him.

'I need my gym kit,' Harry said.

'And I need to leave,' Amanda responded. 'Let's go in together, Aitch.'

He did not look convinced.

'Come on,' she took his hand, sticky with sweat. 'How bad can it be?'

Both children were brittle and nervous. Amanda opened the door. Their mother was sitting at the table, head in hands, crying. Their father was standing behind her in his dark blue suit, white shirt, red tie, his patriotic Union Jack uniform. He was pleading with her.

'Elizabeth, can I ...' He looked up and yelled at the children in the doorway. 'What on earth do you want?'

'Robin!' his mother screamed, like a whip in the air. 'Don't talk to them like that. They are only children for god's sake, and they live here too. I take it you did not give a moment's thought to them, either, when you embarked on this ... this ... adventure?'

Then she changed tone.

'Yes, my darlings.' She started drying her eyes. 'What is it you need?'

Harry started to explain about his gym kit. Their father stomped out of the room. Ten minutes later they heard his black ministerial car pull up outside and a lot of shouting from the reporters as he left. Their mother took them into the hallway. Harry bit at his blazer cuff. Amanda danced on her toes. His mother quickly put on her coat and sensible shoes, then opened the front door.

The sound of camera lenses and flashbulbs hit them like machine-gun fire. And the shouting. The start of the siege. Harry wanted to take cover in his burrow, or to die. Either way, to get it over with.

'Mrs Burnett, just a quick word ...'

'How did you find out, Mrs Burnett?'

'Did your husband tell you why he did it?'

'What do you think of the girl?'

'... male menopause ...'

(Laughter.)

'... Carla Carter in her knickers?'

'Can he really expect to keep his job?'

'... midlife crisis?'

'... Victorian values ... would this be one of them, then?'

'She says he was a great and considerate lover ...'

'—did you ...'

'—boob job?'

'Slapper?'

'... Carla Carter ...'

(Laughter.)

'... can you ...?'

'...lover...'

'... how are the children taking ...'

'... lover ...'

Harry's mother stared at the cameras, big-eyed like a seal about to be clubbed. She grabbed both children by the collars of their jackets and pulled them back into the house, slamming the door on the marauders. They stood for a moment together, unsure what to do, then his mother fell to the floor in the hallway and began sobbing uncontrollably on her knees. Harry went towards her and put his arms round her neck. He fell on her, in tears. Amanda did the same. None of them noticed the letter box opening. Fingers pushed inside, with exquisite slowness. Then a camera lens stuck through. The camera captured the moment for the following morning's newspapers. The by-line for the story was for Stephen Lovelace, and above it the word 'EXCLUSIVE' in big black letters. The headline said: 'BETRAYED!' The photograph showed what looked like a protective circle of the three of them, arms round each other's shoulders, the heap of a broken family. The lingerie model pictures were on pages 3, 4 and 5. Sometime later that year at the UK Press Awards the photographer won a prize. The picture was described as 'one of the iconic images of the twentieth century.' One art critic compared it to Canova's Three Graces, under the headline: 'Three *Dis-Graces*.' Another called it 'a twentieth century political *pieta*.'

A columnist in the *Guardian* described it in his book about Mrs Thatcher as 'the symbolic moment when Thatcherism began to hollow out from the inside, like a meringue. Though it took several more years to collapse, this was the moment when we knew she was doomed. She probably knew it too.'

Harry stared into the mirror. He thought of himself and his mother and sister together in the hallway of their own home, in tears, and of the moment when Mrs Thatcher was doomed. Like a meringue.

Muslim College, Acton, West London

SEPTEMBER 2004

Rajiv Khan wore a rucksack. Harry later came to the conclusion that Rajiv Khan always wore a rucksack, perhaps even in bed. For Rajiv, it seemed to be an indispensable fashion accessory. The day they collided was early in September 2004, three years after the 9/11 al Qaeda attacks on New York and Washington and ten months before the attacks on the London Underground. The London bombings on 7 July 2005 and then two weeks later on 21 July 2005 were carried out by young Asian men with explosives carried in rucksacks. But in September 2004 no one paid much attention to Rajiv or to the secrets of his large, black, Kathmandu sports rucksack. Raj and Harry collided in front of the gates of Muslim College in West London because Harry saw dog shit on the street. Suddenly he hopped to his right and into the road. Raj had no chance. He tried to swerve but it was too late. He hit Harry hard on his backside with the front wheel of his bicycle.

'Look out …!' Raj yelled.

'What the …?'

Harry fell over, crying in pain.

'Aaah!'

'Sorry,' Raj yelled as he screeched on the brakes and pulled his bicycle to a halt, falling off sideways. He rolled on his back with the rucksack underneath him and the bike on top, wriggling like an upturned turtle.

'Ow!'

'You okay?'

'Ow! No! You?'

'My fault,' Harry replied. 'My fault, sorry. Yes, I'm okay. I should have looked where I was going. I was just desperate to avoid the dog shit.'

'Welcome to London,' Raj laughed and pulled himself to his feet. 'A city which bears witness to man's constant attempts to avoid dog shit.' He lifted his bike up from the ground. 'Maybe I should get myself a bell.'

'Maybe I should look where I'm walking. You going to classes in here?'

'Yes,' Raj responded with a grin showing neat white teeth from under his short beard. 'Extreme Arabic.'

'My name's Harry. Harry Burnett.'

'Rajiv Khan. Most people call me Raj.' He laughed again. 'I guess we just experienced the famous clash of civilizations.'

'Well, it looks like we survived,' Harry replied. 'And is that what they call it now? Extreme Arabic? I thought it was Intensive Arabic.'

'Intensive. Extreme. Whatever. We'll see.'

It was advertised as a 'fast and demanding course'. The students required no previous qualifications, and were promised three two-hour sessions a week from a native Arabic speaker. But the college website warned of a great deal of homework, and no room for slackers. Raj locked his bicycle round a fence post, hitched the rucksack onto one shoulder and walked into the classroom with Harry at his side. There were twenty desks for students, a teacher's desk, and a whiteboard. The room smelled pleasantly of cardamoms. Harry sat down in the middle. Raj placed his rucksack under the desk beside him and stretched his legs out under it. Half the desks were already full. Harry counted the nine students with some satisfaction.

Nine registrations meant more than enough to ensure the course would continue. The teacher walked in carrying a small cup of Arab coffee, the source of the cardamom aroma.

'I am Abdul Aziz al-Barra,' he said, putting his coffee on his desk and bowing slightly. 'And I am Syrian, which means you are very lucky indeed. And why are you lucky, please?' There was no response. Perhaps he did not expect any. He quickly answered his own question. 'You are very lucky because we Syrians speak the best and the purest classical Arabic. However, this comes with a warning. You will discover on this course that everybody – everybody from an Omani sailor to a Moroccan shepherd – will say that they speak the best and the purest Arabic. Even the Egyptians say this, though in the case of the Egyptians you will please understand that the claim is simply laughable. With Syrians it is at least close to the truth.'

There was some laughter from Harry and Raj and one of the two women in the room. She was dark haired and Mediterranean in appearance and sat at the very front of the class.

'This course is not for the faint hearted,' Abdul Aziz al-Barra went on, stopping to drink his coffee in one mouthful. 'If you are not prepared to work hard then, please, may I respectfully suggest you leave now and find a less demanding class. Perhaps basket weaving. If you can keep it up for three years then I guarantee you will be excellent speakers of the Arabic language. If you can't ... well ... we also have Arabic Culture and Society. Very interesting. We have Koranic Arabic. Very religious. We have slower courses. All of them very good. Some even taught by Syrians. We will now go round the class, please, and each of you will kindly give me the idea of why you wish to learn my language. This will help me teach. Please. Thank you.'

He nodded at a slim, petite blonde woman in her late twenties who sat in the corner.

'Please?'

'I am Polly Black,' the blonde woman said. 'I work in the travel business in central London. I think tourism to the Arab world is something which could be developed.'

'She's an optimist,' Raj whispered to Harry. 'Fancy a package tour to Gaza?'

Then came the strikingly pretty Mediterranean woman who had laughed at the professor's attempts at humour.

'My name is Zumrut,' she said. 'I am Turkish.'

Zumrut explained that she wanted to learn Arabic because she was writing a book about the decline of the Ottoman Empire and its implications for the Middle East.

'I already can read Ottoman. I speak French and English, but I need more context – therefore I need the Arabic language as well.'

'Thank you, Zumrut. Please.'

And so it went. A sad-faced black man from northern Nigeria, Mohammed, said he was learning Arabic 'for religious reasons'. That was all he said. The teacher nodded at Harry.

'Please. Perhaps a little more information from each of you, including any languages you already speak.'

'I am a linguist,' Harry replied. 'A translator. At the moment I am working on a translation of some early Milan Kundera short stories from the Czech into English for a British publisher, and I am also helping with the translation of some poems by William Butler Yeats. I work from home. I also translate business and technical documents. I see learning Arabic as two things. Fun – I am interested in the development of language and I know that Arabic is the language of grammarians. And I also see it as a good business opportunity for me in the future. I am interested in Islamic culture too, but I'm not religious. Maybe you could say I'm an ethnic Christian.'

'Fine,' Abdul Aziz said, nodding towards Raj. 'And you?'

'Scholarship,' Raj said. 'I'm not so sure about the fun, but I hope to enjoy it too. I also want to read the Holy Koran properly, because I am not sure how much you can ever trust a translation, or a translator.' He smiled at Harry. 'No offence meant, but even the best translations are bound to miss something. And I would like to explore Arab culture. It's like a part of me – but not a meaningful part. Or not yet.'

'What do you do, please?'

'I'm an immigration lawyer. Some of my clients are Arabs, so it would come in useful at work too. Iraqis because of the war. Algerians. Also Iranians and Afghans.'

'Ah, so George Bush is at least good for business,' Harry whispered to Raj. 'Glad he's helping someone.'

At the back of the class sat two middle-aged Pakistani men neatly dressed in suits and ties. They knew each other. One spoke for both. The one who spoke said they were originally from the same village in Pakistan and now ran a taxi business together in west Ealing. Their first language was Urdu.

'We wish to go on Hajj pilgrimage and we need Arabic,' the one who talked said in heavily accented English. 'Also wishing to understand our religion better.'

Abdul Aziz nodded at the other man who said simply, 'Same.'

He moved on to the remaining two students, who were also sitting together at the back.

'My name is Rafiq,' the first said, with a London accent. He was in his early twenties, with a wispy short beard. 'I want to travel. That's why I need to learn the language.'

'Talal,' the other said. He was also in his early twenties, clean-shaven. 'My name is Talal. And same. Same reasons as him, same as Rafiq.'

'Okay,' Abdul Aziz said. 'I need a little more from some of you, please. Remember that if you are going to speak aloud in Arabic you have to begin by making sense and being less shy in English. Kindly tell me a little more about your work.'

He nodded at Zumrut.

'It's post-doctoral research work at the School of Oriental and African Studies. I have an academic publisher who has commissioned the work. The collapse of the Ottoman Empire of course led directly to the problems we now have in the whole of the Middle East. I think the book might reasonably be expected to sell, if I get it right.'

She explained a little of the historical context. The volatilities of the region were always kept in check by one dominant power. For a time it was the Persians, the Romans, the Arabs, the Turks. Once the Ottomans had gone, so did the domination.

'Except, you might say, for the Americans nowadays,' Zumrut added. 'Though we may debate that.'

'You also have religious reasons?' Abdul Aziz wanted to know. He was pacing through the class, now at the rear. 'You are Muslim?'

Zumrut turned to face the teacher. She was dressed in jeans and a sweater, with a hint of make-up round her eyes and without a headscarf. She had big dark brown eyes, Harry noticed. She coloured pink at the teacher's question.

'I am Turkish,' she repeated her earlier answer, as if that was answer enough. It could have meant 'yes, of course,' but Harry recognized it was simply an elegant way of avoiding the question.

'Turkey is a secular state,' she explained. 'Most Turkish people are Muslims. Like my colleague here who said he was ethnic Christian, I am ethnic Muslim.'

Harry decided he liked this Zumrut.

'And you? Please.'

The professor nodded again to the two young men at the back of the class.

He was now standing alongside them.

'I have always wanted to learn Arabic my whole life,' Rafiq said. 'My whole life.'

'So why take the plunge now, please?' prompted the teacher.

'I went on the Hajj last year,' Rafiq responded, 'and I now see that without Arabic I cannot understand what it is to be a Muslim. I am incomplete. The language is the key.'

The teacher passed on.

'Talal? Please?'

'Same,' he said again, indicating Rafiq. 'Same thing. We have the same reasons.'

Abdul Aziz raised his eyebrows, as if at an echo.

'Well,' he said when he finished going round them all again. 'Fine.'

And so they began. They dived immediately into the Arabic language and Arab culture. From the start of that very first lesson Harry was enthralled. Beguiled. He loved the sounds, the range of the language, its music. Sometimes it was guttural, like a fight. Other times it was so beautiful he could almost weep, especially when Abdul Aziz played CDs of women singing verses, Sura, from the Koran. It was a curiously spiritual experience for someone like Harry who did not actually believe in any type of god. He also liked the idea of a language constructed by grammarians, with logic and love and subtlety. Above all, he adored the flowing shapes of the writing, the calligraphy, the way in which the letters were formed rather like shorthand in English, often without vowels. At the end of that first class they were all exhausted. Polly Black and the two Pakistani cab drivers hurried away. Polly said something about having to get back to her husband and children. The cab drivers said they were going to work. The sad-faced Nigerian, Mohammed, stopped to talk to Abdul Aziz about the homework he had given them for the following night. Raj put on his crash helmet and rucksack.

'You have to go far?' Harry asked.

'North London. Muswell Hill. You?'

'Fulham,' Harry replied.

The opposite direction.

'See you tomorrow night. Best not forget to do the homework, otherwise we might get a Syrian spanking.'

Harry agreed.

'My guess is that our esteemed teacher is seriously into suffering. Our suffering.'

Zumrut was still in the hallway filling out forms as Harry passed. He smiled, and she smiled back, very directly. Her brown eyes opened wide.

'Nice to meet you. See you tomorrow,' Harry called out to her.

'And you.'

'Plenty of homework.'

'Yes. Enough to keep us out of trouble.'

'I … your name has a very nice sound. Does it mean something in Turkish?'

'It means "emerald",' she told him. Then she smiled. 'How about Harry? Does that mean something in English?'

He laughed.

'It means that my parents were very old-fashioned. Goodnight, Emerald.'

'Goodnight, old-fashioned Harry.'

As Harry left the building he saw Rafiq and Talal outside, lighting cigarettes, talking softly, like conspirators, Harry thought.

'Goodnight,' he called out to them. Both men nodded back, but only Rafiq smiled.

'Yes, goodnight.'

There was something about the smile which Harry knew was false. He did not understand why. On the way to the Tube station he rebuked himself for falling into negative stereotypes about two young Muslim men based on no evidence whatsoever. Bugger the stereotypes. He wanted a beer. He pulled into a pub, the Victoria Arms, ordered a pint and sat for half an hour alone in a corner, thinking about why talking to Zumrut had made him smile.

Talal Ul-Haq and Rafiq Chowdhury finished their cigarettes and their conversation, then climbed into Rafiq's battered

Nissan Micra. It started with a throaty roar. Rafiq cursed. There was a hole developing in the rusty exhaust, and he guessed it would be expensive to fix. Rafiq drove Talal to his mother's house in Wembley, and then returned to his own wife and two young children in Greenford. When he stepped out of the car in Wembley Talal Ul-Haq decided to smoke another cigarette, alone on the street, before going home to face the inevitable conversation. He could recite his mother's words in their entirety because he had faced them every night for months, like a CD he no longer wished to listen to but which he could not stop playing. When are you going to get a job? When are you going to do something with your life? When are you going to amount to something? When are you going to get married? When are you going to stop smoking?

The answer to all these questions, Talal decided, was probably never. He paced up and down, drawing on the Marlboro so the tip glowed strongly in the dark, thinking how best to handle the inevitable conversation with his mother with minimum fuss and disruption. Eventually he stamped on the cigarette butt and walked inside. She was watching television. He told her he was going to his room to read.

'Tomorrow,' she called out after him. 'Tomorrow, Talal, you must find work. No excuses.'

'Yes,' he agreed. He wondered why she did not ask about his Arabic classes, his new challenges, the things that interested him, rather than the things that did not. Why was it that she cared about nothing except his ability to make money?

'Yes, of course. I will try.'

'I mean it, Talal,' she yelled. 'Not try. Try is not good enough. Find. You are too old for me to keep you. You want to end up like your father? You take the jobs that are offered you. Unless you want your whole life to be supported by women? What kind of man wishes for such a thing? And at twenty-five years old? By your age, I already …' Yes, he knew. By his age, she already had four children and was pregnant with the fifth.

And so it went on, the familiar, one-sided conversation.

'Yes, mother. Tomorrow I will find work. I promise.'

Talal climbed the stairs. He heard her call out something after him, something indistinct and pointless but with the words 'Job Centre' at the end.

'Yes, mother,' he agreed. 'Yes, indeed.'

Upstairs, Talal washed carefully and said his prayers. Then he switched on his computer, checking for emails.

There was one from a girl, Malika, he had met at his cousin's house in Bradford, a girl who was working in a local bank, and whom Talal had thought shameless in the way she dressed and talked. Malika's email suggested he was right. She wrote that the next time he came north she would like to meet him again. Alone. She would show him around. Talal blinked. At the mosque he attended in north west London, known as the Green Mosque, the imam, Abu Omar, had read from the Holy Koran (4:34) a verse which the imam said was very important to all young men faced with the temptations of women. The imam said it was to be translated as follows:

'Men are in charge of women, because Allah has made some of them excel the others, and because they spend some of their wealth ... And for those women you fear might rebel, admonish them and abandon them in their beds and beat them.'

Talal knew that apostates and hypocrites translated the verses differently, which was one further reason to learn Arabic, to defeat and confound the apostates and hypocrites in the language of the Holy Koran itself. Talal thought for a moment. He could reply to Malika and point out directly her errors, admonishing her. No, he decided. To what purpose? That was for her father, brothers and uncles. Instead he deleted her email without reading further. There would be no more contact. Ever. Then he opened another email from a cousin, Tawfiq, in Dewsbury. Tawfiq was raging against Tony Blair and the Iraq war.

'God *willing Blair will meet his fate*,' the email read. '*God willing, the people of this country at the next election will reject him and all he stands for. We have told the Labour councillors here in Dewsbury that we are not going to vote for them again. Not until they ditch Blair.*'

Talal thought this deserved a proper reply and began to write to Tawfiq.

'*In the name of god, the Compassionate, the Merciful*,' he began. '*My dearest cousin. And what if they don't ditch Blair? If the Labour party keeps him as its leader and then the people of Britain vote him into power again as the American hypocrites did with Bush? What then? Listen, Tawfiq, when we last talked you said we had to separate the warmongers Bush and Blair from the American and British people. You said they were mostly good people. How do you know this? If the British people vote for leaders such as Blair after knowing what he has done, then the British people must be complicit in the consequences. Are they not to blame? Do they not deserve punishment? When the agents of Blair and Bush slay our brothers in Iraq or in Afghanistan, and their people vote for them, then who is responsible for the slaughter? My dear cousin Tawfiq, I love you dearly but you are very naïve. You told me when I last saw you that democracy will solve things. How is this democracy, please? A million of us marched against the Iraq war, and what difference did it make? So much for freedom and democracy. Millions will vote against Blair at the next election and what difference will it make? So much for the 'electoral process'. There are other ways to make a difference. God willing, you will see that, Tawfiq, before long. In the name of god, the Compassionate, the Merciful. Your respectful cousin, Talal.*'

Talal ignored the other emails. He lit a cigarette and opened his bedroom window wide so the smoke drifted out and his mother did not complain. Then he began to check his favourite websites for news and pictures from the battlefronts in Kashmir, Chechnya, Palestine, Afghanistan and Iraq. He put on headphones, then cranked up the volume on the computer. His mother complained when the singing, shouting or sound of explosions was too high, especially late at night. His mother would always find something to complain about. It was in her nature.

Even before Rafiq Chowdhury reached the door of his house in Greenford he could hear his baby screaming. He revved up the engine of the Micra as he parked it. The roar of the broken exhaust pipe (if you closed your eyes) made the tinny little car sound like a Porsche. Actually, he thought, no. It made it sound like a Micra with a bust exhaust.

Rafiq sat in the front seat for a moment, saying a short prayer, asking for patience. He needed patience to deal with what awaited him. He hoped his wife's odious sisters were not there. Unfortunately he was to be disappointed. Rafiq opened the door of his house and the screaming became more intense.

The smell of micro-waved popcorn hit his nostrils. He halted in the obstacle course of the hallway, pushing his son's plastic tricycle – in the image of an American police motorbike – to one side. He stacked a football and a plastic farmhouse beside it. The screaming started to subside. Rafiq opened the door to the main room and saw that his wife was watching an Urdu DVD in the company of two of her sisters, each with a bowl of popcorn in front of them. It made Rafiq think of something he had enjoyed reading at school, before he had been excluded for selling cannabis. The witches in Macbeth. Rafiq even remembered the lines. 'And when shall we three meet again?' Unfortunately when these three met again – Benazir and her sisters – was every night and almost always round at his house. Rafiq had come to believe that the three women grew fatter before his eyes, expanding hour by hour as they sat on the couch, stuffing popcorn and potato chips between their lips and only pausing from time to time to produce more children. He saw them as three enormous inflatable balloons, three large Michelin women getting bigger and bigger until one day they would float away on the wind and never be seen again. *Inshallah*.

'Hello,' Rafiq said. The two sisters nodded silently. Rafiq's wife Benazir uttered no greeting, nor did she take her eyes from the TV screen. Instead she said, 'I need money for groceries.'

Rafiq put his hand in his pocket and handed her ten pounds.

'I need more,' Benazir insisted. 'The baby needs nappies.'

He handed her twenty.

'It doesn't grow on trees, you know,' he said. Benazir turned back to the film.

Since he had stopped dealing in drugs, money in the household was a little tight, but Benazir had refused to cut the family expenditure accordingly. He suspected that she preferred it when he was dealing, partly for the money, partly because he was out every night, so she and her two fat sisters could gorge in peace. The youngest child was now at his wife's breast, suckling noisily, which explained why the screaming had subsided. The older child, a boy, was snuggling on the lap of one of his aunts and picking at the popcorn. Rafiq went upstairs and lit a cigarette. Then he, like Talal, switched on his computer. His screensaver was a picture of the Chelsea football team, though he had not been to see a match for months. He missed it, sometimes. The imam at the Green Mosque preached that football was sinful and diversionary, pulling the faithful away from the *umma* and towards a way of secularism and sin. The blue background of the Chelsea screensaver disappeared.

It was replaced by flowing green flags with Arabic writing, and then moving pictures of a Hamas suicide bomber driving his car at an Israeli check-point near Ramallah. The bomb exploded, killing three Israelis and injuring four others. There was much ululating on the video. Rafiq switched it off and went to bed alone. When he touched himself that night it was like performing an exercise, joylessly.

Rajiv Khan cycled home quickly in the darkness. He had a bright yellow over-jacket which made him stand out on the night streets. After a few miles, when he reached a neighbourhood he viewed as promising, he took off the over-jacket and rolled it up, stuffing it into the rucksack. Then he cycled more slowly, pausing from time to time to glance at the cars parked on the backstreets. Eventually he found what he was looking for. It was a highly polished black, new model, Porsche Cayenne. Raj pulled on his brakes.

'My favourite,' he said softly under his breath with an air of triumph.

Raj looked up and down the road then slipped the rucksack from his shoulders. He rummaged inside for a moment and pulled out a parsnip and a couple of carrots. Raj looked at the back of the Porsche Cayenne carefully, and then again at the vegetables. He selected the parsnip as the best fit. He stuffed it into one of the exhaust pipes of the car until it jammed tightly, and then stuffed both carrots into the other exhaust pipe. Then he remounted his bicycle and cycled off quickly, without looking back. A kilometre away he stopped to put on his bright yellow reflective over-jacket once more.

'Parsnip Cayenne,' he muttered to himself cheerfully. 'Absolutely delicious.'

Zumrut Ecevit caught the Underground to central London and walked briskly to Covent Garden. The road outside the station was full of people. There were a couple of buskers, a drunk and a few beggars, but mostly just people looking for places to eat and drink. She reached Sofra, one of her favourite Turkish restaurants. It blasted pools of orange light into the street. The sight of it cheered her. It wasn't like being in her home area around Galatasaray in Istanbul, but it was close enough for London. Zumrut stepped inside and the waiters nodded to her. They exchanged a few words in Turkish.

'Hello again.'

'Nice to see you.'

'Welcome. Welcome.'

Zumrut's two women friends were already waiting for her at a table loaded with small plates of food.

There was a bottle of good raki, a bowl of ice and three glasses. Two of the glasses had lipstick on them and a little raki left in the bottom. The third glass was still clean, reserved for Zumrut. The friends kissed. One of them, like Zumrut, was also a postgraduate student, completing her PhD in nuclear physics at Imperial College. The other worked as an architect for a British design consultancy with business interests all over the Middle East.

'I'm sorry I'm late,' Zumrut said. 'What a day!'

The nuclear physicist helped pour raki over ice for Zumrut. She took a sip and savoured the alcohol and aniseed on her tongue.

'Was it as bad as we predicted?'

'Two hours of Arabic and I'm brain dead.' Zumrut shook her head. 'And very grateful for the raki.'

She took a sip.

'But how was it?' the architect asked. 'Religious weirds with beards?'

Zumrut nodded.

'Pretty much.'

'I knew it,' the architect said.

'Me too,' agreed the nuclear physicist. 'What else could you expect?'

'Oh yes,' Zumrut continued. 'Half the class looked like aspirant mullahs. But the teacher was fine. Syrian. Sense of humour. One other woman, thank goodness, so I'm not alone.

English, didn't say much. And a couple of ordinary men. But all these bloody idiots with beards who decided god wants them to speak Arabic! Four of them. No, five. Still, they'll drop out before long. They'll decide god wants them to do something else instead. Something easier. Like bash their wives or father a few more children.'

The other two women laughed as Zumrut took a long pull of raki.

'Please, let's talk about something else,' she said. 'God, let's talk about *anything* else.'

The two middle aged Pakistani men returned to their taxi business near west Ealing train station. One of the men relieved the cab dispatcher for an hour, so the dispatcher could have something to eat. The other took a vacuum cleaner and cleaned out his own car and that of his friend. When he finished, he checked his watch. A little after ten thirty. It had been a quiet night so far, but you never knew how it would go in west London, until the pubs closed. That was when the real money was to be made. Taxi driving was fine as long as you didn't mind putting up with the drunks. He hung a new air freshener on the mirror in his car and one for his friend.

The switchboard began to light up with the first of the calls. The Rose and Crown. Party of four, for Hanwell. He sniffed the air. It was going to be a lucrative night after all, he decided. This was a good job, really. And not a bad country. Being your own boss. As long as no one picked a fight or was sick in the back of his car.

Immediately he left the classroom, Mohammed, the sad-faced black man from northern Nigeria, caught the Piccadilly line to Heathrow airport. He arrived at Terminal Four and changed into his blue uniform. He put on yellow rubber gloves, gathered his mop, bucket and disinfectant, and began cleaning the men's toilets. The worst job was picking out the cigarette butts. For some reason European men thought cigarettes should be thrown into the urinals, when all commonsense would have told them they would have to be pulled out again by someone else's hands. Mohammed's hands. When he finished the men's toilets, he wrote the exact time and his initials on the report sheet on the wall, and then moved off to the next set of toilets. Mohammed had a PhD. He had been a university lecturer in Kano, in the Department of Agriculture and Food Science. He specialized in crop rotation programmes for arable land in dry areas. There was not much need for his skills right now in London. No one cared about crop rotation programmes best suited to the edges of the Sahel, or about Nigerian PhDs. Fortunately there was plenty of need for toilet cleaners at Heathrow airport and in the hotels on Airport Way. He had also been offered a part-time security job at a warehouse in Hounslow. He figured he could juggle two jobs, perhaps three, and he could certainly spend three pay packets. Still, Mohammed thought as he refilled the soap dispensers in the next set of toilets, there were compensations in his new life. His daughter was in a good school. She was working hard. She would do well, *inshallah*. She would make them all proud. University, maybe. A doctor? A lawyer, like that young Pakistani man in the Arabic class, Rajiv? And she would make them all rich. Eventually.

Harry stepped out of the Tube at Fulham Broadway, thinking about Raj and his strong sense of humour, and also thinking about Zumrut. The Turkish woman had the most extraordinary eyes. Warm. Sensual. Like chocolate. Seeing her had a strange effect on him. Everything she said interested him. He liked the confident way she had answered the teacher's questions. She had a peculiar beauty. A calming beauty. He thought it was a beauty of the spirit and intellect as well as of the body. Maybe one day he would chance his luck and ask her out, if he could only overcome his shyness.

It had been a long time since the break-up of his last serious relationship with Petra. He laughed. Ah, Petra. God, what an embarrassment, even to think of it now. Harry was determined *not* to think of it now. Maybe it was time to come out of hibernation. He decided on a plan. He would ask both Raj and Zumrut to come to the pub after the lesson the following night. Maybe they would come, if they were the kind of modern Muslims who would not mind to visit a pub. Harry was confident that they might be.

The woman who called herself Polly Black took the Central Line train to Oxford Circus. She got out holding a Tube map and carefully checked to see no one was following her, then she stepped back into the train just before the doors closed and it moved off again. It was a passable acting demonstration, as if she were slightly lost, like a tourist. Since Polly Black had lived in London for most of her twenty-eight years, except the three she spent reading modern languages in Cambridge, it was unlikely that she was lost. When she arrived at Bank station, Polly got out and walked to her apartment. She took a circuitous route, again checking to make sure that no one followed her. Despite what she had told the others in the class, she had no husband and no children. Nor was her name Polly Black. She lived alone.

Once she was safely inside the apartment she opened a bottle of Australian Shiraz and poured herself a glass, sniffing the high alcohol aroma of the wine. Then she sat down at her computer, and wrote her report on the other members of the Arabic class, beginning, as she would do every week for the months to come, with Talal Ul-Haq and Rafiq Chowdhury.

Leila and Robin, 1982 – 1987

Leila Rajar and Robin Burnett fell into a routine well known to secret lovers. The routine of the body was the easy part.

'Secret lovers,' she said to him once. 'Secrets and love. Inseparable.'

He did not know what she meant.

'Both parts of the phrase have to be true,' she explained. 'We can only remain lovers provided that it is a secret. If it is no longer secret, then …'

She did not have to finish the sentence.

'Excuse me, but why?' Robin demanded. 'We're a bit old to play Romeo and Juliet, and we're in bed together which rules out us being Layla and Majnun.'

They were in bed in the apartment in Hampstead. It was a month after they had begun the affair, a honey month of bliss. A Saturday morning. The sun split the curtains as it always did. Sunlight was dancing on the branches of the trees on the heath. Inside, the light made Leila's hair sparkle. Robin had told his wife, Elizabeth, he was making a speech in Stuttgart. Or Frankfurt. Or Bonn. Instead he was making love to Leila in Hampstead, looking at her eyes as she lay on the bed, clutching her to him. He wondered what it would be like to wake up to these eyes washing over him every day of his life. Forever.

'Why would what we feel about each other have to change if it became public?' he persisted.

'You must be joking,' Leila replied scathingly. She sat up and leaned on her elbow, turning towards him so her hair fell across her breasts. She looked at this man she now loved, running her fingers across the broadness of his shoulders and the flatness of his stomach.

'I like your body a lot,' she said.

'I like all of you,' he replied.

'I just like your body,' she smiled, mischievously.

He arched an eyebrow. She began dressing. He found the way she put on clothes even more erotic than the way she took them off. He listened to the silk on her skin. She cupped her breasts into her bra.

'I still don't understand why we would split apart if it became public that we were lovers.'

'Then you understand nothing, Robin. For a man so clever, how can you be so naïve?'

'Naïve? No.'

'Naïve, yes. You work for a Prime Minister who talks about restoring "Victorian Values". And I work for a news network where the biggest shareholders are donors to Ronald Reagan.'

'Reagan's divorced!' Robin protested. 'And remarried. And as for the others I work with in the government, they're at it like rabbits, half of them ... the other half are at it like gay rabbits. They are in no position to ...'

'That doesn't matter,' she interrupted. 'It's not what they do or what they are. It's what they believe and say and stand for and try to impose on the rest of us. In literature that difference is called dramatic irony. In real life it is called hypocrisy.'

'Hypocrisy,' he scoffed. 'It's just the necessary oil to grease public life otherwise everything would come to a standstill.'

'Of course,' Leila said. 'But look at these.'

She had a stack of newspapers delivered to the apartment. Sidney Pearl brought them upstairs and left them by the door

111

every morning. She brought them into the bedroom and threw the *Sun* at Robin.

'Your British journalists show women with their breasts hanging out on one page and are happy to rant about adultery on the next. It's hypocrisy, sure. But it's also the New Puritanism. And it means we are not supposed to do things like this.'

'Things like what?' he asked. He moved his hand to the mound of her belly and rubbed it softly. She raised an eyebrow. He moved closer.

'Well,' she said, deciding to show him. Her lips parted. 'Things like this, I suppose.'

Their lovemaking came as naturally to Robin as breathing.

'It's not something we do,' he said to her, amazed. 'It's something we *are*.'

But everything depended on time. Everything depended upon how busy he was and on whether Leila's news director in New York, Nora Malahide, sent her on assignment outside London. It happened a lot at the start – a series of frustrations as she went to Jerusalem, Moscow, Helsinki – but it was happening less and less frequently.

'Thatcher is your story,' Nora Malahide told Leila. 'Stick with her. You understand her well. Two strong women from London. Just right for the times.'

And so Leila stuck with Mrs Thatcher. And Mrs Thatcher mostly stuck with London. And therefore Leila had plenty of excuses to stick with Thatcher's confidant and adviser, Robin Burnett. Her routine was this. Two or three days a week she would contribute to the network breakfast news programme, and two or three days to the evening news. She had become the Network Thatcher-Watcher, offering insights, explaining the latest decisions of the British government on international politics, the Cold War, the acceptance of Cruise and Pershing missiles, the changes in the Soviet Union, the Lady's (mostly) steadfast support for Ronald Reagan, her irritation over the American invasion of the British Commonwealth country of Grenada, and so on. Given the time difference, the US breakfast show hits were at 12 noon or 13.00 British time. The evening news was at 23.30 London time.

'Perfect show times,' Robin reminded her, 'for illicit lovers.'

They easily filled the gaps between the news programmes, sometimes walking together on the heath, occasionally venturing out into a restaurant, mostly just being together, alone, talking and lovemaking in the Hampstead apartment, which became their everywhere, the Place of Safety.

'I have a confession to make,' Robin told her one January night when they huddled together in front of the fire by candlelight after a late supper which he had prepared for her. They were sipping red wine. She looked at him and brushed a stray hair behind her ear.

'Go on.'

He took a deep breath.

'I love you.'

She looked at him carefully.

'I know.'

'You always know. It is very irritating. Then presumably you also know that I have never been in love before.'

She shook her head.

'Oh, come on, Robin, I don't believe that.'

'I mean it. I'm serious. I have said the words, of course. One does. At the time I said it I always thought that I did love the ... woman concerned. I am not a liar, or not about things like that. I have never said it when I did not mean it.'

'Except to have sex.'

He was offended.

'No, Leila, not even then. Especially not even then. But it was never anything like this. Now everything in my life I see through the prism of knowing you. With you, it is all in colour. Without you, everything is black and white.'

He thought for a moment and poured them some more wine, then he began to explain his theory.

'I have spent my life in a rational world of facts and numbers. I try to persuade people that I have the answers because I have figured things out correctly. There is also an irrational world of mullahs and Ayatollahs and Christian bigots, and I despise it. But now that I have met you, I have come to understand that there is a third option.'

She looked at him quizzically.

'Don't go all New Age on me now, Robin. I can take the adultery. I just can't take it if you're going to tell me about chakras and crystals.'

'No, I'm not. But with you I have also discovered that there is a meta-rational world, a world that is not irrational but is beyond our capacity to reason. You and I are in it.' He paused for a second and also took some wine.

'God help us,' she said finally.

They slept in the same bed together in their place of safety as often as possible, usually twice a week. Robin would rise early the next morning, and spend an hour energetically swimming laps in the pool in the basement under the apartments, usually sixty laps, 1500 metres. It was time he used to think. His ministerial car would collect him for the office. Leila would go off to work at the studios, make phone calls, write her scripts, broadcast to America, and then she would return to the apartment for lunch. And for sex. Robin liked to cook for her.

'I like to show off,' he told her. 'And I like to provide for you.'

He would prepare something simple while listening to The World at One on BBC Radio Four. Leila would walk in, and they would embrace.

'I am always nervous waiting for you,' he told her. 'I think I am terrified that one day you just will not turn up, or that you don't exist. That I invented you.'

'It's my apartment,' Leila laughed. 'The likelihood is that I will turn up, since I live here.'

'Still,' he said, 'the nerves.'

She smiled.

'I'm nervous too. Every time is the first time. Even when your fingers smell of garlic.'

They would go to the bedroom sometimes within minutes of her returning to her apartment.

'If it's a choice between lunch and this, I choose this,' he said.

'The S-Plan diet,' Leila laughed. 'The Sex Plan Diet.'

'You will be the only woman I will love in two consecutive millennia,' he told her. She blinked.

'You mean we are going to keep this up until after the year 2000?'

'I should think so, yes,' he confirmed. 'I don't see why not.'

'Secretly?'

That word again.

'After what happened to Cecil, I am not so sure.'

Cecil was Cecil Parkinson. Looking back at it, Cecil's scandal was the beginning of the unravelling of the moral authority of the Conservative government, though it would take years to be seen that way. At first, beyond the sniggers, no one really noticed. Cecil Parkinson cast a long shadow. He was a favourite courtier of the Lady, one of her potential successors, and a rival to Robin Burnett's own ambitions. Those who did not like him called him Smarmy Cecil. They were delighted when he made a fool of himself with a woman. Despite their rivalry, Robin felt quite the opposite. Sorrow, and anger that a private tragedy became a public farce.

The Cecil Parkinson scandal broke in 1983. It was at the height of the Lady's authority, after the Falklands victory and the thumping re-election landslide. 'Victorian Values' or 'Family Values' had become one of the new slogans of the party, and

115

behind the scenes the Central Policy Review Staff had offered the Lady a plan to roll back the welfare state forever, including the scrapping of the National Health Service and the ending of publicly funded higher education. Robin thought the strategy utterly bonkers, and said so, privately, to the Lady.

'However elegant the strategy one must occasionally focus on the results,' he argued. She raised her eyebrows at him, but said nothing more. He wondered if he had opened up a breach which could only widen with age. The eyes of Caligula, he thought. In her many television and radio interviews at the time, the Lady kept going on about her own family and her father's grocery shop in Lincolnshire, as a lesson in sobriety and thrift for the entire country. She meant it. In many ways, she embodied it. But the newspapers saw it as a challenge. Not long afterwards – just in time for the Conservative party conference that autumn – they caught Cecil Parkinson implementing one well-known Victorian Value, impregnating the servants. In this case, his secretary, Sara Keays. She was to bear him a daughter.

'There's a big difference from Victorian Values,' Leila said, with considerable admiration for the other woman, 'because Sara Keays did not go quietly.'

Quite the opposite. She made a huge fuss. The newspapers loved it.

'Hypocrisy,' Robin told Leila. 'That's what did for Cecil. Not sex. Or adultery. The press got him because he was a hypocrite, signing on to this family values nonsense and then behaving this way.'

'No they didn't,' Leila shot back at him, amazed again at what she thought was his naivete. It was their first real row. 'They went after him *because they could*. That's all. He gave them the ammunition, just as we are doing. And because there is no such thing as privacy. You're all in a fishbowl and you don't realize it. Privacy does not exist any more. Your private life is a saleable commodity.'

Robin shook his head.

'It would not have been a story if we hadn't got all worked up about the sanctity of family life. I never mention it. Ever.'

'You're defending the press in this?' Leila said, amazed. 'They were right to publish this? So they'd be right to be here in our bedroom right now?'

'That's not what I mean, it's different with you and me ...' He hesitated.

'Why? Because I am not going to get pregnant? Because I am not your secretary? Because you never mention family values? Is that what you're saying? Wake up, Robin. They'll go for you in the end for one reason only, just like Cecil. Because they can. You are a piece of meat. And when they are hungry enough, they will eat you.'

There was a tense silence. Suddenly Robin laughed.

'Why does a dog lick its balls?' he asked her.

She looked at him, puzzled.

'I don't know, Robin. It's not something we considered a lot when I grew up in LA.'

'It's something David Hickox told me.'

'So what's the answer?'

'Because it can. A dog licks its balls because it can, and that's what you are saying the press here is like – a dog licking its balls? It exposed Cecil because it can?'

'Yes, if you like,' she shrugged dismissively. 'A dog licking its balls just about sums up the British press, yes.'

He thought it through for a moment, as if it were a problem with the Budget numbers, capable of an inventive solution.

'Well, whoever is right, it won't happen if they don't find out anything. And they won't find out anything if we take precautions. We can enforce privacy here.'

She grew restive and stepped out of the bed. She stood in front of him, her face reddening with passion. The sight of her body stirred him.

'Oh, for goodness' sakes, Robin. I am the only thing – *the only thing* – that could stop you from going all the way to the top, from becoming Prime Minister. I could ruin you, and you could ruin me. This ... this thing of ours is laden with disaster.'

He shook his head.

'I don't agree, but even if you are right, I don't care. You are the one thing that makes my life worthwhile. If it is a choice between being with you and becoming Prime Minister, I want you. I don't care about the rest. I choose you.'

Now it was her turn to be shocked.

'You don't care ...!'

'I could give it all up and run a tea-shop in Devon if you would be with me.'

'No, that's completely wrong,' she responded. 'If we give up everything for each other, everything that we are, it won't be long before we hate each other.'

He shook his head.

'I am not asking you to give anything up for me. If – when – you return to the United States I will come with you. I can get a visiting professorship somewhere, I'm sure. We will figure it out. We've done the most difficult thing, which is to find each other. That is the meta-rational bit. "Of all the gin-joints in all the world, she had to walk into mine." Humphrey Bogart territory, for real. The rest has to be easier than that.'

'We live our life in dreams and movie scripts,' she said to him. 'Because the reality is impossible. The fantasy is what makes it work.'

He laughed.

'Leila, all you are saying is that our relationship does not work in theory, but it does somehow seem to work in practice.'

He stretched out a hand and she took it. He pulled her back to bed.

'God, I love your body,' she repeated.

'I love all of you,' he replied.

'I just love your body,' she said again. Their familiar refrain.

* * *

By the end of their first year together the press stories outing Conservative MPs for sexual and other matters had become a steady flow. There was the flamboyant Tory MP who plied for rough gay trade in Clapham Common and along a canal towpath. There was the obscure lawyer MP who was found by the *Sun* to have shared a bed with another man but who vehemently denied he was gay.

'We were just trying to save money on holiday,' he said.

'*Mean Bugger*,' was the *Sun*'s headline the next day.

There was the Tory MP found dead on a table wearing women's underwear, with a plastic bag over his head and an orange in his mouth. He had asphyxiated himself during an act described in the newspapers as 'auto-erotic'. Things started to change for both Leila and Robin as they grew more alarmed at what might happen. Leila put a sticker on her fridge:

'Just because you're paranoid doesn't mean they are NOT out to get you.'

For a time Robin worried that he was being followed. He was always looking behind him. Perhaps, he considered, British intelligence was taking an interest in his private life. He might be open to blackmail. Perhaps the newspapers. Perhaps the Americans.

His friendship with the Director of Central Intelligence David Hickox, blossomed. They would meet on every visit Hickox made to London or Robin made to Washington. It would not have surprised Robin if the CIA itself were following him, checking him out, despite the supposed agreement with the British authorities not to spy on each other's territory without prior permission. Or perhaps the men Robin imagined behind him in the shadows were from one of the other rival parts of the US intelligence community, desperate to find out bits and pieces about the foreign friends of the DCI.

'You really think you are being watched?' Leila said to him one night when he was edgier than usual. He had been unable to make love, one of the occasional consequences of his nervousness. He shrugged.

'It wouldn't surprise me.'

'Can we do anything?'

'No.' He shook his head. 'Unless you want to stop this?'

She thought for a moment.

'No,' she said, defiantly. 'No.'

'Me neither.'

Leila cradled Robin's head and stroked his hair. She told him that when he was nervous like this he reminded her of the small burrowing animal in a Kafka short story called 'The Burrow'.

'I've never read it.'

'You've never read anything except economics and politics. You're a typical politician. The animal has a secure burrow with just one entrance. It appears to be happy, but suddenly the animal begins to worry that it might be attacked with no means of escape. So it digs a second tunnel. For a while it is again content, but then it frets about being attacked by two predators simultaneously, one down each tunnel.'

'So what does it do?' Robin asked her, sitting up.

'Digs a third tunnel. And then another. And then another and another until the entire hillside is full of tunnels.'

'So,' Robin shrugged. 'When does it feel safe?'

'That's the point,' Leila answered him. 'The animal never feels safe. By the time the hillside is a labyrinth of tunnels the animal is on the verge of a nervous breakdown because it sees that any predator could come in from any direction.'

Robin thought about the moral of the story for a moment.

'Best to stay in the burrow with just one tunnel,' he said. 'And look after the tunnel. A place of safety. Like this apartment.'

She stared at him.

'You understand Kafka,' she said, 'but you understand it like an economist.'

120

He realized that was not a compliment. From that moment Robin stopped using ministerial cars to pick him up from Hampstead. They were like extra tunnels in the burrow, extra avenues of attack. Robin was suspicious of the gossip of ministerial drivers. He would often order his own driver to take him only as far as Edgware Road, to drop him near a Lebanese café, The Cedars, and to pick him up from there too. It was in exactly the opposite direction from his home in Pimlico. The driver knew something was wrong. And Robin knew he knew.

'I'll get out and walk,' Robin would say. 'Need to think – get a bit of fresh air.'

The driver would look out on the rain-sodden streets of north-west London and conclude that Robin Burnett, once called by the *Sun* newspaper '*the cleverest man in Britain*' was a complete idiot.

'Of course, Mr Burnett,' the driver would say. 'As you wish.'

Robin would turn hard left and walk briskly towards Edgware Road Tube station, and catch the Underground to Hampstead, or walk up to Swiss Cottage and do the same.

'And you want to know the worst thing?' he told Leila on one of the nights when he was supposed to be at the Conservative party's Scottish conference in Perth, when instead he lay in her arms in Hampstead.

'The worst thing?' Leila responded, cradling him like a sick child, thinking he was teasing her or joking. 'No, tell me the worst thing, Robin. I need to know the worst thing.'

'The worst thing is that I have become so used to lying, that I have begun to forget where the lies end and the truth begins. I lie to Elizabeth. I lie to my drivers, to my ministerial colleagues, to my staff, and even to my children. You are the only person that I tell the complete truth to. If I ever lie to you, Leila, then …'

His eyes lost focus as he contemplated the idea of lying to everyone. He could not finish the sentence.

'Ah,' she sighed. Now it was her turn to see something from Kafka. For her it was the lies which were tunnels underground, subverting the safety of the burrow. She winced, and then something struck her. 'It's a terrible thing to say, Robin, but the lies are perfect practice for political leadership. The oil to grease your way, as you said.'

Robin looked out of the window towards the trees on the heath. He did not want to think that his life had become so cynical. There was a wet wind blowing in from the southwest and the trees bent and rustled to its power. When he turned back to Leila he noticed that silent tears were running down her cheeks. They lay in each other's arms until they fell asleep. Unusually, neither of them said anything more.

Her Majesty's Treasury, Autumn 1983

'It's time,' David Hickox said.

'Time?' Robin Burnett responded.

'Yup.'

Robin was in his office at the Treasury. It was dark, well after nine in the evening, a few months after the second Conservative election victory in 1983. Robin was working late on the Chancellor's autumn statement. Hickox called on a secure line.

'The Director of Central Intelligence for you, Chief Secretary.'

Oh, he hesitated. Shit.

'Fine,' Robin said, with all the sincerity he could muster in his voice. 'Put him through.'

Robin's mind was far away. He was befuddled by over-work and stress, and a new fear. Of being caught. He was sure someone had followed him from the Hampstead apartment that morning, but when he turned round suddenly to confront the man, he was gone. A Gumshoe, perhaps. A Philip Marlowe. A private detective paid for by Elizabeth to check up on him. A journalist from one of the scandal sheets about to do a Cecil Parkinson on him after all. Or perhaps it was someone from the Security Service, MI5, trying to figure out if he had some liaison dangerous enough to constitute a threat to national security. Or maybe Robin had just imagined it. Maybe he was going mad. Whichever of these unpalatable possibilities turned out to be true, the last thing he wanted that evening was a secure-line conversation with the Director of Central Intelligence.

It had been a gruelling day, the tenth fourteen-hour day in a row. Just two hours before the call from Hickox, the Chancellor of the Exchequer had left Robin's office. The two of them had been celebrating modestly some good signs on the economy.

'Green shoots, Robin,' the Chancellor had said. 'Green shoots of recovery.'

Robin Burnett agreed, but it still was not good enough.

'At great cost,' he said. Growth was up. Productivity, up. Inflation down. The pound, stable. It was all looking good. 'Except for unemployment,' Robin added ruefully. 'The newspapers are fixated by the collapse of manufacturing. They don't understand that we are becoming a post-industrial power, a service economy. They don't get it. All they care about is jobs, jobs, jobs that make things.'

'Unless we get them to care about something else,' the Chancellor said darkly, 'as the Lady wants.'

'Yes,' Robin agreed. 'As the Lady wants.'

For several hours that day as he struggled with the autumn statement figures on his desk, Robin had also been forced to turn in his mind the provocative conversation he and the Chancellor had endured with the Prime Minister that afternoon in her room in the Commons. She had invited them for 'tea and a chat'. That always meant the Lady wanted something, or that she wanted to gauge their reaction to some ideas of her own.

'The autumn statement,' she began briskly, before they even had time to sit down. 'How optimistic can we be? How robust can I be at PMQs?'

The Chancellor replied that there were now grounds for economic optimism provided they kept a tight grip on spending.

'Facts,' she said, turning to Robin. 'I need facts.'

Robin ran through the figures and forecasts, all of which put the Lady in a chipper mood.

'Things are in fact going rather well,' the Chancellor said, 'although we get no credit for it, thanks in particular to the BBC and the newspaper fixation with the jobless total and the shrinkage in manufacturing.'

'Unemployment,' the Lady insisted, clapping her hands together vigorously, 'is collateral damage in the war on inflation. It is the pain one has to endure to cure the disease.'

Robin could see that she was flexing for an argument with someone. He hoped it wasn't going to be him. She went on, straining for metaphors, trying out the answers she would use when she was next interviewed on television, or during Prime Minister's Questions in the Commons.

'You can't make an omelette without breaking eggs, Robin. These people focus on unemployment. Why? Because we've whipped inflation, that's why. We have beaten the cancer and now they are snivelling because they're left with the common cold. I ask you!'

She began to wave her finger. The second term had brought a lot more finger-waving, even at him. The newspapers said she swiped people with her handbag. It wasn't literally true, but you knew what they meant.

'You have to realize that newspapers – the entire liberal media elite – are like dinosaurs,' she continued. The handbagging had begun. 'Hugely powerful, hugely destructive, but with brains the size of peas. They can only concentrate on one thing at a time. It used to be inflation. Now it is unemployment. Tomorrow, if we want them to talk about something else, we have to change the subject.'

She said those last few words as if they were underlined. Perhaps in the Prime Minister's mind, they were.

'Shall I be mother?' she said with a smile, and began pouring the tea.

'To what, Prime Minister?' the Chancellor asked, helpfully accepting a cup. 'To what shall we change the subject?'

The Lady was now sitting primly on her leather sofa in a powder blue suit and white blouse, with the teacup on her lap. She looked very feminine. Robin hoped she wasn't still on about scrapping the National Health Service. He thought he had torpedoed that idea by now, but with the Lady, ideas were never dead until you had driven a stake right through their heart. She put her cup of tea back on a silver tray and arched an eyebrow.

'To the miners.'

Robin was surprised.

'The miners, Prime Minister?'

'The miners, Robin. Yes.'

Caligula.

The National Union of Mineworkers was the best organized, best financed and toughest trade union in Britain. Since World War Two they had made life difficult, at times impossible, for successive governments. They had wounded the Conservatives under Edward Heath in the 1970s, causing severe energy shortages. Heath had no choice but to impose a three day industrial working week. There had been routine power cuts from area to area in rotation. People lit their homes with candles. This was supposed to be late twentieth century post-imperial Britain, one of the richest countries in the world, and for a time you could not use your electric lights. It led to a debate about whether the country was becoming ungovernable. It also encouraged unrest in other industries, with the miners sending 'flying pickets' to help in disputes which had no direct connection to the coal pits. The car industry had become a serious battleground. Steel. Engineering. The docks. Industrial chaos everywhere. In the international newspapers they wrote of 'the British Disease'.

Then the public service unions got the message. They went on to undermine the Callaghan Labour government in 1978–79, leading to the Lady's Conservative victory of 1979. For months, in their private conversations over whisky and soda, Robin had suggested to the Lady that the public sector unions, most especially the miners, in the nationalized pits run by the National Coal Board, were the biggest obstacle to her plans for complete economic restructuring of the United Kingdom. She had nodded and listened and taken it in, but she said little in reply. That was about to change.

'We need to shrink the public sector,' Robin said, 'like a proctologist needs to shrink a bad case of piles.'

The Lady smiled at his earthy allusion, and nodded with understanding.

The year before, in the run up to the Falklands war, the Lady's own position was doubtful. Now, he realized, she was planning to take on the miners. Robin gasped at her boldness. It occurred to him that the Lady needed enemies the way most people needed friends, and that he thirsted for a new battle too. They were warriors, defined by combat.

'You said yourself that we can never get unemployment down unless we introduce flexibility into the Labour market,' she lectured Robin, in his own words. 'Flexibility means taking on the miners.'

She looked at their faces for a reaction.

'Take on, Prime Minister …?' the Chancellor began. 'As in …?'

'Yes, take on,' she snapped back. 'I am told that Scargill is determined to force a national strike.'

Arthur Scargill was the miners' leader, strongly left wing.

'Told by …' the Chancellor began again.

The Lady glared at him but said nothing. Robin concluded that the Security Service, MI5, had been briefing her. They had infiltrated the miners' union, along with all the other strategically important unions. He knew better than to say anything, but his heart pumped with anticipation.

'Scargill wants to bring down what he calls Thatcherism,' she said robustly. Then she laughed. 'I have always wanted to be an *-ism*. How kind of Mr Scargill to name one after me.'

Robin and the Chancellor laughed too, but Robin could see that a cloud passed over the Prime Minister's face.

'If the miners go on strike, Robin, it will be to provoke a General Strike along the lines of 1926. In which case we have no choice but to defeat them. There is no substitute for victory. Of course we could lie down and let Scargill run the country.' She raised an eyebrow, as if to demonstrate how fatuous the idea really was. 'In some ways he already thinks he does. If we win – and we shall – then organized labour in the United Kingdom will be defunct for a generation. We shall privatize the pits – among other things. British Airways, for example. And we shall cease our dependence on deep-mined coal. The free and flexible market will create jobs. Inward investment will soar. And someone else can be the economic sick man of Europe. Italy, probably. Or France. But it will not be us.'

That last phrase was underlined too. The Lady clapped her hands together and rose, signalling the meeting was over. She brushed a few invisible crumbs from her blue suit. Then she instructed them to prepare immediately and in secret for the miners' strike she felt was inevitable, perhaps as soon as the coming winter, but possibly more than a year away.

As she talked, Robin was reminded of her flushed enthusiasm when she made preparations against General Galtieri and the Argentinians, doing a dozen things at once. Without enemies, the Lady could be little more than a hectoring housewife. With enemies, she was utterly amazing. As long as her enemies were the right ones, Robin decided, things would go well.

'A tin-pot dictator in Barnsley,' the Lady waved that finger again, referring to the town where Arthur Scargill had his union headquarters, 'is no more of a challenge than a tin-pot dictator in Buenos Aires. Just a little closer. Now, let's get on with the preparations, shall we?'

The Chancellor and Robin Burnett left the Prime Minister's office in the Commons with her words ringing in their ears like a slap.

'Wow,' Robin said out of the corner of his mouth as they stepped into the fresh air.

'Phew,' the Chancellor added. 'At least it wasn't scrapping the NHS again.'

'Indeed.'

They walked briskly across the road and back to the Treasury. As they did so, they decided whom they would need to bring together in a secret mini-cabinet to deal with the inevitable industrial confrontation.

'All the economics ministries,' the Chancellor said, counting them out on his fingers. 'Board of Trade. Energy.'

'The Home Office,' Robin added. 'And – I suppose – defence. In case it really does take a turn for the worse.'

The thought of the army on the streets as a result of an industrial dispute with the miners alarmed both of them. Echoes of 1926.

'We might be wasting our time,' the Chancellor said, grimly. 'There might never be a miners' strike.'

They were entering Robin's own office. They sat down on the leather sofas opposite each other.

'If we provide the contingency planning, I think the Lady will provide the strike,' Robin said.

The Chancellor agreed.

'It looks as if Scargill is up for it too.'

Robin nodded.

'Scargill and the Lady. A marriage made in heaven.'

And a battle only one of them could survive.

Now, at what he had hoped was the fag-end of a fourteen hour day, Robin was alone and stressed. The Chancellor had gone off to make a speech at a dinner in the City, talking up the economy as a preamble to the formality of the autumn statement, talking down inflation, and sipping claret.

The autumn statement lay in intellectually incoherent pieces on Robin's desk in front of him, as he rubbed his tired eyes. The prospect of a bare-knuckled fight with the men regarded as the vanguard of the working classes was just around the corner. And, god help him, David Hickox was on the secure line.

'It's time, Robin,' Hickox repeated.

'What do you mean, "it's time", David?' he responded sarcastically. Hickox, like a lot of powerful people, seemed to think that the more he said the same thing, the more sense he was making. In Robin's experience the reverse was usually the case. Robin chuckled.

'It's time all right, David. It's time for me to get out of the office and have a large drink. Miller time, I believe you call it in the United States. That's the only time I understand. It's been a shitty day here. And now, you've come to brighten it up?'

The American laughed. Robin imagined him sitting in Langley, Virginia, feet on the desk, yelling at the secure speaker-phone in the DCI's office, relaxed, almost playful. Pulling strings. Reluctantly Robin Burnett conceded that he liked Hickox more than was prudent. And that affection put him on his guard. Charm was a political asset, but a dangerous one. So was friendship.

'It's time for the Devil to claim your soul,' Hickox said loudly. 'What do you think I mean? It's time to call in a few favours, Robin. I'm coming to London and then Paris and Bonn and a coupla other places next week. Something's come up. I'm seeing my counterparts in London,' – that meant the Secret Intelligence Service, MI6 – 'but I also have a favour to ask from you. Personally. *Mano a mano*. Lunch? Winfield House? Tuesday? At one o'clock. It's very important to me and to the President. And to our friendship. Can you do it?'

Oh, Christ. Oh, double Christ. Hickox' words made Robin Burnett think of the line from Virgil's *Aeneid*:

Timeo Danaos et Donad Ferentes.

I fear the Greeks, even when bearing gifts. What would Virgil write now? I fear the Americans, especially when talking of Friendship and Favours. Shit. Double shit. Shittety-shit.

'You are serious about the Devil coming to claim my soul, aren't you?' Robin said. 'You've packed your horns and pointed tail?'

'Yes,' Hickox laughed. 'I am always serious. When I want something.'

Oh, god. Robin changed tone.

'Of course, David. It would be a pleasure. Tuesday lunch. I just have to re-jig a couple of things. But it will be good to see you.'

He took a deep breath. Re-jig, as in cancel. Good, as in having a hernia. Pleasure, as in, a cardiac infarction. Robin didn't have to look at his diary. He knew there was a departmental meeting, followed by preparation for Wednesday's Prime Minister's Questions. It was part of his routine. The Lady liked him to provide her with the best arguments on why, if their monetary policy was the right medicine for the economy, British society remained in such a turbulent state.

'There is no such thing as society,' he lectured her repeatedly in their PMQ prep meetings. 'There are individuals, there are families, and there are over-lapping communities. There is, of course, also the national interest. But there is *absolutely no such thing* as British 'society' outside the minds of social workers. And if social workers are so successful, Prime Minister, you may care to wonder why the rich don't have them?'

The Lady had laughed at Robin's rant. She complimented him.

'Maybe it is time for a promotion?' she teased. A rare glimpse of the mouth of Marilyn Monroe.

131

'I ... well, promotion ...' he did not know what to say. 'Thank you, Prime Minister.'

She didn't say what she had in mind. Perhaps she really was just teasing him.

'Winfield House, one o'clock,' Robin repeated on the phone to Hickox. 'Will the ambassador be joining us?'

Winfield House was the mansion in Regent's Park occupied by US ambassadors. From its rooms in the 1940s, General Dwight D. Eisenhower had worked with Churchill to mastermind the liberation of Europe.

'No,' Hickox replied brusquely. 'Gawd, no. The ambo's only a goddamn pizza salesman, Robin. He'd just get in the way, unless you want anchovies with it.'

The current US ambassador in London had indeed made his fortune with pizza franchises all over the American West. He had donated tens of millions of dollars to anti-abortion causes and also to the Republican National Committee. All he asked in return was to please his wife's most earnest desire – and be made ambassador in London in order that she might meet the Queen. It seemed a fair enough trade. Hickox was clear how the lunch would be conducted.

'No note takers, no flunkeys, no ambassadors,' he said. 'No paper trail. And given the sensitivity of what we might talk about I'd be grateful if you wouldn't mention the meeting to ... to anyone. Just you and me, Robin, old buddy.'

I can't hardly wait, Robin Burnett thought, old buddy, old chum, old pal. Whatever the lunch was to be about, it took no particular genius to recognize it would be politically toxic.

'Fine,' Robin replied, and even found himself smiling at the telephone. 'Good to hear from you, David. It's been too long.'

They hung up.

'Bloody hypocrite,' Robin Burnett muttered to the telephone on its cradle. 'Bloody, bloody hypocrite.'

132

He meant himself. Not Hickox. Hickox was many things, but certainly not a hypocrite. What you saw with Hickox was what you got, Robin thought. A charming man who was also a physical and intellectual bully. He would do more or less anything to advance his own interests alongside those of his president. Robin found it curious that he admired Hickox for this. When he talked about him to Leila he said that it was Hickox's shamelessness which most appealed to him, while at the same time he despised himself more and more for the same traits, especially the lying. Still, Robin thought, there was one person to whom he always told the truth. Leila. One person around whom the truth revolved, and who anchored him to reality.

Robin checked his watch. It was now almost ten o'clock at night. Shit. Shit. Shit. He had at least another two hours' work on the autumn statement. What should he do? He was utterly distracted by the Hickox call. He drummed his fingers on the desk and then decided to call Jack Heriot at home. Heriot picked up. Robin could hear the theme tune for the ITN television news in the background.

'Something has come up, Jack. I need a briefing from your people.'

'My people?'

Robin Burnett paused for a second.

'No, actually I don't. I need a briefing from … another service. But I'd like you to be present for some political advice.'

'Oh,' Heriot replied, suddenly interested. 'Another service' was the government euphemism for the Secret Intelligence Service, MI6.

'Right,' Heriot said. 'What's come up?'

'Hickox.'

'Oh.'

'He's coming to London and wants to see me.'

'Oh.'

'Alone.'

'Oh,' Heriot said a third time, his voice full of curiosity. 'I see the problem. Then I'll fix it. For tomorrow.'

Robin put down the phone and tried to concentrate on the figures in front of him, but without success. Rather like the first moment he saw Leila, he knew that his life was about to change. He sensed that it could not possibly be good. He began to think again about running a tea-shop in Devon or becoming a visiting lecturer at some east coast American university. It was the paradox of government, he decided. Now that he actually knew how it worked, he did not want to do it any more. The more he knew, the more he could. And the less he wanted to do. He stared at the paperwork on his desk for a few minutes, and then went back to work.

HM Foreign and Commonwealth Office, 1983

The briefing Jack Heriot organized took place late the following morning in the Foreign Office. Robin was shown through to one of the rooms that looked out on the inner courtyard, a room placed at the disposal of the Director of the Secret Intelligence Service. The rather grubby old fashioned headquarters of MI6 were just a short walk away. Heriot thought it better for Robin not to go there.

'The Yanks call it "plausible deniability",' Heriot smiled, plump and sweaty in his blue double-breasted pinstripe suit, as they waited for the director of MI6 to arrive. Robin reflected that he and Heriot were heading in opposite directions, physically. Heriot was getting plumper in government, while Robin was becoming leaner and harder. Different ways of coping with stress, he decided.

'And what are we plausibly denying?' Robin asked him.

'Everything,' Heriot responded.

'Why?'

Heriot looked at Robin as if he had suddenly begun speaking Martian.

'For goodness' sake, Robin, if anyone in the House ever asks you whether you had a briefing from the intelligence service, the traditional recourse is to say that we never discuss intelligence matters. But that's hopeless. The press writes: "Minister refuses to deny ..." That kind of thing. Much better to say categorically that you have never, ever, had any briefings on any subject connected with British foreign policy except those conducted by officials in the Foreign Office.'

'You mean I should lie?' Robin said in mock outrage.

'No, of course not. The opposite. It's a non-lie. That's the point.' Heriot paused for a moment. 'Though of course it amounts to an untruth, but that's not the same thing.' Jack Heriot laughed at his own joke, opening his arms wide and gesturing at the office. 'And so here we are. An intelligence briefing with oversight from democratically elected politicians. That means me. I have to keep an eye on Monty in case he corrupts you.' Monty was Sir Montague Hawke, the Director of the Secret Intelligence Service. 'Besides, if he gets you over at MI6 he'll just show you how moth-eaten the whole place is and browbeat you into stumping up more cash for the new headquarters.'

For years MI6 had been fighting an internal battle to build a new headquarters on the South Bank of the Thames. Within Whitehall it was known as 'the Vauxhall Pleasure Dome' because the plans were so elaborate and expensive that the design might be worthy of Kublai Khan.

'Security reasons,' Sir Montague would say as an explanation for the extraordinary ziggurat-like building he wanted for SIS. 'Security is paramount.'

The costs of the MI6 Pleasure Dome did not fit in with the tight spending limits Robin was trying to impose. The project had been delayed, but not yet cancelled.

'I am not that easily swayed,' Robin said. Jack Heriot raised an eyebrow, and said nothing.

Sir Montague Hawke walked into the room a few minutes later, shook hands and made himself at home behind the empty desk. He was tall, a little past the usual retirement age, thin as a rail, with a shock of white hair and so many wrinkles round his eyes it made Robin Burnett think of pictures of the poet W. H. Auden or of one of those sad-eyed Chinese dogs, shar peis. A secretary came in with a tray of coffee and biscuits and put them on the desk. Sir Montague looked at the tray with disdain, as if refreshments were for cissies. Then he began.

'So, Robin,' he said, rubbing his big-veined hands together, 'Jack has told me some of it. A lunchtime treat for you, with our American cousin. He is on his way over to see me next week too, so it is ... shall we say, quite interesting that he wishes to see you as well. Perhaps you'd like to explain the problem in your own words?'

'Quite interesting' was about as colourful a phrase as Sir Monty ever used. Robin Burnett began to speak slowly and carefully. He recounted the phone call from Hickox, including the instruction that it was a personal matter, not to be discussed with officials.

'So naturally, I ...'

'Naturally,' Sir Montague nodded. 'Naturally you did precisely the opposite. Hickox will guess as much. But there's a kind of accepted form with these things. Absolutely correct judgement, Chief Secretary.'

As he stared at the wrinkled face, for the first time Robin felt a thrill of fear. What did these people know? Why did it appear that they knew everything? Perhaps because they did. Did Sir Montague know about Leila? Did Hickox? Jack Heriot? The Security Service, MI5? Was there a security dimension to having an affair with an American national of Iranian background? Was this something they cared about or merely gossiped about behind his back? Was that why he kept feeling he was being followed? Robin swallowed hard.

'Hickox made some reference to being the Devil. He said he had come to claim my soul. Perhaps he's been reading Faust.'

'I think that *very* unlikely, Chief Secretary,' Sir Montague affirmed, stressing the word 'very' until it appeared to have four or five syllables.

'More like an offer you can't refuse,' Jack Heriot laughed. Robin did not understand the reference. Heriot explained.

'*The Godfather*.'

Robin looked at him blankly.

'The Godfather?' he repeated, puzzled.

'That Godfather? The film? The book? No? Not seen it? Great stuff, really. Made me think that dealing with the Reagan administration at any level is like dealing with the mafia. They talk about "consulting the allies", which means you must do what Reagan's people say or they do it without you, and you end up in bed with a horse's head.'

Robin nodded, as if he understood, and then went on.

'Last year I promised Hickox personally that we – that I – would always be grateful if he helped over the Falklands. That I owe him. He has every right to assume I will keep my word.'

'Why?' Sir Montague asked. 'People don't.'

'Because I do keep my word. The question is, what does he want? Or, bluntly, what am I getting myself into?'

The tall, thin man rubbed the wrinkles round his eyes with a tired hand. He stood up from the desk.

'Bad back,' he said as he stretched towards the window. 'Seizes up if I sit. Am getting too old for all of this. Falling apart.'

There was a long pause while Sir Monty contemplated the Foreign Office central courtyard and swayed a little on the balls of his feet, stretching his back. A stray pigeon flew on to the window sill, caught sight of Sir Montague's hangdog look, and flew off.

'Iraq,' Sir Monty said definitively at last. 'Or Iran. Same thing in the American mind nowadays, rather like Tweedledum and Tweedledee. Undifferentiated disasters, I suspect, but that's a personal bias, not an intelligence forecast.

The Americans have taken to calling their policy for the region "dual-containment", meaning they hope to keep both Iran and Iraq in their box, though history might suggest otherwise. But what specifically does Cousin David Hickox want from you, I wonder? What indeed.'

Sir Montague rolled a little more on the balls of his feet and then turned to face Robin and Jack Heriot.

'Well, whatever it is, there might just be an opportunity here for us, Chief Secretary. If you are prepared to take it.'

'An opportunity?'

'Yes.'

'What kind of opportunity?'

Sir Montague pursed his lips into a grimace, but said nothing. For a second, Robin's habitual optimism faded. He sensed that something might be about to go wrong, seriously wrong, and that when the disaster finally occurred, the meeting that he was now attending in Her Majesty's Foreign and Colonial Office would be erased from everyone's memory. Except, perhaps, his own.

'Well,' Sir Monty went on, 'Hickox obviously thinks that you, Robin, can or will do something for him that my Service or the Foreign Office cannot do. Something in the economic sphere, perhaps. Or something involving direct access to the Prime Minister. He will know how much she relies on you for honest advice. Whatever it is that Hickox wants, Chief Secretary, if you do it, then he will be forever in your debt. The current roles – where you are indebted to him over the Argentine business – will be reversed. He will owe you. And he could be even more important in future than he is now.'

Sir Montague paused a little, turning it over in his mind.

'Think of it this way: in helping Hickox you may be making a wise investment for the future. Money in the Favour Bank, if you like. Capital you can draw on. And of course *not* helping him will make a potential enemy of one of the most important people in the Reagan administration, someone who might become Vice President – or even President of the United States.'

This line of reasoning did not cheer Robin up at all.

'It depends on exactly what he wants,' Robin said morosely. 'I know nothing about Iraq or Iran except what I read in the newspapers. Tell me more about David Hickox, please.'

'You have already met him several times,' Sir Montague replied. 'So you must have formed your own judgement?'

Robin nodded.

'Of course. He plays the affable, back-slapping all-American guy, but he is much more intelligent than that and, I suspect, much more ruthless. I mean that as a compliment. You sniffed at the idea he might have read Faust, Sir Monty. I wouldn't be too sure he hasn't. He's a lot sharper than he appears.'

'A fair summation,' Sir Montague conceded.

'But I am asking for your judgement, Sir Montague. For a start, why is he Director of Central Intelligence? What's his USP?'

Sir Montague laughed.

'Where to begin?' he said slowly, pacing a little behind the desk. 'Where indeed is his Unique Selling Point?' He cleared his throat. 'In David Hickox, President Reagan has chosen someone with a long history of links to the Middle East. In 1976 – three years before the fall of the Shah and the Pahlavi dynasty – David Theodore Dubois Hickox was a member of the US Congress for northern Virginia. There was not much to distinguish him politically from others on the right of the Republican party, except his hard work and constant net-working. Oh, and his charm. He has a kind of legendary charm, as you have pointed out. If you like that sort of thing.'

Sir Monty made it abundantly clear that he did not like that sort of thing. Charm was like homosexuality, Sir Monty reflected. All right in its way. Never entirely to be trusted.

'Hickox first came to our attention because the Congressional district he represents – around Arlington – is home to many workers at the Pentagon and the CIA. He was well plugged in to the defence and intelligence community and also to the high tech industries and contractors that you find in northern Virginia. As a freshman Congressman he secured a seat on the House Intelligence Committee.'

'So?' Robin prompted.

'So, we began paying attention to him. Among other things, David Hickox was the foremost advocate in Congress of supplying Iran with a secret nuclear energy programme in 1976.'

Robin Burnett gasped.

'What?'

He was not sure he had heard correctly. Heriot also looked stunned.

'A … a nuclear programme? To Iran? In 1976?'

'It was intended to be for peaceful purposes,' Sir Montague said stiffly. 'We're not talking bombs, here. We're talking nuclear power.'

Robin Burnett laughed.

'In a country afloat on oil and gas?'

'Indeed,' Sir Montague coughed a little. 'You have to remember, Chief Secretary, that those were the glory days of the American relationship with Iran. They had supplanted the British as the key regional power ever since the Mossadegh coup of 1953. By 1976 we were talking of thousands of years of Persian power and culture. The 2000th anniversary of Persepolis. The Iranians were buying tanks and weapons systems so quickly that we ourselves were awash with oil money almost as much as they were. An arms bazaar developed. And then it went pear shaped after 1973. The Arab–Israeli war. The Shah tried to help the West by keeping oil prices down and production up. By '76 the Iranians were looking for a reward. And the reward was the transfer of US technology to a Persian nuclear power programme. David Hickox was going to get it for them.'

'But, I mean,' Jack Heriot exclaimed, just as surprised as Robin. 'Nukes? They couldn't seriously have expected to get nukes? I don't remember that.'

'No one remembers it,' Sir Montague said loftily. 'But of course, in the Service we do. Hickox argued for up to eight nuclear reactors capable of enriching uranium to weapons grade. And the fuel, of course. He almost got his way, too, though the Ford administration had more sense than they are sometimes given credit for. You can imagine what would have happened. Events have consequences. The Islamic Revolution overthrew the Shah just three years later. If Hickox had got his way then Ayatollah Khomeini and his chums would have inherited the ability to make nuclear bombs. I don't believe nuclear deterrence would work with a regime led by a religious fanatic, more interested in the next world than this one. Do you? I think the Americans would have been forced to consider their own pre-emptive strike.'

Robin Burnett breathed deeply. The world of macro-economics, the autumn statement, unemployment forecasts and even the prospect of taking on the miners in a national strike, had never seemed more appealing. Ayatollah Khomeini with nukes. Organized by his new best friend, David Hickox.

'Go on, please, Sir Montague. I am sure there is more.'

'Oh, yes,' Sir Montague nodded, his wrinkles cracking into the hint of a smile. 'There is more. During the Carter years David Hickox was one of the leaders of Team B.'

Heriot and Robin Burnett looked at each other blankly.

'Never heard of it, I'm afraid,' Robin admitted.

'Me neither,' Heriot said.

'Ah, Team B,' Sir Montague sighed, longingly. 'Team B, Team B. What a delight for those of us who have been involved in intelligence matters in a professional capacity for many years. Team B included names you might be familiar with – Paul Wolfowitz, Donald Rumsfeld, and others. Ronald Reagan and his California friends had argued for years that

CIA intelligence assessments of the Soviet Union were too friendly. Too soft. So, enter Team B. They provided … let's call it a *different* perspective, shall we? Reflecting a more paranoid style. Russians with snow on their boots were about to invade Kansas, apparently. That kind of thing.'

'And a less charitable view of Team B?' Robin asked.

'Lunatics in charge of the asylum,' Sir Montague replied briskly. 'Absolute nutters. Dismissive of anyone who did not share their delusions. They seemed to think the CIA was full of commie pinko bedwetters.' Here he gave a full-throated laugh. 'The CIA has its problems, from time to time, but in my experience lack of enthusiasm for taking on the Soviet system has never been a characteristic of the people at Langley.'

Robin and Jack Heriot exchanged glances. It was rare to see Sir Montague so exercised.

'Who exactly are these Team B people? I've not really heard of any of them.'

'Oh, you will,' Sir Monty enthused bitterly. 'They are loosely grouped followers of Senator Henry Jackson, the Senator from Washington State – known to some of my younger colleagues as the "Senator for Boeing", because he delivers so much business to that company. He's nicknamed "Scoop" Jackson. He appears to believe it is his life's work to make US tax payers purchase as many weapons systems as possible. His people call themselves "neo-conservatives" for some reason which escapes me. Apparently to distinguish themselves from paleo-conservatives or Jurassic conservatives or some such primitive Washington tribes. Still, whatever they call themselves, it's American taxpayers' money they are wasting so perhaps one shouldn't grumble.'

Robin Burnett laughed at the mandarin wit.

'You have me enthralled,' he said. 'I thought David Hickox was just a hamburger-eating ex-footballer with a penchant for falling to the ground and doing one-armed push-ups.'

'Oh, he did that for you?' Sir Montague smiled, rearranging the wrinkles round his eyes in amusement. 'How lovely! You must really have got under his skin. I have never seen it myself, though they say it is an amusing diversion. Useful for distracting the press and other children. At any event, Hickox was nominated Director of Central Intelligence by president-elect Reagan in December 1980 immediately after the election, to signal to the intelligence community that – what is the phrase Hickox himself used? – No More Mister Nice Guy. The gloves are coming off. The Cold War just got a few degrees colder. He encouraged the press to call him "Wild Bill Hickox", which I believe endeared him to many Americans. And now my understanding is that David Hickox has ambitions to run for the presidency of the United States one day. And since he is your new best friend, how nice that may be for all of us. An opportunity, as I say.'

Heriot and Robin laughed again at Sir Montague's patrician attempt at American cadences.

'So Team B has now taken over Team A?' Heriot wondered.

'Precisely. Team B runs the CIA. It *is* Team A. In June 1981 Hickox personally ensured that the Israelis were able to use their F16s to attack Iraq's nuclear reactor at Osirak. US intelligence assets planted guidance transmitters under Iraqi and Jordanian radar so the Israelis could hit Osirak without being detected until the last moment. Then, shortly after you met him at the barbecue of the Navy Secretary, Don Hall, in Middleburg, the President made David Hickox his secret and special envoy to the Middle East.'

'Really? Secret *and* special? Meaning?'

'Meaning, he is not coming here to London to see you, Chief Secretary, even though he may flatter you otherwise. Nor just to see me. This is a stop off. My understanding is that David Hickox is on his way through London to Baghdad, where he will meet Saddam Hussein.'

Robin's eyes widened in surprise.

'Why?'

'To stop Iran winning the war against Iraq.'

Robin was growing increasingly alarmed.

'And my role is …?'

Sir Montague shrugged. He turned back to the window and jiggled a little on his feet.

'Well, indeed. That is the question of the hour. What is your role?'

He paused and then changed tone, turning to Jack Heriot.

'D'you know, Minister,' he said, 'that this building is increasingly grimy with age and traffic fumes. It might be worth seeing whether the courtyard could be cleaned properly. Even with the tightness of departmental budgets, surely we can afford to spruce the Foreign Office up a bit without the Chief Secretary to the Treasury bursting his spending plans in the forthcoming autumn statement?'

There was a pause. A silence fell between the three men.

'Well, Sir Montague,' Jack Heriot answered eventually, 'we'd welcome it of course, though Robin here has some fairly tough spending caps on all of us.'

'Thumbscrews,' Sir Montague said.

'Necessary to keep inflation under control,' Heriot went on.

Robin said nothing. He was still morosely pondering what he had learned about Hickox. Sir Montague continued.

'Then, of course, the plans for my service's new headquarters on the South Bank are taking longer than we expected because of the thumbscrews and the spending caps.' Sir Montague turned back to Robin. 'I don't suppose any of this could be expedited, Chief Secretary? It would be very helpful to get on with our new home. Unless you are minded to cancel it in the name of short term bean counting?'

Robin coughed with embarrassment. He had reached the highest level of British politics and was now arguing with Sir Monty as if over the price of carpets in a Middle East souk. He looked at his watch and signalled that he had to go. They all stood up at once.

'Thank you for your briefing, Sir Montague,' he said with a smile. 'In the spirit of inter-departmental cooperation, I will see what I can do about the matters you have just raised. Consistent, of course, with bearing down on inflation through reducing public spending.' He hesitated. 'But there are … There are always exceptions, especially for matters connected with national security. I am sure we can work something out.' He looked at Heriot and Sir Montague. 'To everyone's benefit.'

Sir Montague Hawke smiled briefly, an enigmatic smile that flickered across the lines on his old, grey face. They shook hands. Robin left. He stepped down the main staircase and looked at the glories of the great Empire which surrounded him, the marble, the tapestries, the paintings, every inch of which exhaled the word 'power'. He felt just as he had done that day he first saw Leila. His life was about to change, irrevocably and forever. This time he was not so happy about it. Behind him in the sterile room set aside for his use, the Director General of the Secret Intelligence Service turned to the deputy Secretary of State at the Foreign and Colonial Office.

'Robin Burnett could be Prime Minister one day,' Sir Montague Hawke said slowly. 'If he doesn't burst into flames first.'

Heriot nodded.

'It could be a close run thing,' Heriot answered.

146

Regent's Park, London

AUTUMN 1983

Winfield House is one of the finest houses in London. A short walk through Regent's Park from Baker Street, the acres of private gardens make it seem like a country home, except it is in the heart of England's biggest city. It's the official residence of the Ambassador of the United States to the Court of St James. The Tuesday of Robin Burnett's meeting with David Hickox was the last warm day of the autumn of 1983. The leaves were already gold and brown, and some had begun to fall. Robin awoke early in the apartment in Hampstead and looked out over the changing colours on the heath. He could smell Leila on his body and in the bed and that made him smile. She had woken before dawn, kissed him and then left for the studios to edit a film for that day's American breakfast television news. Robin went down to the pool in the basement and swam his customary sixty laps, rhythmically beating out each stroke as he arranged the day in his mind. He shaved carefully, showered, dressed, and worked for an hour or two at his papers in Leila's study. At exactly nine o'clock he called his office to issue instructions to the staff.

'I intend to sign off on the new SIS building,' he told his PPS.

'Right,' the young man said, unable to keep the surprise and amusement from his voice. 'So Sir Monty gets his Pleasure Dome?'

147

'National security reasons,' Robin snapped back.

'We'll need to find savings elsewhere,' the PPS reminded him. Robin was in no mood to be lectured about basic principles of arithmetic.

'Indeed. Just get the paperwork ready.'

He put the phone down and then called Elizabeth. He felt it necessary to preserve the lie that he was on his way back from Edinburgh by train.

'Is something wrong?' she wondered. He denied it.

'No, all is well. Just very, very busy. Exhausted. I'll be working late again tonight.'

Another set of lies on his account. This time *raison d'etat*.

'Of course you will,' Elizabeth responded. He put the phone down.

'Meta-rational,' he murmured. 'Even the world's most truthful person probably only tells the truth 99 per cent of the time. And the world's biggest liar probably has to tell the truth 98 per cent of the time, to keep up his credibility. I'm somewhere in the gap. That's where all the fun is.'

He tidied his papers, put them in his attaché case and prepared to leave for the lunch with Hickox.

'Good morning, Mr Burnett,' Sidney Pearl called out to him in the hallway.

'Good morning, Sidney. Fine morning. I believe Miss Rajar will be back around one thirty. Unfortunately I have a lunch engagement.'

'I notice that you always use the word "unfortunate" when you mention working lunches,' Sidney reminded him. Robin laughed.

'Yes, I don't do much work at them, and I never enjoy the lunch either.'

Sidney halted him for a moment.

'Let me just check the security cameras, before you leave, Mr Burnett. Best be safe.' Sidney flicked through the black and white CCTV screens on the monitors behind his desk.

Nothing. 'All clear, sir. No one about. I hope you have a productive day.'

It occurred to Robin that Sidney Pearl was a rare character, a man content with life, content with his lot, a man who – unlike those people Robin met daily at Westminster, and certainly unlike Hickox – wanted nothing from him, nothing at all, except to be of service. From time to time Robin would show his appreciation. He had twice invited Sidney and his family to the Commons. They sat on the terrace facing the Thames, and Robin watched as the concierge flushed with pride in front of his wife and two teenage sons.

'The heart of British democracy,' Sidney kept repeating to his wife and children, as if to convince himself he wasn't really dreaming. They were sipping tea and watching barges ply up and down the Thames. The sun danced on the river. 'That's what this is. What a rare treat. Thank you so much, Mr Burnett.'

The teenage boys did not seem convinced. They exchanged knowing glances, embarrassed by their father's behaviour. A few weeks later Robin saw Sidney Pearl's two boys standing outside Hampstead Tube station in full punk rock gear with CND badges and others which read: 'Fuck the Filth' and 'Anarchy in the UK'. They were swigging from cans of Carlsberg Special Brew, and smoking roll-up cigarettes which may or may not have contained tobacco, standing in a circle with three or four others whose mouths and ears and noses were mutilated with metal pins and jewellery. The girls in the group wore tartan mini-skirts and had carefully laddered black tights and Doc Martens. They stared back at Robin with dead eyes. He passed by, quickly, wondering what Sidney Pearl made of his sons. Wondering what his sons made of Sidney Pearl. Wondering whether there had always been such a gulf between parents and their offspring, or whether it was new. His own children increasingly treated Robin as a stranger, his time with them like a visit from the vicar, awkward and stilted.

'Our children always judge us,' Leila told him she had read somewhere. 'Seldom, if ever, do they forgive us.'

A month or so later Sidney confided to Robin that both boys had left home and were living in a squat in Hoxton in north London.

'They're in a band,' he said sombrely.

'A band. Right.'

'They call it punk music, whatever that is. Very loud. Very political, apparently. But I'm sure they're not involved in drugs.'

'Oh, I'm sure of that too,' Robin said, trying to keep the doubt out of his eyes. 'Set your mind at rest on that, Sidney. They're fine lads, well capable of looking after themselves.'

Robin Burnett was touched that despite Sidney's troubles with his own family, he was solicitous for Robin's own welfare, especially in ensuring that no one was lurking outside the building. The IRA had murdered one of the Lady's closest confidants, Ian Gow. An Irish republican splinter group, the INLA, had blown up another confidant, Airey Neave. Plus there was the constant risk of what journalists called a 'doorstep' – a reporter grabbing him at the entrance to the building for a surprise interview. Robin knew with absolute certainty that one day it would happen.

'One day,' he told Leila, 'I will become a scandalous man.'

'You are already a scandalous man,' Leila responded. 'It's just that you haven't been caught yet.'

'All clear,' Sidney confirmed again. Robin nodded and then strode briskly out of the rear door. He looked left and right. No one. Absolutely no one in the street waiting to expose the scandalous man. He walked up to the main road and flagged a black cab to Edgware Road. Another part of his routine. Robin would take a coffee in the convenient Lebanese café, The Cedars, behind Edgware Road Tube station, where he waited for his ministerial driver. The waiters, Maronite Christians exiled from Beirut, would make him welcome. They recognized him from the television and would occasionally engage

150

him in a short and polite political conversation. They fretted about the arrogance of Israel, the duplicity of the United States, the wickedness of the Syrians, and the influence of the Iranians. So – though he never told them as much – did Robin. Today he was due to meet Hickox. He sat at the back of The Cedars and sipped a large espresso, correcting his notes by hand. He saw his official driver pull up outside, as arranged. He paid the coffee bill, and climbed in the car.

'Winfield House,' he said. 'Drop me off then take the boxes and files to Joan in the office. Pick me up at two thirty unless I call you before.'

'Yes, sir,' the driver responded.

All the drivers were used to the strange routines imposed by the Chief Secretary to the Treasury. All of them guessed why. Sex. It was always sex when ministers acted in this way. None of them – so far – had sold the story to the newspapers. The driver steered the ministerial Jaguar towards Regent's Park, wondering whether Robin Burnett's piece of skirt was worth the terminal damage which would be done to his career when it all came out. And it always did come out. A bit on the side never remained on the side. It was just a matter of time before it came to centre stage.

Robin looked out of the window at the litter on the streets and the graffiti on the walls, trying to focus on the meeting with Hickox.

'Be particularly wary if your meeting is out of doors,' Sir Montague Hawke had warned, as a final piece of advice. 'We, of course, do not eavesdrop on our good friends, the Americans. That would be bad form. But you can be assured that they do indeed bug each other. If Hickox takes you outside, what he wishes you to know will be supremely sensitive – meaning that he does not want any of the myriad US intelligence agencies to hear about it.'

Robin twisted his face as if in pain. *Supremely sensitive*. He stepped out of the car at Winfield House and passed through the security check, then strolled down the drive, feeling the late autumn sun warm his back. As he approached the house through the rose garden he heard a hearty voice call out.

'Yo! Robin! Good ta see ya. Over here.'

Hickox was wearing a dark grey suit and white shirt. He had taken off his tie. He was holding something in his hand. A putter. He had been practising on the ambassador's private green next to the rose garden. Nine little red plastic flags stuck out of holes on the perfectly manicured grass, short as the baize on a snooker table. Hickox held the putter towards Robin.

'Wanna try?'

Robin shook his head.

'I haven't golfed in months, David. Don't have the time. Maybe I need to get back to it.'

'But you work out, right? You look toned.'

'Well, I swim a bit in the mornings, but I don't get as far as one-armed push-ups if that's what you mean.'

Hickox laughed.

'And you fuck,' Hickox responded, almost as if it were a joke.

Robin Burnett felt he had been struck by lightning. Hickox turned away towards the ball on the ground. He putted it towards the hole. It stopped inches from the pin.

'Hot damn,' he said. 'These English greens get so wet, I need to hit the putts harder.'

Robin tried to smile, but his head was spinning. What did Hickox really know about him? Why did he say, 'And you fuck?' What did he know about Leila? And what did he really want?

'I do all that may become a man,' Robin replied, as if thinking aloud. 'Who does more, is none.'

'Macbeth,' Hickox said. 'Approximately. A study in man's ability to delude himself over his talents while colluding with the forces of darkness. Pretty much the story of politics in Washington and London right now.'

152

'Yes, indeed,' Robin smiled. He tried to recover with a joke of his own. 'And while fucking is a great deal of fun, David, there are those of us who believe that working in Her Majesty's Treasury is among the world's greatest contraceptives. Besides, the British press tend to think we fuck the country, rather than any one particular individual.'

Hickox had the grace to laugh. He handed his putter and baseball cap to one of the Winfield House staff.

'Lunch will be along in a moment, Robin. Let's take a turn around the grounds. Get some air. I want to ask you something. Out in the wide prairies of Regent's Park.'

Robin felt a surge in his blood. Sir Monty's words 'supremely sensitive' filled his mind.

'Of course.'

The lawn undulated away from the house towards the public park and the zoo, behind a hedge and security fence.

'I am on my way to the Mid East,' Hickox said bluntly. 'Eye-raq. For a one-on-one with Saddam Hussein. Your people at MI6 and the Foreign Office already know. I expect they have told you.' Robin said nothing. 'Thought so. Anyway, I'm aiming to fix a few wrinkles and I am here to call in a few favours.'

'So, am I one of the wrinkles? Or one of the favours?'

Hickox smiled.

'You're more like a hot iron,' he said. 'To smooth things over. The wrinkle is resistance from within the ... British bureaucracy. From my counterparts, you might say. From the Wrinkle-in-Chief, Sir Montague Fuddpucker and his Merrie Men.' Hickox put on a phoney and rather constipated upper class British accent in mimicry of Sir Montague Hawke, which made Robin laugh.

'Top hole, old chap. Tickety-boo. But caaaan't poss-ibly expect me to do such a thing. Wouldn't be prop-ah.' Hickox pulled a face. 'Fuck, you know, Robin, sometimes you gotta remind people that we are all on the same side.'

They stopped walking.

'What do you want from me, David?'

'That's why you're not like the usual Brits,' Hickox replied, laying a big hand on Robin's shoulder. 'That's why I like you. That's why I can do business with you. You skip the foreplay, and I appreciate that. You always cut to the chase.'

He cleared his throat, as if making an announcement, but when he spoke it was almost in a whisper.

'Robin, I want you to make sure that shipments to a country in the Middle East of engineering materials and chemicals currently held up by red tape are expedited through the United Kingdom.'

Robin was taken aback. What had this to do with him?

'Shipments?' he said. 'Chemicals? Red tape?'

'Some of the shipments are sensitive and need special export licences. My people tell me you can do this through the Board of Trade.'

'I am not in charge of the Board of Tr—'

Hickox brusquely interrupted.

'But you can get this done, Robin. I trust you. I trust you more than I trust some of the people who work for me at CIA. And you owe me. And – this is a big plus – there is no downside for you. You have no Congressional oversight to worry about. No one will walk back the cat. You don't even need to know what I am talking about, you just have to make sure it gets done. If necessary the President will talk to the Prime Minister, but you can make it happen without it going all the way to the top, and then I will be very grateful. For obvious reasons, it's best if our principals do not have to get directly involved in this.'

Robin really did not know what Hickox was talking about, especially the bit about walking back cats.

'In case it goes wrong?'

'Correct.'

'It's that important?'

'Yes, but like I say, you don't need to sweat the small stuff.'

'Don't I?' Robin shook his head in protest. 'I think I do. Chemicals? Engineering materials? It's not really my line of business. I'm an economist. I don't understand exactly what you …'

'You will,' David Hickox said. 'Let's go to lunch.'

He led him back to Winfield House. As they reached the door, Robin said, 'Which Middle East country gets the shipments?'

David Hickox opened his arms in an expansive shrug.

'Iraq. But you knew that too. Let's not speak of it directly inside here, okay? You … well, you never know who is listening. Just general conversation, you with me?'

Robin nodded. He was with him. Oh, yes.

The Iran–Iraq war had its roots in the Iranian Revolution of 1979. Ayatollah Khomeini's return to Tehran on a plane from Paris threw the country into chaos. President Jimmy Carter watched impotently as a great American ally collapsed into the hands of a theocratic cleric. The Iran–Iraq war started a year later, in 1980. Scenting weakness in Iraq's historic Persian enemy, Saddam Hussein ordered an invasion. It was a catastrophic miscalculation by Saddam, one of many to come.

Washington and various Arab regimes saw Saddam as the bulwark against the Shia revolution of Ayatollah Khomeini. Saddam saw the possibility of an historic land grab. The Arab conquest of Persia. The Americans saw a way of sticking fingers in the eyes of Iran. What none of them had considered was the patriotism and courage of ordinary Iranians who rallied to their country's defence whatever they thought of the regime in the Islamic Republic. Instead of resulting in the overthrow of the mullahs, the Iraqi invasion of Iran merely ensured the Islamic regime's survival in power for decades to come.

By the time Robin met Hickox at Winfield House the war had been going on for so long it had fallen out of most British and American newspapers. Those newspapers which did cover it were the worthy, All-Bran types. News of the war was relegated to a few paragraphs on an inside page. Sometimes they showed photographs that reminded Robin of archive material from the Somme in 1916.

Hickox led him to a small table in the ambassador's private dining room, stiff linen, cut glass.

'Where is the war now?' Robin asked. 'Who's winning?'

'The Iranians have turned it round,' Hickox replied, tearing at a roll and pulling a forkful of prawns towards him. 'You gotta give them credit for it. They're brave. And desperate. And very patriotic. But mostly desperate. They are sending in waves of kids, sometimes unarmed, often as young as fourteen.'

'Kids?'

'Kids. They attack the Iraqi positions and get chewed up like in a meat-grinder. Human waves, groups of six or seven. One of the kids will have a rifle – one rifle for six of them. They charge the Iraqi positions. When the one with the rifle is hit – which doesn't take long – one of the others picks the rifle up and calls out that god is Great or some such, and keeps on running toward his own martyrdom.'

Robin shook his head almost in disbelief.

'Despicable.'

Hickox disagreed.

'Effective. We have not seen this kind of human-wave warfare since the eastern front of World War One in 1917,' Hickox continued, 'just before the Russian Revolution. Nor this kind of fanaticism since Japanese pilots committed suicide on US ships in the Pacific. The Iraqis are losing ground. In Iran the mullahs are inciting the kids to prepare for the final sacrifice. Martyrdom. It's a big Shia thing, goes back to the roots of the religion. And the Iraqis can't drive them back fast enough.' Hickox paused and leaned forward confidentially.

'Saddam Hussein could lose this war. He's worried, Robin. We are all worried.'

'We care?'

'Oh, yeah. We care.'

Robin Burnett said nothing. The main course arrived. Robin had selected poached salmon. David Hickox opted for rare Scottish beef.

'I personally would never under-estimate the Iranians,' Robin Burnett said, thinking in part of Leila. Not a woman to be under-estimated. 'The Persians are what they have always been – the true regional superpower, in terms of economics, population, size, culture, competence and intellect. Iran is the country we should get on-side. There are subtleties about Iran ...'

'Don't think we're not trying,' Hickox said, attacking the steak with a sharp knife. 'Things have been happening.'

'What kind of things?'

'Things – as you said yourself – that you don't need to know about. Things that I don't even need to know about. Related to Lebanon.'

American and other western hostages had been seized in Lebanon by Shiite activists from Hezbollah, the Party of god. Hezbollah was financed and to some degree controlled by Iran. The *Quds* section of the Iranian Revolutionary Guards was set up to extend the Iranian Islamic Revolution – *Quds* meant Jerusalem. The Iranians were spreading around a lot of cash.

'But it isn't easy,' Hickox continued. 'Some of my people think there are moderates in Iran. Me, I'm not so sure. Moderates? I mean, it's like reading Mario Puzo, *The Godfather* – you might think there's good and bad mafia, but they are all still fucking mafia. *Capisce?*'

Robin Burnett laughed, mostly at the thought of Jack Heriot and David Hickox both taking lessons in life from the same literature. He made a note that he had better read the book or see the film when he had time. But he never had time.

'To get the Eye-ranians back on side we'd need the Shah back,' Hickox said. 'Any kind of goddamn Shah. That's why we can deal with Saddam. He has no religious angle. He just wants the money. Oh, and the power. What was the old saying about Trujillo, the dictator in Panama? He may be a sonuvabitch but at least he's our sonuvabitch? I think Saddam's the same. We can help him. I think we may have to. And I think we can use him. We need to stop the Iranians before they win this war. If they win it'll be a disaster for everybody for generations, everybody in the Gulf, everybody who uses oil. You know what the Russians think?'

'What do the Russians think?'

'Some of their generals with experience in Afghanistan think that before too long the United States and the Soviet Union will be on the same side in a war against Islamic fanatics.'

Robin thought the idea absurd, and said so.

'And what do you think, David?'

Now Hickox laughed with a whoop of joy.

'I agree with you. Absurd. I think the Soviets are hurting in Afghanistan. It's gonna be their Vietnam. The Pakistanis and Saudis are being real good at making sure the Islamic fighters get plenty of weapons. There's even Saudis doing the fighting – leading the fighting. There's a multi-millionaire Saudi guy called Osama bin Laden. He's given up the family construction business in the Mid East to go live in an Afghan cave and fight the Russians. Can you believe that? With help from good people like him, we're gonna do for the Soviets in Afghanistan what Vietnam did for us. Payback time.'

'We?'

'Yes, Robin, "we". You and me, and maybe even Sir Montague Fuddpucker, whether he likes it or not. In this you are either with us or against us. Black or white. We don't do grey any more.'

Robin stared at the big heavy man in front of him but did not reply. The newspapers said that Hickox worked out with weights most days, pumping iron. He was proud that he could bench press 200 pounds. Prior to their lunch, Robin had asked the Treasury press office to do a cuttings search. They had circled a quote from Hickox in which he said that doing a bench press was as much fun as having sex with a woman. Robin thought that maybe Hickox had not met the right woman. The two of them sat with their elbows on the crisp linen tablecloth, leaning towards each other, talking softly. Robin was sipping sparkling water, Hickox had a Diet Coke.

'This poached salmon is terrific. How's the Scottish beef?'

Hickox nodded in appreciation.

'Good,' he said. 'Very good. Now here's the deal.' He held up the steak knife, its stained tip towards Robin Burnett. 'The Iranians win, they get their hands on a fifth of the world's known oil reserves – more if they push on into Saudi Arabia and the Gulf states. That happens, the United States is at war with Iran.'

'You're joking?'

Hickox shook his head.

'Do I look like I do jokes about going to war with Iran, Robin? We'll turn Tehran into a fucking car park. I have personally told the Saudis as much. Tehran – car park. Totalled.' Hickox spoke in a low tone, slowly, jabbing his knife rhythmically at Robin. 'So, anyone who has any reason in their lives to care for Eye-ran or Eye-ranians should do all in their power to prevent that from happening. Y'got me?'

The words fell on Robin like cold rain. So Hickox did know about Leila. Christ. When the Director of Central Intelligence finished talking he sat back hard in his chair and put his knife and fork loudly down on his plate. A silence fell on the meal.

'I don't do dessert,' Hickox said eventually. 'You?'

'No.'

'Then let's go walk off the lunch outside while they fetch us some coffee.'

Once they were safely outside again walking side by side on the lawns Hickox said, 'So, I need an answer. Are you with us on this, Robin? The export thing? Or against us.'

Robin raised an eyebrow.

'David, let's be clear. You are talking about the export of precursor chemicals for chemical weapons?'

Hickox at first said nothing, but nodded slowly.

'Sure, the Iraqis are making nerve gas,' he answered, after a moment's thought. It was as if he were talking about chocolate pudding or soap powder. 'Sarin. Tabun. That kind of thing. Works real good on human-wave attacks. If the Iranians are going to fight World War One, the Iraqis need to fight it too.'

Robin Burnett did not know what to say. A vague historical fact crept into his mind.

'You know that Hitler didn't use chemical weapons in World War Two?'

David Hickox shrugged.

'Sure I know. That's because Hitler understood that the Allies had more chemicals than he had. It wasn't like he was exactly queasy about gassing people. Our information is that the Iranians do not have any Weapons of Mass Destruction capability. No chemical weapons, no biological, no nukes. If the Iraqis hit 'em with gas and hit 'em hard, then Iraq will change the course of the war.'

'You want Iraq to win?'

Hickox shook his head.

'We want them both to lose, Robin. I thought I explained that. If Iraq looks like it's winning, we turn off the supplies of precursor chemicals. We want them to fight until they are exhausted, meanwhile we want the oil to keep coming out. *Capisce*?'

Robin tried not to react. He was appalled, but also filled with a kind of admiration.

'At least you're an honest cynic,' he said eventually. 'We don't get many of those here. Are you telling me that you have already approached Sir Montague and they don't want to take responsibility for allowing nerve gas into the hands of an Arab dictator? But that you think I'm an easy touch?'

When Hickox replied, every word was clear and soft and slow.

'I just want the job done, Robin ...' and then he banged his hands together. 'This is not about easy. This is about winning. And preventing a full scale war with Iran. We need to stop the Iranians getting to Saudi Arabia and threatening the Gulf. We're prepared to go to war to stop it. That happens, all your economic policies are down the tubes. Everything you've worked for. When you're Prime Minister, and I make it to the White House, we will both remember this day, with pride.'

Robin Burnett blinked. The words washed over him.

'You've planned for that too?' he scoffed.

'Yes,' the American replied without any irony. 'Yes I have.'

He noticed that David Hickox's hands were so large and pudgy that the knuckles were like dimples.

'I'll see,' Robin said.

'A stroke of the pen will do it. Talk to people. You can push it through.'

'I'll see,' Robin repeated, checking his watch. 'I'd better go.'

Hickox walked him up the path to the gate of Winfield House where his ministerial car was waiting. At the security gate they shook hands. Robin felt Hickox's vast fist close round his own.

'We are talking about preventing the price of oil from reaching a hundred dollars a barrel by Christmas. We are talking about hyper-inflation like you've never seen before and the collapse of the world economy. We are talking about preventing World War Three. A few thousand gassed Iranian fanatics is neither here nor there. Y'got me?'

161

'I got you,' Robin Burnett said.

'Oh,' Hickox said as a parting shot, 'I understand that your Prime Minister has an interest in selling tens of billions of dollars in military aircraft and other weapons systems to the Saudis.' Robin looked at him blankly. His surprise was genuine. He knew nothing about it.

'Very good for high-tech industrial jobs,' Hickox said. 'If you help me on this, my understanding is that the contract with the Saudis will be easy to get through. Otherwise, there could be problems with technology transfer. The Lady will be very grateful to you, Robin. So will the President. And so will I.'

Robin shook hands and nodded, then he walked to his car as if sleepwalking. David Hickox took his coffee into the secure room in the ambassador's residence and picked up the phone to call Washington.

That night Robin slept at Leila's in Hampstead. At dinner he ate very little. When Leila questioned him he said it was because he had endured a long lunch with David Hickox.

'Oh,' Leila said.

'Oh, what?'

'In 1979,' Leila explained, 'I was assigned by CBS News to go to Paris and get on the plane with Ayatollah Khomeini. He was returning from exile to Tehran.'

'So?'

'So I found out later that David Hickox was one of the people agitating in Washington for the plane to be shot down, to assassinate the Ayatollah and kill all the other people on board, including me.'

Robin stared at her.

'I guess he thought it would save everybody a lot of trouble,' Leila said, without bitterness. 'And perhaps he was right.'

Hampstead, London, April 2005

HARRY BURNETT'S STORY

Compartmentalization. That was the secret, Harry decided. The key. He was sitting in the Hampstead apartment on the leather sofa. The detectives had gone. He had a dreadful sense of foreboding, as if something terrible was about to happen, as if a ghost had entered his life. He needed to prepare, even though he had no idea what he was preparing for – except that it was probably something very bad. He needed to be ready. He felt as if his body had been bounced around inside the drum of a tumble dryer and was struggling to escape. He decided, above all, to stick to his routine. Com-part-ment-al-iz-a-tion. He would divide up the different bits of his life and put them in separate boxes, store them in airtight Tupperware containers marked: Family, Friends, Work, Arabic, Other Stuff and, inevitably, things being what they were, Shit. It was the only way to survive.

Harry called Sidney Pearl.

'I'm going to get my things from my flat in Fulham,' he said. 'I'm going to move in here for a while, Sidney ... and ... and I'd like the locks changed on the apartment please.'

'Certainly.' Sidney hesitated. 'Anything wrong?'

'No,' Harry lied. Lying was becoming a habit. He adapted to it with surprising ease. 'Just a precaution. It's ... well ... the ...

163

the police suggested I should … maybe … think about it, and I have. It's a good idea. I mean, you never know …'

'It won't be a problem.'

'Good. Could you make three copies of the keys, please? One for yourself, and the cleaners, and the other two for me?'

'I'll get on to it right away. I know just the people. You can rely on Sidney Pearl.'

Harry returned to Fulham to pack a suitcase and a rucksack. He threw together some clothes, his laptop, his Arabic books and homework plus the papers and notes he required for his most urgent translation work. He needed to re-open the Tupperware box marked 'Work' and get something done. The past two days had knocked him off his timetable for finishing the Kundera translations, though the money from the up-himself New York corporate lawyer would pay the bills for a few weeks. By the time he arrived back in Hampstead, the locks on the apartment had been changed. Sidney Pearl proudly handed over two sets of new keys and showed Harry the third set hanging up in a locked cupboard behind the concierge's desk.

'There you go,' Sidney beamed.

'A place of safety, indeed,' Harry complimented him. 'Thank you, Sidney. I can rely on Sidney Pearl as you say. You're a marvel.'

'My pleasure. Oh, yes. My pleasure.'

The only person Harry told about the burglary was Amanda. No one else. Again, a matter of instinct. The right thing to do, even if he could not explain why.

'Very convenient,' she responded when he finished telling her. He didn't like the sarcastic tone.

'Eh?'

'Very convenient.'

'Explain.'

Amanda had just undergone her own interrogation by the police and was in a nervous mood. They had admitted to her that there was no reason whatsoever to think that what happened to Robin Burnett had been anything other than a suicide attempt.

'Then why are you treating me like a criminal?' Amanda had shot back. 'I'm the daughter of someone who is gravely ill in hospital and for no reasons that you can explain to me, you are acting as if I was a suspect.'

At that point the police backed off and left her alone.

'So, explain,' Harry repeated.

Amanda took a deep breath.

'Well, little miss spiky hair from the bench on the heath gets into the apartment and removes the only proof of any connection with Leila Rajar from right under your nose? Plus the computer? You sure you didn't hallucinate the whole thing, Aitch?'

'Hallucinate it?' Harry felt the heat rising in his neck. 'Amanda, I didn't hallucinate the apartment, did I …?'

'Was there really a photograph?' she interrupted. 'Was there really a little miss spiky? Maybe you're cracking up? You smoking anything?'

'Oh, come *on*, Amanda, …' He spluttered in anger. 'That really isn't funny. Or helpful. We're both stressed out …'

'Seriously, Aitch, what have we got ourselves mixed up in? I mean with? And who? Oh, you know what I mean. What other skeletons are in the closet?'

'I don't know,' he snapped back. 'Maybe he ran a string of international call girls and his entire client list was on the computer. Nothing would surprise me.'

That wasn't true. Everything surprised him. The suicide attempt. The Hampstead flat. Leila Rajar. The burglary. How did all this start? This season of surprises?

'It's like all the shit that's been piling up since I was born is getting together to hit us now,' he suggested. 'Bad karma.'

'I really don't understand what you mean,' Amanda replied. She was now sitting in her office in a large solicitors' practice in Cirencester, also trying to restore some sense of routine.

'Just think about it,' she told him. 'Just think about my life. The most excitement I get in one normal day is drawing up a will, or a mucky divorce, usually involving the husband having it off with the Polish au pair, or the wife running off with her tennis coach. And then suddenly, boom! All this! Father in hospital, headlines in the newspaper and on TV, and the police acting like some scene from *The Bill*. And it's not over yet, is it? Now, you're telling me about a burglary. I'll need to lie down in a darkened room or something.'

'Not a burglary,' he corrected her. 'That's the point. The girl had a key ...'

'She had a key – and you think her having a key somehow makes more sense? I don't even know what normal means any more. What are we mixed up in, Aitch?'

Harry sighed.

'It's just some residual shit left us by our esteemed father,' he replied, 'on the grounds that he hasn't done enough damage. How is Lord Voldemort, anyway?'

Amanda had spent a frustrating hour at lunchtime at their father's bedside.

'Condition stable,' Amanda said. 'That means he is not about to die. But he's not about to recover any time soon, either. Who knows? I just wish you'd told the police about the burglary, because next time they interview me I'm going to have to lie about it.'

Harry grew irritated again.

'Maybe I would have told them if it had been a burglary,' he snapped. 'How many times does it need to be repeated? The girl had a key. Maybe she was a ... friend of his. Maybe she had a right to be here.'

Amanda knew exactly what her brother was thinking.

'Maybe it was another of his girlfriends and you just couldn't face the thought of another scandal.'

'Maybe,' he conceded. 'At first I didn't want to be kept up all night by the police asking stupid questions. Then I thought, why should I trust them, anyway? They leak to the newspapers, don't they? A story about Leila Rajar and dad together would just open it all up again. Then the mystery girl. Tell no one about any of this, please. *Whatever you say, say nothing, Amanda.*'

'It's up to you,' she replied harshly. 'But sooner or later it'll all come out. It always does. And then the police'll be pissed at you. And maybe me, now I know.' She paused for a second and then changed tack. 'So – when are you coming out here to see him?'

'I'm still thinking about it.'

'Well don't think too long. He might die any time, and then you'll regret it for the rest of your life.'

That was absurd. He started to sing a bit of the old Frank Sinatra song.

'*Regrets, I've had a few, but then again, too few to mention ...*'

'Harry, stop being so juvenile. I mean it. This is not about him. It's about you. It's about ending the damage to you, once and for all. Don't you get it?'

And then she rang off.

'The damage?' he wondered. Harry wasn't damaged. He was sure of that. He got it. Of course he did.

Compartmentalization, he repeated. Keep the bits of his life separate. And so that evening, Harry decided, it was off to Arabic as usual. He had worked too hard at the language to give up now. He would not allow himself to fall behind because of his father. Robin Burnett had done enough damage in his life. And there was something else. Harry had discovered something quite unexpected in Intensive Arabic. A social life. Something he had not experienced much since Petra left him. Ah, yes. That sealed Tupperware box marked 'Petra', the box which still gave him nightmares. Another bit of shit he could trace back to his father. Petra. Harry put his Arabic

167

books in his rucksack and walked to Hampstead Tube to begin the long journey towards Muslim College. Petra was in his mind again, like an old and familiar dream. It had been a year since she walked out for good.

'You are congenitally unable to commit,' she yelled at him. 'You're fucked up by your father and it's time you got over it.'

She slammed the door of the Fulham flat. Harry opened it and ran out behind her as she tried to jump into the waiting taxi, a suitcase in either hand. The taxi driver did not bother to get out to help her. Instead, Harry helped her put the suitcases inside.

'Thank you,' she said scornfully, 'for being a gentleman to the last.'

'I ... Petra, don't go! Please! I ... love you ...'

'You love me?' she scoffed.

The taxi driver suddenly was paying attention to her domestic drama where he had not bothered paying attention to her luggage.

'Have you forgotten the day with Leo Blair? I haven't! I should have dumped you then. That was the day it really ended. Think about it. Goodbye, Harry. You've got plenty of growing up to do. Just get out from under your father's shadow and get a life.'

The taxi door slammed, and the cab drove away. He watched the back of her head, facing stiffly forward. Petra never looked back. She never would. He waved, a desiccated gesture. He walked back into the Fulham apartment and poured himself a whisky, even though it was four in the afternoon.

'That day with Leo Blair,' he murmured. 'Oh, god.' And then, 'Oh, yes.'

Harry met Petra at university, at a Labour party meeting. It was October 1997, a few months after Tony Blair was first elected. It was acceptable to play the song 'Things Can Only

Get Better' at the start of Labour Student meetings. Irony had not yet been invented. All the best looking women students were Labour, then, Harry thought. And the best looking of all, was Petra. After a few months he asked her to live with him. Petra said no.

'That's a shared commitment,' she told him.

'It's a shared maisonette,' he laughed back. 'And I own it. The rent would be very reasonable.'

Petra moved in.

'Where did you get the money for this?'

He explained about his family circumstances, his father's disgrace, mother's death, and the modest inheritance of the Pimlico house split between him and his sister.

'Enough for a two-bed flat in Fulham for me, and a three-bedroom farmhouse in Gloucestershire for her. Our father's legacy, among other less desirable things.'

As he replayed the conversations with Petra in his mind, Harry changed trains at Tottenham Court Road and took the Central Line west to Acton for the Arabic class, thinking how far his life had already changed. He sat in the Tube staring out the window into the blackness. It was one of the mysteries of the London transport system that the trains all had big windows – and yet mostly they ran underground where there was nothing to see. And then in the blackness he saw something. A vision of himself and Petra in bed together. He was glad of her company, glad of her warmth. The Fulham flat was not in a good area. Outside there was dog shit on the streets. A big messy family lived in the run-down house opposite, and they were always making a noise, or making trouble, or both. There was an ailing black father and a miserable looking white mother plus an indefinite number of children, maybe six or seven. You could never tell.

Harry knew the name of the oldest child, Carlton, because someone was always shouting it out as he did something bad on the street.

'Carlton, get in here.'

'Carlton, switch that off.'

'Carlton, did you eat your father's lunch?'

'Carlton, muthafucka fuck you ...'

Carlton was fifteen but even bigger than Harry, around six foot three inches. Carlton would skip school most days, wake at noon, hang around outside the house with his mates, playing on an untaxed motorbike, roaring up and down the street, bouncing along the pavement. Most days Harry would try to study in his flat in the mornings, then as soon as Carlton and his gang woke, he would be forced by the noise to head to the university library. Best to keep his distance.

A couple of times Harry and Petra returned from Tesco loaded down with carrier bags to find Carlton careering down the pavement on the motorbike towards them, almost clipping one or other of them. Once Petra had to jump into a doorway to avoid being hit. Carlton would kill someone – or someone would kill him first. Harry sat by his desk looking out on to the street where the fifteen year old pointlessly revved up the bike or rode it on the pavement, or handed the bike over to one of his teenage mates who would do the same. Then another. Then another. When Harry fumed in frustration, Petra said, 'Stay out of it.'

'I can't,' Harry said. 'I need to work.'

'Go to the library.'

'I can't be bothered. Besides, this is supposed to be my home.'

Petra said, 'Welcome to London. Be happy. At least it's white, black and Asian kids all together. It's a good thing.'

'White, black and Asian kids all behaving like multi-cultural fucking dickheads,' Harry replied heatedly, 'it's hardly my idea of progress.'

He did nothing. Then one day, when Petra was at the university and Harry was at home trying to complete a complicated Czech translation, he snapped.

'Fuck it,' he yelled, throwing his dictionary on to the bed as one of the kids revved up the engine until Harry thought it would explode. Or that Harry himself would explode. 'Fuck you. Fuck you.'

He burst out of the front door of his flat and crossed over to the group of teenagers. It was – as Petra said – a mixed race group, white, black, Asian, six boys in all, in Nike trainers, hoodies and baseball caps. Carlton was the biggest. He was sitting on the wall, smoking a cigarette and watching another boy aimlessly twist the accelerator on the motorbike as grey smoke poured from the exhaust. The boys looked at Harry but said nothing. Harry walked past and rang the doorbell.

'It don't fucking work, is it?' Carlton told him helpfully. 'You need to bash it.'

'Yeah, bash it, is it?' one of the white boys said, though he made it sound like 'baaa' and 'sheet'.

The boy with the motorbike handed it to Carlton who roared away, leaving behind a pool of blessed quietness for a few minutes as Harry hammered at the door knocker. A beaten looking black man, Carlton's father, appeared in the doorway. He was stooped. He looked sick. There was a smell from the house, the smell of fried food and of too many people and not enough money. Harry almost lost the will to continue. He could hear Carlton roaring behind him on the bike, but did not turn away from the old man.

'Erm, excuse me, sorry about this,' he apologized, wondering what he was apologizing for. 'It's just that I work at home and the noise from the motorbike is so much that I can't. Work, I mean. Is there anything you can do?'

Harry could hear Carlton behind him, revving up the bike before handing it over to one of his friends, an Asian boy. Two overweight white girls arrived. They were wearing crop tops, their fleshy bellies bulging out over their tracksuit bottoms, muffin waisted. They sat on the wall on either side of Carlton, fat white stomachs exposed, and asked him for cigarettes. The old man shrugged.

'I'll try,' he said, nodding in the direction of the teenagers. 'But … pheeeew.'

He let the air out of his lips. Harry thought about this beaten old man and his huge son. The old man's tired eyes washed over him. Harry felt small and pointless. He made an attempt at conversation.

'Where you from? Jamaica?'

The old man shook his head.

'Trinidad.'

He explained he worked on the buses but was now on the Sick, permanent disability benefit.

'Di-a-beet-eez,' he opened up his arms.

'I'm sorry,' Harry apologized again. 'I really didn't mean to add to your trouble…'

A woman called from inside the house.

'Joe!' she yelled. 'Joe, I need you. This stupid fucking sink's blocked again.'

'Coming,' he yelled back at her. 'No problem,' he said to Harry, closing the front door. 'Any time.'

Harry returned to his study. He looked out of the window where the fat white girls were chewing gum and smoking at the same time. The man – Joe – had returned to the front door. He called over to the boys. Harry watched as he dug into his pocket and produced a ten pound note. Carlton took it quickly and stuffed it into his own pocket.

He switched off the motorbike and propped it against the wall, putting on a security chain. Then he signalled to his mates and the girls. They walked off in the direction of the shops. Harry felt guilty. Like a fool. What was he thinking? He made himself a coffee and sat in a chair. School? These kids didn't go. Work? They wouldn't hold down any kind of real job with no qualifications. Crime? Was that all that was left for them?

Harry was still feeling uneasy when Petra returned from the university. She put her bag to one side and took off her coat. She was wearing jeans and a tee shirt. He remembered that he put his arms round her and began to kiss her, feeling her hips arch towards him the way that always aroused him, like pushing a button. He ran his hands over her thighs and hips.

'Bed,' she said. 'Bed. I need something to go right today.'

'Me too. You've no idea what ...'

'Talk later,' she said, kissing him to keep him quiet. 'Sex now.'

'Nnnn,' he agreed, and her lips were all over him.

They shed their clothes quickly and began to make love, vigorously, as if it were an Olympic sport.

Now as Harry stared out the window of the train in the blackened tunnel somewhere near Notting Hill Gate, he remembered exactly how Petra felt to his touch. She had small breasts, a tiny waist and very strong thighs. She was exactly the opposite of the flabby white girls who hung around outside the house opposite. Petra would push hard against him to dictate the rhythm of their lovemaking. His hands were all over her as he tried to kill off the frustrations of the day. He remembered that they were moving towards a climax, when it happened. Suddenly there was a loud beeping noise.

'Shit,' Harry said.

'Oh, leave it.' Petra pulled him back to her, arching and then dipping her thighs.

'My beeper,' he said.

Petra knew what it was. The beeper had been given to Harry by the Labour party. It was part of the new communications strategy so that key party workers could always be contacted in an emergency.

'Mmmm, leave it,' she repeated and pulled him towards her again, but Harry broke away. He stood up. Petra looked at him, blankly. He checked the beeper. He was naked and still visibly aroused. He stood at the end of the bed. Suddenly he turned towards her and punched a fist into the air.

'Yesssssssssssss!' Harry called out. 'Yessssssssssssss!'

'What is it?' she said, clutching at a sheet to hide her nakedness.

'She's pregnant!'

Petra was puzzled. She blinked.

'Who is?'

'Cherie!'

'Cherie?'

They stared at each other in mutual incomprehension. Petra pulled the sheet tightly around her while Harry strutted with his hand in the air at the end of the bed.

'Cherie Blair!' he said. Then he read out the text message. It said that the Prime Minister's wife was about to have another child.

'It means that the next election is in the bag!' Harry yelled out, dancing a little jig with the beeper in his left hand and his right hand saluting the air. 'Yessssssssssssssss!!!'

Petra looked at him in amazement and then pulled the sheet over her head, throwing herself back on the bed. Outside Harry could hear the sound of the motorbike starting up again. Carlton and his mates had returned from the shops with cans of fizzy drinks, packets of crisps and some cigarettes, but it no longer mattered. The next election had been won, by a simple act of conception.

'Yesssssssssssss!' he repeated. 'Yessssssssssssss!'

The Central Line train rattled towards Acton Town. He remembered that he had tried to go back to bed with Petra. He lay beside her and tried to kiss her, but she would not pull the sheet away from her face. When he tried to take it away, she turned, roughly and pressed her face to the pillow. Then she got up and told him he was seriously fucked up and should get help. She ran into the bathroom. Harry remembered the sound of the motorbike outside. He lay back and the pillow where Petra had been was wet with her tears.

'Carlton,' someone was calling, as the motorbike revved up again. 'Carlton! For fuck's sake!'

In May the following year, Tony Blair's re-election victory was assured, his second win. A child was born, Leo Blair. He was the first child born to a sitting British Prime Minister in Downing Street in living memory. Now he was going to infant school, unaware of the part he had played already in Harry's life.

Harry walked out of the Tube station, hitched the rucksack with his Arabic books on to his shoulders, and headed towards Muslim College. Since that day with Leo Blair, the day when the beeper went off, much of his life had changed.

That day, Harry put on his clothes and got ready to leave the house.

'Where are you going?' Petra called after him, still angry.

'Just a moment,' he replied. He found an envelope in the desk in the main room and put a £20 note inside and wrote the word 'JOE' in block letters on the front. He put on some flip-flops, opened the front door and checked no one was watching. He loped across the street and stuck the envelope through the door of Carlton's family home.

Now, several years later, Harry never saw Carlton any more. Sometimes he wondered what had happened to the big lump of a lad. The army? Maybe in Iraq or Afghanistan? Possibly. In jail? Sometimes he thought he had seen the two fat white girls, one of them pushing a stroller with a pudgy baby of indeterminate race. Maybe it was Carlton's. Joe, the sad eyed father from Trinidad, had died, though Harry wondered what had happened to his bedraggled wife and the other children. The neighbours said they could not keep up with the

175

rent and had moved away. He wondered what had happened to Petra who had burst into his life and left him so empty, and he wondered why friends and family and people he loved turned out to be so disposable, so transient.

He walked through the gates of Muslim College and told himself, it does not have to be this way. It really doesn't.

Arabic for Beginners, April, 2005

Harry entered the classroom for Intensive Arabic (Beginners), and it was like coming home. A familiar routine. Polly Black was already there, sitting at her desk, writing. Talal and Rafiq were together at the back of the class, talking in low voices. Talal nodded at Harry. He sat next to Zumrut, as usual, and her face broke into a wide smile. As usual.

'How are you?'

'Fine,' he said. 'Where's Raj?'

'He texted me to say he'd be late.'

Harry, Zumrut and Rajiv were a class within the class. Polly was mostly on her own, Rajiv and Talal together. Everyone else had dropped out. Three times a week at seven o'clock, promptly, they gathered. The teacher, Abdul Aziz al-Barra, strode in with his coffee and cardamoms. The whole session was now supposed to be in the Arabic language, though Harry always joked that in New Labour-speak it was 'an aspiration, not a commitment'. The only one who occasionally arrived late was Raj, when he had legal emergencies with asylum cases. On those nights he would turn up hot and sweaty from cycling at double speed across London.

'Good evening, welcome,' the teacher said. Each lesson began with a formal greeting in Arabic, and then Abdul Aziz would demand a minute of personal news from each of the students. How was their work today? Their family? Their social life? Then he would broaden it to a casual conversation. How did they react to some item of news that had broken that day, a particular crime, a big sporting event.

'Do you think this city has any chance of securing the 2012 Olympics?' he asked them, as Rajiv arrived, sweaty and puffing, his cycle clips still on his trouser legs, just five minutes late. They began to debate the issue of London's bid for the Games. It would be decided at the beginning of July.

'It will go to Paris,' Harry suggested. 'The French are much better at organizing these things.'

'Yes,' Rajiv agreed. 'And all Muslim countries will want it to be in France because Chirac opposed the Iraq war.'

The conversation often turned to the Middle East, and most especially Iraq.

One of the first phrases Raj had asked Abdul Aziz how to say was: 'George Bush is a halfwit.' The others laughed. Abdul Aziz offered a suitable translation. Harry asked for the Arabic for: 'Tony Blair is Bush's poodle.' It was Rafiq who had asked how to say: 'George Bush is a murderer.' Abdul Aziz answered their questions, but then grew serious.

'Please, this is an Arabic grammar and vocabulary lesson,' he had smiled at Rafiq. 'This is not a class in political theory or opinions. I may share your views, I may not. Either way, please to do that on your own time, not mine. I am not here merely to extend your vocabulary of abuse.'

Each class he asked one of them to volunteer to lead a discussion. That night's topic was a suggestion from Zumrut: 'Can Muslims be Europeans?'

She began the conversation with her short prepared statement in Arabic.

'What does it mean to be a European? Is it a matter of geography – or of culture? Or even of religion? And under what circumstances might Turkey become part of the European Union?'

They attempted to debate in Arabic, but it proved too tough for them, and eventually Abdul Aziz pulled them back to a grammar lesson for the rest of the first half of the session. He checked his watch.

'Take a break,' he said. 'Fifteen minutes, please, back here.'

They filed out for a quick lavatory break and then sat with their coffees for a few minutes.

'Maybe we asked the wrong question,' Harry argued with Zumrut. 'It's not whether Muslims can be Europeans but whether British people can be Europeans. Mostly we pretend we are not.'

'I am,' Raj replied strongly, heaping some sugar in his black coffee. 'I most certainly am both a British Muslim and a European.'

'How can you be?' Rafiq demanded. He was standing on the edge of the group and his expression was a mixture of disbelief and horror. 'How can you say that you are a European? Or be British and a Muslim?'

'Are you not?' Raj shot back.

'Of course not,' Rafiq responded, frustrated. 'I'm just an effing Paki.'

Harry looked shocked. Rafiq went on, heatedly.

'Well, that's what I've been called.' He turned again to Raj. 'And you are too. You're just an effing Paki. Don't tell me you've never been called that.'

Raj pulled a face.

'If they called me a dog, that does not mean I have to bark.'

Abdul Aziz broke in. He had another coffee with cardamoms in his hand and was smiling with good humour.

'In Arabic, please.'

'Sorry,' Rafiq apologized. 'But this is coffee break.'

Abdul Aziz shrugged.

'I am not defined by what other people think of me, or what stupid people call me,' Raj said forcefully. 'Racially and ethnically I am not a European. Culturally, I most certainly am. In fact, Rafiq, I am more of an effing Londoner than I am an effing Paki. I was born here. This is my city. I want the Olympic Games here in my home town, and I don't even know what it would mean to be a Pakistani any more.'

'People *think* you are Pakistani though,' Talal argued heatedly. 'People see you as a Pakistani. Why? Because you are. That's why. I was born here too. So was Rafiq. It doesn't mean we are Europeans in any way. Not European by race, not culture, not religion. Not part of it.'

He shook his head very forcefully. Harry did not understand what Talal meant by 'it', but was unable to break in before Rajiv did.

'Maybe,' Raj insisted. 'But I am! I am absolutely part of it – I am part of the same culture as Beethoven and Shakespeare. And the Spice Girls and *Big Brother*, for that matter.'

'So am I,' Zumrut said. 'Most definitely. European and Turkish.'

'The question was European and Muslim,' Talal said sourly. 'Not European and Turkish.'

'That too,' Zumrut answered, though there was an edge to her voice as she stared defiantly back at Talal. 'You do not have a monopoly on knowing what it is to be a Muslim, so please do not try to dictate to me or to any Turkish person.'

He blinked. Harry watched Talal and Rafiq exchange glances. Neither of them said anything more. Polly Black also watched the interchanges quietly.

'Fine,' Abdul Aziz said, holding up the front page of *Al Quds Al Arabi,* an Arab language newspaper produced in London. 'Back to the class please for a little more vocabulary-building, from this newspaper front page story about Gaza ...'

* * *

It had taken only three or four lessons before Harry, Raj and Zumrut began to socialize together after the class. It came after they discussed Arab attitudes to alcohol in one of the earliest vocabulary-building sessions.

'From an Arabic word, please,' Abdul Aziz lectured them, '*al-kuhl*. Alcohol. And even the word for the equipment for the distillation process is Arabic, *al-embic*.'

Raj and Zumrut both admitted that they drank alcohol. That night Harry suggested they go to the Victoria Arms for a beer. Now, most nights after class, they would do so.

'You don't see some kind of contradiction here?' Harry asked Raj that first time.

'What?' Raj laughed. 'Between my religion and my pint of Stella? I don't think so. Despite what Rafiq and Talal think, I am every bit as much a Muslim as they are. Maybe more.'

'What *is* their problem?' Zumrut wondered. She was drinking beer too.

Raj giggled.

'Lack of sex,' he said. 'They are saving themselves for the seventy-two black eyed virgins they are to meet in Paradise.'

Some believers thought that martyrdom in the service of religion would lead immediately to Heaven and to seventy-two virgins.

'Paradise must be a long way from London,' Harry suggested. 'There aren't seventy-two virgins in the whole of this city.'

'What is this thing with the virgins?' Zumrut objected, sipping her beer, and lifting an eyebrow, archly. 'Most Turkish men would prefer a woman in her twenties who knew what she was doing. I have an aunt in Izmir who is a virgin. She is fifty-seven years old and has a moustache.'

Harry and Raj laughed. Harry watched her animated, intelligent face, the way she brushed back a few stray hairs. There was something about the way she carried herself, something in her conversation, which unnerved him.

'Drinking alcohol has also been lost in translation,' Rajiv added. 'That's why we need to learn Arabic. So we can translate the bits about alcohol for our benighted Muslim Brothers Rafiq and Talal.'

'They really don't think we are Muslims,' Zumrut said. 'Not me, anyway.'

'Of course they do,' Harry protested.

'No,' she said very firmly, pursing her lips. 'Rafiq and Talal really do not believe that I am a proper Muslim. They are utterly intolerant, Harry. And to be honest, they are more our problem than they are yours. I mean, a problem for Muslims. If they saw Raj with that half empty pint glass in front of him they would think of him as an apostate. And god knows the words they use for me.'

'She's right,' Raj agreed. 'I believe in god. I pray. I fast. I offer *zakat*, charity. One day I will go on the Hajj. I am not especially devout but I believe, and I perform all the obligations of a Muslim, but that is not good enough for them.'

'How do you know?' Harry said.

Rajiv shrugged.

'Can't you feel it? The hostility?'

Harry shook his head while Zumrut agreed enthusiastically.

'How did we get to this?' she said. 'How did they get to this?'

She began to recite in English a verse of the Persian poem, the *Ruba'iyat* of Omar Khayyam.

Since in this sphere we have no abiding place
To be without wine and a lover is a mistake
How long shall hopes and fears persist whether the world is created or eternal?
When I am gone, created and eternal worlds are the same.

'Written nine hundred years ago,' Zumrut said. 'And what has happened to us since? Where is the poetry like this? Where are the questions? The reasoning? The philosophy?'

Harry looked at this Turkish woman sitting across from him in the pub. Her eyes were flashing with passion. He put his hand out for his pint of beer, and it began to dawn on him that if he was lucky enough to have some kind of relationship with this woman, no beeper would get in the way. There would be no Leo Blair moment ever again.

'So how do you make a living?' Rajiv demanded of Harry.

'I translate books and technical documents, plus some literary works. There is not much money in the literature, but a lot of fun. And no fun in the technical stuff, but a bit of money. It keeps me sane.'

'What kind of literature?' Zumrut asked.

He explained about the Milan Kundera short stories. The last of them was proving difficult, familiar ground for Kundera fans, a lot of sex in a grim Czech hospital.

'Kundera is exactly the opposite of the seventy-two Virgins,' Zumrut said. 'The women are just as sexually active as the men. Sometimes more so.'

'Correct,' Harry responded. 'The Czech doctors and nurses use sex as a means of escape from Soviet repression. But the problem is how to translate sex for a twenty-first century audience without making it laughable. There is now a literary Bad Sex Award, and I don't want to win it.'

'You could try it out on us,' Raj suggested. 'If we laugh, you have to change it. We will do the Bad Sex test for you.'

Harry nodded, and bought some more beer.

And so, the week before his father was found close to death in the cottage in Tetbury, Harry arrived at the pub with a sheaf of A4 paper and his latest translated story. He read parts of it to Raj and Zumrut.

'Just the dirty bits,' he said.

He kept it sparse and lean. They did not laugh, thankfully.

'Actually it is very beautiful,' Zumrut said, when he finished reading a particularly tricky scene. 'The sex is tender, and desperate. And political.'

'Bad Sex Award?'

'No,' she said. 'It's fine.'

Raj agreed. 'Make Love Not War, sex as political rebellion. I like that idea. Sex and love as the things the authorities – the government, the Communist party, religious leaders – just cannot control. Although, they certainly do try.'

'Of course sex is subversive,' Zumrut responded. 'That's why so many cultures are frightened of women.'

'Sex is also a consolation,' Raj said. 'Sex is the nearest thing a poor person gets to heaven.'

'It's the closest an ordinary man comes to poetry,' Harry decided. 'Or true freedom.'

'That's why all extreme Islamists are sex-starved.'

'Oh, Raj, that again,' Harry laughed.

'Maybe we should ask Talal and Rafiq,' Zumrut suggested. 'They'd be the experts.'

'Do you think they are pretty extreme?' Harry wondered. 'It sounds like a tired old stereotype to me.'

'Deobandis,' Raj said, referring to a conservative religious group with a big following in the English Midlands. 'Or their fellow travellers. The people who meet in the Green Mosque in north London. Abu Omar's people. I'd bet they have contacts in Dewsbury. There's a mosque there which is ... way out ... Scary...'

'They scare you?' Harry said.

Raj nodded.

'Sure. They scare most British Muslims. I wish I was as certain about anything as they are about everything.'

'Such as?' Harry asked.

Raj thought for a moment.

'I went to school in Hounslow. In English A Level we studied Tennyson's poem *In Memoriam*. It's religious – Christian – about the death of a young friend of the poet's. But what is important is not the quality of the Faith, but the quality of the Doubt. That's me. That's Britain, isn't it? We are a nation of Doubters. But not Rafiq and Talal. They have no Doubts, only Beliefs. That's why they will never fit in here.'

Harry disputed this.

'They are as British as you or me.'

Raj shook his head.

'No,' he said. 'Trust me, Harry. Really they are not.'

And so, by the night of the class two days after his father's attempted suicide, the students had improved sufficiently for many of the conversations to begin, at least, in Arabic, with occasional dips into English, which Abdul Aziz joked was a new hybrid language fit for multi-cultural London. He called it 'Arablish'.

'So, *yanni*, Blair finally called the election,' Polly said in Arablish during the last period of conversation, just before the end of class. 'No surprise.'

'No surprise about the result either,' Harry said. 'He'll win.'

'As if it will make any difference,' Raj responded.

'Elections always make a difference,' Zumrut said emphatically in English.

'Speak Arabic!' Abdul Aziz clapped his hands in desperation. 'Now, homework,' he said, and reeled off a list of things for the next class. 'Goodnight to all of you, and thank you.'

They said their goodbyes and filed outside, continuing their discussion.

'What did you mean when you said elections change things?' Talal demanded of Zumrut in the hallway outside the class. 'They didn't stop the invasion of Iraq, did they?'

Zumrut squared up to him, talking calmly, though Harry detected an edge of anger.

'Elections are the only civilized way to change things. They are not perfect, but they do work. In Turkey we rely on the Army to intervene to sort out our problems. But that's like expecting your father always to take decisions for you. Military coups infantilize us. Politics means making mistakes. I happen to agree that the Iraq war was a mistake, but democracy means letting mistakes happen.'

Talal blinked at her. They clearly despised each other.

'I'm not against politics,' Raj said. 'Or democracy. I'm just against politicians. Talal has a point. A million of us marched against the Iraq war. And what difference did it make? The politicians say they want to listen, but they never do.'

Suddenly Talal intervened with a passion that surprised Harry.

'So what is it then? This democracy? This new election Blair has called? What does it mean?'

Raj turned towards him, surprised he had spoken.

'Democracy is more than just winning elections,' he said.

'That's not the point,' Talal grew heated. 'Iran has elections. Is it a democracy? Nobody in the West thinks so. India stamps on the people in Kashmir. Is it a democracy? Everybody in the West tells me so. Democracy is what people in the West like. What they don't like cannot be democracy. Pah! They don't want Muslim democracy. They want Muslim docility.'

He crossed his arms over his chest as if all further argument were superfluous. It was the longest speech any of them had heard from Rafiq or Talal in any language, English, Arabic or Arablish. Harry was impressed, and surprised. He also agreed Talal had a point.

'Democracies often get things wrong,' Harry admitted. 'I mean, Bush's War on Terror. How can you make a war on a tactic? And in Iraq, how can you force democracy on people? Though I confess to you I thought getting rid of Saddam Hussein was a good idea, but ...'

'Bush is a stupid man,' Talal interjected.

'Whatever,' Harry continued. 'But he had no choice but to defend America by attacking Afghanistan. He did have a choice about attacking Iraq. I thought he got it right at first, but I've changed my mind. That's allowed too.'

Zumrut stepped in.

'The real disease in the world is dictatorship. In Egypt or Pakistan or Iraq. Violence is just the symptom. We need to attack the disease. Then the terror will fade away.'

Talal stared at her.

'How?' he said. 'How do you do that?'

Raj butted in.

'Democracy is about the majority understanding that minorities have rights too,' Raj explained. 'We are all, at times, in the majority. But we are also all, at times, in the minority. The test of a democracy is whether minority rights are respected. India does. Iran doesn't.'

Talal shook his head.

'Democracy is a con,' he answered hotly. 'Like you said, a million marched against the Iraq war in 2003. That means fifty-nine million British people did not march against the war. Those fifty-nine million will allow Blair to get back in for another five years. She –' he nodded in the direction of Zumrut, 'she said democracy is about making mistakes. But making the same mistake three times with Blair is ...'

Talal could not think of the word. He ran out of steam.

'Criminal,' Rafiq helped him out.

'Criminal,' Talal repeated.

'What's the Arabic word for criminal?' Raj asked Abdul Aziz, who was walking past on his way out the door. The teacher responded.

'Good night to you all. May your passion for Arabic be as great as your passion for argument.'

'There has to be a middle way between violence and apathy,' Raj said as soon as Abdul Aziz left the building. 'We just need a more active politics.'

'Such as?' Zumrut wanted to know. Raj looked uncomfortable, as if he wished he had kept his mouth shut. Rafiq, Talal, Zumrut, Harry and Polly were all staring at him. He stuttered. Zumrut continued.

'What kind of active politics? The politics of violence is just narcissism. The plane hijackers of 9/11 were the ultimate narcissists, saying to the whole world: Look at me! Aren't I clever! That's not what you mean, I hope?'

Talal looked desperate to say something, but Rafiq glared at him, and both men stayed quiet. Polly's eyes flickered around the class, standing in the hallway.

'No, not that kind of politics,' Raj agreed. 'Absolutely not. I completely reject violence.'

'What then?' persisted Zumrut. 'Not violence, not apathy, but a more active politics. Like what?'

The others again looked at Raj. He scratched his neck in embarrassment.

'I am not sure I can explain it … I just feel we need to do something …'

His words died away. Harry engaged Zumrut in a conversation as Talal and Rafiq looked at each other and then left to have a cigarette outside. As soon as they left, so did Polly Black, hurrying off to see her devoted but non-existent husband and children.

'Goodnight,' she said. Talal and Rafiq mumbled something in response and then moved towards the battered Micra car and headed north-west towards Wembley and Greenford. Raj, Harry and Zumrut nodded at each other.

'Pub,' Raj said.

'Oh yes,' agreed Zumrut. 'Please!'

Zumrut bought a round. Harry smiled at this delicate, beautiful woman, lifting a heavy pint of beer to her lips.

'Cheers,' she said.

'Well,' Raj went on, 'I've been reading Persian poetry, thanks to Zumrut. And she's right. It's always, "use the wine, take the girl, enjoy life to the full", because nobody asked us if we wanted to get born and nobody will ask us when we want to die.'

'It sounds like Samuel Beckett,' Harry said. 'Make the best of it, because one day Godot will arrive. Except they wrote this stuff nine hundred years earlier than Beckett.'

'Wouldn't you just love to get Omar Khayyam or the poet Rumi together with the leaders of Iran right now?' Zumrut offered. 'With Khatami and Rafsanjani? I wonder what they would find to talk about?'

They supped for a while and then Raj said, 'Anyway, you're the sly dog. Aren't you, Harry?'

'Am I?'

'Eight months of lessons, and you never once told us about your father.'

Harry put down his own pint. The compartments of his life started running together, the Tupperware boxes opening up and becoming jumbled.

'My father?'

Raj stared at Harry's shocked face and wondered if he had gone too far.

'There's ... there's not much to say,' Harry stuttered.

'We are all entitled to a bit of privacy,' Raj said quickly. 'I am very sorry to hear what happened. If you don't want to talk about it, I shouldn't have ...?'

'No, no,' Harry said, unconvincingly. 'It's ... it's fine...'

There was a short pause and Zumrut looked concerned.

'What's wrong with your father? I don't understand.'

Harry stared at her full in the face. He could see her concern, and it touched him deeply.

'He's in a coma after a drugs overdose,' Harry blurted out, then began to tell the story, briefly. 'And slashed wrists. The police say it looks as if he tried to commit suicide.' He stopped and thought for a moment. 'But the way they act, it's like they think someone tried to kill him.'

He gave an account of the previous forty-eight hours.

'Now I really don't understand,' Zumrut said when he finished. She ran a hand backwards through her long brown hair. 'Why does your sister want you to make up with your father? For what?'

Zumrut spent most of her days researching in the British Library. She caught up with the news only at weekends. There was an embarrassing pause.

'Did I say something wrong?'

'No, Zumrut,' Harry replied. It was impossible for this woman to say something wrong. 'It's just that ...'

Raj helped him out.

'What Harry didn't mention is that his father is a very famous politician.'

Zumrut still looked blank.

'Robin Burnett,' Raj explained. 'One of Mrs Thatcher's bright young things. Member of the British cabinet in the 1980s. Tipped for the top. Then he got caught up in an idiotic scandal with a girl and had to resign.'

'Oh,' Zumrut said, laying a hand gently on Harry's arm. 'I'm so sorry, Harry. So very sorry.'

He shook his head and took a sip of beer. He liked the touch of Zumrut's hand. He tingled with desire. She took her hand away.

'How did you know he was related to me?' Harry asked Raj.

'One of the papers had a picture of you and your sister, taken years ago. But the same names – Harry and Amanda. I figured it had to be you. You even look a bit like Robin Burnett in his younger days. You've got the square jaw and striking hair.'

'Oh, god, what an insult,' Harry replied with a laugh. Then he sighed and turned to Zumrut. 'The weird thing is, we have not had any contact for years and yet since it happened, right now, I'm living in his flat.' Harry explained about the Hampstead apartment, telling them most of the details, except about the picture of Leila Rajar and the burglary. 'And very nice it is too. Though I expect when he recovers he will want it back.'

'You think ... he will recover?' Raj asked.

Harry thought for a moment.

'I ... don't know. Though ...' He was not sure what he wanted to say, but suddenly the words were in his mouth, '...though once upon a time I would have said that I didn't care what happens to him. Now I do. I ... would like him to pull through. I am ... intrigued ... yes, intrigued. I want to meet him. I have a lot to ask him about. And he has a lot to answer for.'

He blurted out the words and then began to think about what they meant. They all drank their beers in silence for a few moments.

'Now you know my dark secrets,' Harry nodded cheerfully at Rajiv. 'I'll get another round, and you two tell me yours?'

Raj laughed.

'I am far too boring for dark secrets.'

'Oh, really,' Harry said. 'Then what about when Zumrut asked you what kind of "active politics" you think we need nowadays?' Raj sucked in air. 'You were embarrassed.'

Raj looked embarrassed again.

'You see? Just like now?'

'Get the drinks and I'll think about telling you,' Raj said.

Harry did as he was told. When he sat back at the table, he returned to the point immediately.

'So what are the dark secrets of that rucksack that you cling to like it was your only child?'

Raj laughed.

'Do I really?'

'Yes.'

Raj looked at his glass. Now Harry was the one to wonder if he had gone too far.

'I'll answer all that in a minute,' Raj said. 'First let me ask you something, Harry. Will you really be working for the Labour party in this election, despite what you think of Blair?'

'Yes,' Harry said. 'I expect so. I'm supposed to go canvassing the Peabody Estate this weekend, depending on what happens with my father. Want to come?'

'No thanks. But does it change anything? Leafleting the Peabody Estate? Knocking on doors of people who want to watch TV instead? Getting Blair back for five more years?'

191

'You should praise Harry for the effort,' Zumrut said. 'At least he is engaged. At least he is involved.'

'Look,' Harry added, finally, with a touch of exasperation. 'I am going to work for the re-election of the Labour party because all the other possibilities are much worse, that's all.'

'A fine speech of true British *realpolitik*,' Raj laughed, and then wrinkled his forehead. 'Okay, maybe it really is time to show you the secrets of my rucksack.'

Raj drew it out from under his feet and put it on his lap. He opened the rucksack slowly. First he withdrew his bicycle helmet and a small pump and put them on the table next to the beer. Underneath there was a plastic bag. He angled it towards Harry and Zumrut and opened it so they could see inside.

'Carrots?' Harry said, surprised. Half a dozen fresh carrots.

'Shhhh. Keep your voice down,' Raj warned them.

'Keep my voice down about carrots?' Harry hissed.

'And potatoes,' Zumrut added.

'Carrots and potatoes?' Harry repeated. 'I don't get it.'

'He's making some kind of stew,' Zumrut suggested.

'Not exactly,' Raj said. 'I sometimes use parsnips or leeks too. Leeks are good.'

'What – because they're organic or something?'

'No,' Raj said seriously. 'Because they are long and thin.'

They exchanged puzzled glances.

'Look, Harry, you do your political work with canvassing and leaflets. I do mine with these.'

He held a carrot up for inspection. It was fat, about fifteen centimetres long, unremarkable in every way.

'Do you want to see a potato, too?'

'I don't think that will be necessary,' Harry said. 'I have seen potatoes before. Explain yourself, Raj.'

Zumrut was also puzzled. Raj tried to explain.

'I read it in a book and I thought it was a good, non-violent way of making a point, one vegetable at a time. When I'm cycling late at night I look out for the worst polluting cars I can see – Chelsea tractors, 4x4s. I select from my range of organic weaponry, then I stuff their exhaust pipes full of vegetables. It takes a while but it really fucks up the engine. Really – fucks – it up.' He took a long pull of his pint.

Harry felt his jaw had dropped and his mouth was open. Zumrut's eyes sparkled with amusement. They looked at each other.

'You're not serious?'

'Very serious. I try to limit it to one car a night. Sometimes I get carried away and do a few more.'

Harry shook his head.

'But that's … That's …'

'Illegal,' Zumrut said.

'And you're a lawyer.'

Raj nodded.

'Technically,' he agreed. 'You are right. It is illegal. Direct action usually is. But it is non-violent. And it really does make a point.' He drained his glass.

'Look, I must be off now. See you tomorrow in class.'

'You have work to do with your political vegetables?' Zumrut laughed.

'Yes,' Raj said. 'And do you have time to hear one more secret?'

'Go on,' Harry said, laughing.

Raj pointed at them both in turn.

'This is even more subversive,' he said. 'But here goes. You two should go out together.' A silence fell over the table. 'For goodness' sake get on with it. Okay? It's so obvious how well you get on. You make each other laugh, which is good enough. Now, good night.'

Raj strapped his cycle helmet on to his head, hitched the rucksack on to his back and left the Victoria Arms. Zumrut and Harry did not know what to say. Eventually they looked at each other and burst into laughter.

'While he's off saving the planet,' Harry said, 'would you care for another beer?'

Zumrut nodded.

'If it helps,' she said, 'you can tell me more about your father. If you don't want to, that's fine too. I didn't mean to pry, earlier.'

Harry nodded.

'He's right, you know,' Harry said, plucking up courage at last.

'About destroying gas guzzling cars with vegetables?'

'Not that,' Harry responded. 'I have been thinking about you for ages.'

'Oh.'

He looked at her, embarrassed. Her eyes were oval, and so very dark brown. It made him think again of rich, dark, chocolate. He remembered the briefness of her touch when she laid a hand on his arm, and the feeling of his own arousal.

'Would you ... would you like to come back to my father's place in Hampstead? I mean, we could talk. I could get us both something to eat?'

Zumrut said nothing. Then she stretched her hand towards the lager and lifted the beer to her lips, all the time watching him. Then she nodded.

'Yes,' she said. 'I would like that very much.'

The Visitor, April 2005

They sat side by side talking on the Tube journey to Hampstead. Almost as if in competition, Harry was talking and Zumrut interrupted, Zumrut talked and Harry cut in. Laughter and stories and observations, and occasionally her hand on his arm to make a point, or the flash of her teeth, or her hair carefully placed by her fingertips behind her ear. Harry could not take his eyes off Zumrut. Not once did he stare out of the window into the blackness of the tunnels. She glanced at him and cocked her head sideways and he thought of her brown almond eyes like pools into which he would throw himself. He wondered what it would be like to wake up next to those eyes. He blinked and imagined she was gone. But she was still there, beside him, hand on his arm, laughing.

'And the joke is?'

'The joke is that Raj isn't the only one who wondered if you would ever get around to asking me out.'

She giggled girlishly. He swallowed.

'Oh, you did too, did you?'

Now it was her turn to blush.

'Yes. I did.' She looked down at her feet. 'Sorry.'

'I'm a bit shy,' Harry confessed. 'My last relationship ended ... Well, pretty disastrously. My fault. And ... this will sound ridiculous, but I so much enjoyed your friendship and your conversation after the classes that I did not want to risk spoiling it by hitting on you for a date.'

'That's one of the things I like about you,' she smiled.

He felt her hand on his, the fingers cool to the touch, squeezing him.

'You are … considerate. Turkish men are … Well, I love my country and the men are very nice, but they are very rarely shy.'

He wanted to kiss her. They fell silent. They were somewhere on the Northern Line just north of Tottenham Court Road station.

'What are you thinking about?' he wondered.

'Same as you, probably,' she responded. He nodded. Not on the train, he thought.

Zumrut said, 'Why did your last relationship end so badly?'

He blushed. And then he whispered to her about Petra, about Leo Blair. He gabbled the story and Zumrut was baffled.

'I don't get it.'

Harry tried to explain it again.

'I was very committed to my work with the Labour party,' he said. 'So was Petra – or at least she had been. We met when we were student activists. She … she grew out of it. I took a bit longer. We went our different ways. And I'm not like that any more, Zumrut. I promise. Reality has set in …'

Now she laughed out loud.

'Reality? You mean when you have sex nowadays you switch your pager off?'

'I don't have a pager any more.'

'We all do stupid things, Harry. All of us. I was married for a year.'

He was shocked.

'Married?'

'Yes. It's not unusual to marry young in Turkey, even for university graduates. I was twenty-one. It was … a complete disaster in every way. I'm divorced now. Your beeper incident sounds quite small in comparison.'

They stepped out of the Tube at Hampstead. There was a drunk leaning against the wall of the station exit, vomiting on the ground. They hurried past him. The drunk was performing a difficult trick. He was vomiting while still holding a can of lager, which he managed not to spill. He was about Harry's age, but dressed in an expensive pinstripe suit. The vomit splashed all over his Church's brogues. When he finished vomiting, he stood upright and took a sip of lager from the can, to refresh himself. Harry grimaced and offered Zumrut his arm.

'An old-fashioned English tradition.'

'What is?'

'Puking in the street.'

'Really?'

'Probably. But what I really meant was that a gentleman offers a lady his arm, like this.'

'Oh, really. And the lady?'

'The lady grasps it gently. And with gratitude.'

'Thank you, sir. I think I understand.'

Zumrut grasped it gently, and they walked on a few metres until she stopped and looked at him. He felt her hands grasp his, and shuddered with pleasure.

'So if you no longer have a pager,' she asked, 'then there is nothing which will beep and interrupt us?'

He shook his head.

'I am a lot less interested in politics than I used to be,' he answered. 'At least that's one way of putting it.'

He fell gently into kissing her, as if into a whisper. Her lips were hotter and softer than anything he could have imagined, and her scent rose in his nostrils until he swayed in the kiss. When they stopped, they looked at each other silently.

'I ... I ...' he coughed. 'I ... wish we had done this months ago.'

'It's better now,' she told him. 'Better because we have begun with a long conversation. That was why my marriage did not work. Because we never really talked properly.'

'I suppose we had better ...'

'... we had better get to the apartment,' she said. 'And quickly. I need a pee.'

'Me too,' he laughed. 'Too much beer.'

They raced up the hill. This late at night, the concierge desk was empty. Harry hit the codes on the keypad at the front of the apartment block in a mixture of desperation, anticipation and relief, pulling the newly cut apartment keys from his pocket. The art deco lift sped to the correct floor and they bounded across the blue carpet. Harry turned the key.

'Where is it?' Zumrut pleaded. 'The bathroom?'

'There's two.' Harry pointed to the toilet nearest the door. 'That's yours. I'll use the other one.' He walked quickly towards the main bathroom, relieved himself, washed his hands, looked at the mirror with unaccustomed vanity. What would she see in him, this wonderful, beautiful Turkish woman? Maybe something that he could not even see in himself. He called out to her as he stepped into the hallway.

'Zumrut, so what do you want to eat?'

'So what can you cook?' she yelled from behind the toilet door.

'Everything. And anything. I'm the master chef. I'll check what's in the fridge and create.'

Harry grinned as he turned towards the kitchen. Then he saw something move, and the grin froze in a rictus of fear and surprise. The movement came from the main room. It was exactly the opposite direction to where Zumrut was, so it could not be her. He flooded with panic. Not again. Not after he had changed the locks. Surely not the spiky-haired girl? Or something worse. He turned towards the movement. Someone was there, he was sure of it. Harry looked for a weapon to defend himself and Zumrut – a stick, a club – but nothing came to hand. Then the intruder moved again. Harry stepped back and raised his right fist, ready to strike as hard as he could. It was a woman. The woman stepped from the shadows in the main room. She stood out boldly in front of Harry, placed her left hand on her hip and stared at him. She was wearing a black trouser suit with her dark hair tied back. In her right hand she clasped a crystal glass of white wine.

'So, then, master chef,' she said softly. 'What *can* you cook? I mean, for real?'

'What can I ...?' he mumbled.

'Yes, cook,' the woman went on. 'Looks like we're all hungry here. I got some things at the market on my way, including a very good white Macon. I'll pour you a glass while you do the cooking.'

Harry's heart thumped. He blinked, sucking in air. Even in the half-light she was beautiful, with a feline sensuousness, well aware of the effect she had on men. She stared at him, unafraid. But there was a surprise.

On television and in her publicity pictures, Leila Rajar always had straight hair. Now it had given way to curls. Harry looked down. Beneath the trouser cuffs, she had bare feet. Her toe-nails were painted dark red. It occurred to him that he had never considered a newsreader to have feet before. They were like mermaids, different under the waist.

'Jesus Christ!' he blurted out. Now it was her turn to look him up and down.

'Sorry to startle you,' she apologized, without sounding particularly sorry about it. 'Let me get some wine for you and your friend.'

Zumrut came out of the bathroom at the front of the apartment.

'So ...?' she began, and then blinked in surprise. 'What the ... who ...?'

She ran out of words. Harry looked from one to another, and stumbled into an introduction.

'Eh … um … this is Leila Rajar, please meet my friend, Zumrut Ecevit.'

They nodded towards each other. Leila held out a hand and smiled.

'Very pleased to meet you, Zumrut. Lovely name. Turkish for "Emerald", I think.'

'Yes,' Zumrut agreed, now even more surprised. 'That's right. Emerald. You speak Turkish?'

'A little,' Leila said.

'I was going to try to contact you,' Harry blurted out to Leila. 'To tell you about …'

'There's no need,' Leila shook her head. 'I knew. Maybe even before you did.'

'I'm …'

He was about to apologize to Leila for some act of omission or commission, but it was as if she could read his mind.

'I know,' she repeated. 'We are all sorry. Not just you. And we all share the guilt for why he did this to himself.'

Harry sucked in more air, like a fish in a stagnant pond.

'We do? Guilt?'

'Yes. All of us.'

They stood in an awkward silence. He didn't know what she was talking about.

'Well,' Leila said eventually, 'shall we at least have that glass of wine and see if it releases our tongues, while the master chef plans his meal?'

She had taken control. Harry decided it was probably wise to do exactly as Leila Rajar wanted.

The three of them had almost finished the first bottle of wine by the time Harry began to throw together the ingredients for supper. They were standing in the kitchen. The two women had struck up an easy and instant friendship.

200

Harry's opinion of Zumrut rose even higher when she acted as if this was the normal way for first dates to proceed – to return to a strange apartment to find an even stranger American woman, apparently some kind of celebrity, drinking a bottle of wine. Harry washed the salad. He felt tense, not able to think properly, flushed by the wine. He compensated by doing several routine things at once – boiling water for pasta, peeling cloves of garlic that he knew he would use in something but wasn't sure what, bringing different cuts of cheese from the fridge to warm up to room temperature. He was aware the women were watching him closely.

'I like a man who knows his place,' Leila suggested. 'In the kitchen.'

'Me too,' Zumrut grinned slyly. 'Very much.'

'This is our first date,' Harry pleaded to Leila. 'I'm trying to impress Zumrut, and she's wondering what on earth is going on. So am I.'

'But I am impressed,' Zumrut admitted. 'I've known you for about six months and now I find out, on the same evening, that your father is a famous politician, that you are friends with one of the best known TV people in the world, and that you can cook. Truly, Harry, I think you may be crazy but …'

'It runs in his family,' Leila said. 'They are all crazy. Talented, but weird. Trust me.'

Harry's stress disappeared around the time they started sharing the second bottle of wine. Now it was almost midnight. They sat around the table in the kitchen eating his simple creation. Pasta and a sauce Harry made from garlic blended with peas, olive oil and pepper, plus the salad and cheese.

'This is terrific,' Leila said.

'Good,' Harry said, pushing back from the table. 'Because now we've eaten, I need you to tell me how you know my father. What's going on, Leila?'

Leila looked at her wine glass, and emitted a long, slow sigh.

'This sounds private,' Zumrut said. 'Why don't you take your glasses into the main room and I will wash up.'

Harry shook his head.

'That's not fair.'

'I'm used to being very straight in the way I speak,' Leila Rajar interrupted him. 'So I will be real blunt now. I am sorry to rain on your first date, but Zumrut is right. It will be easier for me to speak to Harry alone for half an hour. Then I'll leave you kids in peace.'

'I can go home now,' Zumrut said. 'Call a taxi.'

'Please don't,' Harry pleaded. She cocked her head a little and the brown eyes looked at him. He felt a surge of desire.

'No, please don't,' Leila insisted. 'Call a taxi for me instead. Half an hour and then I'll leave. If you don't mind loading the dishwasher? I have checked into a hotel, not far from here, in Swiss Cottage. Harry – you need to hear a few things from me tonight. We'll talk more later but it is important for both of us to be straight now. Very straight.'

Leila sounded stern. Harry thought she was using the television voice she kept for announcing American dead in Iraq. Zumrut nodded.

'I'll do the dishwasher.'

Harry and Leila left her in the kitchen and took the wine into the main room.

'Well, go on, Harry,' Leila said, pouring another glass of wine as they sat on the couch in the main room. 'You ask. I'll answer.'

'First, how did you get in here?' Harry began, trying to keep the irritation from his voice. 'I changed the locks.'

'I know.'

He began to get annoyed.

'Stop saying that,' he said irritably. 'You keep saying you know this and you know that. You know everything, obviously. It's beginning to piss me off.'

'I do not know everything. And I understand why I annoy you. Like all journalists, I have my sources. And like all journalists, I don't reveal them.'

'And like all journalists you come in to places where you are not invited. Or is that burglars? Journalists. Burglars. It's so easy to get confused.'

'I'm sorry. But the owner of this apartment usually invites me.'

'Oh, does he? I suppose you have keys?'

'Actually, I do, yes.'

'Right,' Harry went on: 'So, do I have to change the locks again?'

Leila shook her head. She appeared contrite.

'No, you don't. I'm sorry. I thought it was for the best. That I would surprise you.'

'You did surprise me.'

'I did not know you would have company.'

'Neither did I.'

'Zumrut's beautiful, by the way. And very clever. You're a lucky man. But I promise you I will not enter this property again without asking your permission, or, better still, seeking an invitation.'

'Thank you,' Harry sighed.

'Sidney Pearl is an old friend,' she added by way of explanation. 'We go way back.'

Harry appeared mollified.

'Very well. Will you please tell me about you and my father?'

'About me and your father?' she repeated, putting her hands together and resting her head for a few seconds, as if praying for some kind of guidance. 'Where to begin? At the end, perhaps. I saw him at the hospital today. I drove out from the airport, as soon as I landed. They said there is hope, though it might take a few days for him to pull through. His vital signs are good, much of the poison is out. His wrists are bandaged. The blood transfusion was in the nick of time. He looked surprisingly at peace, I thought … though I … I don't mean that in a morbid kind of way.'

Harry studied her face. She had a few lines, but in all the right places, where she laughed and where she thought, and where she showed she had been loved by men. She was a woman at ease with herself. Her skin was taut and healthy like that of someone years younger; her cheeks rounded almost like those of a young girl. She wore no rings, no jewellery except a pair of simple gold earrings.

'You still love him, don't you?' Harry blurted out. Leila blinked.

'That's not something I can easily answer,' she murmured softly. 'I stopped asking it years ago. A matter of self-preservation, probably.' She looked down at the floor and sighed. 'We have never really stopped loving each other, your father and I, though at times we could not bear to speak. Not for months. He has been in my life for such a very long time, much of it at a distance. There is not a day passes but that I think of him.'

'I would call that love.'

She shrugged.

'Then call it love.'

'So…?' he asked.

She sighed.

'So. Events pulled us apart. There were things we could control, and things we could not. Your father was the love of my life … Is. Is the love of my life. But …'

Harry stared at her as her words drifted away.

'No one has ever told me that they loved my father,' he said simply. 'No one I knew ever did. I thought he was a total shit.'

She nodded.

'I know. Ooops. Sorry.'

A long silence fell between them.

'How long are you staying?' he said eventually.

She took a breath and snapped back to normal.

'A few days is all I can manage,' she said. 'This time. I thought he was about to die and so I came. To say goodbye. I don't think that will now be necessary. He is a very tough man.'

'And yet he tried to kill himself? Or was it really someone else?'

She did not respond. Instead she looked Harry up and down.

'Do you realize how much you look like him?' she said.

Harry blanched.

'I don't think so.'

'Oh, yes. You are big and tall, broad in the shoulders, you have hands like him and even have the same mannerisms.'

'Absolutely not!' he protested. 'Mannerisms are acquired, not inherited, and I have never been close enough to learn or acquire anything.'

'The way you lean your face on your fist when you are listening to me. The way when you are feeling awkward you stare at your shoes. Like now. The way you just rubbed your forehead in frustration at me being Little Miss Know-it-all. The way you used your hands when chopping the tomatoes in the kitchen, like a surgeon, precise but very macho, very firm. The way you opened the head of garlic with one sharp blow from the flat of your hand. Your father cooks like that, too. Do you want me to go on?'

Harry looked at her, stunned.

'I have nothing to do with him,' he blurted out angrily. 'Beyond the accident of DNA.'

'As you wish. You have that, too, of course. You have a big physical presence, and women like that. Zumrut does, certainly. You are more like your father than you would care to admit. I bet you even have an emotional hunger, too, and it scares you more than you can say. When you fall in love, it is rare, but it is total. You keep the scars. Am I right?'

Harry was offended by her arrogance in presuming to know him. Or maybe the accuracy with which she clearly did. He spluttered.

'I ... I ... how dare you ... I ...'

'I think that the very beautiful young lady in the kitchen needs to spend some time with you, and I need to get going. We'll talk more tomorrow – if you would like.'

She moved to the phone and dialled a cab, giving the apartment address and phone number easily from memory.

'Fifteen minutes,' she said. 'There are things I need to tell you, though they are hard for me. Things you need to understand.'

'What do I need to understand?' he shot back at her.

She clapped her hands together angrily.

'That your father is not the complete bastard that you take him for.'

Harry sucked in a deep breath.

'Did he really try to commit suicide, or did someone try to kill him?' he repeated. He was surprised to find out that he cared.

'I don't know for sure,' she replied. 'But if it was a suicide attempt, he had his reasons. We all contributed to Robin's depression.'

Harry was astonished.

'Depression?'

'Yes.'

'Him?'

'Yes.'

'I don't have any reasons ...'

'You most certainly do, Harry.'

He grimaced.

'Who stole the photograph and the laptop?'

Leila smiled.

'My property,' she said. 'So I made arrangements to recover it. Now, my cab will be here in a moment so I suggest we tell

206

Zumrut that she doesn't have to hide away any more. And I strongly advise you to treat her well. She's a fine young woman.'

Harry felt numb. He went to the kitchen and found Zumrut stacking the last of the plates in the dishwasher and wiping down the work tops.

'Thank you, Zumrut,' Harry whispered to her, and snatched a kiss. She shrugged and put her arms around him.

'For what?'

'For being you. For being here. For putting up with the weirdest first date in history – and for doing the washing up. I'm sorry.'

She smiled.

'There's no need to apologize. This is a time for family. I understand that.'

'The Dragon Lady's about to go,' he said. 'Will you stay?'

Zumrut nodded.

'Yes. But don't call her the Dragon Lady. I think she's lovely.'

Everybody was lovely, apparently. Including his father. It made Harry feel sick. They returned to the main room. Leila had put on her coat.

'I love London, you know. I had such happy times here.'

'But you come back,' Harry said. 'Often.'

'Yes,' she admitted. 'Often. I don't do nostalgia, but I like walking around the heath. Your father and I used to walk around here hour after hour … Well, anyway, I come here and I fade into the background. In New York or Washington I get recognized a lot, but here, most people don't know who I am.'

'I noticed your hair,' Harry said. 'It's straight on television and all your publicity pictures, but not straight now.'

'The curls are natural. This is how I really am. The straightness, like a lot of things on TV, is pure fake. Every day of my professional life they take out the curls and put in the straight. Every day I make sure I don't eat too much, don't put on weight, don't drink alcohol, don't have much of a life, don't have affairs, make sure I sound sincere, even when I feel completely phoney. What you see is a slim, dark-haired woman with a straight coiffeur. Lurking inside is a curly-headed Tele-Tubby, who wants to behave disgracefully. I can do that here – in this apartment – but not in America.'

Zumrut said, 'You make it sound like being a nun. You're in the nunnery of television. A life of deprivation.'

Leila laughed.

'Yes. But then, every few months, I escape the nunnery and come to London.'

'And meet my father?'

'Yes,' she said. 'And meet your father.'

'Oh,' he said. 'I see.'

When the taxi arrived, Leila kissed Zumrut on both cheeks. Harry walked her to the door. She paused and turned to him.

'Harry, I know this is hard for you.'

He felt dizzy. Another shock of realization floored him.

'It has just hit me that you are the woman who broke up my family. Not the other one. The … lingerie model, or whatever she was, the one in the papers, the woman that I have hated all these years. It should have been you that I hated.'

He did not say it as an accusation.

'Yes.' She looked embarrassed. 'Perhaps. It's not easy for me, either, if that helps. And I will tell you … everything, eventually.' Her tone changed to one of pleading. 'Your father has done many wrong things. So have I. So – and this seems to shock you – have you. It's called being human. And if he does die, do not think badly of him. He always loved you, in his way.'

Harry wasn't sure exactly when Leila shut the door behind her and walked away to find her taxi, but he was sure that Zumrut was coming towards him. He was standing by the door, weeping. She put her arms around him, turned her head a little to the side and held him like a child as he continued to cry without shame. He remembered the softness of her kisses on his face and the heat of her lips, and he felt safe. For the first time in his life he felt he was in his own place of safety.

208

Harry awoke at dawn the next morning with the sun splitting the curtains and lighting the room. It glinted on Zumrut's hair. There was the scent of almonds and of sex. He turned towards her and noticed she lay in the middle of the bed. Her tiny frame held the centre ground of the mattress like an occupying army. He lay over her, his body cramped towards the edge, watching her breathe. Her musky scent was in his nostrils. He wanted her again.

'The middle of the bed,' he whispered, kissing her shoulder blade gently until she murmured something in her sleep. 'Emerald, you prefer to sleep alone.'

She moved. Sighed.

'Nnnnnnnurgh?'

'Or, like me, you have become used to being alone.'

He kissed her shoulders, then her breasts. She moved again, this time stretching as if her whole body smiled. His lips moved downwards, caressing the mound of her belly. His tongue touched her hot skin. She rolled away from him, still asleep. How different from Petra, he thought. How different this woman was. And how different he himself had become.

A precious emerald. He was determined not to lose her.

He padded naked into the study and connected his laptop to the router, where his father's laptop had once been. He logged on to check his emails. There was one from Redknapp, the constituency party secretary in Fulham, calling on all party workers to gather at the constituency Labour party offices to start work on the election campaign. Harry responded that he would be there. Then there was a big surprise, from an unfamiliar email address. Petra. It was his first contact with her since they broke up. It was headlined: 'Romantic Mathematics'. She, too, had perfect timing. Everyone in his life had impeccable timing. He had heard nothing from her for months, tortured himself with guilt about their break up, and now that he felt he had begun to get over her, on the very day he was in bed with someone he knew would be important to him, Petra had written him an email.

'*I'm abroad,*' the email said. '*A long way from London. Travelling. I saw this and thought of you, for the first time in months.*'

He looked further down the email. In bold letters she had written:

Smart Man + Smart Woman = Romance.
Smart Man + Dumb Woman = Affair.
Dumb Man + Smart Woman = Marriage.
Dumb Man + Dumb Woman = Pregnancy.

'*It made me laugh. Also I heard on the BBC World Service that your father has tried to kill himself and that Blair has called the election. I hope that your father wins his fight. I hope that Blair loses his. You have always been too hard on your father and too soft on Blair. I hope you will not work for the Labour party until they get rid of Blair, and get out of Iraq. Is this what we worked so hard for? Is this it???!!! Good luck in whatever you do. Petra x*'

He was still sitting in the chair looking at the email when he heard Zumrut behind him.

'*Askim*,' she said. She had told him when they made love that it was the Turkish word for 'darling'.

'*Askim*, is something wrong?'

He shook his head.

'Just a ghost from the past,' he said. 'But the moment will pass.'

'Are you okay, *askim*?' Zumrut put her arms around him.

He grasped her hand and turned to her and kissed her.

'Yes,' he said, 'when I am with you.'

He made a simple breakfast and they spent the morning together. He told her about the email from Petra.

'The beeper girl?'

'Yes, the beeper girl.'

'You loved her?' Zumrut said.

'Yes.' Then he paused. 'I did. My first love.'

'And now? Do you still love her?'

He sighed.

'No,' he said flatly. 'No, I do not.'

Zumrut nodded. They talked all morning and then at lunchtime Zumrut returned to her own apartment in Hammersmith and to her research. They agreed they would meet again that night at the Arabic class.

'Raj will know immediately what has happened between us,' she said.

'Yes,' he agreed. Raj would know immediately.

Harry shaved and showered and took the Tube to Fulham. He walked along the high street to the constituency Labour party offices behind the Post Office, wondering why Petra had bothered to tell him not to work for the party in the election, when she knew he would. Absolutely, he would. What was the point of being in a political party if you could not turn up and help it at election time? When Harry arrived at the CLP offices, there was Redknapp at the front door with a bucket and mop. He had pulled back the security grill and was working a short hose, squirting at the doorway, and then mopping. There was a strong smell of urine.

'Good morning,' Harry called out cheerfully. 'Smells like an election victory to me.'

'Smells like piss to me,' Redknapp responded. 'Still, things can only get better, eh?' He sprayed across the doorway. 'Bloody dossers,' he muttered. 'Pissed in the entrance again.' The jet of water washed the smell away into the gutter.

A couple of empty Carlsberg cans and cider bottles bobbed towards the drain. Redknapp switched off the water and put the hose back on the reel. He and Harry walked inside together. There was a loud hum from the photocopiers, clicking and printing, and a few people, looking busy. About half were students, the other half retired people. Harry looked around the room.

'Where is everybody?'

'This is everybody,' Redknapp admitted. There were far fewer volunteers than Harry remembered from 1997 or 2001. 'Difficult to motivate. Third victory on the horizon. Iraq war. Can't be arsed.'

Redknapp was a short man with a greying beard and out-of-control eyebrows. He had taken early retirement from the local high school where he had been deputy head teacher. Now he devoted all his time to the party. He offered Harry a mug of milky tea.

'Put me down for canvassing,' Harry volunteered. 'As much as you like.'

Redknapp made a note on a list in front of him.

'Harry Burnett,' he said aloud, 'laid down his life for the cause.'

If Redknapp had other names, they were a secret. All constituency papers were signed J. T. Redknapp. Jesus Tiger, was one guess. Jehosophat Tit. Jehovah Tush. Josiah Trotsky. Redknapp refused to confirm the truth. Harry always suspected it was something irredeemably middle class, like Julian Tobias.

'We'll need a much bigger effort from those that do turn out this time,' Redknapp lectured Harry. 'You'll get a lot of slammed doors.'

'Maybe,' Harry said. 'But the British people will never elect the Tories. People always vote for the more optimistic party. And that's us.'

Redknapp jerked a thumb at the Labour party workers behind him.

'Maybe, but only if these people here get out and get people to vote at all. I'll put you down for the Peabody Estate, since you're so keen.'

Nobody called the Peabody a 'sink estate' any more. The new jargon was of a housing estate in 'special measures'. And 'a challenge'. These were polite New Labour words for a shithole. It was just as dangerous now as the first time Harry had canvassed it, with Petra, as students, only now it was branded differently, as if that in itself made a difference. The Peabody was where most of the local undesirables had been housed. When Harry was mugged and had his iPOD stolen, the muggers ran off into the Peabody.

'That's great that is, Redknapp,' Harry said, thinking of the meaning of Redknapp's words. 'Come Saturday, I'll knock on doors in the Peabody and the pitch will be: "Blair: yeah, he's a bastard – but at least he's *our* bastard. Not a Tory."'

Redknapp's eye-brows shook at Harry's attempt at a joke.

'Maybe you should tell them that you were born the day Thatcher first got elected. That ought to be worth a few votes.'

'Sure,' Harry said. 'Fine. I just hope there'll be a lot of us on the Peabody, for our own protection, as much as anything.'

'I'll see what I can do,' Redknapp promised. 'You're not scared, are you?'

Harry shrugged.

'Of course not.'

Queen Margaret's Hospital, Gloucester

APRIL 2005

Amanda walked into the hospital alone. The stake-out from journalists had disappeared. All the TV trucks had gone. So had the police. They all had other priorities. Good. The local newspaper said that the Prime Minister was to be in the centre of Gloucester near the cathedral later that morning giving a speech about the strength of the economy. He was also opening a new school, sponsored by a local business, part of the initiative to get private money and expertise into the public sector. Most of the TV trucks from the hospital had relocated to the school playground. The Chancellor of the Exchequer was in Cardiff, also talking up the economy. The leader of the Opposition was in Oxford, complaining about illegal immigrants and asylum seekers.

'*Are you thinking what we're thinking?*' his party kept saying.

Amanda didn't think it very likely that she was thinking what the Conservative party was thinking at the moment. In fact, as slogans go, '*Are you thinking what we're thinking?*' was about as annoying to Amanda as any advertising concoction could possibly get.

She walked in through the hospital doors, steeling herself for the sight of her father comatose in his bed, and the strange mixture of emotions, led by pity, that she would feel. Pity was never a good part of any relationship. She also pitied her brother, which was not good either. He was impossible, sometimes. Most times. Harry did not seem able to get it through his thick head that if their father died, Robin Burnett's personal suffering would be over, but like a classical Greek tragedy it would pass to the next generation, to her, and more especially, to Harry himself. Despite his bravado and studied indifference, Amanda knew that Harry would bear the burden of guilt of not making up with their father for the rest of his life. She sighed. He just bloody didn't get it, which meant that she would have to talk to him again and try to reason with him. Whether Harry would listen to reason was a different matter. He, more than she, had inherited their father's genetic defect of stubbornness. As Amanda entered the private ward next to the Intensive Care Unit, one of the ward sisters, a Filipina, said hello, with a warm smile.

'Morning, Miss Burnett.'

'Hello, good morning, Sister Esmeralda.'

The nurses were mostly Filipinas or East Europeans, with some West Indians or Africans, brought in to fill the gaps in the National Health Service. It was the same story in the fields around the city where the agricultural workers were mostly Portuguese, Poles and Russians.

'Are you thinking what we're thinking?'

Amanda was thinking: where are all the British people who used to do these jobs? She looked at the smiling face of the Filipina ward sister and was thinking about who would empty her father's bed pan or catheter bag if all the immigrants in Britain went on strike simultaneously. There were not many British people volunteering for piss and shit duty in the NHS in Gloucester. She could not remember the last time she met a British-born nurse.

'Are you thinking what we're thinking?'

Her stream of incomplete thoughts was interrupted by the Filipina ward sister, who was saying something in a heavy accent which Amanda did not quite catch. She nodded towards the private room where Robin Burnett lay.

'You seester,' it sounded like, 'she weeth father.'

Amanda scrunched her nose in puzzlement. There ought to be some kind of English test before they got the job, surely.

'Sorry, I'm what? She who?'

As Amanda tried to make sense of the Filipina's words, she caught sight of someone moving out of her father's private room at the end of the Intensive Care Unit. The Filipina nurse beamed and pointed.

'You seester. See! She meeess you. She going odder way.'

'My sister?'

Puzzled, Amanda turned from the nurse to see the back of a young woman with spiky hair. She was carrying a small rucksack and hurrying off down the corridor.

'My sister?' she repeated, taken aback. Then she blurted out, 'But I don't have a sister.'

The smile died instantly on the face of the Filipina nurse. She looked crushed. Amanda stared at her for a second and then turned quickly and ran after the young woman with the spiky hair. The girl was now disappearing at great speed at the end of the corridor, darting into the crowds of visitors and away through the tangle of passageways, into the bowels of the hospital and perhaps out into the sunshine of the car park and away. Amanda ran blindly this way and that, then she stopped breathlessly at a junction between two corridors, not sure which way to go, realizing her pursuit was pointless. She was chasing a shadow. She cursed softly and then headed back to the nursing station in the Intensive Care Unit. The Filipina nurse had by this time raised the alarm. Half a dozen nurses and doctors were gathered around Robin Burnett's bed, checking his vital signs. They had called the police.

'Is he okay?' Amanda asked.

'More than okay,' one of the doctors replied. 'He's stirring. He's coming round. Miss Burnett, would you mind waiting outside?'

The words buzzed round Amanda's head once more.

'*Are you thinking what we're thinking?*'

Maybe this time she was.

Three hours later, Amanda's text to Harry read:

'*He's out of coma. Talking!!!! U need 2 come 2 c him, Aitch!!*'

Harry was in the apartment in Hampstead, sipping coffee with Zumrut, suffering the happy exhaustion of new lovers. He had a slight stiffness in his back and in his shoulders, and it made him feel good. He and Zumrut had been lying in each other's arms on a lazy morning when they were awakened by Amanda's first frantic call.

'The spiky-haired girl, Aitch,' Amanda said breathlessly, 'she just got away from me.'

'What?'

'Yes, her! In the hospital! The one who stole the laptop computer.'

'You saw her?'

'Yes! Here in the ICU! Coming out of his room! She does exist! It was like chasing a deer, or something, you know?'

He knew. She gabbled an explanation.

'Down the maze of corridors. I just lost her completely. It's like you said about the night in the apartment, like chasing a gazelle. Really.'

'It sounds like the same girl. About twenty?'

'About that, yes.'

'Pretty? Dark hair with blonde spiky highlights?'

'Couldn't see her face but spiky hair, yes.'

'Light perfume. Moves fast when cornered.'

'That would be her, then, Aitch,' Amanda gasped. 'But who can she be? What can she want with him? He had nothing with him that she could steal. And whatever she did do in the room, it didn't harm him as far as the doctors can say. Perhaps the opposite. The nurse called the doctors and security and when the doctors checked him they said he seems to be fine. Nothing stolen, nothing tampered with. They said he's now in a shallow kind of sleep.'

'He's what?'

'He's coming out of it, they think. He could awaken properly at any time. They are going to move him to a room right next to the nursing station, where there is better security and they can watch him more closely. The police have been here but they – surprise, surprise – don't know what to make of it. They've given him a police guard, at least for now.'

Amanda started to calm down. She told Harry that she would wait at the hospital for a couple of hours to see if the doctors were right, that he was coming out of the coma.

'Fine,' Harry said, deciding reluctantly that he had better get out of bed and start the day. He and Zumrut showered and made coffee and sat together in the kitchen and then desire took them again and they returned to the bedroom. An hour or so later they were still in each other's arms when another text message from Amanda suddenly interrupted them, ringing on Harry's phone. Harry looked at Zumrut guiltily.

'I ...'

She laughed.

'This isn't the Cherie pregnancy moment,' Zumrut laughed. 'If that's what you are thinking. And I am not ... whatever her name was ...'

'Petra.'

'Whatever. It's not about the Blair family. It's about your family. Get up and get the message. Read it, for goodness' sake!'

Now Harry laughed too. He stretched from the bed to his mobile phone, reading it aloud excitedly.

'*He's out of coma. Talking!!!! U need 2 come 2 c him, Aitch!!*'

He shivered. It suddenly occurred to him not only that his father would live, but that Harry would meet him, as if for the first time.

218

'Should I … should I go down there to Gloucester?' he asked Zumrut. 'To the hospital?'

Before she could offer any advice, the telephone rang.

'Harry, I have a car,' Leila Rajar said decisively. 'I will be outside the apartment in an hour to pick you up. I've just been talking to the hospital. You have heard the news?'

'That he is out of the coma?' he responded. 'Yes.'

'Then I think it would be good if you come with me to see him. We can talk on the way. I know you have questions. Can you be ready in an hour?'

Harry felt excited but nervous. Yes, he had questions. Twenty years of questions. Leila seemed to know everything that went on in the most private parts of his mind. He felt cornered by the fact that she was right. She was nearly always right. He did want to talk with her. And, he admitted to himself for the first time in his life, he also wanted to talk with his father.

'Okay, Leila, okay,' he said on the telephone. 'See you in an hour.'

As he hung up he turned to Zumrut. She was big-eyed with curiosity.

'Come with me?'

She shook her head.

'Not this time,' she replied. 'There will be other chances to meet your family. But not under these circumstances. For now, you need to be with your father alone and to figure out who each of you are, and what kind of relationship you might have. And to talk more with Leila, without me being in the back seat acting as some kind of brake on the conversation. Besides, I have to be getting to the library. I have work to do.'

'But you are my safety blanket,' he said with a mock shiver. 'Protection against the monsters.'

'No,' Zumrut said firmly. 'You don't need a safety blanket, and you don't need to fear any monsters. You need the truth, and to be with your family. Believe me, I am right about this.'

Harry nodded.

'Yes, you are right about this.'

He kissed her and held her once more, and then they both got ready. Exactly on time – another of Leila's irritating habits, Harry decided – a black Mercedes saloon arrived at the Hampstead apartment with Leila behind the wheel. She was wearing a black trouser suit and white shirt and had large sunglasses perched on her nose. Her hair was even more curly than before, tied back from her face with a black ribbon. Leila Rajar was a remarkably beautiful woman, Harry thought. He could understand exactly what his father had seen in her. The moment he closed the car door, even before he could clip on his safety belt, she had gunned the Mercedes and they sped off westwards towards the M40 motorway. Leila needed no directions. She knew the way. Obviously.

Harry said, 'Amanda told me that a young woman intruder was in the hospital in my father's room when she arrived early this morning.'

'Yes,' Leila agreed. 'The ward sister told me that too. They were all a bit shocked by it, though no harm was done.'

He could not see Leila's eyes behind the dark glasses. She was looking straight ahead, concentrating on the road. But there was something in her voice – that calm, mellifluous American TV voice – which unnerved him.

'From Amanda's description,' Harry persisted, 'it's the same woman who entered the apartment when I was sleeping and stole the computer and the picture of my father with you. The one who recovered your property, perhaps I should say.'

'Oh, yes?' Leila repeated, with even less conviction than before.

'Slender, moves like a gazelle, dark short hair with blonde spiky highlights. Twenty-ish. Ring any bells?'

There was a long pause. Leila said nothing. They were reaching the open stretch of the M40 motorway at Denham, just inside the M25.

'Leila, who is she?' Another long pause. Harry persisted, 'The nurses in the hospital said that she claimed to be Amanda's sister.'

Leila Rajar sucked in her breath and turned away from the road to look at Harry for a second.

'Harry,' she said quickly, and then turned back to the road ahead, 'the nurses are right.'

Harry blinked.

'What do you mean they are right?'

'She is Amanda's sister,' Leila explained. 'Of course that means she is your sister too. Half-sister, if you want to be pedantic. Her name is Maya. She's my daughter. And your father's daughter. She's a little bit younger than you said. She's not yet twenty. Coming up for eighteen. But very grown up in all sorts of ways. I hope you will learn to like her. Love her, even, when you get to know her. Which you will, soon. Very soon. I can tell you that Maya very much wants to meet both of you.'

London, May 1987

It was the day on which Leila Rajar was preparing to telephone Robin Burnett to tell him that she was pregnant. She was also going to tell him that their relationship was over, knowing that it would make him very unhappy. Leila had woken up early, and had then been sick. She had no TV assignment that day so she dressed in jeans and an old sweater and walked on Hampstead heath to get some fresh air. At every step she turned the plan that she had already formed over and over again in her mind. She took a heath path and felt the glory of the sharpness of the colours and the smell of the wet pine needles, diminished only when she had to stop to retch behind a tree. Morning sickness made her feel as if she was on a ship, tossed on the sea. The more she walked and the more she thought, the more Leila was absolutely sure about what to do, and equally sure Robin would object to her plan. She steeled herself. She would do it anyway. Alone. She strode quickly down the heath paths as if on a military march. She had waited five years for Robin Burnett to leave Elizabeth, and he hadn't. It was time to explore the inevitable consequences of what she thought of as the syllogism of her unhappiness:

It has not happened.

There is no sign of it happening.

Therefore it will never happen.
And again:
It has not happened.
There is no sign of it happening.
Therefore it will never happen.
And again:
It has not happened.
There is no sign of it happening.
Therefore it will never happen.
And therefore ...

And therefore. And therefore it was time to move on, with Robin's baby growing in her womb. And yet. And yet she loved him. The trees on the heath and the birds and the grass which flowed like a river down from the house at Kenwood to the lake, every part of this heath knew that she loved him still. It was a Lover's Paradox. She loved him not *despite* the fact that he refused to desert his children for her, but *because* of it. Did that make sense? Of course it made sense. Had Robin Burnett been the kind of man who could easily walk out of a marriage and a family with children, then Leila Rajar would not have loved him at all. How strange, this Lover's Paradox. An irony.

The word made her smile, alone on her path, nurturing her morning sickness among the beech and oak trees. Robin always blustered that Americans 'didn't do irony'. He was wrong about that, too, of course. Leila loved him for his faults and she decided that she would probably love him always, with the unconditional love that she already felt for their unborn child. *Meta-rational*, as Robin put it, with his funny way of ordering and classifying every human emotion. Just like an economist. But her mind was made up. She had to go. Soon. To stay any longer in London waiting for him to leave Elizabeth and his children would – Leila knew – destroy her. She was not cut out to be the Other Woman. She was not cut out for doubt. She would not be destroyed.

223

On those mornings when Robin had gone early to his office in Whitehall, and Leila had no story to file and nothing better to do, she would often walk on the heath like this, as if on autopilot. Her mind would rage, her feet would follow whatever whim struck her as the best route of the day. She passed the ponds where the hardy men and women of London bathed in mud-brown water the colour and texture of English gravy no matter how chill the air. Now she was climbing the hill to Kenwood, marvelling at the great house and the view of the London skyline. It was a place to think, in its way, another Place of Safety. She decided that she would return to the apartment, call Robin and explain her plan about the way ahead very, very simply, without any negotiation. It would take just four words, even if it had taken her five years of walking on the heath paths to formulate them.

Love is not enough.

She repeated the four words to herself as her feet felt the softness of the spring growth, marching now with fierce determination.

Love is not enough.

Love is not enough.

Love is not enough.

She felt another twinge in her belly, and paused until the nausea passed. Her only real fear was that Robin would think she had allowed herself to get pregnant to trap him. She hadn't. The pregnancy was a mistake. A glorious, wonderful, magnificent, delightful mistake – but definitely a mistake. They had talked about having a family together – five children, two of them adopted, plus at least one dog – and yet – another irony – Leila had not ever truly contemplated pregnancy, though she knew her time was getting short. She hated being a cliché, but for a woman in her thirties, the old wisdom that each day the clock ticks more loudly happened to be true. Now it was ticking towards giving birth to a child.

A child without a father for a woman without a husband. Leila strode back to the apartment and grabbed at the telephone, punching out the familiar telephone number, reciting under her breath:

Love is not enough!

Love is not enough!

Robin Burnett was, as usual, in his office. But now it was a different office. A much bigger office. On the back of a series of ministerial successes, including his role in facilitating the multi-billion-dollar Al Yamamah arms deal, Robin Burnett had been promoted to Secretary of State for Defence. Al Yamamah was the name of the biggest arms deal in British history. It was, the official announcement said, aimed at improving the security of a key ally, Saudi Arabia, in a troubled region, with troublesome neighbours like Iran and Iraq. British Aerospace, later to be renamed BAe, said it guaranteed thousands of British high tech jobs for years to come. The Americans smiled on the deal. So did the Lady.

'Congratulations.' Leila had flung her arms around Robin on news of his promotion to Defence Secretary. 'On the promotion. And on the arms deal.'

Robin kissed her and let his hands rest on her hips.

'Thank you,' he replied. 'Though rather like the production of sausages, perhaps it is best not to inquire too closely into the ingredients of my current success.'

She stepped back and looked at him quizzically.

'Meaning?'

'Meaning ... meaning, that nowadays I do that which is necessary or expedient. I am not always sure I do that which is right.'

Robin refused to tell her any more. Leila could not help thinking that keeping her as a mistress, fantasizing about a future together, but doing nothing to make it happen, might have fallen into the same category of expediency.

* * *

'As soon as the Lady steps down,' Robin Burnett's colleagues whispered, 'the job is yours, Robin. *Yours.*'

Robin kept telling Leila how some of his colleagues had become absurdly polite to him.

'Why?' she asked, naively.

'Jockeying for position in the Burnett Government,' he laughed, 'whenever that might take shape.'

The prospect of the Prime Minister's job meant – another paradox – that Robin himself was full of gloom. He told Leila repeatedly that the closer he was to seizing his ambition to be Prime Minister, the more he doubted whether he really wanted the job. Why did he want it? What for? Could he withstand the scrutiny? Could anyone? Robin paced the corridors of the Ministry of Defence planning the amalgamation of traditional infantry regiments or discussing the building of a new generation of aircraft carriers, barking out orders, the very model of ministerial efficiency, and yet convinced that his job had become tedious beyond belief. From time to time the fantasy of running a tea-shop in Devon with Leila would come to him again. Or more seriously he would think of going into the City to earn a barrow-load of money. At least – as he told Leila – in the financial markets of the City of London in the late 1980s, no one would question their relationship because no one expected any morality whatsoever. Greed was Good. Anything that you could legally get away with was acceptable, providing it made a profit. He could take the directorship of an investment bank, and be with Leila, publicly, his high-powered trophy wife. No one would expect anything else of him.

'The real scandal in the City of London or Wall Street is not what is forbidden,' Leila told him, 'it is what is allowed.'

Robin turned silent. When he had helped free up the markets, he had not expected some of the consequences of unregulated ruthlessness. What he did understand was that 'family values' in City circles meant simply the cost of alimony or of sending unwanted children to boarding school. And that provoked more personal gloom.

As he stalked the corridors of the Ministry of Defence or the Commons, Robin Burnett knew somewhere in his heart or his brain that the relationship with Leila was doomed. The certainty of this depressed him more than anything. He kept asking himself why would god, or Destiny or Fate bring together two people for such happiness and then allow it to die? He knew it was about to end. Leila knew. Yet they continued as if nothing had changed, except the growing shadow of sadness around his heart, made even worse by the fact that Leila had been acting strangely, in ways that he could not easily describe. For the first time, early in 1987, Robin Burnett recognized that they had secrets from each other, and it tortured him.

One night in early 1987 they made love, as usual, and afterwards were lying together in her bed in the darkness, like spoons, their bodies curved together in perfect harmony. Leila was facing the wall. Robin was holding her from behind.

'Mmmm,' she sighed in bliss.

Robin kissed her naked shoulder and then got out of bed to have a shower.

'What's the matter?' she asked him, stirring.

'I have to go home,' he told her, pulling on his underpants.

'Home?' She sounded sleepy. Fuzzy.

'Did I not say? I'm off before seven tomorrow. Ministerial car with the Lady to Northolt and then to Brussels. European summit, plus NATO ministerial. A three shirter. Bloody French will try to stitch us up as per usual with the idea of a European Defence Force, without committing any more money to defence. It's total bollocks, again as per usual, but I have to waste my energy arguing against it.'

A 'three shirter' was diplomatic jargon for three sweaty overnights of diplomacy. Leila was irritated.

'Stay, Robin. You can leave early tomorrow.'

'I would love to but …'

He never managed to finish the sentence. Leila sprang out of bed and was at his throat, crazed, claws out, like one of those lionesses he had seen in a wildlife film. Once the male lion mated, he would spring away quickly, otherwise the lioness would turn and claw his face off.

'What do you mean you would "love to, but"?' Leila snapped. 'What do you mean? "Love" and "but" don't go together in the same sentence. Not with me they don't.'

'But I was …'

'But … but …? You sound like a motorboat engine. Just look at yourself. You are a fully grown man leaving the bed of the woman you love to go back to a woman that you say you do not love, and …'

Leila was molten with fury, waving her hands in the air. He could not recall the rest of her harangue, but it was unanswerable. Leila was right. Leila, in his experience, was more or less always right. There was nothing in his life that made him feel more inadequate than disappointing her. They said nothing more to each other that night. He finished dressing and she returned to bed. Robin kissed her on his way out. She lay still on the bed, and did not respond. Robin left the Hampstead apartment shortly after midnight and returned to his own family house in Pimlico. As he entered the hallway Leila's words flooded through him. He had indeed left the bed of the woman he loved for the bed of a woman that he did not love, and so Robin did not go to bed at all that night. He sat up on a sofa in the drawing room drinking whisky, and then fell asleep to troubled dreams. A dark cloud had formed over his life, and the cloud refused to move. It had become part of him, a malignant growth.

During the next few days while Robin was in Brussels for the 'three shirter' European summit and NATO ministerial, he had appalled the French Defence Minister Marcel Bertrand by the ferocity of his public attack on the plans for a European Defence Force.

'A Defence Force created by a government in Paris which wishes to spend less on defence in the future is the shabbiest of con tricks on the people of Europe,' Robin told a news conference. 'The French government wishes to create a European pillar of defence, it tells us all. But it is a pillar built of the cheapest cardboard. M. Bertrand should be ashamed of himself. He is promoting a confidence trick – a *trompe l'oeil* scheme in which a great European nation acts as a parasite on the taxpayers of the United States of America. As a European I am ashamed. So should M. Bertrand be, though shame and he would appear to be unacquainted.'

The attack was front page headlines in all the British, French and American newspapers. Bertrand complained about the bluntness of what Robin had said. *Le Monde* described it as a verbal '*force de frappe*'. The Lady called Robin Burnett to congratulate him, but there was an edge in her voice.

'Everything all right?' she asked at the end of the conversation.

'Yes, Prime Minister. Everything is all right. Why do you ask?'

'Mmmm,' she weighed up her thoughts. 'I saw your press conference clips on TV. You made an absolutely correct argument, Robin, but ... but you looked unusually irritated with the French.'

'Everything is fine, Prime Minister,' he re-assured her, and then blushed. She was mothering him, he realized. It was one of her extraordinary characteristics. But he wondered if he had overstepped the mark.

During those three days in Brussels, Robin and Leila held snatched and unsatisfactory conversations several times on the telephone. They planned to meet and stay together at her apartment the following weekend. It was half term. Elizabeth was scheduled to take Amanda and Harry to Cornwall for their school break, a family tradition. Robin was too busy to go down to Padstow with them. Another family tradition. He knew he was not seeing the children enough. Not seeing them at all, mostly. The boy, Harry, was behaving strangely. The girl, Amanda, was distant as if he was an irrelevance in her life, which perhaps he was. Robin realized he could fix the French on defence, but he could not fix his own family, and it troubled him. He was a bad husband. A bad father. An increasingly inconsiderate lover of Leila. And a very successful and ruthless government minister. Perhaps all those things went together.

He felt that whatever remained of his humanity was being squeezed from him, like a lemon in a press, sucked dry and increasingly bitter. Gloom upon gloom upon gloom descended upon him and he could do nothing to shake it. Even the supposed bright spots merely made him feel worse.

Robin's continuing closeness to the Americans was one bright spot. It was welcomed by everyone within the British establishment. Sir Montague Hawke and the others at MI6, the Foreign Office, the Prime Minister's Office and even the Lady herself, were astonished at how highly regarded Robin Burnett had become at the highest levels of the Reagan administration. Most of them did not know exactly what had been required to solidify this closeness, which added to Robin's air of mystery. It was a trans-Atlantic success too.

'You have a lot of juice,' the Director of Central Intelligence David Hickox told him bluntly, during a snatched conversation in the wings of a NATO ministerial event in Brussels. 'When the time is right, use it.'

'Use it to do what?'

Hickox looked at him as if he had gone crazy.

'To become Prime Minister, maybe?' he suggested. 'Yo? Burnett? Hello?'

'Oh,' Robin replied. 'That. Of course, yes.'

As part of his growing relationship with the Americans, the Vice President of the United States had invited Robin and the Burnett family to spend some time at his holiday home on the coast of Maine. Robin, naturally, agreed. The two men went fishing together. Robin pretended to enjoy it. All the political briefings he had received from Hickox and others suggested that the Vice President was almost certain to succeed to the presidency when Ronald Reagan's term expired in January 1989.

'It is always very difficult to follow a charismatic leader,' the Vice President told Robin as they cast for rockfish just north of Kennebunkport. 'As you yourself will know.'

Robin took the hint.

'When the Lady goes,' Robin replied, 'I think the British people may content themselves with a certain dullness for a time, as long as the dullness also includes competence and honesty.'

The Vice President nodded.

'*The Era of Charisma is Over*,' he intoned, as if making a State of the Union speech. Both men laughed.

'At least you have a date certain,' Robin said. 'You have something to work towards. You know that the next election will be in November 1988. In Britain we have no idea when the Lady will choose to depart.'

The Vice President nodded.

'She may not *choose* to depart,' was all he said. 'Others may have to choose for her.'

Then the two men returned to their fishing rods.

'They love you in Washington,' the Lady told Robin on his return from fishing with the Vice President. 'Everybody I meet has a good word to say about you.'

The Lady herself had enjoyed a particularly warm private summit with the President at the western White House in California. In an unguarded moment when they were together, the President had flirted with her. He told the Lady that she had the best legs he had seen since Betty Grable. The Lady blushed. She enjoyed the compliment, and enjoyed telling her male colleagues about it afterwards.

'And we love you here too, Robin. That's why I am going to promote you to Defence.'

Damn, he had thought at the time. He wanted to be Chancellor of the Exchequer, but the Lady had extended – what would Jack Heriot call it? – an offer he couldn't refuse.

'Defence? Well, thank you, Prime Minister,' he said. 'Thank you very much.'

And so Defence it was.

In his new role Robin Burnett now had in front of him weekly intelligence reports from Sir Montague Hawke and defence intelligence assessments or 'estimates' on Iran and Iraq. They made him feel sick. An unreported but catastrophic slaughter was taking place day after day, some of it from chemical weapons. There was no one Robin felt he could discuss his feelings with. Not Sir Montague. Not Jack Heriot. Not his colleagues at the MoD. And certainly not Leila. It would simply inflame her Iranian passions. She knew some of it, however. Night after night over supper she would rage at the mullahs in Tehran, sacrificing so many young Persian lives for a bankrupt Islamic revolution. Then Leila would turn her anger to the criminals in Baghdad, the mass murderers who had started the war and who were known to be using poison gas, as well as a campaign of direct attacks on Iranian civilians in the cities.

It had become known as 'the War of the Cities' because Tehran and Baghdad were deliberately targeted. The result, of course, was that the autocratic regimes in both countries now enjoyed more popular support than ever before, for patriotic reasons.

'Hickox told me that people who are terrified always support their governments,' Robin told Leila. 'He says it's a lesson for all of us. Build fear, build support.'

Those few worthy British newspapers that hadn't completely given up covering the fighting between Iran and Iraq carried stories of the war's disastrous progress.

'Why don't you do something about this, Robin?' Leila said to him late one night, with great fury after reading out reports of thousands of bloated bodies twisted by the heat and exposure to gas, lying in the desert in southern Iraq. 'Why don't you speak out?'

'Words,' Robin protested weakly. 'Just words. An empty gesture. No one in Britain cares, and we don't have any real leverage with either side.'

'Really?' she shot back at him. 'No leverage?'

'Really,' he confirmed.

Robin bit his lip, and turned to another glass of wine. It was the first time he had directly lied to her. He had lied to everyone else, but lying to Leila was a new and rather terrible sensation, like some kind of personal grief. Was he now incapable of telling the truth to anyone? Did he tell the truth even to himself? Perhaps the truth had become very simple: that he loved Leila but would never leave Elizabeth for her? And in his public life, he would do anything – anything – to advance himself. He blanched in shame. At least, he thought, I still have a conscience. I still *know* what I do is wrong even if I cannot stop myself.

'That doesn't matter!' Leila challenged him. 'It doesn't matter if you have no leverage. What matters is that there is no point in being in a position of political leadership if you cannot give a lead. Reagan – god help him – has at least challenged the Soviet Union on being the Evil Empire. And it is. Evil. And these atrocities in Iran and Iraq, Robin, on both

233

sides, are evil too. Completely immoral. Why can't you say something – anything – to condemn the use of nerve gas? Or the human rights violations of conscripting children into armies to be slaughtered? Is it really too much to ask? If it is, then you are complicit. You are just as much a war criminal as the people who are doing the killing.'

He blanched at the ferocity of her attack.

'British policy ...' Robin began, but even he was bored by his own words as he struggled to complete the sentence. 'British policy is ...'

Leila stood up, glared at him and walked away. It was the first time that he had seen her so angry. She slammed the door and went to work alone in her study. Robin poured himself two fingers of malt whisky and a little taste of water. He sat back in the chair and contemplated whether he was indeed a war criminal.

'A war criminal,' he said softly, sipping the malt. 'A war criminal.'

He shook his head. He had a bizarre feeling of being disconnected from reality. He could talk honestly to no one any more. No one. He could not tell Leila anything about the war. He could not tell anyone else about Leila. And – this was the truly bizarre point which kept him awake at night – the only real risk of his own career being destroyed was exposure in the press over his relationship with her, a very private, sexual matter. He laughed bitterly into his whisky. He had absolutely no reason at all to fear any kind of exposure of his role in helping tens of thousands of people be gassed by Weapons of Mass Destruction, far, far away. It was ludicrous. Ludicrous. And it ate away at him.

'I am getting away with ... murder,' he whispered to himself as he refilled the whisky glass. 'Murder. And I can't get away with ... love.'

Robin drained the whisky and went to bed.

That night Leila refused to let him touch her, and then when he whispered apologies and kissed her gently and repeatedly, she relented. As he raised himself upon her and she moaned with pleasure, he looked into her open, brown eyes, and he knew that it could not last. Their time was coming to an end.

Early in 1987 Robin heard in the tea-rooms at Westminster that one of the tabloids thought they had a sex story connected to him. He was summoned to a meeting by the Chief Whip, Gordon Currie. The Chief Whip's office is a gothic parlour designed to intimidate. Robin was not in the mood to be intimidated or bullied.

'You wanted to see me, Gordon,' he said brusquely.

'Robin, it's a routine question, just between us,' Currie said to him. He was an old-fashioned Shire Tory who loved gossip but always looked uncomfortable when forced to talk about sex. Girls were something of a mystery to him. He pulled at the collar of his shirt as he spoke, as if it were too tight.

'The newspapers,' Currie went on. 'They claim they are on to something.'

'Yes,' Robin had responded, immediately suspicious. 'I see.'

'The newspapers are determined to find any evidence of any member of the government having sex with …' Currie hesitated, again running his finger round the rim of his collar. He laughed nervously. He hated tackling Cabinet ministers in this way because he was certain that they always lied to him. For his part Robin could see that the Chief Whip regarded him as a possible future Prime Minister. Robin was the one who was doing the intimidating. Currie made it into an awkward joke.

'… They are interested in anyone in the government having sex with … well, anyone really. Women, men, animals, various types of fruit, or indeed with themselves. So I have to ask this of you formally, Robin, I'm afraid. Is there anything you need to tell me that could bring embarrassment to the government?'

'No, Chief Whip,' Robin responded equally formally. 'There is nothing I need to tell you.'

'The story is that … well, that it is you and a Commons researcher.'

'Absolutely not true. You have my word.'

'Good,' Gordon Currie responded in a businesslike tone, appearing to be convinced. He studied the papers in front of him and made a brief note with a Meisterstuck ink pen. 'Very good. Thank you, Robin.'

'Thank you, Gordon.'

Robin left immediately and strode back up Whitehall towards his office whistling a jaunty tune. He remembered Winston Churchill's comment, that nothing cheers up a man more than facing death, and surviving.

At least once a week during the first few months of 1987 the Ministry of Defence press office told Robin they had received an inquiry from one newspaper or another about his supposed 'friendship' with any number of young women. Robin Burnett had been named by one newspaper as '*The Government's Mr Sexy*'. To his amusement, and to Leila's, a magazine had called him: '*The Sexiest Mind in the Cabinet*'.

'Fuck me with your mind,' Leila had said to him in bed that night.

'I'll do my best,' he responded. 'But failing that, there are other parts of me which remain available.'

Curiously, the more false stories about the more women the newspapers researched, the safer Robin felt he had become. It was as if he was being inoculated against the real disease by a number of weaker, phoney strains. Around this time Robin first started keeping a diary, or rather two diaries. One was a contemporaneous account of what was happening in government. He would type out, rather painfully, a few hundred words a day. The other was more complicated, a reconstructed diary of the previous few years, as far as he could remember them, beginning with the Falklands crisis of 1982 and his trip to Washington when he first met David Hickox. Robin told no one about the two diaries, not even Leila. He cast back in the reconstructed diaries to try to make sense of why he had become so disillusioned, despite the many successes of the government. He wrote of the Falklands, and of the newspaper strike at Wapping.

He wrote of the preparations for the miners' strike, and the way that Scargill had played into their hands, fallen into the trap, completely discredited himself. He wrote eloquently of the changes to the British economy as it left behind its industrial past and moved towards the core of the modern service economy, underpinned by sound money and aggressive City practices. He wrote – glowingly – of the Lady. And then he wrote of Hickox. He wrote a great deal about David Hickox. There needed to be a record of all of this, he decided. All of it.

In March 1984, Robin Burnett met David Hickox again. Hickox was once more passing through London on his way to another secret meeting in Iraq. He was in ebullient form. They ate beef in an old fashioned restaurant in Jermyn Street and then savoured a couple of late night drinks at a private gentlemen's club nearby. Hickox put his arm around Robin and told him that his personal assistance in ensuring the disputed export licences for chemicals to Iraq had been 'vital' to their shared strategic objectives in the Iran–Iraq war. It was a success.

'Congratulations,' Hickox said, with a slap across Robin's shoulder blades.

'Define success?' Robin asked, rather doubtfully.

'Success is the fact that nobody is going to win this war,' Hickox replied. 'Nobody. Except maybe us. The combatants both lose. That is success.'

Robin nodded and agreed. There was something truly exhilarating about what they had done, like a shot of whisky, or induction into a secret priesthood. They had changed the world.

* * *

Later that month, after Hickox had visited Baghdad and returned to Washington, Robin was given a briefing by two intelligence officers, a man and a woman, working for Sir Montague Hawke. He never found out their names. It wasn't necessary. They showed Robin a number of photographs. One had David Hickox shaking hands with Saddam Hussein. Both men were smiling, hands clasped, their other hands on each other's shoulders, like old friends. Robin thought of the way Hickox's hand had been on his own shoulders in the London club.

'Promiscuous bastard,' he said aloud. The two intelligence officers working for Sir Monty grinned, but said nothing. The photograph of Hickox with Saddam was dated 19 December 1983. The MI6 briefing went on to outline the current state of the war. They handed Robin a printed version of extracts from the MI6 intelligence report.

'The United Nations is about to announce publicly that Iraq has used mustard gas and the nerve agent tabun against Iranian troops. American diplomats are privately briefing US newspapers that they are, nevertheless, satisfied with Iraq, and suggest that normal diplomatic ties have been established, without any formal or public notification of the fact. Iranian casualties from the gas attacks are not known. Iraqi sources suggest at least seven thousand dead or permanently disabled. We believe from our own sources that at least a third of these casualties would be boys aged 14-18, though an East European intelligence agency has been told by one of its sources that boys as young as 9 have been used. Girls are also used to walk into minefields to clear them before the Iranian forces advance. The East European intelligence service has further been told that in some areas groups of boys are roped together, so the fainthearted have no choice but to advance. Needless to say, they have no protection against the gas attacks ...'

Needless to say, they have no protection. Seven thousand dead or permanently disabled. Boys aged 14-18. Nine year olds. Girls. Roped together. Needless to say. Robin re-read the briefing and then put it to one side. He rubbed his forehead and thanked the two intelligence officers who returned to their desks in MI6. Robin sat back at his own desk and took a sip of water. He suddenly felt very, very tired. He remembered the lines from Wilfred Owen on mustard gas in World War One:

'If you could hear, at every jolt, the blood
Come gargling from the froth corrupted lungs
Bitter as the cud
Of vile, incurable sores on innocent tongues ...'

He thought of a nine year old boy dying like this. He thought of his own son, Harry, dying like this, chewing the bitter cud of vile incurable sores. Robin Burnett recorded in his reconstructed diary that as soon as the two MI6 agents left the room, he marched towards his private lavatory at the side of his own office, dipped his head towards the toilet bowl and was violently sick.

By the spring of 1987, now that he was Defence Secretary, his contemporaneous diary entries showed that Robin's stomach for such things had grown stronger. He found himself less and less affected by the content of the intelligence briefings.

'I think I am more "professional" these days,' was how he put it to Leila.

'You mean you are better at your job?'

'Better at some parts of it,' he replied. 'Like lying. I suspect you become used to it. You might even say, you become good at it.'

'How bad are the briefings about what is going on in the war?'

He shook his head.

'I can't tell you in detail, but we have reliable accounts of children killing children, conscripts killing conscripts, in a war which no one can win. We have bodies literally exploding with the chemicals of decomposition inside them. It is like Passchendaele every week in the heat of the desert. It ... disgusts me.'

He noticed that as he said it Leila looked away. For a second, he thought that maybe he himself had begun to disgust her.

In January and February 1987 David Hickox contacted Robin directly several times with progress reports on 'American and British objectives in the Middle East' which apparently were still in the process of 'being achieved'. Hickox gave few details, beyond what was already known publicly. British and American hostages had been freed from Lebanon.

'Best not to ask precisely how and why,' he said.

No one was winning the Iran–Iraq war. It was still a successful stalemate. And of course most of the world seemed content with this state of affairs provided that there was minimal disruption to the oil tankers coming out of the Gulf. There was no significant outcry from even the most vocal human rights groups about the use of nerve gas. The Campaign for Nuclear Disarmament and other pacifist groups had a different focus – getting Cruise and Pershing missiles out of Europe. This caused Robin Burnett great and bitter amusement. From his office at the MoD he occasionally watched the brigades of CND activists marching up and down Whitehall, picketing here and there, shouting their slogans. He would view the evening news pictures of the women tying their Teddy bears to the fence at the US base at Greenham Common with disgust. He would appear on *Newsnight* or the *Today* programme to defend the government's position and deride the Greenham Common Women as 'apologists for Stalin, naïve defeatists and dupes.'

One night in a televised debate with a group of women's peace activists he caused uproar by calling them 'narcissists in love with their own irrelevance'. They shouted him down in the studio. Robin sat calmly as the women shrieked in his face and the hapless *Newsnight* presenter attempted to restore order. A few tens of thousands of dead foreigners in Iran and Iraq did not appear to trouble their sensitive consciences, Robin told the newspapers later.

'They could, of course, take their Teddy bears to Baghdad. Perhaps Saddam Hussein will give them a sympathetic hearing.'

By May 1987 the intelligence memos had become so complicated Robin tended to skim them rather than read them. But he was drawn to one curious economic fact. Almost every significant industrial country seemed to be making money out of the Iran–Iraq war, except of course Iran and Iraq. Because everyone was making a profit, Robin decided, there was no one left to complain.

'*One company (name redacted) has delivered 60 tons of DMMP, a chemical used to make sarin, to Iraq. Precursor chemicals have been exported to Iraq from Singapore (4515 tons) the Netherlands (4261 tons) Egypt (2,400 tons) and Germany (1027 tons). One of Italy's largest banks, (name redacted) is funnelling sums we estimate to amount to $5 billion by 1989. These funds are in part guaranteed by the United States. France has concluded a deal to provide Iraq with 133 Mirage F1 fighters over ten years. We estimate the total French arms sales to Iraq will amount to 40% of France's arms exports. The bulk of Iraq's military supplies come from the USSR, but the contributions from the People's Republic of China and Brazil are also significant.*'

And so it went on.

'*Ad nauseam*,' Robin once told Leila, while again sparing her the details. 'Literally makes me sick.'

In April 1987, David Hickox became US Defence Secretary, Robin's counterpart in the Reagan administration. At that point he was – for a time – tipped as a potential running mate for Vice President Bush in 1988. George H. W. Bush decided otherwise. He settled on the apparently far more tele-genic (and significantly far less intelligent) Senator from Indiana, Danforth Quayle.

'Commiserations,' Robin had telephoned Hickox when Quayle's name was announced as the Vice Presidential nominee. 'I can't think what Quayle's got that you haven't – except for staringly empty blue eyes.'

'Oh, Robin, Quayle's just Impeachment Insurance,' Hickox commented with a huge laugh. 'If Bush gets into trouble, nobody'll ever impeach him if we know Quayle could make it to the presidency. As for me, well, maybe I'll get to the White House in the end. They say ninety-nine per cent of success in life is just sticking around. I'll be around for a while, like a bad smell.'

'Somehow, I believe you,' Robin said.

On his first trip in his new post as US Defence Secretary, to a NATO summit in Brussels with President Reagan, Hickox and Robin again made time to talk. The two Defence Secretaries agreed to play golf at a private club in Surrey used by US Embassy personnel. Robin protested that his game was extremely rusty.

'Good,' Sir Montague Hawke commented when Robin told him about the golf meeting. 'The special relationship with the United States requires that you play Greece to America's Rome, and that you also play golf to lose.'

'I don't think that losing at golf will prove to be a problem,' Robin replied. 'You can count on me.'

The clubhouse in Surrey was monstrous. It was a mock Tudor Edwardian mansion near Guildford, and at the back there was a large, wood-panelled dining room, empty except for a couple of waiters in white formal jackets. David Hickox sat with his security guards, sipping coffee, waiting for Robin. He was already dressed in his golfing gear, Black Watch tartan trousers and mis-matched tartan baseball hat, yellow and white checked sweater, tight over his thick-set body. Robin thought he looked like a heavyweight harlequin from a medieval pageant.

'Let's do it,' Hickox said, standing up immediately and leading Robin outside. 'Let's get some air.'

They played the first two holes talking about nothing except golf, mutual friends and families. At the third tee Hickox hit a huge drive up the fairway. Robin hit his drive the same distance but into the rough on the right.

'I told you I was rusty,' Robin cried out mournfully. 'I'd better do something about this slice.'

'Wanna play for money?' Hickox laughed.

They seemed to be the only golfers on the course that weekday morning, though they were tailed at a discreet distance by two American and two British protection officers, all four of them looking vaguely ludicrous in their smart business suits.

'I have something to say to you,' Hickox said as they searched for Robin's ball in the long grass. 'Something you won't like.'

Robin straightened and looked at him.

'Go on.'

'We've been backing both horses in the Iran–Iraq war in ways that we have not shared with you.'

Robin looked at him, puzzled.

'So?'

'So – it's going to get out,' Hickox explained quickly. 'Be made public. Big time.'

'Oh,' Robin said, a thrill of fear running through him. Perhaps the scandal that would expose him might be the real scandal after all, he thought. Not anything to do with Leila. 'How much is going to get out?'

Hickox shook his head.

'We've … we don't know, exactly. That is … look, Robin, I gotta level with you. You know that there's been an operation to engage with Iran, working out of the Old Executive Office Building next to the White House?'

Robin nodded. He knew some of the details.

'Some of it,' he said. 'You tell me your version.'

'It's been run in part by a Marine Colonel called Oliver North. He and the others were tasked with getting our hostages out of Lebanon. And they succeeded.'

'Yes, it was good work.'

British hostages had been released too.

'Yes,' Hickox agreed. 'It was good work.'

The Lebanese kidnappers were members of the Party of god, Hezbollah. They had managed to put the fear of god into most people in the region. They were largely financed by Iran, and it was necessary to engage Iran to ensure the hostages were freed.

'But ... there was a price,' Hickox went on, putting his ball towards the hole on a slow green. The ball stopped more than a metre short. 'I would lose my job if anyone knew I told you this, Robin – you being a foreigner, and all.'

Robin also putted. His ball stopped close enough for Hickox to nod that he would give him the hole. Robin started to relax. Of course the Americans had paid some kind of price to secure the release of their hostages. It would be done through intermediaries – called 'cut-outs' in the trade – so no direct American contact with terrorists was provable. Paying a ransom was no big deal, if it saved lives, Robin thought. Expedient. Necessary.

They walked together to the next tee and Robin placed his ball ready for the drive. He could not understand why there was such alarm in Hickox's voice unless something terrible remained to be discovered. The hole was a par four. Robin altered his grip slightly to try to counter-act the slice. He drove badly, a low-flying ball which bounced along the fairway. Hickox teed up his own ball and hit it with undisguised fury, some two hundred and fifty yards.

'Go on,' Robin encouraged him as they walked on. 'Tell me about the price.'

Hickox sighed.

'Robin, it's mixed up with other stuff. You ever heard about the Contras in Nicaragua.'

Robin Burnett did not know what Hickox was talking about.

The question of Nicaragua was a matter of indifference in Europe, but it amounted to an obsession within the Reagan administration. Reagan's people kept muttering about a Communist regime just a day's drive from Texas. In the 1980s Nicaragua was run by the Ortega brothers and their Sandinista movement which had overthrown a particularly nasty pro-American dictator. The Sandinistas called themselves nationalists, socialists and anti-imperialists. It meant anti-American. Whether you thought of the Ortega brothers as Communists was a matter of debate. Certainly they were on the Left. They were close to Fidel Castro in Cuba. The Reagan administration, unable to get rid of Castro, was convinced they could roll back communism by using Latin American allies to overthrow the Sandinistas and the Ortega brothers. For years the United States had backed the Nicaraguan Contra guerrillas – a bunch of right-wing mercenaries and thugs who were out to destabilize the Sandinista government.

'The President,' Hickox continued, 'has been having big trouble with the Democrats in Congress. They are constantly trying to tie our hands in the making of foreign policy. They stopped us giving money to the Contras in Nicaragua. Made it illegal.'

It was called the Boland Amendment. It meant that the Reagan administration could no longer legally fund the anti-Communist Contra guerrillas with US taxpayers' money.

'So?' Robin played his second shot towards the green. It rolled into a bunker. He swore softly under his breath, surprised at how competitive a golf game with Hickox had become. He wanted to win.

'So,' Hickox continued, playing his own second shot on to the green. 'So, we had this neat idea. We approached the

Iranians to get our hostages out of Lebanon and away from Hezbollah. The Iranians said they would do it, but they wanted weapons in return.'

'Weapons?'

Hickox nodded.

'We ... we made a deal.'

Robin Burnett tried twice to blast his ball out from the sand in the bunker, and both times failed. He conceded the hole. Both men had reached the next tee, but neither showed any sign of wanting to play golf.

'You made a deal on weapons with *Iran*?' Robin repeated, in amazement. 'As well as with Iraq? You whore. What kind of deal?'

'From memory,' Hickox replied, counting out the weapon's systems on his fingers, 'we let them have two thousand TOW anti-tank missiles. Then there were, I guess, some two hundred parts for MIM23 Hawk surface-to-air missiles. Plus we okayed the sale of further weapons from a third country ...'

'A third country?'

'Israel.'

'Fucking hell, David. How much more of this is there?'

'A lot,' Hickox responded. 'We're in deep.'

Robin was astounded. Nothing Sir Monty or his own defence people had told him prepared him for this conversation. For eight years, ever since the Iranian Revolution of 1979 and the kidnapping of more than 400 diplomats and their families in the US embassy in Tehran, the United States had publicly been trying to destroy the Islamic Republic of Iran. Destroy. Now Hickox was telling him that the Reagan administration was secretly propping up Iran with weapons shipments. And so were the Israelis. It was almost incomprehensible.

'And Israel?' Robin Burnett gasped. 'You are telling me that the Israelis are sending weapons to Iran?'

Hickox nodded.

'The shipments first went out in the summer of '85. The Israelis have been dealing with Iran since … since forever. 1981 at least. We just, kinda, put more enthusiasm behind it, y'know?'

'Jesus Christ, David.' Robin shook his head, still trying to come to terms with what he heard. 'If this is true we are fucked. Completely fucked.'

'Don't,' Hickox said, waving a pudgy hand in his face. 'Don't say it. It is true. All of it. And it gets worse. You need to know it all before it comes out. Which it will do, very, very soon.'

Robin felt another wash of panic hit him at the words 'before it comes out'.

'So why is it coming unstuck?' Robin asked.

'Money,' Hickox sighed. 'The deal was that the Iranians would pay us something extra for the missiles. In cash. We would get the hostages in Lebanon released. Which we did. There are plenty of people breathing free air now who would still be chained to walls in south Beirut if it wasn't for us. That's the one bright spot that we will keep mentioning. But … then there's the catch.'

'The catch?'

'Yup. A big snafu. Our Marine Colonel North and the others involved didn't just leave it with Iran. They wanted to put the Iranian money to good use. So they gave the profits, all the money left over, to fund the Contras in Nicaragua, and buy them weapons and other war *materiel*. Ollie says it was a neat idea. Get the Iranians to fight communism! Yeah, that's neat, right? I'd buy that. Just like we've got the Muslims fighting the Soviets in Afghanistan, let's have the Muslim money from Iran fighting the Commies in Nicaragua. What's not to like?'

Robin felt as if he was having an attack of asthma.

'Why … but … why didn't they … just steal it?' he blurted out. 'It would have been simpler.'

Hickox looked at him.

'Because they are patriots, Robin. Honest men. Look, reality check. Nobody in Congress gives a shit about a million people dying in Iraq or Iran, nor are they gonna lose any sleep over nerve gas in someone else's war. But the one thing that gives the Democrats a hard-on is the idea that we are funding the Nicaraguan Contras. They've gotten wind of it. I don't know how. Maybe from within the CIA. And they're real pissed that we're breaking their Boland fucking Amendment. So what I came to tell you is that there will now be full scale Congressional hearings. They will *sub-poena* witnesses. People could go to jail. Documents will be turned over. We will do our best, you have my word on it, to keep your name out of all this if we can. But it is going to be a major-league clusterfuck. If anyone can prove that the President knew anything about it, he will be impeached. It will be Watergate all over again, and I don't think the country could stand that. High Crimes and Misdemeanours. It's our Falklands War, Robin. An existential threat to the government. It's that serious.'

Robin felt dizzy. Each word was like a punch to his head. He looked around the golf course. The whin was in brilliant yellow flower. The grass of the fairways was a stark green that hurt his eyes. He blinked at the big man in front of him with his yellow checked jersey and mismatching tartan cap and trousers. Hickox bent down. For a moment he thought the American was about to do some more of his one-armed push-ups. Instead he placed his ball on the tee, stood up again and smiled.

'Still, there is some good news.' He hit his drive and watched his ball bounce along the middle of the fairway.

'Good news? How can there be good news?'

'Oh,' Hickox replied. 'In Washington there is always good news. Nobody at CIA sanctioned anything. And in my new role as Defence Secretary I am of course outraged – *outraged* you hear me? – if anyone broke the law. I'm clean. The Veep is clean. The President ... he doesn't know anything about anything these days, poor guy. Barely remembers what his wife looks like. Colonel North and a few other munchkins will take the rap. They're loyal. They won't speak. They'll be burned at the stake, like witches. Every so often the Republic demands a renewal through human blood, human sacrifice. And besides, whatever anybody thinks, the oil in the Gulf just keeps pumpin', right? So, you gonna drive now, or you just out here for the walk?'

Late in the afternoon of that day in May 1987 when she decided to tell him it was over, for ever, Leila Rajar called Robin Burnett on his private line in the Defence Secretary's office.

'I know you are busy,' she apologized. He suddenly felt alarmed by her tone. Her voice was so expressive. Now it was almost formal, as if they did not know each other very well. 'I'm sorry to bother you, but I didn't want to wait until the weekend.'

He felt a blush come over him. Her voice, even after five years of clandestine lovemaking, calmed and energized and aroused him. He knew then as he knew every time they spoke, that he loved her. He loved her above everything.

'I'm pregnant, Robin.'

Uncontrollably he began to smile, as if the sun had come out.

'You're what?'

'Pregnant,' she repeated. 'Plural. With child. Just a few weeks gone, but it is definite. I did a test a couple of days ago and had confirmation from the doctor first thing this morning.'

'That's ...' he struggled to find the right words. His heart leapt with joy. 'That's fantastic news! I'm so pleased. I ... I want to get on the desk and dance, I ...'

'Don't.'

Leila dropped the word like a bomb. She was very formal now, cold, as if she was reading from a news script. In a way, she was.

249

'Robin, I am going to spend the weekend with you as we planned, but next week I am returning to the United States. For good. Without you. I won't be coming back. Nora Malahide wants me to anchor the Iran–Contra hearings for the network from Washington throughout the summer. It's a big break for me. She says it's a step towards becoming a permanent news anchor. I can do it, and still manage my morning sickness. The hearings will likely go on right through July maybe August. Then I will take leave to have the baby. I know you will try to persuade me otherwise, and I also know that I love you. But I cannot be persuaded. It's over, my darling Robin. It's over between us, forever.'

She paused. 'Love,' she said finally, 'is not enough.'

Robin Burnett felt a dead, cold hand grasp his heart and squeeze with chilled fingers.

'I see,' was all he said.

Gloucester, April 2005

For the rest of the journey to the hospital in Gloucester, Leila mostly talked and Harry mostly listened. He had dozens of questions buzzing around in his mind like insects, but the more she spoke, the more the insects disappeared. Leila's voice was beautiful, hypnotic, full of colour and emotion, and he didn't like to interrupt her flow. She told him everything, more or less. She spoke of how she and his father had fallen in love, of Robin's guilt, and their desperate desire to do nothing which would harm the children.

'You mean me and Amanda?' Harry said.

'Of course,' she confirmed. 'And, eventually, Maya too. Whatever you may think of your father he was – is – desperate – utterly desperate – to protect you. Otherwise he would have left your mother for me right at the start. I respect him for that, even if I didn't like it.'

'I am surprised that my father is capable of loving anyone.'

'Don't be.' She spared him nothing. 'He loved me, for example. He loves me still. He loves you and Amanda. He loves Maya.'

'How do you know?' Harry protested.

'Because you, Maya, Amanda and I are the only people who can really hurt him,' she answered with a show of finality which kept Harry silent for a while. 'And we all have, believe me.'

He stared out of the window at the fields flickering past.

'And you loved him too?' he said eventually.

'Of course,' Leila nodded again. 'He is – was – is – the love of my life. But …' Leila sighed, remembering her old slogan. 'Love is not enough. Love is not enough to ensure that things work out. Your father would never have left his children. He was incapable of doing so, or if he was forced to leave, he would always have been unhappy. I made the decision for him. I made the break. Someone had to change things. It could not go on. It was driving me mad to be the Other Woman. What is it you English say? "The Bit on the Side". That isn't me, really. I went back to Washington and pursued my career. It's a different culture there. No tabloid newspapers, or not the same as here. Investigative journalism in Britain used to mean something else, but now it's just investigating who is sleeping with whom, because that, apparently, is what sells. To me it seems so much effort for so little point. Journalistic masturbation. Here's the difference. If I had been a British news anchor, unmarried and pregnant to a Cabinet minister in 1987, I'd have been ruined. As it was, I returned to Washington, I got on with my career. No one pried into my pregnancy or my privacy. I married later anyway, and it was never an issue.'

Leila paused.

'Oh?' Harry said. He noticed she was not wearing a ring. 'You're married?'

'No, but I was. Well, technically I suppose I still am. We've separated. We're divorcing. It didn't work out. I guess I was on the rebound from your father and I made a mistake. As your father did too, after me. Boy, did he make a mistake.'

Harry noticed her knuckles had gone white on the steering wheel and the speedometer was clocking more than ninety miles an hour.

'You mean with the lingerie model? Carla Carter?'

Leila said nothing.

'And ... and Maya?' Harry said. 'My ... sister?'

'Yes. Maya. She's almost eighteen now, on her way to Princeton. We decided ...'

'We?' he interrupted.

'Maya and I ... and Robin. He's been a hands-on father, Harry, as much as he could. As much as I'd let him. He cares for her just as he cares for you, only you won't let him. We decided Maya should take a few months away from school in New York to come to London and study at the International School. She's been doing languages. Farsi and Spanish. She wants to do law and international relations at Princeton. It must run in the family.'

'She's been living here? In London?'

'Yes, of course.' Leila seemed genuinely surprised by his slowness. 'I thought you had worked that out. In the apartment in Hampstead.'

Harry realized he had worked out almost nothing about anything.

'The apartment in Hampstead is yours?'

'No, I gave it to Robin as a present, years ago,' Leila explained. 'After the scandal with the ... after the scandal broke, he was on hard times financially, whereas I started to make a lot of money. At first he stayed down in Tetbury in seclusion – he called it "Splendid Isolation" – and he let out the apartment in Hampstead to make a bit of money. He had no other source of income. Then a few years ago when one lot of tenants left, he started using the place again. It was a big breakthrough for him. It meant the shame had gone, or most of it. So when Maya came over to start the language courses, he moved to Hampstead so he could look after her.' Leila broke into a proud smile. 'You know, he really did look after her, cooked and cleaned. Helped with her homework! Can you believe it! Your father playing the domestic god for his daughter?'

She laughed and then accelerated past a row of trucks, taking the Oxford by-pass. Harry looked away again, out of the window at a field of sheep, white dots on the green. He wiped his eyes, and hoped that she did not notice the tears.

'He's actually a good father,' Leila went on carefully, glancing at Harry to gauge his reaction. 'Or he tries to be. There are certainly worse ones.'

He looked back at her, raised an eyebrow but said nothing.

'Sidney Pearl knew,' Leila went on. 'Obviously. He's been such a loyal and good friend. When Robin could not be in Hampstead, Sidney helped look after Maya. Then when it happened ...' She sighed.

'When what happened?'

'The attempted suicide.'

'You are sure that's what it was?'

She thought for a moment before answering.

'As sure as I can be. We'll let Robin tell us, but I think so. Anyway, when it happened, Sidney and his family took Maya in to live with them until I could get over from New York. Then you turned up and the police were on their way ... she had to get back into the apartment to pick up a few of the things that she'd left behind. Mostly her computer. She and Robin have been working on a book of his life. The true story. Everything that he did in government. Writing up his diaries and adding things. Not surprisingly, she didn't want anyone else to see what was in the computer – including you.' She hesitated. 'In fact, especially you, Harry.'

'She knew all about me?'

'Yes. Of course. I hid nothing from her. Why would I? But we're grateful you did not mention anything to the police. Keeps her out of it, as much as possible.'

They switched to country roads near the hospital. Harry was strangely excited. The dread he had once felt about meeting his father had given way to reluctance, and now to curiosity. The Robin Burnett that Leila had described was utterly unknown to him. Perhaps there was a different father lurking out there somewhere, someone that he had never known and never even guessed at. And now he was about to meet him, this new man, this different father, this Robin Burnett, for the first time. And what would he say? How would he look? How do you open a conversation after eighteen years of silence?

'Hi, dad. How's it going? How's things?'

Should he, Harry, apologize? And if so, for what? Sorry for being such a shitty son? Don't mention it, son – I'm just sorry for having been such a shitty father? Harry was puzzled.

'But if all this was going on right now in his life, living with Maya and so on, plus your divorce,' Harry said eventually, 'then why would he try to commit suicide?'

They had arrived at the hospital grounds.

'I don't know, exactly,' Leila admitted, reversing the car into a parking space. 'That's a big question. Maybe he'll answer it for us all today. Something tipped him over, and I can guess at part of it. A return of the shock which hit him when the scandal first broke.'

Harry looked at her. The idea that his father could suffer from any weakness other than arrogance and indifference had never occurred to him.

'Shock?' he scoffed.

Leila sighed.

'The moment we split up eighteen years ago – Robin said it was like being hit by a truck. Think about it, Harry. In the space of a few months in 1987 he lost me – his best friend, the woman he loved. At the same time he lost Maya. Then he lost you and the rest of his family, plus his marriage, and his career. What do you think that would do to any normal person? Well, it did exactly the same to your father. But he's strong. He coped. Mostly. Recently he took a big dip. Maybe he'll explain what caused it. Maybe he won't. In which case, don't press him.'

'But it really was a suicide attempt, right? Nobody tried to ... Tried to ...'

He could not say the words.

'Kill him?' Leila shrugged. 'Robin has many important friends and many important enemies. But none who would ... At least I don't think ...' She recovered, and then said with an air of finality, 'No, my guess is, he did it himself.'

The walk from the car park to the hospital ward where his father lay felt like the longest Harry had ever taken in his life. He and Leila walked side by side. She took his arm gently, which gave him something approaching courage. He trembled. They did not talk as they walked down the corridors. In the Intensive Care Unit a Filipina nurse steered them towards a Jamaican ward sister. She greeted them in a lilting voice.

'He's sitting up,' she beamed. 'He's doing really well, isn't he, doctor?'

The doctor was sitting at the nursing station, a brassy blonde Russian woman in her early thirties, with sharp black lines drawn for eyebrows.

'Veery weell,' she confirmed in a strong accent.

'Will he be okay?' Leila asked.

'Yees, we are hoping so,' the Russian doctor nodded. 'A veery good prognosis. He has eaten breakfast a leetle. He will make full recovery, though he is weak and sore in the stomach. When the consultant comes, she will say more.'

'We've moved him,' the Jamaican sister said, with a knowing smile. 'So we can keep an eye on him. And make sure he gets the right visitors.'

The ward sister took Harry and Leila through two sets of double doors to a room opposite the nursing station. Outside the room sat a hospital security guard, bored but pretending to be alert.

The room had enormous picture windows, so the nurses could easily watch what was going on inside, and check on unwanted visitors. Harry looked at the man on the bed, with bandages on his wrists and a drip in his arm. He was a stranger, Harry thought. A complete stranger, though made suddenly human by the conversation Harry had just had with Leila. Robin Burnett was grey and thin, very thin, but there were some familiar things about him. He had imposingly broad shoulders, a big chest, handsome face and shaggy grey hair falling over his pale skin. The man was sitting up in bed with monitors connected to his body. He was talking animatedly to Amanda who sat in a chair in the far corner. Harry sensed his body was shaking. His father was alive, awake and alert. Almost as if in a dream Harry felt Leila's hand grasping his arm, insistently pushing him towards the door of the hospital room. His father was still caught up in conversation with Amanda. Leila strode towards the bed.

'Robin!' she cried out, excitedly hurrying towards him. 'Oh, Robin, I am so pleased you're awake. So very, very pleased.'

'Leila!' His face lit up.

She bent over the bed and kissed him on the lips as they embraced. His father's left hand came round her back and Harry could see he had a cannula inserted above the wrist, a drip attached. Harry walked a little further into the room and stood beside Amanda's chair.

'We thought we had lost you,' Leila said.

'I know,' he replied, consolingly. 'I know. I'm sorry.'

'I'm sorry too.'

Leila hugged Robin Burnett in an embrace which lasted minutes. Harry could not see their faces, but it was obvious that they were both crying tears of relief. It reminded him of the black and white photo of the two of them in evening dress, and clearly in love. Whatever had happened between them, the love was still there. Leila finished hugging the man in the bed, and stood back.

'Robin,' she said softly, 'Harry came with me.'

The old man looked at him. His lips trembled noiselessly. Harry suddenly felt a surge of strength in his own body as he looked at his father for the first time in years.

'Hello,' he said softly, almost like a breath. 'How are you?'

'Hello, Harry,' his father replied from the bed. 'I am very glad to see you. Very glad.'

They stared at each other for a moment. Harry did not know what to do, so he stepped forward and they shook hands briefly and formally, and then separated.

'Well,' Robin Burnett said, attempting to be cheerful, 'now that the gang's all here, what shall we talk about?'

Harry smiled. Still the raconteur. Still cracking jokes. Maybe not so different from what he remembered. Leila took charge.

'We shall talk about you, Robin. We're all here because, in our very different ways, we love you. So, how are you?'

She took a seat by the bed and he stretched out his hand towards her, gripping with all the strength he could manage.

'Alive,' he said. 'Not much more. My guts feel as if they have been put through a blender. But the doctors told me I should make a full recovery.'

'Dad,' Amanda said, with a nervousness in her voice at using that word. 'Dad, when you get out of here, can we ... I mean would you ... You said in the card you sent me a couple of weeks ago that it was time to try to mend things and maybe to start again somehow. I didn't say it to you at the time, but I will say it to you now. Yes, of course. I agree. Shall we try?'

Robin nodded. Harry could see tears in his father's eyes and felt prickling in his own. He shuffled his feet and looked at his shoes. He could feel his father's gaze upon him, the gaze of all of them upon him, but he could not bear to say anything at all. He bit his lip and blinked at the tears and looked at his shoes.

'That would be wonderful,' Robin Burnett said slowly.

Leila stretched her hand out to him across the bed and he grasped it.

258

'They say there are no second chances in life,' she said. 'But maybe in some way we could start again. All of us.'

Robin looked at her and a smile split his face.

Harry found himself nodding in agreement.

'Yes,' he said. 'All of us.'

Harry and Robin looked at each other, as if for the very first time.

London, May 1987

It was the day on which Leila Rajar had planned to leave Britain for the United States, forever. She had discussed it with Robin on a dozen occasions in the apartment and turned it over in her own head a thousand times in walks upon the heath. 'For ever' seemed such a long time for two people who had promised that they would love each other 'for ever'. It was a word without end, Leila thought. Like 'never'. The day on which she was to catch the British Airways flight to Washington, Leila woke early in the apartment in Hampstead and turned to Robin Burnett in the bed. He was lying on his back, with his hands over his chest. Cadaverous, she thought. Like a man prepared to enter his coffin. Love is not enough, she whispered to herself, and then snuggled beside him, nuzzling into his animal warmth. He woke. He put his arms round her, rubbing her belly and into her groin with familiar ease, arousing her. All those years and his touch still made her wet in seconds.

'It's a girl,' he said.

'How do you know? Have you turned into a mystic?'

He shrugged.

'I just know.'

'I'll tell you,' she said, 'if the scan picks up the sex.'

'Did you mention sex?'

His hand moved deeper. She arched an eyebrow as his fingers began to explore her. They kissed slowly and made love for what they both accepted was the very last time, with a quiet desperation. When it was over they held each other like victims of a shipwreck enduring the storm.

'This was always the best bit,' he said, after a while. 'Afterwards. The hugs. The stroking. The conversation, the pillow talk. The way you nuzzle into me. The idea that this is our place of safety.'

'I think you liked the sex as well,' she said. 'I know I did.'

'Oh, yes,' he admitted. 'I liked the sex as well. I am sure I must have told you that I always went for ecstasy over happiness.'

'What will you do about that now?' she wondered. 'The sex?'

He shook his head. It was not something which had even crept on to his list of things to worry about.

'I have no idea,' he confessed. 'And I have never thought about it until now. What I do think about all the time is who I will talk to – I mean talk to honestly. Who will I trust? I don't trust anyone except you. I don't really talk to anyone properly except you. There's a big Leila-shaped gap in my life from today onwards.'

She sighed. She had always known that his real betrayal of Elizabeth was not sexual. It was emotional.

It had begun with that long and uninterrupted conversation they had started five years earlier at the end of the Falklands War. It was a conversation which had continued every day since. The emotional connection was the piece of the puzzle that could never be repaired. It was lost, she feared. Forever. That word again. She began to worry about Robin, more than about herself.

'I could call you,' he suggested.

'Don't,' she said.

He nodded.

'No. I won't.'

For the best. A clean break. *Love is not enough*.

'You will have the baby to think of,' he said. 'Do not concern yourself with me.'

She shook her head.

'But I do. I love you, Robin. Still.'

'And I have loved you since the very first time I saw you.'

He touched the familiar roundness of her, kissed the softness of her neck, and then the growing mound of her belly. Her smell was in his nostrils.

'If it is any consolation,' he said slowly, 'I think that what you are doing is the right thing. It is definitely the right thing for you. Maybe I will eventually come to see that it is the right thing for me. We both know that I could never easily leave Harry and Amanda.'

'You should try to make up with Elizabeth,' she advised him. 'As best you can.'

'I know what I should do,' he agreed, but his voice sounded hollow. 'But I can't. And I won't.'

She didn't say anything more. They had a desultory breakfast, as if it was the last meal before a funeral or an execution. He drank orange juice and sipped coffee but could not eat anything. She tried some oat cereal but moved away to throw up in the toilet.

'Morning sickness,' she said. 'It feels just like sea-sickness. Queasy. Dizzy. I hope it doesn't last for long.'

He felt like throwing up as well, but held it in. By the time she had to leave for the flight, they had already decided that he would not go to the airport.

'You'll just make a scene,' she said. 'And so will I. Besides, having kept it secret for five years, blowing it now in public at the moment it is over would seem a little careless.'

'Five good years,' he suggested.

'The best,' she agreed. 'I think you were – are – the love of my life. It's just a pity that …'

262

She began to cry and then caught herself, and then laughed through the tears.

'We agreed no tears,' he smiled. 'In your master-plan for how to handle this moment I believe it was point number three.'

'No tears,' she repeated, drying her eyes. 'Obviously. Though for something so real, it feels almost as if it is not happening – or happening to other people. It is as if I am spectating on what we are doing.'

'It's a pity we can't live our lives like an experiment,' Robin replied. 'In one test-tube we separate. You go to Washington and have our baby. In another test-tube, we stay together. And then we come back in five years to find out which experiment worked. I still find it hard to believe that two people who love each other as much as we do are unable to make this work. Love maybe is not enough – but it is something. Something big, in our case. Don't you ever ask yourself why did god … fate … whatever … bring us together if it is to end like this?'

She sighed. She was busy checking her passport and tickets.

'We've been over this, Robin, and …'

'I know. I am not trying to start an argument. It just runs around my head, that's all.'

'We will keep in touch,' she said. 'At a distance.'

'We'll talk.'

'We will always talk. But you must give me time and space. Lots of time. And lots of space.'

'I want to be father to my child.'

'You can't be,' she said, stuffing the passport and ticket wallet into her handbag. 'Not really. You have to be a father to the ones you have here in England.'

'Please don't exclude me,' he pleaded.

'I will never exclude you,' Leila replied. 'And I will never lie to our baby. He or she will be told the whole truth. That she was conceived in love, that her mother and father love her, but that events conspired to make it impossible. Big events. I will not hide it. And there will never be a time when I will forbid you from contacting me – or your child. But you must give me time.'

She emphasized the last six words.

'You will find someone else,' he said sadly. 'Get married. Have more children. You will forget me.'

She touched his face with her hand.

'Robin, neither of us know what is ahead of us. Don't make it any harder. Come visit, sometime. Preferably when you are Prime Minister. You could give me an interview.'

'Oh,' he laughed, 'funny thing about that. The Lady called me last night at the office. Said at the next re-shuffle she wanted to make me Foreign Secretary.'

It had not seemed important enough for him to mention the previous night. Leila jumped up and down on her toes with excitement.

'Fantastic, Robin! Fantastic! Right now with all the negotiations over nukes with Gorbachev it couldn't be better. You'll be the one to bring the Cold War to an end! I can't believe it.'

He shook his head and spoke in a flat voice.

'I said I would need to think it over a little and then talk to her about it. She seemed surprised.'

Leila was astonished.

'Of course she was surprised. What's to consider? It's the last piece of the puzzle before you become her successor.'

Robin Burnett took a deep breath.

'Leila, I have … I have tried never to lie to you about anything. But there are some things about my professional life – some decisions I have had to take in what I believed to be the national interest – that I think you would find … upsetting. They upset me, anyway.'

She blinked at him.

'Like what?'

He let the breath out of his lips and shook his head.

'You are going to Washington to anchor what they are now calling the Iran–Contra hearings, beginning with the testimony of Colonel Oliver North?'

She nodded.

'I know a little about this, from the inside,' Robin told her. They had agreed over dinner the previous night that Hickox was correct in predicting that it promised to be the biggest scandal since Watergate. It could bring down the Reagan administration. President Reagan had promised never to deal with terrorists, yet he presided over an administration which had done precisely that. Hypocrisy. Lies. Duplicity. Law-breaking. And more.'

'Ollie'll take the Fifth,' Leila said without any doubt. 'They're calling him the Mute Marine. He's saying nothing, which means they'll be the shortest hearings in US political history. What's he gonna say? That he was party to negotiating with Hezbollah? Arming the Iranians? Funnelling money illegally to the Contras? Only an idiot would say anything. He's not an idiot. And he has the right not to incriminate himself, so he won't.'

Robin shook his head.

'That's not what I hear,' he said slowly. 'I've been told by ... some people ... that Colonel Oliver North is going to tell everything that he knows. Everything. He's going to go through it all. Lance the boil.'

She stared at him wide-eyed with astonishment.

'How do you ...?'

'Don't ask. I can't tell you the truth and I don't want to lie. There have been enough lies. The fact that Colonel North will testify is a good thing for you, because it gives your job a focus. And it's a good thing for me because while Congress and the media are distracted by his little shenanigans, nobody is going to pay any attention to the Big Picture.'

'What Big Picture?'

'The Big Picture is that we have been arming Iraq for years.'

265

'We?' she said.

He nodded.

'Yes,' he confirmed. 'We. Or to be more precise, me. Me, Leila. For some years now we – I – have been enabling both sides to kill each other so that neither side could possibly win the war. I have that on my conscience. Blood on my hands, the same hands that I use to touch you. I am fairly sure that once you go, I will not want to go on with my political career. I feel like what you once called me – a war criminal.'

Leila Rajar looked at the man she loved, the man she was leaving. Something profound had changed within him. His assuredness, his ease with himself and his ambitions. He was a clever man, she thought, but not a naturally devious one. And now he had learned to dissemble and master the craft. Dishonesty had grown like a parasite within him and was now close to killing its host, and she could do nothing to save him. It was time for her to make her own life. It was time. Leila burst into tears and he put his arms around her in a tight embrace. They clung together for a long time, until the phone rang. It was Sidney Pearl announcing that Miss Rajar's taxi for Heathrow airport was waiting on the driveway outside the mansion block.

'Thank you, Sidney,' Robin said, and then turned to her. 'It's time.'

'Yes,' she said, 'it's time.'

Leila dried her tears and picked up her bags. He stayed in the apartment as she walked down the hallway towards the elevator without ever looking back, walking out of his life. Forever.

Gloucester, April 2005

Harry, Amanda, Leila and Robin Burnett had been chatting in the hospital room for twenty minutes when the consultant arrived. There were three junior doctors trailing in her wake, including the bottle-blonde Russian, a Filipina nurse and the Jamaican ward sister. The consultant was a short and stout German woman in her fifties with her hair tied back so severely it could almost have been an attempted face-lift. She introduced herself as Dr Heidi Krause.

'Well, I am glad to see you are sitting up, Mr Burnett,' Dr Krause said. 'And that your family is here. You appear to be doing very well.'

'Thank you, Dr Krause,' Robin Burnett said, 'for all your efforts on my behalf.'

'The important thing,' she turned to Leila, Harry and Amanda, 'is that there must not be too much excitement. I know that you have a lot to talk about, but I suggest that you limit your visits to one person at a time, and no more than two people a day for the next seventy-two hours. Perhaps two of you might think of leaving now, and the visit of the remaining person should go on for no longer than another half hour? I am sorry if you have travelled a long way, but it is really for the best, for Mr Burnett.'

Amanda and Harry decided that Leila should stay with their father and they would go and have a coffee in the hospital café. Leila did not protest. She had travelled longest, needed to get back to work in the United States and, though nobody said it openly, she had by far the strongest connection to Robin Burnett.

'We'll figure out a visitation rota,' Amanda told Dr Krause. She bent to kiss her father on the cheek. 'See you tomorrow, dad. I'm glad you're getting better.'

Harry stood and stared for a moment, then moved forward. He stuck out his hand and his father grasped it in both of his own. Harry gripped with his other hand. He was shaking with emotion.

'Me too,' was all he could say. He saw tears in his father's eyes through tears in his own.

'Leila, we'll meet you in the café when you are finished,' Amanda said, as they left. 'Goodbye for now, dad.'

'Goodbye,' he croaked, never once taking his eyes from Harry.

'Goodbye,' Harry repeated, 'for now.'

Amanda and Harry walked as if in a dream towards the hospital café. He was still trembling. The café was mostly empty, except for a few patients in blue hospital robes sitting with their visitors.

Amanda ordered cappuccinos and she and Harry sat sipping them at a table by the window in the brightness of the sun which beat on the glass with a heavy glare.

'He looked well,' Amanda said, almost as if she were trying to make conversation. 'Considering.'

'Yes,' he replied. 'Considering. Hell Freezes Over.'

'What?'

'Oh, you know, *The Eagles*. They broke up fifteen years ago and swore they would never play together again until hell freezes over. Now they've got a new album and are on tour, making millions. *Hell Freezes Over* is what it's called. It happens.'

Amanda looked at her brother, and her face crinkled with affection.

They were too absorbed in their thoughts to notice the two men who entered the hospital café behind them. One of the men was in his fifties, grey haired and with a waist thickened by too many large suppers and too much alcohol. This man had strikingly bright blue eyes, cornflower-blue eyes, and while he wore a suit, shirt and tie, the only part of him that seemed without a crease was where his belly filled the shirt until the buttons looked as if they might pop. His colleague was wispy and thin, with short brown hair. He wore an open-necked denim shirt and jeans and had two Nikon digital cameras slung around his neck. As they approached where Harry and Amanda sat talking by the window, the thin man with the cameras began to shoot a series of pictures. Harry was the first to sense their presence, but only because the two men grew emboldened as they closed in on him and Amanda. By the time Harry paid them any real attention the two were five metres away, the camera shutter clicking rapidly.

When he realized he had been spotted, the older, fatter man with the cornflower-blue eyes strode boldly towards Harry and Amanda, preceded at half a metre by his gut. A big smile split across his face, like a gash in a watermelon. He extended his right hand in an exaggerated gesture of friendship.

'Hello, Mr Burnett – Miss Burnett,' the fat man said with forced jollity.

Harry stared straight into his eyes. He knew immediately. The eyes were unforgettable. Harry felt like a small boy in a house in Pimlico peeing himself on the floor, except that he was a fully grown man in his early twenties, suddenly suffused with anger.

'Stephen Lovelace from The Whisperer column in the *News of the World*,' the man with the blue eyes called out loudly, rocking from side to side with bonhomie. 'Good news about your father, eh? So, how is he? Did he say anything about why he tried to kill himself?'

'Sorry,' Harry said, staring at the blue eyes as if at a serpent. 'What did you say your name was?'

'Stephen Lovelace,' the tubby reporter repeated with a grin.

Harry noticed the greasy wetness of the man's lips, and he pushed back his chair to stand up and face him. The cornflower-blue eyes met his gaze and then looked up at him as Harry rose to his full height. Lovelace's hand was still outstretched, as if expecting to be greeted with affection. His upper lip and forehead were stippled with beads of sweat. Harry was not conscious of taking a decision about how to react. All he remembered when the police questioned him afterwards was the sun beating on the window, the thud of his own blood in his ears like the roar of a waterfall, and the sweat on Lovelace's upper lip. Lovelace's pudgy fingers were still extended towards him. When Harry thought about it later, it was as if someone or something was controlling him, some primitive instinct, something visceral. Whatever it was, Harry pulled his right arm back and turned his hand into a fist. The cornflower-blue eyes flickered in alarm. Harry used his left hand to push away the outstretched fingers of Stephen Lovelace, and then he hit the reporter as hard as he possibly could with his fist on the bridge of his nose. There was a crack. Harry felt the grease of the sweat on his knuckles as Lovelace's nose exploded across his face. The blood gushed through his broken nostrils, over his wet lips, and splattered on to the floor.

Lovelace turned and fell backwards, clutching at his face and writhing on the floor as the blood poured through his fingers. Harry took a pace forward, paused for a second and then kicked Lovelace hard between the legs. The reporter jack-knifed, clutching his groin. Blood gushed from his face. At first Harry was only vaguely aware of the photographer, snapping away at him. The thin man in blue denims stepped back a couple of paces to film what the newspapers were later to call 'the incident'. In fact he filmed the incident only until Harry turned towards him and grabbed at one of the cameras round his neck, twisting the strap into a garrotte.

'Greeuccch,' the photographer choked. He twisted to protect himself, but Harry kicked him at the side of the knee like a scythe bringing down blades of tall grass.

According to witnesses from the gathering crowd in the cafeteria, Harry appeared to be the calmest person in the room. Amanda and a few other women held their faces in horror, while others called for hospital security or rang for the police on their mobile phones. Harry calmly took the two cameras from the photographer's neck and smashed them repeatedly on the tiled floor until they were reduced to shards of metal, glass and broken plastic. The value of the two Nikons and their lenses was later put at £5,000. The hospital reported four cracked floor tiles, with a notional value (including the cost of the employment of a tiler) at £200.

Four hospital security guards arrived and took Harry to the management suite where they sat with him until the police arrived. They reported that he behaved calmly, offered no resistance and merely asked for a glass of cold water which they happily provided while they waited for the police cars to arrive. The photographer in the blue denims was named in the following morning's newspapers as Alistair Sergeant. It was reported that he had recovered from what was described as his 'ordeal' after a short medical examination of his bruised neck. He said he was considerably shaken, but he recovered sufficiently to drive back to London with the bits and pieces of his cameras rattling in his camera bag. Despite the apparently terminal damage to the Nikons, the photographs of the attack were intact in the camera memory. Two photographs were released that evening to the *Sun* newspaper which published them in the following day's paper. The *Sun* is a sister paper of the *News of the World*, both owned by Rupert Murdoch's News International. The rest of the photographs were kept for a splash in the *News of the World* the following Sunday, alongside Alistair Sergeant's first person account of his 'traumatic ordeal'. Other photographs, taken on mobile telephone cameras by bystanders, appeared in most of the morning papers and on the 24-hour TV news channels.

Stephen Lovelace was detained in hospital. His nose was broken. He was concussed. His testicles were severely bruised and swollen. His cornflower-blue eyes were bloodshot. His clothes were torn. His shirt buttons had popped. He had lost two teeth – two crowns – at the front, and when he spoke to the television and radio reporters who soon arrived at the hospital, he did so with a kind of whistle through fattened lips. He told them that he had been chatting '*amicably*' to the family of '*the scandal-hit Tory MP*,' when suddenly one of them launched a '*savage and unprovoked attack*.'

A TV reporter asked him a question which television viewers could not quite catch because it was off-microphone.

'*No*,' Lovelace replied with a whistle, '*I can't think of any reason why he would do this. It was like he was mentally unhinged.*'

'*Could it be to protect the privacy of his father?*'

'*He should have thought of that,*' Lovelace whistled through his broken teeth, '*before he got himself caught up in the scandal. Some people,*' Lovelace went on, '*think they can get away with anything, just 'cos they are in positions of power. This country doesn't work like that. That's why we're free.*'

There was another question which was more or less inaudible.

'*No*,' Lovelace replied. '*It's not against the law to ask people questions. I was just doing my job.*'

* * *

When the police officers arrived at the hospital management suite, Harry was cautioned and then formally arrested. He accompanied the arresting officers to Gloucester police station where he was formally charged with common assault and criminal damage. Then he was offered a cup of instant coffee and put in an interview room. He said he would talk to the police and answer all their questions, but only after he had first had the opportunity to talk with a lawyer. Amanda called her solicitor's offices and they dispatched one of the criminal law specialists to the police station. The solicitor was only a couple of years older than Harry and advised him that it would be best to plead guilty to common assault and then to offer a plea in mitigation, in the hope of receiving a soft sentence. He would have to pay for the damaged cameras.

'Harassment. Balance of your mind upset. Protecting your father ... that kind of thing.'

'No,' Harry said, firmly. 'You don't seem to understand. I'm pleading not guilty.'

'But ...' the solicitor began to argue gently. 'You just told me that you hit Lovelace in the face as he tried to shake your hand. That's an open and shut case of assault.'

'Not guilty,' Harry repeated, sternly. 'Stephen Lovelace provoked this assault. He stalked me and my family as if we were animals. What I did was ... self defence.'

'You hit him first,' the solicitor prodded gently. 'He did not hit you at all.'

'Okay,' Harry said, 'then we'll call it pre-emptive self-defence. Pre-empting another one of his shitty lying stories about me and my family.'

'Well,' the solicitor responded, bemused by his strange client, and searching his memory for law-school defence possibilities. 'There is a crime of criminal libel. It's very rare. It means that you were driven to strike the alleged victim as a result of something he wrote about you which was untrue and drove you to violence. To be honest, I'd have to look it up. I don't think anyone has argued this for years. But in theory we could launch a private prosecution, or at least use it in your defence. But I have to advise you that punching someone in the face in front of dozens of witnesses would tend to be a signal to most of the magistracy in this part of the world that you assaulted him. Even tabloid reporters have the right not to be beaten up.'

'Please do look it up,' Harry said, suddenly cheerful and ignoring half of what his solicitor had to say. 'Yes, indeed. Criminal libel. That was it. From years ago. A festering wound.'

The solicitor left Harry in the interview room, convinced that some kind of commonsense would assert itself in his client's befuddled head after a few days' reflection. In the meantime he would work on the assumption of a not guilty plea. And he would check his law books for Criminal Libel.

While Harry was getting himself arrested, Leila sat with Robin Burnett in the hospital room and held his hands. He looked upon the face that he had known and loved for so many years, and she looked at him.

'So,' she said, eventually. 'Do you want to tell me why? Or do I already know why?'

He looked down at their entwined hands.

'You already know why,' he replied.

She looked into his eyes, and she immediately understood.

'Of course,' she said.

'Yes,' Robin told her. 'Hickox.'

Harry was held in jail overnight and then released the following day after a brief appearance at the local Magistrates' Court. The reporters' benches were full of journalists, inspired by that morning's newspaper headlines. Amanda picked Harry up from the court. They walked to the car park past half a dozen TV crews and twenty or thirty photographers.

Microphones were shoved in his face but Harry said nothing. Amanda drove him back to the hospital, and as they stopped at traffic lights she reached to the back seat and handed him a sheaf of newspapers. He laughed at the images on the front pages of most of the tabloids. They gave all the appearance of being relieved that some different and much more entertaining piece of news meant they could escape from the tedium of putting the General Election campaign as their lead story.

'What's so funny, Aitch?'

He started to read aloud.

'*News of World Man beaten by son of Tory Scandal Minister,*' one broadsheet front page trumpeted, with undisguised delight.

'*Nose for News,*' said one of the tabloids, focusing on the pictures of Stephen Lovelace holding his bloodied face.

'*Tory Scandal Suicide Son Smacks Hack,*' said another.

Many of the papers carried the same large photograph of Stephen Lovelace with white bandages across his nose, looking obviously distressed. Inside, many of them had devoted several pages to rehearsing the original scandal with pictures of the lingerie model, Carla Carter, plus two personal accounts from Alistair Sergeant and Stephen Lovelace. Lovelace spoke of the '*frenzied attack*' on him '*from the deranged son of the scandal minister*' as he '*politely inquired about the health of the boy's father*'. Other newspapers had similar coverage, though some carried in great detail accounts of the physical damage inflicted on Mr Lovelace, but with the implication that Lovelace and The Whisperer column had been harassing the family for years. The *Media Guardian* offered a series of articles on what it called '*Victims of Tabloid Harassment*'.

Harry was still laughing.

'It's just the way they keep saying it's Tory Scandal Minister's Son,' he told Amanda. 'It's like they are delighted to remind people how sleazy the Tories are. I'm winning Blair more votes by hitting Lovelace in the face and stirring it all up again than when I go out canvassing the Peabody Estate.'

Amanda started to laugh too.

'You're a devious lot, you political activists. You'd do anything to win.'

Harry agreed.

'Where are we going, by the way?'

She said she was taking him back to the hospital.

'I think you should see dad one more time, then you can return to London. Only, no punching anyone today, okay? Lovelace is still in the hospital somewhere. Best you avoid him.'

Harry agreed. The knuckles of his right hand were bruised and sore. God knows what Lovelace's face must be like. He could hear in his mind the sound of the reporter's nose being broken and the splat of the blood on the hospital floor. Harry felt calm. He knew he had expiated something. Guilt, probably. The blood on the tiles partly made up for the pee on the parquet floor when he was eight years old. He smiled and was content.

Nowhere in any newspaper was there any mention of Leila Rajar. As the fighting in the café subsided, the Jamaican nursing sister came into the hospital room and told Leila and Robin Burnett that there had been what she called 'a bit of an altercation' in the café between Robin's son and a reporter from the *News of the World*. Robin appeared concerned for a moment and then a smile crossed his face.

'You'd better go ...' he said protectively to Leila.

'Yes,' she replied. 'I'd better go.'

'We'll talk.'

'Yes,' she said again. 'We'll always talk. We always have, haven't we?'

He nodded. Leila slipped away. She walked briskly to her black Mercedes and returned to London. When she arrived at her hotel, she spoke briefly with Amanda by telephone and got the full story. They agreed they would meet again soon.

The following day Leila travelled to Heathrow airport. She checked again on the phone with Amanda for the latest about Robin and Harry, the miscreant Burnetts, and then returned to the United States.

The day after the fight with Lovelace, Harry and Amanda walked into the hospital room together. Harry could see his father's eyes catch fire as they entered.

'Good morning,' Robin Burnett said. 'How's the Contender? Punched anyone so far today?'

'Not yet,' Harry laughed. 'But it's early. Come on and have a go, if you think you're hard enough.'

Robin Burnett also found himself laughing, a full-scale belly laugh which only stopped when he felt the pain in his bruised stomach.

'I'm going to leave you two together for an hour,' Amanda said. 'I'll come and say goodbye, then I'll visit you properly tomorrow, dad, okay?'

Robin Burnett nodded. Harry thought his father looked considerably stronger and younger than the previous day. His voice had recovered some of the impressive timbre Harry remembered from the library film of him campaigning for Mrs Thatcher in 1979.

'Yes, fine,' he said.

Harry sat in the chair next to his father. The two men looked at each other.

'I've been reading about you in the morning papers,' Robin Burnett said, and then started to laugh. 'I'm very proud – very proud of my son. I should have done what you did years ago. A punch to the nose! Of course! And a boot in the balls! Just perfect!'

Harry found himself laughing again at the shared joke. Eventually his father straightened his face.

'We need to talk,' he said. 'Seriously. Harry, I am so very, very sorry for … everything. I hope in time you can forgive me.'

Rather like the incident with Stephen Lovelace and the photographer, Harry was not aware of deciding anything at all. It was as if some instinct guided him. He found himself nodding, enthusiastically. The words came from his soul, not from his mind.

'Too long a sacrifice makes a stone of the heart,' he answered.

'You read the card I sent you?' Robin Burnett said.

'Of course I read it,' Harry responded. 'And of course I forgive you. Of course, dad.'

Amanda wanted a coffee but thought it unwise to attempt to sit in the hospital café again. The hospital authorities had told her they would try to keep journalists away from the premises as far as possible, but they reminded her it was a public place, not a fortress. Lovelace, they said, would be discharged later that day, but it might be better for everyone if Amanda and her brother stayed well clear.

'Yes of course,' Amanda agreed.

The morning was sunny and bright and she went for a stroll in the grounds, still trying to come to terms with her father's recovery. In her heart she felt optimistic that at last, perhaps for the first time, they might function as something approaching a family. Maybe. All kinds of unimaginable things were now possible. As she sat down on a bench in the grounds, Leila called her again on her mobile.

'I just wanted to say goodbye,' Leila said. 'I'm about to board for New York. I really enjoyed meeting you and Harry.'

She repeated that she hoped they would all get together again soon, and then rang off. Amanda continued to sit on the bench feeling the strong morning sun wash over her. She was lost in thought, considering how all their lives had changed in

278

just a few days, and that it was only the beginning of the changes. She sat on the bench staring at some azaleas that were just coming into flower, her mind elsewhere. She did not hear the person approaching from behind her, until her name was called.

'Amanda,' the young woman said, with an American accent. 'Amanda, mom said I would find you here.'

Amanda turned and stared at the young woman with the pretty face and spiky hair.

'Oh,' she said. 'It's you.'

'Yes,' the girl replied. 'It's me. Do you mind if I sit down?'

The hour Harry spent with his father passed quickly. Too quickly. They agreed Harry would pay another visit in a few days. They also agreed that as soon as Robin Burnett was well enough they would meet and talk and go through everything. Everything. They even agreed that it was a good thing for Harry to canvass for the Labour party.

'At least you are involved, Harry. Theodore Roosevelt used to say that the important thing was to be in the arena, to take part. I respect that far more than if you were apathetic.'

'I do care,' Harry said. 'Though I suspect that one of the reasons I joined the Labour party in the first place was because you are a Conservative.'

Robin Burnett laughed.

'Of course,' he agreed. 'That's completely logical.'

'Will you vote?'

Robin Burnett shook his head.

'After my little speech about being in the arena, well, maybe I should confess that I am disillusioned with all of them, though Blair is quite interesting. One of us, I suspect.'

'One of us? One of who?'

'A Tory hiding as a New Labour leader. He has done what Clinton did in America – triangulated his party. That's why voters find him attractive – he is not really a party man. He's a chancer.'

279

'Oh,' Harry responded. 'I hadn't thought of it quite that way.'

'It doesn't matter if the cat is black or white so long as it catches the mice,' Robin Burnett said. 'One of my favourite sayings.'

'Theodore Roosevelt again?'

Robin Burnett laughed and shook his head.

'Deng Tsao Ping. Close enough, though. A Chinese reformist Communist leader and a maverick American politician.'

A silence fell between them. It was time for Harry to go but something was gnawing at him. He had to say what was on his mind, even at the risk of upsetting his father.

'D-dad,' Harry began. 'Why did you do it?'

Robin Burnett looked down at his hands folded across his stomach as he lay on the bed. He sucked in some air and sighed until his chest trembled.

'I did it because I truly believed I had nothing more to live for. That I had wasted the past twenty years of my life. That's it, really. All there is to tell. The details … well, I will maybe go through it all later, after I am out of this place and no longer officially a sicko.'

'No one,' Harry began, 'no one tried to harm you?'

Robin shook his head. 'Not in that way,' he replied. 'The pills, the wrists, all my own work.' He smiled grimly. 'I have not been much of a father to you, so far, Harry. But I will be in the future. I promise. If you'll let me.'

Harry was puzzled. His father had answered a question he had not asked. When he asked 'why did you do it?' it was not about the suicide attempt, but about the scandal years before. Why did he go off with the lingerie model? What was that about? But perhaps now was not the time. Or perhaps it was a deliberate politician's evasion of a difficult question on his father's part.

Harry was contemplating whether he dared ask the question again when Amanda walked in. Behind her was the spiky-haired girl.

'Maya!' His father sat up in bed with delight. 'Oh, darling, it's so good to see you!'

The girl bounded across the room and hugged and kissed her father. Harry watched closely. It was a lesson in zoology. He was watching a strange species, a species in which a child and its father clearly had always loved each other. He watched, and learned.

An hour or so later, after Amanda dropped them at the station, Harry and Maya were on the train heading back to London together. They were chatting about everything from the promise of her future studies in Princeton university to the bizarre episode involving both of them on the night of the supposed burglary in Hampstead.

'I saw you looking up at me from the heath,' Harry said. Maya laughed.

'I know! And I saw you. Then I ran away like a rabbit.'

'Gazelle,' Harry corrected her. 'I thought you were like a gazelle. And I felt as if I had a strange bond with you. It was very weird.'

'You're my brother,' she said. 'So looking up at you had a very peculiar effect on me, too. I wanted to save dad from any further trouble. I knew that anyone who saw the photograph of him with mom, or who read what was in the computer, would ... well, it would open up the scandal all over again at a time not of his choosing. I did it to protect him.'

'What's in the computer?' Harry wanted to know.

'Everything,' she said, her eyes opened wide, as if in amazement. 'You just won't believe it.'

Harry nodded and then said, 'Try me.'

'I will,' she said. 'You just have to read it.'

The moment Leila Rajar landed at New York's JFK airport she switched on her mobile phone and called the hospital in Gloucester. They put her through to Robin's room. He was alone, sitting up, watching news of the election on a 24-hour news channel. They were about to cross live to a speech from the Prime Minister justifying his foreign policy decisions, specifically on Iraq and Afghanistan. Robin put the news channel on mute.

'I am so sorry, Robin,' Leila told him. 'I have been thinking about nothing else for the past eight hours on the flight. I will never lie to you again. Never. Can you forgive me?'

Robin Burnett thought for a moment. On the screen in front of him the Prime Minister was goldfishing words about the struggle against terrorism and why the world was a far better place without Saddam Hussein running Iraq. The strapline under the Prime Minister said he had robustly defended his decision to go to war even though no Weapons of Mass Destruction were actually found in Iraq.

'War in Good Faith says PM,' the strapline said.

'It's a time for truth from both of us now, Leila,' Robin answered. 'Only the truth is good enough.'

'Yes,' she agreed. 'Only the truth.'

As Harry arrived back in Hampstead with his sister, Maya, they separated. She was still staying with the Pearls, though they discussed whether she would move back upstairs to their father's apartment. He kissed her on both cheeks and said goodnight. He had given Zumrut a key and she was waiting for him upstairs in the flat.

'I like it when you are here,' he told her as he kissed her.

'I like it too,' she replied. 'Would you like a drink, or are you in training for your next fight? I got a bottle of wine.'

'Drink,' he demanded. 'And enough boxing jokes, okay? I had an hour of them from my dad.'

'Oh,' Zumrut said, pouring him a glass. 'There was a message for you. From your friend Redman?'

'Redknapp, you mean? The constituency agent?'

'Yes,' Zumrut confirmed. 'That's the one. Redknapp. He said it would be best if you didn't help them out with the canvassing in the election this time. He said that he can use you on polling day, but he doesn't want the press making a story out of you working for Labour in the run up to the vote. He said that you getting charged with punching that journalist wasn't helpful. Maybe you should call him in case I got it all wrong?'

'Oh,' Harry said, sinking into a chair and sipping his wine. 'I don't think you've got it wrong at all.'

He began to laugh.

'You see, my darling Zumrut, I have now become a political scandal in my own right.' He sat back in the chair and laughed at the ceiling. 'Fantastic! Like father, like son!'

Hampstead, April 2005

'You just have to read it,' Maya told Harry again. 'His book is awesome. Explosive. It explains everything.'

'Everything about what?' Harry asked.

'Everything about everything!' she replied, not very helpfully. 'Everything to help you understand why we are where we are today.'

They were in the sitting room in the apartment in Hampstead, finishing a bottle of wine, Maya, Harry and Zumrut. They were watching the television news, and it was and endless stream of fact, supposed fact, speculation and commentary about the election. Harry was growing increasingly irritated. He had called Redknapp back and the agent confirmed that 'the party' thought it was 'for the best' if Harry did not do any canvassing this year. He had checked 'with headquarters'.

'But you're okay for polling day,' Redknapp said. 'In fact we could use you at one of the polling stations.'

'Why am I okay on polling day?' Harry asked him. 'But not before it?'

'Because we don't want any negative stories before the election,' Redknapp told him. 'Afterwards, who gives a shit?'

Harry suggested that being known for punching a tabloid reporter would definitely be worth a few votes in the Peabody Estate, but Redknapp did not rise to the bait.

'It's not my decision anyway,' he said. 'The Masters of Spin have decreed, and we lower mortals must obey.'

Harry turned grumpily to the television again. The opinion polls showed Labour steady at over forty per cent. In a three-party split it was more than enough to win a third landslide victory with a margin of sixty to a hundred seats. It had been the same story for days.

'This election lacks a degree of dramatic tension,' Harry suggested. 'We all know who is going to win.'

'At least it doesn't go on for two years,' Maya said, 'like at home. Here it's three or four weeks and then, boom! Over. I like that.'

Despite the near certainty of another big Labour win, the three main political parties, various nationalist groupings in Scotland, Wales and Northern Ireland, plus an army of journalists, pundits and TV commentators, acted as if their sense of expectancy was almost unbearable.

'Now, what would it take for a hung parliament?' a particularly excitable-yet-smoothly-condescending presenter on the BBC clapped his hands and shouted at the camera.

'It would take a bloody miracle,' Harry answered him. 'As you have just explained to us with your polls, you daft tit.'

The excitable-yet-smoothly-condescending presenter continued his exposition, explaining what it would take for the utterly unlikely to happen.

'Well, let's just have a look!'

A television graphic of enormous columns appeared on the floor by his feet and exploded into life showing precisely what it would take for no one party to be able to form a majority government. Columns of blue, red and yellow ascended skywards on the screen until they tied themselves in knots.

'NOW JUST LOOK AT THIS!' the presenter bellowed.

'Oh, for god's sake, can it,' Harry shouted at the screen. 'You've just predicted a Labour landslide, so why are you buggering on about a hung parliament you tosser.'

'Is it always this dull?' Maya said. 'I'd rather watch *The Simpsons*.'

Harry shook his head.

'Not always. Sometimes there's a real fight. Not this time.'

'Interesting elections don't always end up with good results,' Zumrut insisted.

'You are such a defender of British democracy,' Harry teased her. 'I think you love this country more than I do. Maybe that's one of the reasons I like you so much.'

'No, Harry,' Zumrut persisted. 'I'm just thinking of ...'

'... George Dubya Bush in 2000!' Maya interrupted. 'Boy, was that an interesting election! The first one I paid any attention to. But I don't think it was all that good, do you? The Accidental President.'

Harry reached for the remote and switched off the TV.

'Think about it this way,' Harry said. 'As a Game of Consequences. Unintended Consequences, but Consequences nevertheless. We would not have had George W. Bush as a viable candidate in the year 2000 if we hadn't had the Iranian Revolution discrediting Carter in 1979.'

Maya didn't understand.

'What has Carter got to do with it?' she said. 'That's a stretch. I mean, Dubya was drinking and partying all through the Carter years like in an alcoholic daze. I wasn't even born yet. And I don't see what the Iranians have got to do with anything – you're sounding like my mother, Harry. She thinks Iran is behind everything. Spooky ... you're creeping me out.'

'Okay, okay,' Harry started to explain. 'I know it sounds like a stretch but hear me out. The Iranian Revolution in 1979 discredited President Jimmy Carter, right? Made him look weak?'

'I guess,' Maya agreed. 'The hostages and everything. Desert One.'

Desert One was the failed attempt by the US military to rescue the US hostages held by Iranian students in the American embassy compound in Tehran.

'Yeah, exactly,' Harry said. 'So the Iranian Revolution helped get Reagan elected President in 1980, with – guess who? – George Bush senior as his Vice President.'

'So?' Zumrut argued and rolled her eyes at Maya.

'So,' Harry replied defiantly. 'That's the only reason any of us ever got to hear of Dubya, because he was the son of the President of the United States.'

'Sure,' Maya said. 'But so what? It's not like the Iranians planned it or something.'

'No,' Harry admitted, 'but that's not the point. The point is that we are still playing the Game of Consequences from the Iranian Revolution in 1979, and that's why so many people are getting themselves killed. We're playing it here in Britain too. We would not be lining up for a third Labour victory if Britain had not elected Thatcher in 1979, because she ended up dividing first Labour and then her own party. Quite something to be important enough to destroy not just one but two political parties, don't you think?'

'You are taking this too far, Harry,' Zumrut protested again. 'You cannot see the roots of everything we're now suffering stretching back to 1979. Just because you happened to be born that year.'

Harry laughed.

'Well, that too. But look. Everything from the Iraq war to Afghanistan to the Tories in a mess to Blair and George W. Bush – they all really do have their roots in 1979. That's where it all started. It's like the assassination of the Archduke Franz Ferdinand in Sarajevo in 1914 leading to the First World War and then after twenty years the Second World War, a total of thirty years of misery, and then the Cold War. Our generation's years of misery – decades of misery – started in 1979, and we haven't noticed it yet. The Iranian

Revolution was just as important as the assassination of Franz Ferdinand, because it brought all the pus of the world to the surface.'

'I get it!' Maya announced. 'That explains why dad was so obsessed with all that stuff.' She looked as if she suddenly realized there might be something in Harry's arguments after all. 'There's a lot in his book about precisely that. He calls 1979 the year of the Break with the Past, and the beginning of the New World Order. He talks of ATL and BTL – After The Lady and Before The Lady.'

Harry smiled.

'Well, looks like dad and I agree on something after all,' he said. It made him feel strange to think that it might be possible to inherit a genetic pre-disposition to *think* in a certain way. 'And he's right,' Harry responded with a smirk. 'Obviously. Absolutely on the button. Maya, you said I should read his book. Do you have a hard copy?'

Maya shook her head.

'All in the computer, and I have back ups. It's more or less done. Just a few literals and a bit of copy editing, plus maybe a few bits of explanation. Shall we print it out and you can tell me what you think? Sounds like you and he are soulmates.'

They drained their wine glasses and went to the study. Maya connected her Sony Vaio laptop to the printer and began running off the pages of Robin Burnett's autobiography.

'What does he call it?' Zumrut asked, as the sheaves of paper spun out from the printer. Maya handed her the title page.

'*A Scandalous Man*,' Zumrut read aloud, laughing. 'What a great title.'

Maya laughed too.

'Dad says that it's the supreme joke about his career and about his life. He says he really is a Scandalous Man but that the scandal that he is famous for and which destroyed him, is not the real scandal that he feels guilty about.'

'Oh?' Harry blurted out. 'What's the real scandal?'

Maya shook her head with a grin.

'I'm not going to explain. You are going to have to read his book, Harry. I can't tell you. It's complicated, and it's rooted in what you were talking about. I haven't even told mom the whole thing. I think she'd be shocked, and she's unshockable about most things – except when I got my belly button pierced.'

Harry's eyes widened. And it was not at the thought of Maya's pierced belly button.

'You mean he kept secrets from Leila?'

Maya nodded.

'I guess so, if that's the way you want to see it. Some of the stuff in the book is pretty weird. Arms shipments, chemical weapons, Iraq. I guess I need to re-read it. Very complicated, like I say.'

They stacked the chapters neatly and clipped them together, a bit more than 100,000 words in all.

'I'll start to read it tonight,' Harry said. 'Will you stay for dinner, Maya?'

Maya nodded.

'I'd like that.'

'In fact,' Harry returned to something he'd been thinking about since they returned from Gloucester. 'Would you just like to stay? You can move back in here until you need to go back to America at the end of the summer. It's more your home than mine. We're … family, supposedly.'

Maya blushed.

'I'll think about it. I mean, yes. Yes, please. I'll tell the Pearls tomorrow. They have been so kind to me. I think they miss their own children a lot. Mrs Pearl always wanted a daughter.'

Maya explained that the Pearls' sons had moved out. The younger son, David Pearl, was thought to be living in a squat in Dalston or Hoxton and was mixed up in drugs in some way. The older son, Jez, had cleaned himself up and emigrated to Israel. Sidney Pearl had lost touch with David, and was quite distraught about it, Maya said.

When the printing was finished, Harry put the pages to one side for reading later and prepared a simple supper. Zumrut and Maya were cleaning and chopping salad and making small talk when suddenly Harry blurted out, 'D'you know, I hated him.' The women stopped talking and looked at him. 'I know it's shameful,' he went on, 'but I really did.'

The words were said without any bitterness. Harry was grating parmesan cheese on the pasta with a great deal of vigour.

'Really?' Maya said. 'That bad, uh?'

'Yes. Hate. It's the only word which does justice to how I felt. I hated my father. I never called him dad. I called him father because that was a way of keeping him apart from me, like the Old Testament god – someone to be feared and absolutely never to be loved. And I know that hatred corrodes the vessel in which it is contained. Amanda used to tell me that all the time. But I couldn't help it.'

He put down the cheese grater.

'And now?' Zumrut said, stretching for the salad bowl. 'Are you corroded?'

'Yes, probably,' Harry admitted. 'But as for him – well, for the first time I have come to understand that he must have suffered too, and how much he must have suffered.'

Maya nodded.

'Yes, he did suffer. A lot of that is in the book too. Think about it, Harry. He is the father of three children and cannot see two of them at all. The third child – me – is being brought up by her mother in Washington and then in New York. She gets married. Plus, he has destroyed his own career, and many of his former friends and colleagues avoid him as if he had some kind of virus. He says in the book that what he called his "pariah status" made him understand what it must have been like for all those people in the eighties who had AIDS. At the moment you are most in need of friendship, it disappears. That's the man you called father.'

'I never really thought about it,' Harry admitted. 'All I thought was that he had made me and Amanda very unhappy, and helped destroy our mother. We ... we used to come down in the morning for school and there would be empty vodka bottles on the floor and our mum was lying on the couch – still drunk, or hungover ... it was ... humiliating.'

He trembled, unable to finish the sentence.

Zumrut interjected, 'Did he come to see you in the United States, Maya?'

Maya nodded.

'Often,' she said. 'Five or six times a year. Or we would come to see him, sometimes at his cottage in Tetbury but mostly here. Mom let him have this place.' She gestured around her. 'Dad had no money to speak of. Mom hit the big time as a news anchor. She wanted him to have it, rent it out for a while, which he did. They had happy memories. I loved it too. I loved London. Loved the heath. Loved the shops and the theatres and the museums. What mom loved was the anonymity. She would let her hair curl, not wear make up, put on jeans and a baseball cap and no one – no one – would recognize her. She said it was heaven. Whereas when father came to New York we always had to be careful ... and of course that got more difficult when mom married ...'

Her voice now trailed away.

'It wasn't a happy marriage?' Harry asked.

'No,' Maya said simply. 'It was a mistake.'

Maya explained that Frank Doolan, her stepfather, was a senior official in the World Bank. Doolan knew all about Robin Burnett, but had kept Leila's secret and treated Maya as if she were his own.

'It didn't work out because mom always knew it would never work out. Dad cast such a big shadow. Mom used to say he was the most interesting man in the world. He had the most interesting brain that she had ever encountered and she wanted to climb into it. Frank ... well, he's a nice guy. And he tried. But mom ... always loved dad. A tragic love story.' Maya laughed. 'Like Romeo and Juliet in yuck-o middle age. In the book you'll see he compares it to a Persian folk tale of two star-crossed lovers.'

'Leila and Majnun!' Zumrut said.

'Yes!' Maya responded with delight. 'That's it! You know it?'

Zumrut nodded.

'Everybody knows it. It's almost a cliché.'

'Maybe in Turkey it's a cliché,' Maya turned serious. 'But not here. In a weird way the news of mom's divorce might have been the thing that pushed him over the edge into trying to take his life.'

Harry was puzzled.

'Surely it should have been just the opposite? Wouldn't he have been happy at what she was doing?'

Maya shook her head.

'I'm going to have to ask mom, but I think ... well, the last time I saw him before it happened was here, in this apartment. He was real upset. I mean *real* upset. He was drunk. Real drunk. I had never seen him that way before. I asked him what was wrong and he said he was going to leave for a couple of days and go back to Tetbury ... Maybe I should have got the message ...'

Maya started to cry, noiselessly. Harry stretched out his hand to his little sister and she took it. Zumrut put a consoling arm around Maya.

'Don't blame yourself, Maya,' Harry said. 'It was nobody's fault except his own.'

As he said the words, for the first time in his adult life it occurred to Harry Burnett that he really was part of something which looked like a family, a dysfunctional, weird, bonkers, nutty family, but a family nevertheless. The thought made him smile inwardly. Maya recovered.

'The way it happened was this,' she said. 'I'd been out at my Farsi class, then I went for a bite to eat with friends at a Persian restaurant off Tottenham Court Road. Anyway, I arrived home and dad was sitting on the leather chair – right here – in front of the gas fire. Sipping whisky. "Hi," I said. He said, "Hi, Maya." But he sounded real beat up.

'He looked terrible. I'd been living in the apartment with him for almost four months, so I got to know his moods. He would dictate the book and I would key it into the computer just as he spoke. So ... articulate, you know? He met all these people that I read about. Gorbachev. Thatcher. Reagan. Bush's father. He knew Brent Scowcroft. Colin Powell. Cheney. Rumsfeld. Vice President Hickox when Hickox was Reagan's CIA Director. It's all in the book – awesome. Totally.

Maya took a deep breath, as if it was a relief to tell someone all this.

'Anyway, that night I get home and I can see he's upset. "Maya," he says, "I'm ... I'm going back to Tetbury tomorrow for a few days. You be okay here on your own?"

'"Sure," I nod. "I've got work tidying up the book – mostly your bad syntax, dad."

'Teasing would make him laugh but not that night. I asked if he was okay for, like, the tenth time, and he says, "No, I'm not," and pours himself another whisky. When I ask him what's up, he sighs and tells me, "Everything."

'You know anything about depression? Me neither. But the way mom explained it was that if being sad is having a cold, depression is pneumonia. In psychology class they say there are people who are drains, and people who are radiators. Dad is a radiator. Until that night. So I say, "What do you mean, everything's up? What's wrong?" Nothing. He says nothing. I lay it on. "Stop being Mister Misery." So he cracks. Kinda. He tells me that all his life is collapsing, just like it did before, and he can't take it a second time.

He starts on about how mom is having a divorce and how what he wants more than anything is to get back together with her and me, and I say I know, I know. Then he starts on about something else.

'"I got this call," he says. "Out of the blue." Some guy from his past had come visit him. "Like a ghost," he says. "Or the devil. Come to gather up the promised souls."

'"Who is he, this guy?" I say. But dad won't answer.

'So I'm like, "Dad, what's up?" And he's like, again, "Everything."

'The next day he goes off to Tetbury. And the day after that he tries to kill himself. I call mom and tell her, and she's like, oh my god. "*Oh my god, Maya!!! Oh my god!!!!!*"

'And then she tells me to get everything out of the apartment that might make another scandal about dad for the newspapers, and that she'll get on the London flight the next day, but Sidney Pearl says we've got a problem. You're upstairs, Harry, and I'm like, fuck. What do I do now? So I talk with Mr Pearl and we come up with something, and I am to wait until late and you're asleep and then ...'

Harry was listening wide-eyed, trying to take it all in.

'Jeez,' was all Harry could say, like a teenager not sure how to swear. He was thinking about his father, and his demons from the past, his private hell. 'Jeez, Maya.'

Zumrut put her hand on his.

'Are you okay, *askim*?' she asked softly.

Harry nodded.

'All along I just assumed he didn't care,' Harry cried out. 'God-the-Father. Smug, all-powerful, a very, very bad god. How can I have got him so wrong?'

'Don't blame yourself, *bitanem*,' Zumrut consoled him. 'You said yourself, it was his own decision. Nobody made him do it.'

'None of us stopped him, either,' Harry said.

He sat in silence with Maya and Zumrut for a long time. Then he picked up the manuscript of his father's book and sat in a chair under a reading light, looking for clues.

London, Autumn and Winter, 1987-88

ROBIN BURNETT'S STORY

After Leila left London for good I had a breakdown. Not a total collapse, not a catastrophe, not utterly debilitating, but a wave of profound sadness hit me. I went to the doctor who suggested various pills which made me feel nauseous or thirsty or suicidal, or all of these things in various combinations, so I stopped taking them. I lost weight, probably about ten or fifteen pounds, though I didn't bother to weigh myself. I didn't care. I was in shock. Grief. I later heard Her Majesty the Queen say something remarkable after the September 11th attacks on New York in 2001. She said that Grief is the price we pay for Love. I thought that was a wonderful way of putting it. It summed up how I was feeling by the end of 1987, paying the price for love. Leila had given me the Highest Highs of my life. Now she was gone, I was going through the Lowest Lows. Alone. It was almost as if love were an exercise in Newtonian physics, in which every action eventually does have an equal and opposite reaction.

Curiously, I became better at my job. I was never a pushover, but now I was brutally decisive. I had a reputation for never suffering fools gladly. By late 1987 it was widely known that I did not suffer them at all. The Service Chiefs – those hard nuts who had become heads of the army, navy and

Royal Air Force – were somewhat in awe of me, as were my staff at the Ministry of Defence, many of my colleagues in the House and much of the Cabinet. I always had a ruthless edge, where necessary. Now it was always necessary. Politics is like economics – the two basic stimuli are Greed and Fear. In the past as Chief Secretary to the Treasury I was good at playing on Greed. Now I became exceptional at Fear. We were expecting the Lady to re-shuffle the Cabinet early in 1988, with me now publicly tipped for the Foreign Office. I behaved with great indifference towards the idea, because I was indifferent to more or less anything.

'I am surprised you don't get ulcers,' Jack Heriot said to me after a particularly stormy Cabinet meeting during which I had openly attacked the Chancellor for his stupidity in shadowing the Deutschmark. We were supposed to be detached from European currency agreements – the precursor to the euro. But we weren't. Instead we were semi-detached. The Chancellor was pursuing a policy of secretly shadowing the main group of European currencies at a value of three Deutschmarks to the pound. It was bound to come apart.

'Are you challenging the value of the pound?' he snapped at me in Cabinet.

'No, Chancellor,' I replied. 'I am challenging the intellectual coherence of any one individual who thinks he can set the value of the pound.'

There was a buzz around the room.

'We have brought stability ...' he began to defend himself.

'It will come apart,' I persisted, 'when the markets decide you have got the value wrong, not when I – or with respect, you – decide anything whatsoever.'

I could see Jack Heriot was listening intently. He was now Home Secretary, I was at Defence, and we had made a private pact. When we ran against each other to succeed the Lady, we would keep it clean, not bear grudges, not allow Our People to brief against the other – and each of us would agree to serve in the other's administration, rather than sulk in our tents in a huff. It wasn't to be like that, of course. But we tried.

'I would far rather you stand aside to give me a clear run at the leadership,' Jack told me over lunch at the Cinnamon Club, a mouth full of tandoori fish.

'Ditto,' I said. 'You blink first.'

And we both laughed. I always admired Heriot, and my new brutality since Leila left meant he was slightly in awe of me, particularly after the row in Cabinet about the Deutschmark. At the following week's Cabinet meeting the Chancellor returned to the subject of the Deutschmark like a dog which returneth to its own vomit. I suspected that he had been having a week of briefings from the Treasury staff on what to say to defend their position.

'The new stability of the pound created by our policy,' he began, 'is allowing manufacturers and exporters of all kinds to plan ahead. It will enable us to maintain our options about the creation of a common European currency in future without committing to it prematurely.'

Codswallop, of course.

'If you insist on this policy of shadowing the mark, then the markets will unpick you,' I rebutted the Chancellor. 'And when they do – when they bet against the pound – we'll be ruined as a government.'

'I really ...' he began, but I cut him off savagely.

'A run on the pound means you'll have no choice but to raise interest rates through the roof to keep the currency stable, since that apparently is your policy. The markets will see your bet and double it and double it again until you crack – which you will – with catastrophic consequences.'

The Chancellor started to backtrack and protest that he had merely consented to an informal arrangement which could be abandoned at any time. Poor chap. He had delusions of competence.

'Abandon it now, then,' I suggested helpfully, 'because now would be a really good time.'

There was more huffing and puffing, waffle about stability and predictability for British businesses in – effectively – handing over control of our economy to the Germans. I had said my piece. I did not intend to argue further. The Lady looked at me strangely but she said nothing. She had signed on to the policy of shadowing the mark reluctantly – but she had done it.

I think she knew it was bonkers, but in attacking the Chancellor I was, in a way, also attacking her leadership. For the first time.

'I am surprised you don't get ulcers,' Jack Heriot said again after the meeting.

'I don't get ulcers, Home Secretary,' I responded a bit pompously, 'I give them.'

Jack moved away from me.

'Be careful, Robin,' was all he said. 'Don't make unnecessary enemies.'

'The hand that wields the knife,' I replied, quoting the old cliché, 'shall never wear the crown. You should be pleased that I am doing it for you. Clearing your path. I may not have the stomach to take you on after all this is over, Jack.'

Heriot said nothing.

I was conscious of turning inward. In the moment that Leila left London I had lost my lover. I also lost my best friend, and my only confidante. I was, to be frank, inconsolable. Someone – I can't honestly remember who – some kindly soul suggested I seek professional help and recommended a therapist with the appropriate security clearances. I would trudge up once a week from the Ministry of Defence to a place in Harley Street where at first I said almost nothing, as if I were enduring an interrogation at the hands of the KGB. Eventually, after a few weeks of prattling about nothing, I started to give the therapist some hint of the catastrophe that I was still enduring. He was called

Dr Greenbaum. If he had a first name, I never knew it. A small Jewish man who had the slightly neurotic mental characteristics of Woody Allen, even though physically he could not have been more different. He was not thin and tortured, but thick-set with a contented pot belly and short black beard. After six sessions or so I finally told Greenbaum the name of my lover – ex-lover. He had never heard of Leila Rajar, I am delighted to say. No one in Britain had heard of Leila Rajar, whereas everyone in the United States, by the end of 1987, had most certainly heard of her. Her anchoring of the daily Congressional hearings on the Iran-Contra scandal had become a phenomenon – a serious daytime television ratings success. Tens of millions of Americans watched the hearings every day, or listened to them on their car radios, and were then glued to the follow-up criminal trials, including that of Colonel Oliver North. The guts of the Reagan administration were being dissected on a slab, and it was as compelling as a made-for-TV drama. More compelling, perhaps. In the criminal proceedings Colonel North was convicted but then eventually acquitted on what the press called 'a technicality'. It was more or less as David Hickox had forecast.

The American courts ruled that all the public coverage of the Congressional hearings into the Iran–Contra affair made Colonel North's conviction unsafe. What a wonderful system! Imagine it here in Britain! A future defendant talks too much on television about all the bad things he has done, but then the courts cannot punish him – because he has incriminated himself! Superb! Wondrous! A triumph for democracy! Anyway, he got off. Colonel North, in typical fashion, referred to the 'legal technicality' by a different name.

'We call that legal technicality the Constitution of the United States,' he said, more or less. 'The right not to incriminate yourself.'

It makes me laugh to think of it now, though I had reason to celebrate as David Hickox soon reminded me. He telephoned the night Colonel North was finally acquitted, full of joy.

'Looks like we just saved our sorry asses,' Hickox told me. 'Small tragedy – nobody hurt. Nobody blames the President, and nobody much cares about the others, including you and me. Hoo-aaah.'

I imagined that after he finished the conversation with me, David Hickox had got down on the floor and pumped a few one-armed press-ups. There's no doubt we were all relieved. At first I wondered if my own name would come up in testimony, but it didn't. Or if it did, it was only tangentially, and therefore never made the newspapers. I was untouched, and I was thankful. The Congressional committee called David Hickox himself as a witness and – while he definitely didn't fall to the ground and start doing one-armed press-ups under oath on the witness stand – he did do the next best thing. To every question about what he knew and when he knew it while Director of the CIA, the new US Defence Secretary snowed them under with such detail about the terrorist threat from Hezbollah and the Iranians and the weapons shipments that the members of Congress on the panel were begging him to stop.

'Thank you, Mr Secretary,' they praised him. 'Thank you for your candour.'

'Candour' is American political slang for talking too much. They were bored rigid.

'You are welcome,' Hickox smirked at the end. 'And may I praise the rigour and integrity of this inquiry, Senator.'

'Thank you, Mr Secretary.'

They hadn't laid a glove on him. It must have been the late summer of 1987. Not once did any of the Congressional interrogators mention our covert support for Iraq. Nobody talked about the shipments of precursor chemicals or nerve gas or Weapons of Mass Destruction. Nobody questioned the fact that we were pumping up Saddam Hussein's arsenal.

Nobody suggested that within three years of the Iran-Contra inquiry ending, by August 1990, Saddam would invade Kuwait – assuming, quite reasonably on his part, that American acquiescence or indifference would continue. The US Ambassador in Baghdad had even told Saddam face to face that Washington had no interest in intervening in disputes between Arab countries, which Saddam – again, quite reasonably – interpreted as the official US go-ahead to invade Kuwait. And of course nobody could have foreseen that the following year, by January 1991, Saddam's troops would be shooting at British and American soldiers using some of the military equipment we'd been so keen to help him obtain. In all this the one person who acted rationally and consistently was Saddam Hussein himself.

There was one other surprise. Despite all the condescension endemic here in Britain about ordinary Americans, the American people proved themselves desperate to be informed. American viewers were transfixed by the TV spectacle of the Iran-Contra hearings. From the start of Colonel North's testimony – facing the press as if a firing squad of camera shutters and exploding flashes – Leila's shows got higher Neilsen ratings than the daily soap operas. She became a star. By the time that her weight had gone up and her pregnancy would have been obvious to viewers, the hearings were completed. She was able to take a few months off, basking in her glory, reading her good newspaper reviews. Leila had the baby – Maya – in Columbia Hospital for Women on the edge of Georgetown. There was no scandal. It was regarded as a private matter. I was so pleased. The birth signalled the time when we started talking properly to one another again. It was her move. We had agreed it would always be her move. I gave her what she had asked for – space and time – and one day – to my astonishment – she called me on my direct line in the office.

'You're a dad,' she said, the sunshine back in her voice. 'Your daughter is to be called Maya. Your name is on her birth certificate. Do you approve?'

I remember that day as if the clouds had parted after months of rain.

'Yes,' I cried. 'Yes, I do approve, oh, I approve.'

So we talked. At first Leila was jumpy. We kept the conversations short and she did not call me back again for two weeks. Then it became more frequent and eventually – though this would take two years – it was every week, sometimes several times a week, and I was permitted to call her anytime too. Our friendship restarted, although the weeks after Maya was born were very difficult for me. Every instinct meant I wanted to be there, to be with her in Washington, to hold my daughter in my arms. Instead, I was tied to my desk at the Ministry of Defence, as if to some Sisyphean labour. Whatever basic humanity I possessed was squeezed out of me by the exercise of power.

Leila refused to let me see her or Maya. She said she was moving to New York to anchor a network breakfast show and that once her own life was stable, I would be welcome to visit if we could bring it off without any publicity. I remember she told me her new contract was for seven million dollars a year. I found it difficult to believe, but that is what they pay people on American network TV.

'I am Her Majesty's Secretary of State for Defence,' I said to her boldly. 'I have to be in Washington and New York on a regular basis. I am sure that I should be able to find time to dine privately with the hottest new presenter on American TV, and her baby.'

'No,' Leila said. And then more hopefully, 'Not yet. Soon.'

With Leila's consent, I made plans to travel to the United States in early January of 1988. Unfortunately in the late autumn of 1987 I also made some serious mistakes which were to undo me and scupper the planned visit. My personal life had come apart. My political life was on the cusp of coming apart. I could see the future clearly. The only big surprise was how little I cared. I was to become A Scandalous Man.

* * *

I first realized it was starting to unravel in the therapy sessions. They were generally fairly useless. After eight or ten weeks of therapy I was considering cancelling them. It seemed that I talked endlessly and pointlessly with Dr Greenbaum about why I had not left Elizabeth and the children, rather than – more usefully – why Leila had left me.

'You believe in the sanctity of marriage?'

'I wouldn't call it "sanctity" but I do believe marriage is important, and that the marriage vows are important.'

'Even though you broke them?'

'Yes. But I did not do so lightly, as if they meant nothing. They are an aspiration, as well as a commitment.'

We went round and round in circles like this, Dr Greenbaum and I, until I was fed up talking about it.

'You believe that Leila is the love of your life?'

'Yes,' I agreed.

'Then what was it that stopped you from leaving Elizabeth to be with the love of your life? Your career?' He questioned me quite rigorously like this. 'Was that what prevented you? A conflict between ambition and the woman you loved?'

'No.'

'Well it looks like it.'

I did not agree. I would have given up my career for Leila, but did not have to.

'A political career can survive a divorce,' I told Greenbaum. 'But it cannot survive indecision.'

Greenbaum clearly did not understand. At around that time – the autumn of 1987 – the Lady had been faced with another minister having an affair. I won't say which one. The Lady had been told that the man could not make up his mind whether to leave his wife for his mistress, or vice-versa. The Lady lost her temper and yelled at the poor hapless chap: 'For god's sake, Stand Up or Sit Down. It doesn't matter which. What matters is that you Don't Wobble, Man.'

304

The poor chap finally decided to Sit Down – he dumped his mistress and stayed with his wife. The affair did not become public, but the Lady sacked him anyway.

'No guts,' was all she said when asked for a reason. 'I don't like a man with no guts.'

Dr Greenbaum was relentless.

'So – ruling out your career – why then did you not leave Elizabeth, Robin?'

I searched around for explanations.

'Maybe I could have – should have – but I dithered too long. Isn't that what men do with their mistresses? Think they can have it both ways? What is it that shit Goldsmith says? You know, the financier?'

Greenbaum didn't know. James Goldsmith was a big player in the City and in the bedroom.

'Goldsmith once said that a man who marries his mistress is "merely creating a job vacancy". I was never like that, but Leila eventually lost patience and left. She wanted a clean break. Maybe ... maybe if I had more courage – more guts – we could have been together in a way which did maintain my political viability.'

Greenbaum shook his head.

'You cannot become Prime Minister in this country after a divorce involving another woman, especially not ...' He chose his words carefully. 'An exotic foreign woman. The British public would not stand for it.'

I disagreed vigorously.

'You do the therapy, Dr Greenbaum. I do the politics. I tell you that properly handled, I could have survived a divorce. What I would not be able to survive are the affairs.'

'Oh,' he said, triumphantly, like a miner who had finally found gold. 'The affairs?'

The affairs. Remember, these were the beginnings of very different times. President Reagan himself was divorced. We were about to enter an era where Bill Clinton could survive an affair with the White House intern Monica Lewinsky.

Princess Diana survived her numerous and energetic affairs to become a national treasure. Prince Charles survived his affair with Camilla Parker Bowles to go on to marry her. John Major and Edwina Currie ... Well, who would have thought it? Around a third of the British population had gone through divorce and many more were having affairs or never married the people with whom they had children. The press worked themselves up into a lather, but the British people were – again, as usual – way ahead of the morality of the chattering classes. And yet it was pointless to discuss this with Dr Greenbaum. He was probing as he saw it, into the deeper reaches of my psyche. He was beginning to piss me off.

'The affairs?' he repeated. My face showed that I realized I had been caught out. 'You have had affairs subsequently?'

'Yes.'

'Subsequent to Leila?'

'Yes.'

'You are having an affair now?'

I took a deep breath.

'Yes, Dr Greenbaum.'

'Oh,' he said. 'I see. Perhaps you had better tell me about it? Or them?'

'Perhaps not,' I replied.

But I did. I suppose there seemed little point in paying £70 an hour for a Harley Street therapy session and then remaining silent, so I relented. I told Greenbaum that since Leila had left London I had been with one or two women, women I cared about, nothing casual, but nothing emotionally too serious either. I was damaged and was not going to allow myself to be hurt in the same way again.

One affair was with a special adviser – that is, a political appointee, in my department. That could cause me problems, I acknowledged to Greenbaum, since technically I was her boss.

It was an on-and-off sort of thing. She had problems in her marriage, we had to work a lot together, we liked each other's company and we managed to have quite a lot of sex. It was all very affectionate, and that was all. But it was nothing compared to Leila. And then, of course, there was Carla. Carla Carter. Sounds like the name of someone from a made-for-TV movie, doesn't it? That really is her name. The newspapers, when it all broke, called her a 'lingerie model', which – in the way of British newspapers – was not a total lie, but was so far from the real truth that it might as well have been.

Carla was completing her PhD at Keele University at the time we met, a junior lecturer in the politics department. She was – as the newspaper pictures faithfully show – very beautiful. She had done a bit of modelling since her late teenage years to help pay for her time at university, and continued with it even when she was studying for her PhD. One of Carla's assignments – just one out of dozens and dozens she told me she had undertaken for fashion catalogues and holiday companies – had been for a lingerie company. It was all very innocent – knickers, bras, bikinis – in a catalogue aimed at twenty- and thirty-something women. Not exactly porn. But somehow, 'Carla the Politics PhD' didn't sound as good in headlines in the tabloids, and so she became Sizzling Carla the Knicker and Basque Lady, the Lingerie Model. A scandal, of sorts, was born.

It was by now late November or early December 1987. I remember it as being the lowest point with Leila. We had renewed contact, as I said. Maya had been born, and I had been flushed with new hope that we might rebuild our relationship. Then Leila insisted on keeping at a distance until – at the very least – January of 1988 and my scheduled visit. I kept thinking of what I was missing – the first months of my daughter, my lovely daughter Maya. This is not an excuse, but I was low and lonely and over-worked and therefore susceptible, you might say, to some kind of affection. Carla and I met for the first time at her request. It was to be in my constituency office. Her PhD research was on the political power of pressure groups, and their ability to shape and influence top-level political decision-making. By the time we met, Carla had already written chapters about the civil rights movement in the United States and in Northern Ireland. There were also chapters on the trades unions, animal welfare campaigners and environmental groups ranging from Greenpeace to the Council for the Preservation of Rural England. She's a very talented woman, Carla Carter. Specifically, she contacted me for the chapter about the Campaign for Nuclear Disarmament.

By that time, the late 1980s, the Cold War – though almost nobody predicted it, and certainly not the CIA or MI6 – was almost at an end. The Reagan administration was talking about building anti-missile shields, anti ICBM systems, which everyone referred to as Star Wars. We had happily accepted mid-range Cruise and Pershing missiles in Europe and were gradually tightening the rope around the neck of the Soviet Union. Our rope, their neck, not the other way around as they had for so long predicted.

Carla Carter had written to me about CND because I had been scathing about them publicly. I had called them irrelevant narcissists, in love with their own sense of moral superiority, because they acted as if no one but their good selves desired peace.

'Please let me interview you for my book,' her letter ended. 'Any time. Any place.'

I wrote back saying: 'CND have no influence whatsoever with me or with anyone in the Ministry of Defence, ever. None. This should be a very, very short book, Miss Carter, or at least a very short chapter, if it relies on how far CND influence British policy or public opinion.'

Carla persisted. I liked that about her. I admire persistence. It is the most important political virtue. Without persistence, nothing is achievable. She sent me another letter arguing that the Greenham Common Women – the frightful harridans who protested outside the US airbase – really had informed the public debate. Carla's letter said they gave a human and moral centre to something which otherwise was merely for technocrats – dull statistics about missile throw-weights and missile kill-counts. Her argument was that the Greenham Common Women showed that ordinary British people cared what was being threatened in their name to ordinary people in the Soviet Union. We corresponded for a couple of weeks and then – although I suspected that Carla herself might be a left-wing harpie – I agreed to meet her. The most convenient place was in my constituency office. Carla had shown me that her arguments were worth engaging, even if I was sure they were wrong. I firmly believed then – and insist now – that CND was a self-regarding waste of time. A diversion. Nobody was going to Ban the Bomb. Nobody was going to dis-invent it. Quite the opposite. The challenge – which seemed to escape the Bearded Ladies at Greenham – was to stop other countries like Pakistan, India, Iran and Iraq – from getting the Bomb. Besides, I could see every day in Iran and Iraq and elsewhere, tens of thousands of people being killed without so much as a whimper from the portly moustachioed lesbians of Greenham Common.

When Carla turned up at my office, I was very surprised. She was anything but my image of her. Glamorous. Beautiful. Much younger than me. Soberly dressed. And of course nothing like one might imagine a lingerie model would be. She was not particularly left wing either. She had a flexibility of mind that I admired. Our conversation caught fire beyond the allotted half an hour. Two hours later I invited her for a drink, which turned into dinner, and then human nature took its course and we became lovers. I try to regret all this, but of course I don't. I regret getting caught. There is no scandal unless you get caught. As to my own state of mind, well, Leila was three thousand miles away with Maya. I was increasingly estranged from Elizabeth, and there was no way our marriage could be rebuilt. Instead, I feared that Elizabeth was turning the children against me. There were snide remarks, sniping rows over the breakfast table. She would turn the radio off in the mornings and I would turn it on. Little things, stupid things, which pointed towards the decline in respect and the inevitable end of the marriage. I was extremely busy, under pressure, and still regarded as one of the two best hopes to succeed the Lady as Prime Minister. My elder child, my lovely daughter Amanda was mostly all right despite the tension at home, but the younger one, Harry, was just eight years old and he sensed something terrible was wrong. When Harry did see me, which was very infrequently, he began treating me as if I were an interloper in the family, a pariah. Dr Greenbaum would say I was emotionally starved. He told me there was a Bruce Springsteen song of the time, *Hungry Heart,* which summed me up. I had a hungry heart, desperate to consume. The affair with Carla fed me. We had a lot of sex, a lot of conversation, a lot of fun, at a time when I had forgotten what fun was like. It was a holiday from reality. I never thought it would last, but that did not matter. Holidays don't last, do they?

Unwisely – looking back on it – I wrote Carla a few notes and called her frequently on the telephone, spending time with her when I could. Then, one day as if out of nowhere late one Friday evening – *Newsnight* was on the television – I received a telephone call at home. It was a man called Stephen Lovelace. I remember that he described himself as 'an investigative reporter from The Whisperer column on the *News of the World.*' I had always assumed that one day someone calling himself an 'investigative reporter' would call me and say he had checked the files and the export licence records and uncovered proof that I had authorized the shipment of precursor chemicals to enable Saddam Hussein to make nerve gas. But that did not happen. Instead I had an 'investigative reporter' on the line telling me I was having an affair with a 'lingerie model'.

I started to laugh.

'With a what?'

'A lingerie model.'

Giggles from me.

'You mean ...?'

'Knickers, lacy underwear.' He spelled it out.

'I think I would remember, Mr Lovelace,' I responded, still in good humour. Then he dropped the bomb.

'Are you telling me, Mr Burnett, that you have never heard of or met a woman called Carla Carter?'

Oh, god! When I recall it even now I still have the sensation of falling into a bottomless pit. Somehow – I never entirely understood how – Lovelace had discovered something. Maybe we were seen by people near Carla's home. She had a little flat near the university, and I occasionally slept there overnight. Or we would go to a country pub and drink discreetly in a corner, or have a late-night meal in a cheap and cheerful Indian restaurant, flock wallpaper, candle light, lager. Who knows? In the great scheme of things it doesn't matter. Being discovered merely seems inevitable. For years my life had been rather like driving on a motorway with numerous exits which I did not take until I was faced with only one marked: SCANDAL. There was no alternative route, no way out.

'Miss Carter has told me everything,' Lovelace said pitilessly, 'and shown me the notes you wrote her.'

I was still falling into the pit. Of course Carla had told him everything. She was – is – a very clever woman. Academically very bright, the first in her family to go to university – just the kind of person I most admire. But she was utterly guileless in a bright, academic sort of way. Carla was not used to the world of lies and duplicity that I now inhabited.

'Are you denying that you know Carla Carter?' he repeated.

'No,' I said. 'I am not denying anything – nor am I admitting anything, or discussing anything – about who my friends, colleagues or contacts might be. Nor am I prepared to discuss with the *News of the World* any private meetings I have had with anyone on any subject, ever. It is simply none of your business, Mr Lovelace.'

'So it's a "no comment" then, Mr Burnett?' he persisted, unable to disguise his glee. 'Don't you want to know what she has been saying about you?'

I pretended not to be interested, except in so far as to correct the libel he was about to commit.

'Of course I am curious,' I snapped. 'It's my reputation you appear to be trying to destroy.'

Lovelace read me a list of things Carla was supposed to have told him, some of which were true, some of which were false, some of which seemed to be like a fishing expedition, to encourage me to speak.

'Given the embarrassment you will be causing the Prime Minister by this, Mr Burnett, do you think you need to resign?'

'Mr Lovelace,' I replied, 'you clearly believe you have a story. Whether you print it is up to you. But I am amazed that in a world where more than a billion people exist on less than a dollar a day, you think your readers need to learn any of the things you have just told me. Goodbye.'

How stupid of me. How arrogant and pompous, but there you are. I hung up the phone and felt rather like one feels as a child when wetting the bed. There was a moment's warmth and pleasure and then an awful feeling of chill and discomfort. *Newsnight* was still blathering away and I switched it off. I made myself a whisky with a taste of water, and sat down in my chair at peace for the last time. The storm broke that Sunday morning. Actually, it broke late on the Saturday night when the first editions of the *News of the World* had Carla in her knickers on the front page, looking very glamorous. The telephone rang at home and rang until I disconnected it, and the siege of the house in Pimlico began more or less immediately. I tried to tough it out, but of course I could not. Elizabeth said she would stand by me and then said she wanted a divorce, and in the weeks that followed she vacillated between the two. The children were very upset. After a few days, when I thought it had begun to quieten down, the newspapers published pictures taken through the letterbox. The pictures showed Elizabeth and the children holding each other in tears on the floor. That was the final straw, for me. I knew it was over. Some colleagues – to his eternal credit Jack Heriot was one – urged me to make a stand and tough it out.

'If they get you on this, they will come for the rest of us soon,' he said.

I'd always suspected he was having an affair, and now here was proof of a sort, although the details of it all did not come out until much later. But that's another story.

'Don't quit, Robin,' Jack insisted. 'Some of us are trying to get the PM to draw a line and say there is a difference between what is private and what is public. This has in no way affected or undermined your performance as a minister.'

I listened to Jack's arguments and was very moved by his concern. Then I resigned anyway.

I was offered a lot of money for my story. I refused. I was surprised – very surprised – by Carla. I could not believe she would betray me. And I could not believe that an assistant lecturer at Keele University would want pictures of herself in her underwear all over the tabloids. I contacted her. The university said she was on leave of absence. I called her at home. She was in a terrible state. Tears. Absolute agony. It was worse for her than for me, much worse. At least I was in the public eye and used to the intrusion, whereas she was an obscure but talented academic trying to make a serious career for herself writing an academic book. Suddenly she's all over the newspapers in bikinis and stockings and suspender belts, treated as if she were a whore, which she most certainly was not.

'They were waiting for me,' she told me in our last conversation, sobbing into the telephone. 'Outside my flat. Two of them. They took pictures and started asking me questions and I panicked and thought I could handle it. They asked me if I knew you, and I said yes, of course I knew you, that you were helping me with my PhD. I should have lied, Robin, of course I should. But I didn't. Then they asked how long had we been lovers. One of them said they had already interviewed you about it and you had confessed everything. And so I ... I ...'

Well, Carla was in a mess. We agreed it was over. We agreed neither of us would talk any more to anyone about this, though in fact a couple of weeks later she did talk to the *News of the World* again, this time possibly for money. It did not matter to me by then. It was already the end. I resigned and I had to cancel my visit to the United States. I was no longer Her Majesty's Secretary of State for Defence. I was just Robin Burnett, A Scandalous Man, and I thought it best to stay as far away from Leila and Maya as possible. My career was destroyed. My family broken apart. I should not be bitter, but British newspapers act as if they would prefer the United Kingdom to be governed by *castrati*, or celibates. The newspaper proprietors and editors are no more moral than the rest of us, perhaps much less so. But dog does not eat dog. They never send their 'investigative reporters' to feed off each other.

As for me, well, I have always been a normal man, with normal desires and normal needs. I have some talents and I have some flaws. I thought I should serve my country as best I could. And I tried to do so. I made mistakes. I made terrible mistakes with my family, and with Elizabeth, with Leila and with Carla. I bear the guilt of everything which followed, the problems with Harry and Amanda, the collapse of everything that I held dear. And I am sorry. But the real scandal associated with me and the phoney scandals which surfaced in the newspapers are two very different things.

Carla Carter, incidentally, left the country when her PhD was awarded and her book was finally published. I read it. It was a bit dry, a rather earnest academic work, but cleverly argued. I found some of it convincing. My own contributions were kept to a minimum but were just enough to help make Carla a bit of money as a result of the scandal. People who had no interest in the political power of pressure groups bought the book presumably in the hope of hearing more of Carla's Confessions. When last I heard, Dr Carla Carter was a post-doctoral research fellow at a university in Canada. I have always wished her well.

Hampstead, Spring 2005

The Vice President of the United States David Hickox bounded out of the elevator, along the bouncy blue carpet and towards Robin's Hampstead flat. His Secret Service detail almost broke into a run to keep up with him. The Secret Service joke was that Hickox really wanted to play American football, and ran everywhere at full speed in the hope that some imaginary quarterback would throw the ball to him.

'Nice place you have here, Robin,' Hickox boomed as he strode into the apartment, while the Secret Service searched the rooms. 'Real nice. Very private.'

Robin Burnett nodded.

'Thanks, David. I like it a lot for precisely that reason. And it's good to see you. Where's the limo?'

The Vice President grinned. He had arrived at the apartment door preceded by four Secret Service minders, with four others trying to keep up from behind, and another detail downstairs in the lobby where Sidney Pearl was already supplying them with endless coffee and biscuits. The first four agents walked brusquely through Robin's rooms searching for hidden al Qaeda terrorists. When they found none, Hickox was allowed to visit his old friend. The Vice President told the

Secret Service guard to leave them and return to the Hampstead Mansions lobby.

'Mr Vice President, we need to stay in the corridor outside,' the lead special agent protested. 'We can leave you alone for your private meeting but ...'

'Okay, okay,' Hickox agreed. 'Whatever. Wherever.'

Then he turned to Robin's question.

'It's not a limo nowadays,' he said. 'It's a goddamn convoy. Seven cars in all, including two identical limos so our friend Osama is never precisely sure which one to hit. Ever seen a shell game? Well, I'm the peanut.'

'More like a medieval pope or king,' Robin said, 'making his stately progress through his kingdom. How long do you have here?'

'Two hours,' Hickox said. 'Then I have to go see the Prime Minister. Then France – Chirac. Then Moscow – Putin. Then Israel and Saudi and Egypt for a few hours each, and then home, thank god. You're looking good. The life of a retiree agrees with you.'

Robin smiled.

'You're looking pretty sleek yourself, Mr Vice President.'

'Busy, busy,' Hickox laughed. 'Keeps me young.'

'Better get on with it then,' Robin said. 'What was it you wanted to tell me?'

Hickox shrugged and looked a bit coy. Robin thought back to their talk all those years before at Winfield House. Hickox with something on his mind was definitely a man for the great outdoors.

'It's a nice day. Do you want to walk outside? On the heath? I'll show you around.'

'A walk sounds good, but being Vice President is like being in a children's playgroup,' Hickox nodded in the direction of the Secret Service agents outside. 'I can't go anywhere without my adult supervision.'

'We don't get a lot of al Qaeda around here,' Robin responded, putting on his outdoor shoes and grabbing a coat. 'Though we do have a few lunatics at the Green Mosque up the road in Finsbury Park. But they're all talk, so Her Majesty's government lets them rant and they leave us alone.'

'For now,' Vice President Hickox said, as they left the apartment. 'But I wouldn't count on it. I see Intel which says al Qaeda-linked terrorist attacks in Britain are inevitable.'

'Nothing is inevitable,' Robin Burnett responded, as the two of them emerged from the elevator into the main hall trailed by the agents who had been in the corridors. At the concierge desk Hickox announced his intention to walk on the heath. There was much muttering into hidden microphones. Eight of the bodyguards left their coffee behind and were despatched to provide security.

'My Secret Service codename is Lynx,' Hickox whispered. 'Lynx on the prowl.'

'Here in Britain Lynx is the name of a kind of aftershave much favoured by adolescent boys,' Robin responded. 'Perhaps the US Secret Service has more of a sense of humour than I had assumed?'

They walked out of the back entrance of the mansion block and were soon on the heath paths. The Secret Service agents fanned out and kept their distance.

Robin Burnett said: 'So, what's up, David?'

Hickox stopped and looked at him.

'I'm about to resign,' he said bluntly. 'This is my farewell trip on behalf of the President. Actually, I am being fired, but to save everybody's sense of honour, they are going to let it look like my decision. Health reasons. I'm sick.'

'Really?'

'No, of course not,' Hickox scoffed, exasperated. 'But starting Monday I have unexplained heart murmurs. They require a stress-free existence, apparently, which was news to me, and to my doctors. But then I am supposed to be a heartbeat away

318

from the presidency of the United States so maybe they want someone fitter.' Hickox looked as if he was about to strangle someone in the name of a stress-free existence. 'Surprised?'

Robin Burnett shook his head.

'Not really. It takes a lot to surprise me nowadays. Somebody has to carry the can, and it mustn't be the President. As we say here: *deputy* heads must roll. You always told me that the Great American Republic from time to time requires a human sacrifice. It's your turn.'

It was almost two years since the President of the United States had declared an end to major combat operations in Iraq. He had done so while bouncing around on a US warship in the Pacific under a banner that read: 'Mission Accomplished'. It was the peak of American presidential hubris. Since then, the United States and Britain had been fighting at least three different insurgencies.

'And as I always told you, David, never in human history has anyone ever re-structured a political system and an economic system in a country simultaneously. That's what you tried to do in Iraq and it just can't be done. Ever.'

Gorbachev and Yeltsin had tried it in Russia and the result was a disaster. In Iraq it was even worse – millions of discontented people with guns, but without jobs and without any regular source of income. Poor and hungry people with guns and a grudge. It did not need al Qaeda or Iran to light the fuse, though, of course, they also did their best.

'But I am sorry to hear it, David. We didn't always agree, but I respect your energy and your patriotism.'

'Don't deliver a fucking eulogy,' Hickox snapped. 'I haven't died, Robin. I'm just about to quit, is all. It will come out on Monday, like I say, so in the meantime don't tell anyone. The party are thinking about candidates for the Republican nomination for 2008, and I had hoped to be one of them, but I'm not. The President wants to bring someone in as Vice President who might stand a chance of beating whatever anti-war Democrat they finally throw up to meet us. I have agreed to fall on my sword for the good of ... well, you know the bullshit.'

'Of course. I know the bullshit. And I also know that you might stand a better chance of the Republican nomination in 2008 if you are out of the White House and well away from a disastrous war.'

'Hmmm,' David Hickox said with a grin, 'I never thought about it like that, Robmeister. Maybe you should have gone into politics.'

They started walking again. The trees were in bud and in many the leaves had already burst open. It was going to be a long, warm spring. There were a few dog-walkers, and some courting couples walking hand in hand in the sunshine on this most perfect English day in this most perfect of English parks. It was difficult to believe that half a world away British troops were at war in southern Iraq and in Afghanistan, or anywhere else for that matter. When Vice President Hickox spoke again his voice was calm and quiet, almost humbled.

'Robin, we can't win in Iraq. I got it wrong. Team B became Team A and we blew it. The irony is that Saddam was bluffing. And he didn't know that we weren't.'

Robin looked at Hickox with a flash of anger. Hickox's frame was still big, his movements muscular, but there was something hollowed out inside him.

'You had a forty billion dollar a year US intelligence budget and you couldn't do a psychological profile of Saddam Hussein?' Robin responded savagely. 'Now this really is bullshit. You couldn't figure him out for a bluffer? You met Saddam Hussein twice, David. For god's sake, what did you think he was like? His whole career was a series of bluffs interspersed with brutality.'

Hickox was quiet.

'Sure, he was a thug,' he replied eventually. 'A convenient thug, as good as any other. Until he started to cause more problems than he solved. But ... there is something worse, Robin,' he said. 'And I need to tell you, now. As friends.'

Robin said quietly, 'Go on.'

David Hickox took a long sigh. They sat down together on a bench in the sunshine. In front of them a dog-owner with a racquet hit a tennis ball for her retriever to fetch. The dog bounded away. The Secret Service bodyguards had fanned out around the Vice President and were trying to look inconspicuous, but Robin noticed that they eyed the dog-walker suspiciously.

'Do you think your minders believe that woman's tennis ball is a racquet-propelled grenade?' Robin said.

Hickox gave a slight smile.

'British humour,' he said. 'I always liked Benny Hill.'

The Secret Service agents in their formal suits made Robin think of a group of gay businessmen searching for rough trade on the homosexual side of Hampstead heath. The dog-walker again hit the tennis ball hard into the woods. The dog bounded after it. David Hickox started to speak again.

'We think al Qaeda attacks in London this summer are likely,' Hickox said grimly. 'That's the assessment of the CIA, and also of your people. We're all holding our breath, but it could be a 9/11 type of attack on Canary Wharf. There has been a load of chatter ...'

Robin was puzzled. What was this to him any more?

'I'm not with you. Explain.'

'We've put out a special warning to all US embassy personnel to avoid public transport as much as possible. One theory is that there could be a repeat of Atocha here in London.'

Atocha was the main train station in Madrid. It was attacked during the rush hour.

'It wouldn't surprise me,' Robin shrugged. 'We have a generation of young Muslims in Britain who do not feel at home here, or anywhere else on this planet. But you travelled all the way to Hampstead to tell me this, David? I'm flattered.'

They stood up and started to walk again. Hickox smiled.

'Not exactly. Just a bit of foreplay. To keep you interested. There are two other things that brought about my trip to see you. One is political, the other personal. They might … spoil our friendship, but I want to clear everything up before I go, before they make the announcement of my retirement. You were in on the take-off of all we did in Iraq, so I want you to be there for the landing.'

Robin opened his eyes wide.

'It sounds like a crash landing. Go on.'

'Political first. We've … we've been dusting off plans to confront Iran militarily. Perhaps in 2008.'

Again, Robin was not as surprised as he might have been.

'Just before the election?'

'Yes.'

'You know I always thought that would be a mistake,' Robin told him. 'A war with Iran would be a catastrophic misjudgement which would cause us problems for decades to come – decades.'

Hickox strongly disagreed.

'It would be a preventative war, Robin. A war to take them on before they develop the bomb. Last month I was in Riyadh. The Saudis told me that if the choice was either a quick war against the Persians and dislocation in the Gulf for six months, or having to live forever with the Iranians having a nuclear bomb, they want the war. They want the fucking war, Robin. That's what the Emirates say too. And if we do not give it to them, the Saudis say they will create their own bomb. You want two nuclear powers in the region? One defending Mecca? The other inspiring a Shia revolution?'

Robin looked at Hickox with contempt.

'Three,' Robin corrected him. 'Three nuclear powers in the region. Israel already has …'

'I know what Israel already has,' David Hickox shot back. 'And I know what Israel is prepared to do with it.'

322

A surge of anger swept over both men. Robin felt his face flush hot.

'Fighting a preventative war for peace as you call it,' Robin Burnett snarled, 'is like killing yourself because you are frightened of dying. You are fucking mad, David. Absolutely fucking mad. I'm glad you are resigning. You have fucked up everything – everything – by your arrogance and incompetence. I just hope that whoever succeeds you ...' Robin Burnett grew so angry the words would not come. The saliva in his mouth tasted like poison. He turned away from Hickox and spat in the grass. 'Fucking mad,' was all he could manage. They stood for a few minutes glaring at each other in angry silence.

'We'd better be getting back,' Hickox said calmly. 'Can't keep the PM waiting.'

They turned and walked briskly back along the path towards the apartment, each man glad their meeting was coming to an end. Both were convinced their friendship was now at an end too.

As they neared the road at the edge of the heath the Secret Service guards summoned the limousines and other vehicles in their convoy.

'Don't you want to know what the other thing was that was on my mind?' Hickox asked. Robin glared at him and shrugged.

'Maybe you've pissed me off enough for one day. Go on. Get it all off your chest.'

'I have wanted to tell you for years,' Hickox said. 'Years. Because it touches you deeply. Even if we disagree on a lot of things, I have always tried to play it straight with you.'

'Go on,' Robin said brusquely. 'Get on with it.'

'It's about your relationship with Leila.'

Robin stood up to his full height and looked at him. So Hickox did know about Leila. Of course, David Hickox had always known. Again, he was not particularly surprised.

323

'What about Leila?' Robin asked slowly.

'The time she met you first off,' Hickox drawled, and then stopped. The two men looked at each other in silence.

'Yes?' Robin persisted. Hickox was making him beg for it, and Robin resented it. 'Yes, go on.'

'The time she first met you, I ordered her to do it. Leila was working for me. Us.'

Robin felt the sourness of his saliva rise in his mouth once more.

'We sent her to get close to you,' David Hickox said. 'That was the plan. We were talent spotting and you were one of those we picked for the top. And, of course, she did get close to you. A lot closer than any of us expected, but there you are.'

'Leila is a CIA agent?'

'Was. She was a NOC.'

'Knock?'

'Non Official Cover. An agent without diplomatic immunity. She could have been a star for us in the Middle East, but six months after meeting you she confessed that she had fallen in love and she wanted to quit. And she did. Don't be too hard on her, Robin. I just thought it was about time somebody let you in on our little secret, since Leila herself apparently neglected to mention it.'

Robin took a deep breath. His mind was whirring as he tried to process the past. He put his whole life into categories marked 'Real' and 'Phoney'. Leila had always been 'Real'. Until now.

'She told me that she was on the plane with Ayatollah Khomeini.' Robin struggled for something to say. 'In 1979 when he returned from Paris to Tehran to seize power.'

Hickox nodded.

'Yes, I do believe she was.'

'And she also told me that you wanted the United States to shoot down the plane, to kill the Ayatollah.'

Hickox stared at Robin Burnett, his jaw set and firm.

'It would have saved us a load of trouble,' Hickox said. 'Wouldn't it?'

'You would have killed scores of innocent journalists, including Leila, one of your own agents as well as the Ayatollah?'

Hickox merely repeated the answer he had just given.

'Like I say, it would have saved us a load of trouble. Think how many lives would have been saved. Maybe we'd have advised Leila not to get on the plane. You'd have put a bullet in Hitler, wouldn't you?'

They stood motionless and looked at each other for a few seconds.

'Thanks,' Robin Burnett said eventually, 'for clearing all that up.'

'Goodbye, Robin,' Vice President David Hickox responded. 'I guess from the way you look, you want to kill me. I'd recommend that you don't physically strike me, because apart from the fact that I'm a mean son of a bitch and will fight back, one of my good friends in the US Secret Service will probably shoot you.'

'I expect we won't meet again, David.'

'I expect not. But hey, it's been fun. Maybe I'll take your advice and lick my wounds for a year and then see about the Republican nomination in 2008. My heart murmurs might face a remarkable cure. Who knows? It's a pity you lost your stomach for the fight. You were very good in your prime.'

Hickox moved towards the cars as the Secret Service agents ran around and opened and closed doors. Robin noticed that instead of climbing into either of the two waiting limousines, Hickox was ushered into the back of a bullet-proof 4x4 with tinted windows. The Americans clearly were very seriously worried about an attack in London. They were taking no chances, even in Hampstead. Robin watched as the convoy sped off towards central London. He stood at the edge of the heath, trembling, feeling sick and numb. Somehow he got himself back to the apartment. He did not know what to do. He thought of calling Leila and confronting her, though he wondered what point would be served by a trans-Atlantic telephone row. She had lied to him. He, Robin, had lied to more or less everyone. So maybe that's why they were so compatible. But then the bitter saliva rose again in Robin's mouth. The idea that his relationship with Leila was based on an order from David Hickox was so disgusting to him, it felt as if he had been infected by some kind of disease. What had happened to the woman who had smiled upon him in the Locarno Suite at the Foreign Office? Robin sat in the leather chair in the sitting room of the apartment Leila had given him after they broke up, and he wept.

Hampstead and Tetbury, April 2005

When he stopped weeping, Robin Burnett set out systematically to get drunk. By the time Maya returned home from her Farsi class at the School of Oriental and African Studies that night, he was still sitting in the leather chair, but had at least achieved what he intended. His mind was befuddled with whisky, and yet also clearly made up. He knew what he would do. He would return to Tetbury and take his own life. He and Maya had a late night conversation, the details of which he could not much remember when he awoke the following morning with a thudding headache and a sick stomach. He knew he had told Maya he was returning to Tetbury. He instructed her that if she needed anything she could rely on Sidney Pearl. Maya had seemed amused by his drunken state. She had never seen her father like this before. He had never felt the need of alcohol in her company before. That night, in the way of some teenagers, she was also obsessed with a minor philosophical puzzle she had just heard.

'Okay, okay,' she said to Robin excitedly, before he went to bed. 'Here's a riddle, okay? A man sets out to fail. And he succeeds. So what has he actually done?'

His whisky brain could not understand the problem.

'Nobody sets out to fail,' he replied. 'Although Enoch Powell used to say that all political careers end in failure.'

'No, you're not getting it are you?' Maya responded.

He asked her to repeat it. Slowly.

'Okay, here it is again. A man sets out to fail. And he succeeds. So what has he actually done?'

Robin thought for a moment.

'Well, if you succeed in failing,' he replied, 'then of course you fail. It's a play on words, not a philosophical problem. Succeeding at failing logically is not a success of any sort. It is a failure. But if the words mean something slightly different – that the man succeeded in whatever task he set himself, as opposed to failing in that task, then he succeeded. Which is a real success.'

Maya still thought that he just didn't get it.

'Mom says that you think like an economist,' she told him.

'Of course I do,' he responded. 'It's what I am.' And then he paused and thought a bit more. 'Is that a compliment?'

'I don't believe so,' she giggled.

Robin helped himself to one more whisky and took it with him into the bedroom.

'G'night, Maya, darling,' he called out over his shoulder. 'I love you very much. I have always loved you.'

'Goodnight, dad.'

The next morning Maya awoke around ten. She noticed that Robin had risen earlier and tidied the apartment. 'What's on the cards for you today?' he asked her calmly.

When she thought about it afterwards, Maya could not recall anything particularly unusual. Perhaps he seemed a little subdued, hungover.

'I'm going to complete my research on the timetable of events for the last year you were in the government,' she replied. 'We need a guide for people who don't remember, or who are too young to remember. Two weeks' work max. Copy editing from now on. Your work is done, dad. It's a great read. *A Scandalous Man.* Cool, eh?'

'Yes, cool,' he admitted.

He had checked and re-checked the manuscript. His agent had seen the first draft and she thought all it needed was more historical context, facts and figures about the Falklands War, the Wapping crisis, the miners' strike, the economic performance of the UK and so on. Robin also wanted Maya to do more research on the 1991 Gulf war against Iraq, because he saw it as a pivotal moment.

'Remember, Maya, that it needs to be very clear that the invasion of Kuwait by Saddam Hussein in August 1990 was one of the inevitable consequences of our own failures since the Iranian Revolution of 1979,' he lectured her. 'The US ambassador to Iraq, April Glaspie, had specifically told Saddam ...'

Maya interrupted in a weary voice.

'... she specifically told Saddam that the United States had no views on inter-Arab disputes, which Saddam interpreted as a green light to invade Kuwait. It's there, dad. All of it. We've gone through it a thousand times. It's clear. Clear to me at least and I was – what? – three years old at the time.'

'But the key thing to remember is that it links to Afghanistan and the invasion of Iraq two years ago,' he persisted. 'Our current state of crisis. I want this to be absolutely clear. All the conflicts have their roots in decisions we took in the 1980s and in response to the extraordinary events of 1979 during which ...'

'During which my brother Harry was born,' Maya interrupted him again, slightly exasperated. 'The year you were first elected to parliament and Margaret Thatcher took power. I know. Believe me, dad, I really do know.'

'Indeed,' Robin Burnett said, but again the taste of poison was in his saliva.

'Dad, stop worrying. You'll have plenty of time to nit-pick when I get you the final draft. Just a couple of weeks.'

Robin Burnett said nothing. The one thing he did not have was plenty of time.

'And oil,' he said. 'It was always about oil. We can't stress that enough. An attempt to inoculate us against the repeat of the oil shocks that followed the 1973 Arab–Israeli war …'

Maya rolled her eyes to the heavens and let him talk a bit more, then when it was polite to do so, she left for the day. Robin hugged her and kissed her on both cheeks.

'I love you, you know.'

'I know. And I love you, dad.'

'Whatever happens. I always loved you. Always.'

Maya felt slightly embarrassed.

'When will you be back from Tetbury?' she wondered.

'Oh, soon,' he told her, vaguely. 'Soon enough. Sidney Pearl will make sure you are all right if you need anything.'

'I'm not going to get drunk, get pregnant or get a tattoo, dad. Beyond that, I make no promises. Chill out, gramps.'

Despite his mood, Robin laughed.

'I'm chilled,' he said. 'Yes, gramps is chilled. But, Maya, just one more thing …'

'Yes.'

'Always try to think well of me,' he said slowly.

She wrinkled her brow, puzzled.

'Whatever I did, I did for what I thought was the best. The public good. And I always cared for … loved … you and your mother and Harry and Amanda. Tell your mother that. I always loved her. And I forgive her.'

'God, dad,' she said, 'you *forgive* her? What's she done now? Oh, I don't want to know!'

He laughed again, which surprised her.

'Take care of yourself,' he said as she left the apartment.

'And you too,' she said. 'You weirdo.'

She smiled at her father and gave him a little wave as she walked out the door.

* * *

330

An hour later, Robin Burnett was in his car driving to Tetbury, the hangover still thumping in his head. He had eaten nothing and drunk just a couple of glasses of water. In Tetbury he stopped at an off-licence to buy a bottle of whisky. *The Oban*. He reflected that it would be quite possible to kill himself with a cheaper variety of blended Scotch, but that seemed a rather joyless way to go. It had to be *The Oban*. Then he went to three different pharmacies and in each bought a different set of pills, co-proximol, paracetamol. He opened the door of the cottage and called out for the cleaner.

'Megan? Megan you there?'

Nothing. Good. She was due the following morning, which gave him plenty of time. Megan was a stout country woman who had been brought up on a farm and had given birth to five children. She would not find his death particularly traumatic if he prepared for it carefully. Robin pulled out an envelope and put £200 inside it. He sealed the flap and put Megan's name on the front of the envelope. Then he put the whisky and the pills on the kitchen table, and decided how he would handle things. First, while he was still sober, he would get his will from the filing cabinet and check it over. It left all his property to be divided equally among his three children, Harry, Amanda and Maya. He folded the will into an envelope and addressed it to his solicitor, stuck on a second class stamp then walked out to the post box at the end of the lane.

Back in the cottage, he brought out the title deeds to the apartment in Hampstead, and started to read through them. As he did so, his eyes misted over. The place in Hampstead touched him very deeply. He wondered if Leila had given him the apartment as a result of her guilt. Or as a result of her love? Or perhaps both. Robin sighed. It did not really matter any more.

He checked his watch. Nine o'clock, British time, which meant it was four in the afternoon in New York. Too early to call Leila. She would be preparing for the *Nightly News* which was broadcast first at 11.30 p.m. UK time. He could not possibly call her before she went on air. It would be cruel to make her upset. It would be wrong.

Robin went to the kitchen and took a sharp knife from the drawer, then opened the bottles of pills. He returned to the sitting room and put each bottle on the floor around the chair he'd placed in the middle of the room, with the kitchen knife in front, as if in a pagan religious ceremony. Perhaps in a way it was. He filled a jug with cold water then reached for his favourite Tyrone crystal whisky tumbler. He poured himself a drink from the new bottle of whisky, switched on the TV and watched the late evening news. It was full of speculation about whether the Prime Minister would announce the General Election date the following day, and head for his third election victory, a record for a Labour leader. Robin Burnett was convinced Blair would indeed call the election, and that he would win. The Tories were pessimistic, backward-looking, crabby. Robin shuddered. Ordinary people always wanted to vote for optimism and hope. That was why they voted for Thatcher. And Attlee. And Blair. That was why they rejected Churchill in 1945, Major in 1997 and would reject Michael Howard in 2005. The iron rule of politics was that optimists always won, pessimists lost, because most of us in our hearts believe problems can be solved and that our children will do better than we have.

The screen flickered in front of him. International news, the strapline said. First there was a report about Britain's chances of securing the 2012 Olympics. The results were expected to be announced sometime in mid summer. Then there was a short item about the visit to Europe of the US Vice President David Hickox. Hickox was in Paris.

'Vice President Hickox, regarded as the most powerful Vice President in American history, is on his way to Moscow and then the Middle East,' the report said, following discussions with the British Prime Minister. *'It's thought that the Vice*

President's schedule is taken up with trying to form a united front against the alleged nuclear threat from Iran. Mr Hickox is said to be an Iran Hawk – the strongest voice within the United States administration urging that Tehran be confronted with military power.'

The pictures showed Hickox getting out of his aircraft in Paris and being greeted on the steps by the French Prime Minister. He was scheduled to address the French National Assembly, stay overnight and then meet President Chirac the following day. Hickox waved a big meaty hand towards the cameras. The BBC's diplomatic editor quipped that he was *'one of the heavyweights of the American government – intellectually speaking, of course. Behind the scenes,'* the report went on, *'diplomats are suggesting that Mr Hickox has a double agenda: visiting key capitals in the hope of trying to rescue American policy in Iraq and Afghanistan, as well as the more overt mission of squeezing Iran. Here in Paris, they are speaking of an intense dialogue – though one western diplomat told me it was a dialogue of the deaf.'*

Robin switched off the television. By midnight he was drunk. He had taken none of the pills, but the bottle of whisky was a third empty. He picked up the telephone and called Leila.

'Miss Rajar is still in studio,' her assistant said. 'But I'll get her to call you back, Mr Burnett.'

'Thank you.'

Half an hour, and another whisky later, Leila called. Her voice, as usual, cheered him.

'Hi, Robin. Good to hear from you. How's Maya? She with you in the country?'

'No,' he replied. 'She needed to stay in London. The Pearls are looking after her. She's fine. I am so proud of her.'

'Me too.' Leila noticed the odd tone in the way he spoke. 'Is there something wrong, Robin? Have you been drinking?'

He took a deep breath.

'Hickox paid me a visit yesterday. He said we needed to talk. He needed to talk. Clear up a few things.'

'Oh,' she replied. He detected an edge of suspicion in her voice.

'Hickox said he is going to resign when he gets back from the Middle East on Monday. Heart problems, apparently. That's the cover story. Political problems, is the fact. The President wants him out. He's a liability, too tarnished by the war.'

'Shit, Robin, that's a great story. There's time for me to get it on our West Coast affiliate feed if I ...'

'Yes, it is a terrific story,' he cut her off very brusquely. 'But you can't use it tonight, Leila. And there was something else. Something much more important to me.'

Leila knew what he was going to say. Leila always seemed to know what he was going to say.

'Something about you.' He could hear her breathing at the other end of the line. 'He said that when you and I first met you were working for him.' She made no attempt at a reply. 'When he was Director of Central Intelligence. He made it sound like you were paid to get close to me. He said you were an agent of the CIA, a NOC, he called it. Non Official Cover. Like knock on wood.'

'Yes, Robin,' she responded, her voice weighed down with remorse, 'Hickox is telling the truth. I was told to get close to you. But not that close. That was my decision. And whatever Hickox said, it does not mean that anything between us was false. He did not instruct me to sleep with you or fall in love with you, which I did. He did not instruct me to get pregnant by you, which I did. And he did not instruct me to break it off, which I did. There was nothing false about the way I felt about you.'

'I note you use the past tense.'

'I ... we... oh, come on, Robin ... there *is* nothing false about the way I feel about you now, either, you know that ...'

'You were ordered to meet me?'

'Yes.'

'You worked for the CIA at the same time you were a reporter?'

'Yes. When my father left Iran for Los Angeles, they were very helpful to the whole family. They made settling down in California easy. I'm a patriotic American, Robin, you know that. Why shouldn't I be? Why shouldn't I serve my country? They paid me to get close to the Ayatollah Khomeini too. But I didn't fall in love with him. I guess he wasn't my type. Something to do with the beard.'

'Don't trivialize it,' he snapped. 'You lied to me.'

There was a long pause on the line.

'Yes,' she admitted.

When he responded his voice had a coldness in it that she did not recognize.

'Let me ask you one straight question,' he demanded.

'If you must.'

'Do you still work for Hickox, or for the CIA?'

'As you are well aware,' Leila Rajar replied, 'the CIA is forbidden by law from engaging in domestic intelligence-gathering operations in the United States.'

Robin understood she was not going to answer his question. His blood chilled.

'I think you should come over in the next few days and pick up Maya and take her home to the United States. Goodbye, Leila.'

He put the phone down and grabbed the first bottle of pills. He put them into his mouth in twos and threes and swallowed whisky to make them go down more easily. Then he grabbed at a second bottle of pills and repeated the process. He noticed his hands were shaking and his breathing was uneven. The telephone rang. He knew it was Leila but he let it ring and ring.

He poured another whisky and swallowed some more pills, washing them down with *The Oban* as if the whisky were

335

water. In the Gaelic language the word for whisky, *usquebeagh*, literally means 'water of life'. Or in this case, he reflected, water of death. Robin Burnett repeated the process over and over until he began to feel strange. He sat down in the chair in the middle of the room, surrounded by pots of pills. He straightened his tie and smoothed the collar of his dark blue suit. He took one more slug of whisky and dropped the glass and the bottle together onto the floor, then he picked up the kitchen knife and slit his wrist, quickly followed by a slash to his right wrist. Blood pumped down his fingers and dripped on to the carpet. There was very little pain, just a dull discomfort and the sucking sound of blood in his ears like the sound of sand churned up by the waves on a beach. The last thing he was aware of was that the telephone was still ringing, again and again, like a fire alarm in the night. He slumped back in the chair. His hand dropped the Tyrone crystal whisky glass which rolled across the carpet and then came to a halt against one of the empty pill bottles.

5 May 2005, *Election Day*

The date of the third Blair election victory was 5 May 2005. Propitiously or otherwise, that meant it was 05.05.05. That morning Harry and Zumrut rose early in the flat in Hampstead. There was no point at which they had formally decided to live together. They just fell into it as a kind of routine, and never went back to living separately. Maya awoke too and joined them for breakfast. Harry drank a quick coffee and kissed Zumrut goodbye as she headed for the university library to work on her thesis. Maya left for SOAS in Bloomsbury and a day of Farsi lessons, though she wanted to get up early enough to watch people go into the polling stations to vote. She thought it would be interesting to see how it was done in the United Kingdom compared to the United States. Harry took the Tube to Fulham to go to work as a volunteer for the Labour party. He himself voted just as the polls opened, and then stood outside the polling station – a local primary school – with two other Labour party activists. They held in their hands copies of the electoral register, marked to show the likely Labour voters. Shortly after eight the party agent for Fulham, Redknapp, appeared with half a dozen coffees in paper cups.

'How's it going?'

'Slow,' Harry said, comparing things to the other election victories of 2001 and 1997. 'Very slow. Turnout way down on last time. Our people are taking a win for granted. That could be a mistake.'

'Party activists way down too,' Redknapp muttered. It meant he had spare coffees. He handed them out first to the Labour workers and then offered the extras to the volunteers from the other parties. They smiled gratefully as they began to endure their day of shared suffering on behalf of democracy.

'It looks like I've only got you two till one o'clock. Sorry, but people just don't want to work this time. Is that okay with you, Harry?'

'Sure,' Harry replied.

'And I'm sorry we could not use you for canvassing, but not with the assault charges still pending,' Redknapp went on. 'If there had been more trouble with the press following you around and maybe you belting someone …'

'It's fine,' Harry said. 'Really, it's fine. I didn't mind sitting this one out. Though John Prescott belting someone last time around did us no end of good.'

John Prescott was the deputy Prime Minister and had punched a man who threw an egg at him in the previous General Election. Prescott's popularity went up. Voters, Harry thought, prefer human frailties to robotic machine politicians.

Over the next hour or two a straggle of voters emerged from the polling station.

As they did, Harry and the other party workers moved towards them and politely asked for their polling cards. The way it worked was bounded by British etiquette. The party workers never asked voters which way they had voted. Voters would take great offence at that presumption. But what the party workers did do was to ask for their polling cards so that they could see the identity of those who had turned out to vote and who had not. The lists of who had voted and who had not were then compared with the returns from the party can-vassers. Late in the afternoon, Redknapp would go through the returns and target any supposedly 'certain' Labour voters who had not yet turned out. These were voters who had said 'yes' on the doorstep to the Labour canvassers but who had not yet appeared at the polling station. Between late afternoon and the polls closing at ten o'clock, each one of these supposedly 'cer-tain' Labour voters would hear a knock on the door from a friendly party worker offering to give them a lift to the polling station. This last-minute push could win or lose the seat.

'I can help get you there,' the party workers would announce cheerfully. 'No problem.'

The Tories and Liberal Democrats had their own teams, doing the same thing. The Tory team included a nice middle class white lady and a young Asian man who said he was a student but who was dressed in a smart blue suit, white shirt and blue tie. By mid morning the Tory workers were joined by a fat man with a red face who looked as if he had spent the previous night, indeed most previous nights in the past twenty years, drinking too much red wine. The Lib Dems had a lone-ly thin man with a beard, who refused Redknapp's offer of a coffee. He protested that he could not possibly touch any Starbucks products for some ethical reason Harry did not quite catch. Then by mid-morning a tiny bird-like Asian woman in a hejab also arrived. She told Harry she was from Respect, one of the anti-war parties which, as far as Harry could tell, had been formed by ageing white Trotskyites plus disaffected young British Muslims who liked the party's anti-war stridency. Women in hejabs and thin-faced Trots seemed to Harry to be an odd combination, but at least they had something in common: no sense of humour. The woman in the hejab was cheerful enough at first. She said her name was Abeer and she chatted amiably with Harry and the nice Tory lady, until she was joined later that morning by a thin-faced white man, who whispered something to her, at which point

Abeer moved away to the other side of the polling station gates, and said nothing further to anyone. Harry thought her Trot friend probably did not want to get her contaminated by bourgeois values, like socializing.

By the time the fresh Labour volunteers turned up at one o'clock, a couple of things were obvious to Harry. Labour was going to hold the seat, just. But a majority of people had voted against the Labour candidate. Labour would be returned to office but with the lowest vote of any winning party in modern times. The anti-war vote was split. In Harry's area, the Liberal Democrats took about half, and Respect the other half. If the two had combined with some of the smaller parties or a handful of Conservatives, the Labour candidate would have lost. More than a third of voters – edging up to a half in some solid Labour areas – had decided to stay at home.

'The voters want us to win,' Harry told Redknapp at the changing of his shift at one o'clock. 'But only because they hate everyone else more.'

Redknapp shook his head.

'They don't want us to win, Harry,' Redknapp replied. 'People don't want anybody to win any more. It's like a war in which they want everyone to lose.'

Harry shrugged.

'Can you believe the cynicism of people who simply want everyone to lose?' he said. 'What kind of a country would that be? What kind of a hopeless world?'

Redknapp shrugged, but did not try to answer. It was a day to get the vote out, not a day for politics. He had work to do. Redknapp moved off to the next polling station, while Harry returned to Hampstead.

When he arrived back at the apartment, Sidney Pearl was on duty on the front desk.

'Did you vote, Sidney?'

'Of course,' he said with a smile. 'I always vote. It's my civic duty.'

'And may I ask who you voted for?'

Sidney smiled again.

'You may ask,' Sidney responded. 'But I believe I have a right to secrecy, Harry.'

'Indeed you do,' Harry said. 'So you voted Conservative then. They're the ones who are always ashamed to admit to it.'

Sidney laughed and then looked down at the paperwork on his desk.

The apartment was empty. Maya was still out. She had done a short tour of polling stations on her way to SOAS, and then again during her lunch break, taking the Tube to Camden. She wanted to get a sense of election day in the British capital, thinking it might be useful, in some way, when she began at Princeton. Maya was disappointed to discover it was much like any other day, though she was pleased to find that unlike the United States, voting was a simple matter. It took a few seconds, and involved pencil and paper rather than voting machines. There were never queues at the polling stations. Nor were there hanging chads.

Zumrut worked assiduously in the university library until five o'clock and then also returned to the Hampstead apartment. Harry was sipping black tea in front of the television, watching BBC News 24. She kissed him.

'How is it going?'

Harry replied that it was one of the most boring days in the most boring election campaign that he had ever experienced.

'Boring?' Zumrut scoffed, incredulous. 'You want interesting? Never mind George Bush being interesting as Maya says, what about in Turkey? We have interesting bombs. We have interesting violent demonstrations. We have Islamists. We have threatened coups by the army. Boring politics is good politics, I keep telling you Harry. Boring is a sign of maturity. You really do not know how lucky you are. You should be proud to be boring British in your boring democracy, you boring man.'

Harry laughed and said he would think about it as he got her some tea. Then Zumrut sat on his lap and obscured his view.

'I think I know how to make this a lot more interesting,' she told him as she began to kiss him. She reached for the remote and switched it off. 'Come to bed now. If you are going to watch the results later with Maya, it will be a long night.'

'I think I can be persuaded to take some rest now,' Harry said, and they went into the bedroom together.

The woman who called herself Polly Black also voted early, at around eight in the morning. She voted Labour. Then she travelled to work at the Westminster headquarters of the Security Service MI5, a few blocks along from Parliament and across the river from the much more ostentatious new headquarters of MI6, the Secret Intelligence Service. Polly never quite understood how the foreign intelligence service managed to have a far better building than MI5. One of these days perhaps someone would tell her. She would spend the morning studying the latest intelligence on Talal Ul-Haq and Rafiq Chowdhury. Transcripts of the authorized wiretaps on both men's mobile phones were usually available within twenty-four hours.

They were on the highest possible priority list for transcription and – since they sometimes spoke in Urdu – for translation also. Both men were talking with a growing circle of contacts in Pakistan. Inevitably translating from Urdu meant that some wiretaps took longer to process, but the drift of the conversations was now clear: an attack on London was imminent. Polly fretted. Everything worried her. She was sure she was on to something very important, but was not absolutely clear yet what it was. She worried that the men would buy half a dozen pay-as-you-go mobile phones and would keep changing the ones they used, making life more and more difficult. Fortunately, to save money, Rafiq did the opposite. He used Skype to call his contacts in Pakistan. Since MI5 had placed a Trojan in Rafiq's computer, recording his conversations became very easy.

On election day, Polly arrived in the office shortly after 8.30 a.m. and clicked on her own computer. She called up the latest wiretap transcripts, reading through them quickly, stopping only at those bits already highlighted by the translator. Rafiq and Talal were now often talking in a kind of crude code about 'assignments' and 'product' and 'documents' and 'business meetings up above or down below'. Up above, they took to mean Afghanistan. Down below, Pakistan. It was not exactly clear. Rafiq spoke on Skype with a contact in Quetta about once every ten days, promising that there would be great celebrations when they eventually were able to meet.

'Much joy,' he said. 'Much pleasure.'

Rafiq called this contact 'Samir'. Samir told Rafiq that he would arrange for travel documents and 'plenty of flour' to be delivered to him at the Green Mosque in north London. 'Flour' seemed to be the crude code word for money. The Quetta contact said that 'the entire family would be pleased to welcome them after they had concluded their business in London.' Rafiq asked if there was any date set for the conclusion of the London business. Samir said that his family had indeed decided on a date. It was to be July 7th, with the possibility of a further business meeting using other members of the family on July 21st.

'Good,' Rafiq replied. 'July 7th. Very good. All will be ready by then.'

Polly studied the remaining intercepts. They showed, among other things, that Rafiq and Talal frequently used their computers to visit Jihadi websites and chat rooms, under a variety of identities. Talal had downloaded a vast amount of material on the manufacture and use of explosives, much of it from US right-wing militia websites. He seemed particularly interested in the explosive possibilities of fertilizer bombs, plus those involving various chemicals combined with hydrogen peroxide.

Talal's downloads showed that he was also very curious about Heathrow airport. He had downloaded numerous rather dull environmental impact statements on the future plans to build Heathrow's Terminal Five. Polly noted that all the reports contained detailed maps of the existing four terminals at Heathrow and the key transport routes into the airport, including the Piccadilly Underground line. Talal also used his computer to check two bank accounts, one of which appeared to receive regular donations coinciding with talk of the arrival of 'flour'. The 'flour' came from an account run by one of the leading preachers at the Green Mosque, the man known as 'Omar', who in turn received frequent donations from a madrassa attached to the Red Mosque in the Pakistani capital, Islamabad.

Polly checked through MI6 with its Pakistani sources including those in the ISI, Pakistan's intelligence service. They were not always reliable, and were assumed to be infiltrated by Islamist elements, given that they had spent years helping the Taleban in Afghanistan. But the ISI sources confirmed that the Red Mosque in Islamabad was a centre of militant Islamist preaching. The ISI believed that the men inside had stockpiled enough weaponry to equip a small army. The Pakistani President Pervez Musharraf – according to MI6 – was trying to figure out when, and under what conditions, he could afford to send in regular Pakistani troops to disarm the militants in the Red Mosque, and to kill the agitators. It was, Polly was told, a work in progress. It could take some time.

By around ten in the morning, Polly convinced herself for the first time that the police now had enough information to act, to break up what she was convinced was a bomb plot to attack Heathrow airport.

She needed legal advice on whether they also had enough for successful prosecutions of Rafiq and Talal and several associates who appeared on the fringes of the group, including a man from Leeds called Mohammed Sidique Khan. Polly was agitating for a meeting with her superiors, with Special Branch and the Anti-terrorist Command of the Metropolitan Police to decide how and when to proceed. Pressure on resources meant that the surveillance of Mohammed Sidique Khan and his associates had been suspended to concentrate on others like Talal and Rafiq. The Security Service simply could not do everything. The intelligence on Rafiq and Talal was sound, but did not amount to enough yet for criminal convictions. None of the wiretap intercepts nor the Trojan material would be admissible as evidence in court.

That meant they needed to obtain search warrants for the various premises associated with Talal and Rafiq, including a lock-up garage in Boston Manor, near the Piccadilly line Tube station of the same name. It was on the route to Heathrow airport.

It was a big decision. If armed police went in to the houses of Talal and Rafiq and possibly others, and found nothing, there would be a backlash in parts of the Muslim community. If they did not go in, there could be a bomb at Heathrow airport or on the Tube line out to the airport complex. Polly drummed her fingers on her desk. Her mind kept turning to the comments of the man in Quetta who called himself 'Samir'. The date set for the 'business meeting' she repeated to herself, was July 7th with possibly a second meeting two weeks later. She checked her diary. That was just sixty days away. Just two months to make it stick. Polly rose from her desk and went to talk to her line manager. Someone around here needed to start taking decisions. Now would be a good time.

* * *

Around noon on the day of the 2005 General Election, David Pearl, the younger son of Sidney Pearl was found by one of his friends lying in his own vomit in a squat in Dalston, northeast London. David Pearl shared the squat with a dozen other people, all of them habitual drug users. Someone called an ambulance. David Pearl was still breathing when the ambulance crew arrived. By the time they reached the hospital and cleaned him up, David seemed a bit better, but the doctor told him he should stay in for observation and tests. He agreed. He thought he had been the victim of a bad batch of heroin adulterated with some kind of cleaning powder. It had an unpleasant smell, but David had injected it anyway. The doctors said they were not so much worried about the drugs, as about David's liver. They finally wormed out of him a contact number for a relative – his older brother Jez who had emigrated to Israel and now ran a small tourism business and a night club in Tel Aviv. One of the doctors called Jez and advised him to phone his parents which – after a conversation with David – he eventually did . By ten o'clock on the night of election day, as the counting of votes around the country began, a very worried Sidney Pearl and his wife Rachel sat down with their youngest son in the hospital and fretted about his condition. David Pearl admitted that he was glad to see his mother and father, and glad that his brother Jez was coming back from Israel to see him too. It didn't occur to him that the reason Jez was returning in a hurry was because the doctors had told both Jez and his parents that he might not have long to live.

Shortly after seven o'clock on the morning of election day Rajiv Khan cycled, as usual, to his office in Stoke Newington.

He was inclined to vote, but first he had seventeen separate asylum cases on his desk, and he wanted to figure out where he should concentrate his efforts. Raj made a large mug of black coffee and slumped in his chair. When he voted, Raj decided, he would vote for the Liberal Democrats. He had never done so before and he was not especially in love with the party, but they had consistently opposed the Iraq war. So, of course, had Respect, but Raj was very unimpressed by what he called the 'Islamo-Trots'.

He pushed the black coffee to one side and began sifting through the files of those seventeen cases – Iranians, Afghans, Kurds of various nationalities, Algerians, Sudanese and Somalis. Some of the asylum cases, Raj was sure, were probably winnable. But which? Most, nowadays, were hopeless. The mood had changed. Raj thought of his job as a kind of legal triage. Like the first doctor at the scene of a catastrophic accident he decided which of the cases were worth fighting for, which might survive with an amputation, and which he might simply have to let die. Mostly, Raj thought, he was nowadays not so much an advocate in court as a witness to the suffering of others.

'You voted yet?' May McCarthy, one of the other asylum-case lawyers called out to him later that morning.

Raj shook his head. A voice whispered deep down inside that one vote was irrelevant, one vote was pathetic. One vote changed nothing. 'No,' Raj said. 'Not yet.' Silently he argued with himself, thinking of Zumrut's impassioned defence of the right to vote and her arguments against the logic of Talal and Rafiq.

'They never understand that a vote is a weapon which they can use,' Zumrut had lectured him and Harry, 'and which if they do not use, they can hardly blame the government for treating them as if they were of no account.'

Zumrut was right. May McCarthy was right. Democracy was worth an effort.

'You really should vote,' May nagged him gently. 'Nothing will change if you don't.'

'Nothing will change if I do,' he responded glumly. 'But you are right, May. I will vote. I promise.'

'I voted for Respect,' she said. 'I held my nose, and I voted for that gobshite Don Flockart.'

'Why, for god's sake?' Raj wondered. Flockart was the Respect candidate with the best chance of winning a seat. 'You told me last week you'd rather vote for the Devil. Flockart's a psychopath.'

May made herself a coffee.

'True. But I couldn't vote for Blair this time. And if Flockart does get elected, there's only going to be one of him. What harm can he do? He'll just be an irritant, reminding Blair that we haven't all fallen into line. At least it shows we care. So, vote, Raj, damn you.'

May went to her office and sat behind her own stack of new asylum cases.

'Okay, okay,' Raj told himself. 'I will vote. Argument over. Now get down to work.'

He would vote at lunchtime, he told himself. Definitely. Then the telephone rang.

'The governor of Deetcham Holding Centre,' his secretary said. 'A Mister Craig Falwell.'

'Put him through. Governor Falwell?'

'Yes,' the voice said, 'Craig Falwell. Is that Rajiv Khan?'

'Yes it is. What can I do for you, Governor?'

There was a sigh at the other end of the line.

'I have some bad news for you about one of your clients, an Iraqi man, Mahmoud Alani. We had some trouble here at Deetcham overnight.'

Trouble at Deetcham was not new. Men with nothing to lose locked up twenty-four hours a day prior to being deported were not usually compliant prisoners.

'Yes? What kind of trouble?'

Mahmoud Alani was not one of the seventeen new cases on Raj's desk for that day. He was an old case, one that was already lost. Alani was an Iraqi engineer in his thirties, an intelligent, educated man with a family back in Iraq. He was due to be deported the following weekend. When Raj had last seen him, he was very distressed. Alani's English was about as good as Rajiv's Arabic, but he made it clear that if he were to be returned to Iraq he would face being killed. His family were mostly business people in the Sunni triangle, near Ramadi. Two uncles and four cousins had already been killed because one of the family had been working as an interpreter for the Americans. The stress of trying to avoid deportation had aged Alani greatly. He had a thin, lined face and a sagging mouth which made him look twenty years older than he was. A gum infection led to several of his upper teeth falling out. It gave him a pitiful look, sunken gums, hollowed out cheeks, the shadow of a man.

'I'm afraid Mr Alani is dead, Mr Khan. He appears to have hanged himself during the night using bed-sheets. We are investigating the circumstances.'

'Was he not on suicide watch?'

'Yes, of course,' the Governor replied. 'But do you know how many detainees we now have on suicide watch? Dozens, Mr Khan. It is very distressing for us, but we are simply over-whelmed by the numbers.'

'You appear to be containing your distress rather well,' Rajiv sniped. 'And you also have a duty of care which you appear unable to fulfil.'

If the governor of Deetcham was insulted, he did not show it.

'One does one's best to be professional even under the most trying of circumstances,' he said. 'Perhaps you can tell the family that we are sorry.'

'Yes of course.'

Raj put the phone down. All thoughts of voting in the election now cleared from his head. The seventeen new cases would have to wait. He settled down to try, somehow, to contact the Alani family in Ramadi, and tell them that the British state was sorry about the death of their son.

Rafiq Chowdhury spent much of the morning of election day in bed. He had gone to sleep late and then risen at dawn for prayers, returning to bed for a few hours more. Six weeks before election day he had rented a small lock-up garage in Boston Manor, several miles away from where he lived in Greenford. At around noon on election day, according to the MI5 watchers, Rafiq rose and drove south from Greenford to Boston Manor in his old Nissan Micra. The listening devices in the car revealed Rafiq was cursing repeatedly at the noise from the car's exhaust. It was becoming so loud that he feared it had started to draw attention to him. People stared when he sat at traffic lights, the car farting like a mechanical beast. In Hanwell, near the clock tower in the square on the Uxbridge road, two police officers looked at him aggressively, but the lights changed and Rafiq drove on. He decided he would have to spend money to have the exhaust fixed, though in the great scale of things it seemed a useless indulgence.

He drove through Boston Manor and parked the Micra in front of a row of lock-up garages. He opened the rusty garage door. Then he reversed the car inside, and closed the door in front of him, bolting it from the inside. The car was so small there was plenty of room for it as well as the four dark green wheelie bins at the back of the garage. Rafiq examined each in turn. They contained around a hundred kilos of fertilizer of the type used in Northern Ireland for decades by the IRA to make home-made bombs. It was known in Ulster as 'Co-Op Mix'. Rafiq checked the Co-Op Mix carefully. Each of the bins was intact. Good. They had not been tampered with, as far as he could tell. When he finished he sealed the bins again with grey gaffer's tape and marked the joins with a black pen so that the lines matched exactly. On a shelf behind the bins were two plastic bags filled with detonators that Talal had managed to obtain from a contact in Yorkshire. The bags were sealed tight and Rafiq did not open them. Instead he felt through the plastic to make sure the contents were as he had left them. They were. Rafiq never found out who the contact in Yorkshire was. What he did know was that the detonators were of fully professional manufacture, of the type used in quarries or coal mines.

According to the report sent to Polly Black by the MI5 watchers, Rafiq spent just over fifteen minutes in the lock-up, and then he left. His movements were captured by Security Service cameras which were activated every time the door of the lock-up was opened. At precisely the same time Rafiq was inspecting the Co-Op Mix chemicals Polly Black was in MI5 headquarters in a meeting arguing – successfully – that they should substitute the potentially explosive chemicals for others which looked the same but which were inert. They would leave the detonators, untouched. On their own, the detonators could not do much damage. Then Polly sat down for a second meeting with anti-terrorist officers from the Metropolitan Police to begin the planning of a series of raids to neutralize the threat from Rafiq, Talal and their associates, she hoped forever.

Talal Ul-Haq was wakened by his mother on election day at seven in the morning. She was going out. She had no intention of voting. She had never filled in a polling card and was not on the electoral roll. It had never crossed her mind. Instead she had to rush to the first of her two jobs, cleaning for a private service company at Ealing Hospital. Talal's mother had been cleaning at Ealing Hospital for years, and used to enjoy the work. She had felt part of the National Health Service hospital team, encouraged by the nurses to chat with patients. But more recently they had changed the system. Now she was working for a private contractor who wanted her to do the same work for longer hours and less pay and who grew irritated at any contact between the cleaners and the nursing staff or patients.

'I don't pay you to chat to patients,' the contractor told her roughly the last time he caught her doing so. 'I pay you to clean. Now get on with it. And keep your gobby mouth shut.'

That morning of election day she was already in a bad mood. Too little sleep.

'Come on, Talal.' She shook her son violently. She was a small woman but with strong arms and hands. 'I have not got time for this. I will miss my bus. Get out of bed. Now! Come on. No son of mine ...'

And so it began. What Talal thought was the daily routine of nagging. The maternal harangue. Part of him understood his mother's impatience. She had a dog's life. She would clean in the hospital from eight in the morning until four in the afternoon and then return home and clean and cook. Then most evenings she would also work in a halal fast-food fried chicken restaurant until midnight, returning home with her hair and clothes smelling of fried food and fat. Talal could not bear the smell of his own mother, and it made him ashamed.

He thought she seemed particularly grumpy, her grip on his shoulder unusually rough. He could smell that she had worked late at the fast-food the night before. She had washed herself in the shower, but she still smelled of grease because she had put on the same work-clothes.

'Get up, Talal! Will you get up, boy!'

She pulled the covers from him and shouted at him for his laziness.

'One week,' she shouted at him. 'One week, Talal, and then if you do not have a job, you are out of here. D'you hear me? Out!'

Then she banged shut the bedroom door, and thumped downstairs. His mother had made the same threats before, many times. Talal did not take them especially seriously. Nevertheless, he had reasons for wanting a quiet life for the next few weeks. The man they called 'Samir', the contact in Pakistan, had warned them to ensure there was 'no excitement' in their lives until July. Talal found his jeans thrown roughly across the chair in the corner of his bedroom and pulled out his battered leather wallet. He ran down the stairs in his boxer shorts after his mother. She had put on her coat and was about to go out the front door to the bus stop. He had another whiff of the fried fat smell. Talal handed his mother three £20 notes. She looked at him, surprised, then she stuffed the money into her handbag without asking any questions.

'I did a few odd jobs at the mosque,' Talal said unconvincingly, though his mother had not asked for any explanation. 'Abu Omar paid me. I meant to give it to you last night, but you were out working when I got in from Arabic classes, and then I fell asleep.'

His mother looked at him quizzically. She was sure he was lying to her, but still she said nothing. Then she left to catch her bus to the hospital. Her sour mood was slightly dissipated by the unexpected gift. Talal went back to bed for a few hours, then rose and sat by his computer. He received news pop-ups but closed them all immediately. The British General Election did not interest him. The result was clearly a Labour victory. What interested him was whether he had any emails. He found one from an address used by 'Samir'.

'*My brother,*' Samir wrote, '*please be careful. Take all precautions. These are especially dangerous times. Let us not make mistakes just as we are getting so close to the date of the business meeting. More product and flour available in the usual places, but be more careful now than ever before. In the name of god the Compassionate, the Merciful, may we be successful in our best efforts.*'

'No excitement,' Talal said aloud. 'Until July.'

Mohammed, the Nigerian who had dropped out of the Arabic class, was not entitled to vote. Besides, he had other matters on his mind.

He spent the morning of election day trying to compose a letter appealing against the choice of secondary school offered to his eldest daughter. She was eleven years old and he was sure she was academically gifted. One day, she would make them all proud. But the school his daughter was to be sent to had a bad reputation for violence, indiscipline, poor academic results and for drugs. Mohammed was worried. He had read somewhere that the school was in 'special measures', though he was not entirely sure what this strange phrase might mean. Special meant good, right? Except that this did not seem to be 'special' meaning 'good'. It was a bit of a puzzle. What Mohammed did know, however, was the evidence of his own eyes. Some of the girls walking to the school looked little better than prostitutes. They had heavily painted faces and short, provocative skirts, their bellies exposed and their bodies pierced. Some of them had rolls of fat hanging over their tight skirts in a way he found most unattractive. They smoked and behaved in a foul manner. Mohammed had heard the English term for such girls. It was 'slags'. He forbade the word in his house, where women were to be treated with respect. Mohammed had read in the local newspaper that the school had one of the worst teenage pregnancy rates in England, though he was not sure how they had arrived at such a conclusion. The previous year the head teacher had been stabbed outside the school gates by pupils from a rival school. The newspaper said they had come round for a fight, which the head teacher had bravely tried to stop, but one of the boys had stuck a kitchen knife in his stomach. People said the head teacher had made a full recovery. He was a big man of West Indian origin who many of the pupils found inspiring. He was back behind his desk, but Mohammed had seen the man in the street some mornings and he looked like a ghost, a shadow of his former self. He was not a man able to offer any kind of leadership.

Here was the problem which exercised him that election day. There was a far better school closer to Mohammed's family home. Everyone knew that it was a better school. But it was seriously over-subscribed. Mohammed had heard it said that the way things worked in England was not by family connections or bribery. What worked was that the people who complained most and longest and hardest and who knew how to do so, had a better chance of getting their children into the good school. Mohammed knew he had to do something. He had to complain. But it was difficult for him. Complaints in Kano in Northern Nigeria were like sand in the desert, pointless and omnipresent. But complaints in England, apparently, sometimes did the trick, if you knew how to organize them correctly. And so Mohammed struggled with the letter of complaint to the local education committee, unused to writing in formal English.

He decided to put down as much as he could on paper, and then visit the mosque, to see if anyone there could help him with the correct phrases and vocabulary. When he arrived at the mosque, the imam – who was from Yemen – greeted him in Arabic. The imam had very poor English, much worse than Mohammed's, though he did have a fine singing voice. Mohammed smiled at the man and made a little conversation. Inside he knew there would be a number of young businessmen of Pakistani origin who were completely fluent in English. One of them, he was sure, would help him. The community would stand with him. The previous week the imam had tried to listen to Mohammed's problems and had some of his words translated into Arabic. The imam said through the translator that he would help, though it was difficult to see how a Yemeni-born imam with a poor grasp of English could get Mohammed's daughter into the British state school that he preferred. In fact instead of suggesting the names of men who could write the letter about the good school, the imam offered an alternative.

'The *masjid*,' the imam said using the Arabic word for mosque. 'Here in the mosque. School here soon.'

Mohammed did not understand. There was no school in the mosque. What was the imam talking about? Later Mohammed found out. The news came from one of the Pakistani businessmen he approached to help him write the letter.

'We have made some donations,' the Pakistani businessman said, 'to set up a school within the mosque to educate our children according to strict Islamic principles. One class for boys, another for girls. Your daughter could start here. Keep her away from the slags. It would be very good for her, an entirely separate Islamic education, rather than this state school you want to send her to.'

Mohammed dithered. He was not sure. He wondered whether cutting his daughter off from people in England was the right thing to do, particularly since she wanted to study medicine. Then he remembered the short skirts and the make-up and the teenage pregnancies. He was torn. What should he do for the best? Besides, the Pakistani businessman was being very helpful about the letter-writing business.

'I will think about it,' he told the businessman. 'But please, write the letter of complaint anyway. I do not wish her to go to ...'

'... a school for slags,' the Pakistani businessman said. 'Whores. Of course you must not send her there. I will write the letter, but if it fails to do the trick, please think of sending her here to the new mosque school. We need strength from the *umma*. We need to do things for ourselves, Muslim for Muslim. You are good man, Mohammed. It will work out for the best, *inshallah*.'

Mohammed took the letter of complaint gratefully. He addressed the envelope to the local education department. He licked the flap and sealed it, sticking on a first-class stamp, and said a short prayer as he pushed it into the red letter box. Mohammed thought he should talk to his wife and his daughter to ask their opinions about the mosque school, but he did not like to say so in front of the Pakistani businessman. In northern Nigeria it was normal for a man to consult his wife and daughter. But there were Muslim men here in England who did not understand why a man like Mohammed would feel the need to talk to his wife or any woman about any serious matter at all. It was very confusing. Different people had different views. He walked away from the letter box still saying a prayer, hoping that the English way of complaining would do him some good. He was living here in England now. He thought he should try his best to fit in.

The two Pakistani-born taxi drivers who had started the Intensive Arabic course with Harry, Rafiq and Zumrut and then quickly dropped out, voted that morning in the constituency of Ealing Southall. They voted Labour. They always voted Labour. That was who you voted for. Labour. Then they went to work.

Raj Khan still had not voted. It was not that he didn't have time. By late afternoon and early evening he no longer felt like it. He had spent the day in frustration, trying to contact Mr Alani's family. There was a cousin who supposedly lived in Hackney, but the cousin did not answer his mobile. There were telephone numbers on Mr Alani's papers for relatives in Ramadi, and Raj phoned, but every single line had an unobtainable signal. Eventually, more and more frustrated, he called the Iraqi embassy in London and left a message with one of the diplomats who promised, if possible, to contact the family, or to have the Iraqi police do so. Raj shook his head in despair. Before he left the office that night he called Harry. Arabic lessons were cancelled that evening because Muslim College was being used as a polling place. Raj desperately wanted to talk to his friend about the terrible events of the day.

'I'm really pissed off,' he said and began to explain. He told Harry the story of Alani and the conversation with the governor of the detention centre.

'I had a shitty day too,' Harry said. 'If it's any consolation. Our vote is way down – way down.' He looked at his watch. 'Listen, d'you fancy cycling up the hill to Hampstead? Zumrut and my sister and I were planning to go out for a beer and then order a take-away curry and come back to watch the election results coming in. You're welcome providing you don't heckle too much.'

'Yes to the beer,' Raj said. 'But I'm not sure I could face the results in my current mood. We'll see.'

They agreed to meet in the Hollybush pub in Hampstead. When Raj arrived, Zumrut, Harry and Maya were sitting round a table. Raj was introduced to Maya. He was struck by how attractive she looked. He could see a family resemblance to Harry but Maya had the olive coloured skin of her mother, a spiky hairstyle, and a glorious American accent which made Raj think of a movie star. What also struck him was that both Zumrut and Harry looked completely at ease in each other's company. He was very pleased, and his pleasure helped him uncurl the anxieties of the day.

'Beer?' Harry said. Raj nodded.

'Stella.'

While Maya and Zumrut chatted energetically about the election, Raj was thinking that this was one of the miracles of London. Here was a white English guy and a Turkish woman and a half-American teenager sitting down with a British Asian, drinking beer and about to order a take-away curry, and maybe watch the General Election results for a couple of hours, and that was normal. Completely normal. It was London. Nobody paid any attention. This country wasn't all bad, Raj told himself, as he took the first swigs of the beer. Just shitty and indifferent and full of fuck-heads like the Governor of Deetcham, but not all bad. Zumrut was telling Maya that the Turkish government had sent more than 100,000 troops to the border with the Kurdish regions of Iraq.

'Things could get worse,' Zumrut said. 'If the United States does pull out of Iraq – or when it does – Turkey will not allow an independent Kurdish state in northern Iraq. The Iranians will not allow their Kurdish areas to go independent either.

There is much bitterness towards the Americans, and you could see Turkey and Iran making common cause if Iraq breaks apart.'

'Colin Powell said if you break it you own it,' Maya quoted. 'Looks like we broke it and so we need to fix it. The only trouble is no one has an idea how we do that. No one. You wouldn't start from here, would you?'

Harry scoffed, as he put the remaining beers on the table in front of them.

'If it wasn't for Colin Powell selling the war to the United Nations in the first place, none of this would have happened,' Harry said. 'People believed him because he was credible whereas they wouldn't believe others, like Rumsfeld or that shit Vice President Hickox.'

'Oh, god,' Maya said, 'don't get me started on Hickox. At least be thankful he's quit. Though the word from mom is that he's like Dracula. Never believe he's dead until there's a stake in his heart. They say he might want to run for the presidency.'

Raj was not paying much attention to the substance of the conversation. He was slowly, slowly calming down after his truly odious day.

He looked at Zumrut and thought how she was even more beautiful now she was having an affair with Harry. Her face was glowing. They must be having a lot of sex, he decided. Harry pushed a beer towards Maya.

'Illegal alcohol for my under-age sister,' he whispered.

'Half-sister,' she whispered back. 'And I am barely under age, at least in England.'

'Sister, not half-sister,' he said. 'We don't do things by halves here in London.'

Then Harry turned to Raj and asked him to tell them all about his client and his shitty day. Raj explained.

'He just wanted a better life,' Raj said, talking of Mr Alani's suicide. 'He was an economic migrant. I met him three or four times, before he was carted off to Deetcham. He applied for asylum because he had a genuine fear of persecution or even death in Ramadi, but the real reason he was here was for a better life, and he hated to lie about that. Can you blame him? Is that a crime? Well, yes it is. Because he used his initiative to get in here illegally on a truck from Calais. So they were throwing him out. He got depressed, and he killed himself. Where's the justice in that? It won't even make a couple of lines in the newspapers. He's not some C-list celebrity behaving badly, so it's just not a story.'

They sipped their beers for a moment in silence.

'It's not racism,' Harry said eventually. 'It's xenophobia. The British don't care about a man's skin colour. Or his religion. As a nation we just don't like foreigners. We don't like Germans, French people, Poles, Lithuanians, Iraqis, Afghans. Once it was Jews. Now it is Muslims.'

'It's worse than that,' Raj said, passionately. 'Look at the Cabinet, for god's sake. What's Gordon Brown if not an economic migrant? He came down from Scotland to Westminster to better himself and become Prime Minister one day. Maybe we should hold him in Deetcham and then send him back over the fucking border before he does.'

Zumrut laughed.

'Spoken like a true Little Englander, Raj. Still, I'm pleased to see this country has its ethnic problems too. We have the Kurds. You have the Scots. But what can you do about it? Send in the army? From what I've read the British army is all Scottish anyway. Or you could not vote Labour? They're all Scots too. And if you don't vote Labour, you get something worse.'

Raj sighed. Okay, so he had not voted. He was turning into precisely the kind of Englishman he most despised – the one who whinged but never did anything.

'For the first time in my life I am beginning to understand why people become suicide bombers,' he said slowly. They all looked at him. Harry blinked with surprise.

'Really?'

'Yes really. Voting isn't enough. Putting vegetables in the car exhaust pipes isn't enough. Demonstrating isn't enough. Sometimes, maybe to be taken seriously you just have to ...'

He never managed to finish the sentence. When his words ran into silence he noticed that Zumrut and Harry were holding hands and quietly laughing at him. Maya was looking at Harry and Zumrut, too, then she turned to Raj and she was beaming at him.

'You don't believe that,' Maya said. 'You're bullshitting. You know it is an excuse.'

He smiled back.

'Yes I am bullshitting. But I should have voted. I think apathy is immoral.'

'And you believe that as a lawyer you can change things?' Maya persisted.

'Yes I believe that as well,' Raj said, blushing. She had him figured out. 'Though it feels like the Myth of Sisyphus. Every time I roll this massive rock to the top of the hill, somehow I lose control of it and it rolls down again.'

Maya put her hand on his arm.

'One day,' she smiled, 'you'll get the rock onto the top of the hill and it will stick, and then you'll be proud of your persistence. You'll see.'

'Well,' Raj said, pulling on his pint, 'yes, you are right. I will persist. It's just been a long day and a bad day, that's all.'

Maya looked at him, remembering something strange Raj had said a moment before.

'And what do you mean, putting vegetables into exhaust pipes isn't enough? What's that about?'

Zumrut and Harry laughed at Raj's embarrassment. He started a long conversation explaining to Maya what he had been doing as a kind of environmental political activism. As he spoke and looked at the way she watched him, Raj was thinking that there were many things in life better than being involved in an act of terrorism. He would join Harry and the

361

others in eating their late night take-away curry, and he would sit in front of the television watching the election results come in, and he would whinge about them even though he hadn't voted because he was British. It was his birth-right. It was his country.

At around midnight in a faded NHS hospital in northeast London one of the doctors called Sidney Pearl out into the corridor. David had been sitting up in bed, and seemed fine.

'So what is it with his liver that seems so serious?' Sidney asked, agitated.

The doctor, south Asian with a thick accent, said they could not be sure until all the tests were completed.

'But we think it is chronic hepatitis,' he said. 'Possibly he was infected by sharing needles. We're also testing for HIV and other possible diseases.'

'Will he ...'

'It can be treatable,' the doctor confirmed. 'Depending on which type. But it is very serious. His liver is not in a good condition. He is not in a good condition. His lifestyle ...'

'I see,' Sidney said, and then returned to his son's bedside, to concentrate on the only thing he cared about that election night which was the welfare of his child.

England, Various Locations

6 JULY 2005

The raids took place simultaneously across London and the north of England two months after the General Election, at four o'clock in the morning of 6 July 2005. More than a thousand police officers, most of them armed, from seven different forces, plus advisers from the Security Service, MI5, and with an undisclosed number of SAS soldiers in reserve, entered properties in Essex, Dewsbury, Salford, Bradford and London.

Talal's mother was awakened by the sound of her front door coming off its hinges. She blinked and sat up in bed in her darkened room, as armed police rushed up the stairs. A second later, or so it seemed, she was blinded by a bright light in her eyes. Fearful that she was about to be murdered, or robbed, or raped, or all three, she screamed for her son.

'Talal! Talal!'

Talal himself was in a very deep sleep. He had gone to bed at around two in the morning. When the front door crashed open Talal thought he was dreaming. He was aware of vague noises and then of his mother crying out his name in his dream.

'Talal! Talal!'

Suddenly the dream was over. His bedroom door cracked open and lashed back against his bed. Half a dozen bright lights were in his face. His mother continued to scream from her bedroom. Talal saw guns in his face as he was dragged from his bed on to the floor. He felt the thump on his back from a boot or a knee, and then his hands were pulled hard, his head bumping on the floor of the room. Plastic handcuffs were tightened around his wrists by unseen hands and he was picked up as if he weighed no more than a bag of potatoes and thrown back on the bed, face down. It seemed as if every light in the house was switched on, every light in the whole world had been illuminated, in a series of blinding flashes. There was someone speaking to him, reading something, in a monotone. Slowly Talal realized he was being told that he did not have to say anything, but that anything he did say might be taken down and used as evidence against him. He was being formally cautioned. The man reading him his rights said something about the Prevention of Terrorism Act. Talal tried to turn and get up from the bed but the plastic handcuffs bit into his wrists and something was also restraining him at the ankles.

'Let me up, fuck you,' he called out. He tried to kick up his feet, and as he did so he was pushed roughly down with the butt of a Heckler and Koch.

'Sit there, chummy. Move any more and I'll blow your fucking head off, y'got me?'

Talal said nothing.

'I said, did you understand?' The police officer jabbed him rhythmically in the back with each word. 'Blow – Your – Fucking – Head – Off.'

'N-Yes,' Talal murmured, his face down on the bedcovers. He understood.

At exactly the same time the police were smashing into Talal's house, two other squads entered Rafiq Chowdhury's home through the front and back doors simultaneously. The front door flew off its hinges and flattened into the hallway. The back door was held on by several bolts. It splintered roughly and it took a second attempt before it, too, fell inside. In all the confusion the first two officers who charged in at the front tumbled over the chaos in the hallway, the children's toys scattered everywhere like an obstacle course. They stomped on a plastic American police tricycle and a plastic fort, and cracked them apart, cursing. It was part of the mess which Rafiq always hated, and it was to cost him his life. The first police officer fell over the tricycle and thudded to the floor at the bottom of the stairs, blocking the way up.

'Fuck!'

The second officer fell over the first and tripped on top of him in a heap.

'Fuck!'

The men running in from the back door arrived at a bottle-neck of uniforms, bodies, flashlights and adrenalin. The fallen officers tried to get up, struggling in their body armour like monstrous and ungainly beetles, blocking the stairs.

'Officer down,' someone called out.

'Nobody shot!' countered another. 'Nobody shot!'

'Fuck!'

The noise and the swearing in the hallway awoke Rafiq, his wife and the baby in the crib beside their bed.

Rafiq called out loudly, 'What's that? Who ...?'

Rafiq grabbed the metal American baseball bat he kept beside the bed in case of intruders. He leapt towards the bedroom door, as the armed police officers at last reached the landing at the top of the stairs. What happened next is disputed. The official police version is that there was a sudden movement from the bedroom. There was certainly a noise like a loud crack, which some officers said they thought was gunfire. One officer fell down. Those behind believed the first officer had been shot. Rafiq's wife, Benazir, who was three months pregnant, said she could not tell exactly what was happening because the lights were so bright and there was so much noise.

She thought she saw Rafiq swing his baseball bat at the head of the first intruder, a policeman wearing a helmet and mask. Rafiq clipped the intruder hard and there was a sickening thud of metal on helmet, but Rafiq had no gun, Benazir said. He was merely defending himself and his wife and children from a home invasion by unidentified men in black. Benazir's immediate instinct was to grab her youngest child from the cot beside the marital bed and to flee, but in the darkness and confusion she left the baby and ran into the hallway behind Rafiq. That too was to prove a fatal mistake. Benazir Chowdhury later claimed that she and Rafiq did not – could not – know that the people who had burst into their house were police officers. Yes, they certainly did, said the official police report. From the moment the raid began people were yelling out: 'Armed police! Stand still! Armed police! Armed police!' Was there something about the words 'Armed police' that they didn't get? Were they deaf, or what? All of them?

What is not in dispute is that the leading armed police officer was severely concussed by a blow to the left side of his head. Despite his helmet, he immediately fell to the floor. He may have been unconscious for a few minutes. And it might have looked to the people behind him as if he had been shot. What is also not in dispute is that the second officer fired four shots in quick succession. Two shots went into the torso of Rafiq Chowdhury and one unzipped his skull, killing him instantly. The fourth bullet hit the crying child in the cot by the bed, and also proved fatal. Two other officers crashed into Benazir Chowdhury and threw her on the floor, causing severe bruising and a laceration of her left foot. Later that same day Benazir Chowdhury had a miscarriage. The coroner's report showed that the foetus suffered from a neural tube defect related to spina bifida and would almost certainly have been aborted naturally in the following two weeks, though this was later disputed by the family. Rafiq Chowdhury and his baby daughter were pronounced dead at the scene by paramedics. The official account showed two deaths, but the family counted the baby in the womb as a third fatality. There was much bitterness in the local Asian community at the deaths. An independent inquiry into the conduct of the police was launched. The Metropolitan Police issued a statement regretting the loss of all innocent life, but with the clear implication that at least one of the lives lost was not an innocent person. The local Respect party held a rally the following weekend in a park in Greenford calling for an end to what one speaker, Respect's newly elected west London MP, Don Flockart, called the officially sanctioned Massacre by the Nazi Stormtroopers of Blair's British Gestapo, otherwise known as the Metropolitan Police.

As the raids took place across England, the woman who called herself Polly Black sat in an unmarked police car outside Rafiq's house. When she heard the gunfire, she was startled, but not completely surprised. None of the intercepts had mentioned guns, but perhaps that was part of what the man who called himself 'Samir' meant by 'product'. Polly let out a long, slow breath. Her work was more or less complete, at least on this group. She had done her best. She did not know exactly what she had prevented, but her guess was that the cell including Rafiq and Talal had planned to blow up the Underground train at the stop in Heathrow's terminals 1, 2, and 3. It was the busiest Underground station in the busiest airport in Europe. Polly assumed they would use the explosives they had stockpiled in the garage at Boston Manor, though Co-Op Mix was difficult to use effectively and it required a very large volume of explosives to cause any significant damage. Polly never found out how Talal and Rafiq planned to transport the bomb. A large police van collected the green wheelie bins and their contents, plus the detonators, and a full forensic inquiry began.

Despite all her months in Arabic classes, Polly could not say what motivated people like Rafiq and Talal to hate the United Kingdom so much. After all, she thought, this country had given them every opportunity. It had given them everything, including the freedom to hate us. Why they chose the route of jihad remained a puzzle, especially since her Arabic teacher had repeatedly pointed out that the word 'jihad' was most often best translated to mean 'inner struggle' towards spiritual peace, and not – absolutely not – 'Holy War'. Now that this group was finished, Polly intended to return to her desk at MI5 and write her concluding intelligence report, and then switch her resources to other targets. One of those other targets was Mohammed Sidique Khan, the man from Leeds whom she thought was on the fringes of Rafiq and Talal's group. MSK, as he was known, had disappeared off the radar. It would be good to hear from him again, Polly thought. She'd get on to it when the paperwork on this lot had been completed.

At the time of the raids, four in the morning, Harry was asleep with Zumrut in his arms, snuggled deep in the double bed in the master bedroom in Hampstead. Late the previous night they sat together watching the news that London was to be awarded the chance to host the 2012 Olympics. It was a bit of a surprise. It called for a celebration.

That evening Harry produced a bottle of champagne from the fridge. Maya was out – she had been asked out on a date by Rajiv. It had been a funny moment. Rajiv had called Maya to ask her out to dinner, and she had accepted. Then he had asked to talk to Harry.

'Hi, Raj.'

'Harry,' Rajiv sounded nervous. 'I …'

'Yes?'

'I've just asked Maya out to dinner.'

Harry smiled.

'That's great, Raj.'

'You approve?'

Now Harry laughed.

'Are you asking my permission? It's not up to me to approve or not. If it's okay with Maya.'

'I ... that is ... well, I want it to be all right with you. I'm slightly more than twelve years older than Maya ...'

'Raj,' Harry said, 'Raj, will you shut the fuck up? You are embarrassing me. Of course it's all right. It's more than all right. Have fun.'

That night Harry poured the champagne and handed Zumrut a glass.

'Cheers,' she said, holding the glass towards him.

'Wait a minute,' Harry responded and put both glasses on the table. Then he got down on one knee.

'What on earth are you doing?' Zumrut giggled.

'Zumrut Ecevit, I love you very much,' Harry said. 'Will you marry me?'

Zumrut stared at him in disbelief. Tears came to her eyes unbidden.

'Will I ...?'

'Will you marry me,' Harry said. 'Marry me? You know, marry? Have a wedding? Stay together for ever and ever and be happy? Children, a home, the works. Things like that?'

'Yes,' Zumrut said eventually, when she had recovered from the shock, the tears trickling from her eyes. 'Yes I will marry you, Harry.'

The two of them drank their glasses of champagne and then began making telephone calls. Zumrut woke up her parents in Ankara, where it was already one o'clock in the morning. Harry called Amanda and then his father who was now at home in Tetbury. Robin Burnett had fully recovered from his suicide attempt and was spending every waking hour trying to complete the edited draft of his book. The publishers had offered a very large advance. Three national newspapers were engaged in a bidding war for the serialization rights.

The American publisher was confident there was the possibility of a Hollywood contract and a film.

'I have asked Zumrut to marry me,' Harry told his father. 'And she has said yes.'

It went very silent on the phone for a moment.

'Hello?' Harry said. 'Dad? You still there?'

There was a strange sound which might have been a sob.

'Yes, yes, Harry, I'm still here,' Robin Burnett said. 'It's just fantastic, absolutely fantastic news. I am so pleased for you. She's a wonderful woman. You are a lucky man. So very pleased.'

By this time Maya had returned to the flat with Rajiv. Harry told them the news, and handed them glasses of champagne. Maya bounced on her toes in delight, dancing with Zumrut and Harry, and dragging Rajiv into a kind of a jig in the kitchen. Maya then said she needed to call her mother in the United States. Leila was still at the studios. She had just finished reading the evening news. When Maya told her about Harry and Zumrut she burst into tears.

'Put him on,' Leila demanded. 'Harry! Harry! Congratulations. I am so pleased. That weirdest first date in the world you had with Zumrut seems to have worked out all right then?'

A little later Raj left and the others were preparing for bed when the telephone rang. It was Robin Burnett.

'I will come to London tomorrow,' he said. 'Early train. Let's all meet at Edgware Road. I know just the place – a little Lebanese coffee shop called The Cedars. Nine or nine thirty? Then we can talk and plan and go out to lunch and celebrate. I'll book a place in Covent Garden. My treat. To celebrate. Say yes?'

They made the arrangements. Edgware Road. Around nine in the morning. The morning of 7 July 2005. That night Harry and Zumrut made love and then went to sleep in each other's arms, betrothed. At four in the morning while the raids were beginning in London and the north of England they turned to snuggle into one another.

'I love you,' Harry told her.

'I love you, *bitanem*,' she responded.

Harry thought he had never been so happy.

London, 7 July 2005

At seven o'clock on the morning of the raids, Harry woke with Zumrut still snuggled into his arms. They had had very little sleep but awoke, elated.

'I love you, you know. I really do.'

It was a phrase which bore repetition. She rolled over and touched him. He stirred and was aroused.

'We're going to be late if we do that,' he said. 'We need to get up and go to meet dad. He'll be on the train.'

'You see?' she said to him with a sly grin. 'As soon as we decide to get married, the libido disappears. We've gone from young lovers to boring middle aged companionship overnight.'

'Yes, well, maybe,' he teased her. 'But you are only marrying me for British citizenship anyway, so you can stay here. Typical. There ought to be a law against it.'

'There is, *askim*,' she said with a laugh. 'Ask Raj for the details.'

They switched on the *Today* programme for the headlines at 7.30 a.m. as they made coffee and toast. The lead story was the news of the overnight anti-terrorist police raids, plus more reaction to the surprising win of the Olympic Games for 2012 for London. Most people had expected it would be Paris.

'We can go and watch the games,' Harry said, 'with our children.'

'Children!' Zumrut feigned alarm. 'More than one? Exactly how many?'

'Ten. And three dogs.'

The morning news said that in the anti-terrorist raids police had seized a large quantity of explosives and detonators in west London. One of the suspected terrorists had been shot dead. There was some kind of a row over a dead child, although the details were hazy. Properties in Greenford, Alperton and Boston Manor were sealed off. It wasn't clear if the alleged terrorists were foreigners or British.

'Oh, no, not a dead child,' Harry said. 'How could they be so ... careless?'

The radio suggested that one of the targets of the alleged terrorists was thought to be Heathrow airport.

'Obsessed with planes, Osama bin Laden, isn't he?' Harry said. 'Quite the little transport freak.'

'Modernity,' Zumrut said. 'Anything which brings people together causes him problems, though al Qaeda do use the internet. And they used mobile phones to set off the bombs in Atocha station in Madrid. They are a strange mixture of medieval morality and modern technology. It's difficult to get into their heads. Best not to try. At least the police caught these people before they could kill anyone.'

'Yeah, well let's hope so.'

'Is Maya coming with us this morning to see your father?'

Harry knocked on her bedroom door. Maya stirred but sounded very sleepy.

'Look, we'll call you later when you're awake,' Harry laughed, 'and you can meet us for lunch. And tell us what you really think of Raj.'

'Nggurgh.'

Harry looked at Zumrut.

'Young people of today, eh?'

They quickly ate breakfast. Harry checked his watch as they hurried to Hampstead Tube station, heading towards King's Cross. He hated the idea of keeping his father waiting. Increasingly he wanted to see him. He, Zumrut and Maya, had spent several weekends at the house in Tetbury, walking in the country and enjoying his father's company. Harry had read the manuscript of *A Scandalous Man* several times with a mixture of emotions – tears, anger, compassion, understanding, outrage and, eventually, something he would have called love. He had made some comments which his father had incorporated in the final draft.

July 7, 2005 was a warm and humid summer morning in London, with a hint of wind above ground, but the air in the Tube system seemed particularly stale. Harry and Zumrut changed from the Northern to the Circle line. It was shortly before nine o'clock, on the kind of day when Londoners really wished that the Tube trains were properly air-conditioned. Zumrut and Harry stood up in the crowded compartment at the peak of the morning rush hour. She leaned happily into the curve of his body, as the train rattled through the tunnels. Just as the train was about to stop at Edgware Road, Harry caught the eye of a young man in the compartment who reminded him of someone, but he could not think of whom. The young man was about twenty years old, with African features and the skin colour of someone who had mixed black and white parents. Tall, big, thickset, just like ... The name would not come, but the face was there, somewhere from his past, imprinted in Harry's brain. He had definitely seen this person before. If the young man recognized Harry he did not show it. Their eyes flickered over each other, locked for a second and passed on. The man had a rucksack, which made Harry think for a second of Rajiv. But there was something very strange about this young man. His face was wet with sweat. It was warm in the Tube, but not that warm, even without air-conditioning. The young man was extremely nervous, emotionally upset. Harry became uncomfortable and looked away. Suddenly there was a noise behind him. Harry and Zumrut both turned quickly. The young man was shouting familiar words in Arabic, 'Allahu Akhbar,' god is Great. Other people turned to stare at the eccentric passenger with the rucksack. Nobody said anything.

Nobody did anything. Nobody mobbed him or tried to get away. London Zen. Whatever was happening really was not happening if you pretended to look out of the window into the darkness. Just another morning with just another nutter in the London Tube in the rush-hour. Then the man called out again, 'Allahu Akhbar,' and he tugged hard at something in his sleeve. For a second it made Harry think of pictures he had seen of men leaping out of planes and pulling at the cord of a parachute. That instant Harry turned to look at Zumrut, and she at him. Their fingers intertwined. He saw her wide, beautiful brown eyes and the demure smile of his lover, his fiancée, the woman he would spend the rest of his life with. He turned back to look at the young man with a flush of realization. He knew exactly where he had seen the face before, but in the past it always glared at him from under a hoodie or a baseball cap.

It was Carlton.

Carlton from Fulham. Carlton with the cracked-up black father and broken-down white mother, Carlton who was yelling Allahu Akhbar, and tugging at something in his sleeve. There must have been an extraordinary noise as the bomb exploded. It tore the limbs and the heads from the bodies of those closest to the young man with the rucksack, and shattered torsos with shrapnel. Two hundred six-inch nails placed around the device flew in all directions, punching holes in the roof and the sides of the carriage, ripping it open like the serrations on a cheese grater, unzipping the skulls and chests of the passengers, stabbing at the seats and the floor, gouging the guts of the men and women in the train. There was a paradox here. The explosion was so loud, Harry was aware of no sound whatsoever. He experienced no violence. His last image was of the brown eyes of his beautiful Emerald, the Turkish woman he loved, and then a wave of white, enveloping him, and they were together. His last thought was of the words quoted by his father several times in his book, Layla and Majnun.

Two lovers lie in this one tomb
United forever in death's dark womb.
Faithful in separation, true in love:
May one tent house them in heaven above.

London

THE DAY OF THE LONDON BOMBINGS,
7/7/2005

The bomb that exploded in the second carriage of a west-bound Circle Line train killed six people, plus the bomber.

It was the second of three bombs timed to explode within seconds of each other on three separate London Underground trains shortly before nine o'clock on the morning of Thursday 7 July 2005 – a day Londoners were later to call 7/7, with all its echoes of America's 9/11. A fourth bomb exploded on a bus about an hour later.

The bomber on the Circle Line could have been Carlton, Harry Burnett's neighbour from Fulham. During a prison sentence for a series of robberies, Carlton had converted to Islam and had taken upon himself a new name and a new identity to go with his new religion. He called himself Faisal Islam. In fact the Circle Line bomber was not Carlton. It was of course Mohammed Sidique Khan, who was aged thirty. Around one hundred and twenty people were injured, some of them horrifically, in the attack. Mohammed Sidique Khan was the ringleader of the 7/7 bomb plot and he was also a key link with other plotters, some of whom were subsequently arrested. MSK, as the Security Service referred to him, was at the centre of a web of inter-linked conspirators, including those who were planning to blow up a London nightclub and the

Bluewater shopping centre. The plotters described the women who frequented the nightclub as 'slags'. This was a recurrent theme in their chatter about British society, an obsession with the drinking of alcohol and supposed sexual promiscuity of young British women.

The first bomb also exploded on the Circle Line. It was on an eastbound train in a tunnel between Liverpool Street and Aldgate. It killed seven people plus the bomber, Shehzad Tanweer. He was aged twenty-four, and from Leeds. One hundred people were injured, ten of them seriously.

At first it was thought the explosions might have been due to some kind of electrical fault underground. That was the first announcement made on the morning news bulletins. All public transport in London was immediately disrupted.

The third bomb exploded on a southbound Piccadilly Line train between King's Cross–St Pancras and Russell Square. This bomb killed twenty-six people, plus the bomber, Germaine Lindsay, who was of mixed race and aged nineteen. Lindsay was the only one of the plotters to have no direct family connection with Pakistan.

The fourth bomb detonated on a bus in Tavistock Square, near University College Hospital and the headquarters of the British Medical Association. The Number 30 double decker bus going to Hackney Wick had been diverted when roads were closed as an emergency measure after the Tube bombings an hour earlier. Thirteen people died on the bus, plus the bomber, Habib Hussain. He was the youngest of the killers that day, just eighteen years old.

That morning three of the bombers, the ones with the Pakistani family backgrounds, had travelled from the Beeston area of Leeds to King's Cross Station in London via Luton. They had met up with Germaine Lindsay on the way. Lindsay was of Jamaican descent. He lived in Aylesbury, Buckinghamshire. Lindsay's mother had converted to Islam in 2000 and he himself converted soon afterwards, taking the name 'Jamal'. He married a white British convert to Islam, Samantha Lewthwaite, whom he had met at a Stop the War rally.

Exactly two weeks later there was a similar – but ineffective – attack on London transport. The bomb plotters on this occasion were particularly incompetent and none of the devices detonated as they had planned.

The background of all the bomb plotters of 7/7, in Hannah Arendt's famous phrase about the Nazis, seemed to bear out the banality of evil.

Shehzad Tanweer was born in Bradford, in Yorkshire. He lived in Beeston where he was described by neighbours as a 'nice lad' who 'could get on with anyone'. His family owned that great traditional British institution, a fish and chip shop. Tanweer openly supported the al Qaeda attacks on the World Trade Centre in September 2001. He regarded the plane hijackers as 'martyrs'. He travelled to the Pakistani city of Karachi with Mohammed Sidique Khan in 2004, and had come to the attention of the British Security Service. Mohammed Sidique Khan, the ringleader, was the oldest member of the group. He was also raised in Beeston. He had become a youth worker and an assistant teacher at Hillside school. MSK had a reputation as a studious person and a steady worker. He visited the House of Commons at the invitation of the husband of the school's head-teacher who was a Member of Parliament. Khan was also known to MI5, but manpower difficulties meant officers assigned to investigate him were reassigned to what were thought to be more pressing duties. No one knows exactly why the bombers became bombers, though their radicalization came before the invasion of Iraq by British and American forces in 2003, not afterwards. One theory is that they first became involved in political activity in arguments with drug dealers from within the Pakistani community in their home area. They thought that the drug dealers were contaminating the morals of local Muslim youths, and they resisted.

Whatever their reasons, or supposed reasons, in total fifty-two innocent people were murdered in London on 7 July 2005. And because the attacks took place in London, because it was the rush hour, the dead included Christians, Jews, Muslims, those of other faiths, and those of no faith. The four bombers also died, bringing the total number of dead to fifty-six. It's thought that the bombers had links not just to the leadership of al Qaeda, but to other groups preparing acts of terrorism in Britain.

Immediately after the bombings some politicians speculated that there was a direct connection with British foreign policy, particularly the closeness between Tony Blair and George Bush over the Iraq war. There certainly was great resentment against British foreign policy in Iraq and Afghanistan, though this was not confined to the various Muslim communities of Britain. Former British jihadis, those young men who had been radicalized like Tanweer and MSK and who joined organizations such as al-Muhajiroun, later renounced the path of violence. Several former jihadis and their fellow travellers publicly admitted that even a full withdrawal of British and American forces from Iraq would not have stopped the bombings. The motivation was complex. It included a belief that Muslims around the world were being treated badly, and the wish to destroy the immorality of western life, including drinking alcohol, drug abuse and casual sex.

Robin Burnett's Story

28 JULY 2005

On the day of the bombings my train from Gloucester to Paddington was – unusually – on time. Even more unusual, I remember thinking, was the fact that I managed to get a seat, in a train carriage that wasn't grubby, and in which the windows had not been vandalized. I don't know why this was the case, or why these small things cheered me, but they did. I remember looking out of the window at the green fields and the cows and sheep, the chocolate box picture of bucolic English innocence. I took a deep breath and thought how I was glad to be alive. Glad to be alive and to be an Englishman. Suddenly, I had a lot to live for. My suicide attempt seemed like the doings of some poor deranged soul who had indeed died that day. I was born again in a secular sense. I was still alive, and glad of it. The depression – or whatever one must call it these days – had gone. I was thinking about the future, and I was full of a kind of hope and optimism I had not experienced since my first days in government almost thirty years ago.

Harry had called me the night before and told me about the wedding. I was watching a late night discussion on TV involving a couple of Games-Lovers who were delighted that London had won the Olympic Games. The programme editors had dragged out someone prepared to say she thought spending millions on a sporting event was a stupid idea. It was a fairly tepid discussion. Personally, I was pleased London won the Games. Blair had flown to Singapore for a bit of arm twisting and his presence had helped swing it. I was sure of that. Say what you will about Blair, he's an international superstar, he gets stuck in, and for that I admire him. He had then flown off to Gleneagles for the G8 summit in which he was about to end poverty in Africa, apparently. We were one of the richest countries in the world, and for all our faults, we were still one of the best. Zumrut, Harry's wonderful Turkish fiancée, had told me so. I thought to myself that I had learned more about the good things in Britain in the few short weeks I'd known her than I learned in all my years in parliament. She talked to me endlessly about the strengths of our parliamentary debates, and the scrutiny of our aggressive media. I confess I did not always see it her way, but perhaps a foreigner's eyes can notice things a native takes for granted. I could also see why Harry had fallen in love with her. They were good together.

After Harry called me to say he was to get married I immediately called Leila. She had already heard the news a few minutes before from Maya and had just recovered from some happy tears when my call made her cry again. Leila and I had talked every day since I got out of hospital and every conversation made me realize that I had never stopped loving her.

We spoke of how we were too old for hatred and bitterness. Harry had told me that Amanda frequently lectured him that hatred corrodes the vessel in which it is contained. Harry admitted that he had been corroded by his own hatred for me, and it was time for it to stop.

'My hatred was more damaging to me than anything that you actually did,' he told me. I thought it took courage to say so. He read the draft of my book and made some suggestions. 'You were right to say that to understand is to forgive,' he also told me. 'I had no idea what it might have been like for you. I had no wish to imagine it.'

Flooded by Harry and Amanda's forgiveness, I could hardly then pursue a different course with any of those who had caused me problems. With Leila it was easy. I had felt so utterly betrayed when Hickox told me about her, as if the one rock on which I had built years of my life had crumbled into dust. I loved her. I always loved her. And love always implies a degree of risk. She had disappointed me more than anyone had ever disappointed me in my life before. I did not know how to handle it and instead I chose the coward's way of pills and a knife, whisky and suicide. I regret it, but there you are. It's over now.

In the weeks of my recovery I realized how strong Leila was and I believe I came to love her even more. I began to think of the past from her point of view. Isn't that the point? Any story, any narrative, is like a polished diamond. You see the whole, sparkling thing – but it only really makes sense when you understand that each facet of the diamond is a different way of looking at the same thing. Leila and me. Me and Harry. Maya and Harry. Different facets to the same diamond, different points of view. And so I came to see things as Leila must have seen them – a young, talented, woman in her thirties, attached to a married man with two children. She gets pregnant and knows that the man has not left his wife, indeed he shows no signs of doing so. How should she handle it? A coward like me might have opted for the pills and whisky route, but not Leila. How I must have disappointed her then. And yet she calmly walked out of my life and made a success of her own life with Maya in Washington and then New York. I admire her more than I can say.

'So you forgive me?' she asked me a couple of nights after I left the hospital. I was home alone in Tetbury and waiting for Harry and Zumrut and Maya to come down for the weekend. All in all I was feeling rather chipper.

'There is nothing to forgive,' I responded. 'Do you forgive me?'

She laughed.

'Of course. There is nothing to forgive on either side. We're still talking, aren't we?'

Oh yes, I thought, we are still talking. We always talk.

'After your divorce…?' I began, in one of our other conversations. 'What will happen?'

'Ah,' she said. 'Frank is making things easy. It will come as soon as possible.'

'And after …?' I persisted.

'After, well, then we'll see. What are you suggesting?'

I did not know exactly what I was suggesting.

'Our marriages so far have ended in failure, Leila,' I said. 'Yours to Frank. Mine to Elizabeth. It's not a good record. And yet I think you and I might spend some time together. See how it goes.'

Leila said she would think about it.

'See how it goes,' she repeated. 'I can handle that. When Maya starts Princeton in the fall you could come over to New York for a while. Stay with me. Be a kept man. My sex slave.'

Now I laughed.

'I am a little old to be your Pool Boy,' I said.

'I don't have a pool,' Leila told me. 'You'll just have to be my IFB.'

I had never heard these initials before and asked her what they meant.

'Slang from Maya's friends,' Leila told me. 'It means Intellectual Fuck Buddy. Not someone you love, just someone whose company you … enjoy.'

I told Leila I would look forward to being her IFB.

That night three weeks ago, the night before the London bombings, the night London was awarded the 2012 Olympics, the night when Blair was solving the problems of Africa at Gleneagles, that night when Harry and Zumrut told me of their wedding, I confess I cried too. Harry had got it all worked out. He said they were planning a civil ceremony in Turkey – in Istanbul – with a big party organized by Zumrut's parents. Then everyone who wanted to do so was to be invited to a blessing at the Temple of Aphrodite near Datcha. Zumrut's father was something to do with the Department of Antiquities in Istanbul or Ankara or someplace, and he thought he could swing it. I had no idea where Datcha was, but it sounded a lovely, romantic idea. The Temple of Aphrodite. The Goddess of Love. Harry asked me if I could find a Christian minister who would be prepared to go there and perform a blessing, if the necessary permission was forthcoming from the Turkish authorities. I said I didn't know, but I would try. There was my local vicar in Tetbury, of course, who I am sure would oblige, for the chance to walk over Greek ruins to perform a Christian blessing for a Muslim family. It cheered me up just to say it like that.

That night Leila and I talked until late. One of my favourite Spanish songs has the refrain 'Con los anõs que me quedan por vivir, demonstraré cuanto te quiero.' It means literally: with the years remaining to me to live, I will show you how much I love you. I told Leila that it was something we could try. She said she was willing to see where it got us, but with no promises, and no strings.

'We are old enough to understand it is better to go slowly,' she said.

I liked the sound of that too.

Love, I had decided, never really dies. It is like a fire which may fall back into greyness and embers, but given the right opportunity, it can light up again. It had done so for Leila and me that night of the 6th July 2005. I went to sleep around two in the morning. I do not need much sleep nowadays. I set my alarm for the early train. Just a couple of hours' in bed, but I could manage. I could always manage.

On the day of the London bombings I was sitting in The Cedars reading a copy of *The Times* by 9.00 a.m. feeling a strange wave of nostalgia. The café had been updated, of course, all Bauhaus now, with square chairs and a zinc coffee bar. *The Times* had also been updated. In my grumpy old man stage of life I tend to think most British newspapers are tabloid comics with no real news, but there you are. Changing fashions, changing culture. I suppose the real question for the newspaper proprietors is survival in the internet age. Fortunately the waiters in The Cedars have not been updated. They were the usual mix of delightful Maronites who wanted to talk about the plight of Lebanon and the wickedness of its neighbours. I was sitting drinking a cappuccino shortly after nine o'clock when I first became aware that something terrible was happening underground. I heard a rumbling, but you often hear rumbling noises in central London. Then I saw people spilling out of Edgware Road Tube with black grime on their faces, coughing and spluttering. The Lebanese waiters from the café came outside with me to see if we could help in anyway.

'What happened?' one of the waiters asked.

'Dunno, mate,' an exhausted looking commuter responded. 'Some kind of bang. Explosion. Then it all went pear-shaped.'

The first people out were quickly followed by those who had been cut or injured. That was when we all started to feel a degree of panic.

I saw one man with a nail sticking out of the side of his head, though he was able to walk. It was a bizarre sight. He was middle aged, perhaps fifty, balding, well dressed in a dark business suit, not stained with grime and blood. He appeared normal in every way except for the nail in the side of his head, like some kind of Magritte painting of a Surrealist hell. There was the wail of sirens and the first of the ambulances, police cars and fire brigade units started to arrive. The police began to clear the area.

'But my son!' I protested. 'My son and his fiancée! They are ...'

'I am sure they are fine, sir. Now please move along and don't make my job any more difficult.'

And so I moved along. It was a very strange scene. The police were polite, but insistent. I thought of how Harry's beautiful fiancée Zumrut had kept telling me how helpful the British police were, how they never stopped you for a bribe, never harassed her.

'Your British police act as if I am paying their salary, and I am the boss,' she told me. 'The Turkish police are sometimes like that, but often they act as if they are the bosses. You are very lucky.'

I thought she was sometimes a little rosy in her view of the British police. I would have liked to discuss with her the events of a week ago when the fine and upstanding British police shot dead a Brazilian man in mistake for a bomber, but of course, that discussion is no longer possible. Well, to return to the point. On that day, on 7/7, I allowed myself to be cleared away and stood a few hundred metres from the Tube station until the television crews arrived and I watched dozens of survivors from the blast mill around wearing blankets draped across their shoulders, like a scene from a refugee camp in Africa. I soon realized there was no point standing there any more. I called Harry's mobile number but got nothing. I called Maya at home in Hampstead and she sounded drowsy. Still asleep.

'Late night,' she explained. Maya confirmed that Zumrut and Harry had left to come to meet me in The Cedars and that she was planning to meet all of us for lunch.

'No, don't,' I told her very firmly. 'Whatever you do, stay at home today. Stay in Hampstead. Don't come into the centre. Don't go to SOAS. It is absolute chaos here. Absolute chaos.'

Eventually I called the emergency hotline number and the police were kind and took my details and said they would check if anyone answering my son's description had been admitted to hospital. It was a full ninety-six hours before I had it confirmed that Harry and Zumrut were among the dead in the tunnel. They were identified by their dental records. There was not much left of them, I am sorry to say.

That night I watched on television as one anti-war MP, that viper Flockart, lectured us all that the attacks on London were payback for British support for the war in Iraq. Payback? To murder Harry? And his lovely Turkish fiancée? And fifty other people who happened to be Christian, Muslim, Jewish, Sikh, Hindu, of all faiths and of none? I was so angry, if that particular reptile of a supposed Member of Parliament had been near to me I would have cheerfully strangled him. Besides, how did he know what the motives of the bombers really were? How did any of us know? What made my gorge rise was that he was making excuses for evil, like saying a woman with a short skirt deserved to be raped, or that the Jews deserved *Kristallnacht*. God, how I despise people like that.

The following day Leila flew over from New York. I was staying with Maya in the apartment in Hampstead. We were together in our grief, still waiting for the authorities to confirm that Harry and Zumrut were dead, but without hope of any other outcome. Amanda joined us. So for a time did Sidney Pearl. He told me the full story about his sons. One – the younger one – had died the previous month after a long battle with drugs. Apparently in the end it was pneumonia that killed him but he also had hepatitis C and all kinds of self-inflicted horrors. The other boy, the older one, had sobered up long ago and emigrated to Israel where he was making a name for himself running a small business for tourists and a nightclub. I offered Sidney my condolences for one boy, and my congratulations for the other. It made me think that parenthood, however we try to manage it, is simply a kind of lottery. You never know what might be ahead of you. Ever. One day you wake up and find out your only son has been murdered by a suicide bomber. One day you wake up and find that your only son *is* a suicide bomber.

Zumrut's parents came over from Turkey. I offered to put them up in Hampstead but they accepted hospitality instead from the Turkish embassy. We contrived to help them as best we could but they seemed, frankly, at even more of a loss than I have been. Their darling daughter, researching the impact of the collapse of the Ottoman Empire on the Middle East in the twenty-first century, had been snatched from them in the great and supposedly peaceful city of London. I did not know what to say to them. The first time we met I remember putting my arms around them and weeping.

Now today, three weeks later, here we are waiting for the authorities to release the bodies for burial. In truth we all know that we are taking part in a convenient but necessary charade. The burial we have will be purely a symbolic closure, a gesture. There are no bodies. There are only ashes. I have opted to cremate Harry's remains because ... because they are cremated already. It will be good enough. Zumrut's family are still here, still heartbroken, god bless them. I feel so sorry for them in their grief. They had gone from absolute joy at the news of the wedding of their daughter to absolute and catastrophic despair within a few hours. It made me think of the way all of London had done the same emotional *volte face* in the 24 hours after the Olympics had been announced. The entire city had cheered the news that we had won the 2012 Games, and then the following day we were down in Hades excavating the bodies of our children from underground tunnels, while being lectured by a leprous Member of Parliament that it was all our fault, it was retribution for our manifest sins.

Today Zumrut's family invited me to go to Turkey. I talked to Leila and we promised we would go. We can stay with them in Istanbul, and meet their other three children, two boys and a girl. I said we would also like to travel to this place called Datcha and visit the Temple of Aphrodite. The Ecevits said they would be delighted to take us. Apparently it is at the end of a rather nasty cliff road, but you can take a boat trip along the coast. The site is magnificent.

'All the best Greek sites are in Turkey,' Mr Ecevit joked with me. 'Side, Aspendos, the Temple of Aphrodite.'

Leila and I promised to travel there next summer, perhaps at the anniversary of the bombing. In a way it would be more fitting to remember Zumrut and Harry where they planned to have their marriage blessed, rather than here in London. We shall see. One day at a time.

Leila told me she will come back to London for the funeral whenever I manage to get it arranged. Then I will return with her and Maya to New York. The manuscript of the book is completed and the publishers on both sides of the Atlantic say they are happy. The BBC and Film Four are showing an interest, so even if the Hollywood route does not lead anywhere, it looks as if a film will be made of what Harry called the 'roots of our current predicament'.

Despite everything, I remain hopeful that the book will have some kind of impact. People here are interested. I have appeared on television two or three times since the bombings to speak on behalf of the bereaved, and to correct those with the misguided impression this was somehow 'payback' for British policy. I debated with Flockart and I think I made a mess out of him, though he is so self-absorbed he probably did not notice. As Berthold Brecht says, *Der Furz hat keine Nase* – a fart has no nose.

Leila's name opens so many doors in the United States, there is even greater interest in the book over there. We'll see. For my part, despite the terrible things that have happened in the past month I have a sense of relief at being able to confront the truth for the first time in years. Everything in the book is true, or as close to the truth as I can manage to get it. The only deliberate omission is the nature of Leila's employment with the US government. I do not think it would be helpful to dwell on that.

The publisher in New York has one quibble, which I will try to sort out when I get over there with Leila. He would also like me to add an extra chapter about the neo-conservatives. In particular I think he wants me to dish the dirt on the former Vice President David Hickox. I will tell him that I am not going to do that. Hickox will tell his own story. He made many mistakes, but then so did I. His biggest weakness was that as a hugely patriotic American he really could not understand that other people in other countries would be patriotic about their little part of the world too. Ah, well. Perhaps Hickox is re-assessing his own life as I have re-assessed mine.

We have arranged to meet in New York, Hickox and me. When he heard about the death of Harry, he called me immediately. It was not a difficult conversation. I was pleased that he called. He let slip that it really was true that his political ambitions have not completely died. He said he was thinking of running for the Republican nomination in 2008 after all. His heart is better, he said. A miracle cure. Apparently there are two views in the Republican party: that Iraq was a disaster because it was always going to be a disaster, and the other view which Hickox has made his own – that Iraq was a disaster because it was not prosecuted with enough enthusiasm and vigour. Hickox would certainly be the Enthusiasm and Vigour candidate. However much I try to despise him, I can't. I also have spent a bit of time with a friend of Harry, Maya and Zumrut – a delightful Asian lawyer called Rajiv Khan. Harry, apparently, had asked Rajiv to be his best man – and Rajiv has been dating Maya, though personally I think she is too young to consider anything of a serious nature. Shut up, gramps, as she tells me. And on this matter I will shut up.

I told Rajiv about my book, in a moment of unusual candour, and he promised to read it through for me and give me his opinion before publication. I like him a lot. He is doing good work for asylum seekers and refugees. He says that apathy is immoral and I agree with him. He has asked me if I would be prepared to campaign politically for asylum seekers. He says that as an ex Conservative minister, whose son was murdered in a terrorist bombing, I would carry considerable moral authority. People will listen to me. How strange, but I suppose he is correct. My suffering and my mistakes have given me an audience. I have told Raj I will think about how best I can help. But the offer cheered me. I believe there may be some fight left in me after all. I might yet be able to make a difference, as Hickox would put it.

My literary agent has advised that I accept a ludicrous amount of money in serialization rights for *A Scandalous Man* from a newspaper. I have not yet done so, but I suspect I will, despite my reservations. My agent also forwarded me a passage from George Orwell in his novel *1984*. He said he thought I might find it appropriate, and that selling the serialization rights would amount to 'a kind of evangelism – keeping shit out of the newspapers.' At first I did not know what he meant. We had been talking over lunch about how in Britain there are plenty of scandals but – like my own downfall and that of countless others – the supposed scandals always involve trivial and personal matters. The real scandals never make it to the newspapers. The supposed 'investigative reporters' are interested only in the bedroom, and only rarely venture into the boardroom or the Cabinet room. Pity.

Maya has been showing me how to do a Wikipedia search of my own name. It was an illuminating experience. My few weeks of sex with Carla Carter were clipped to my name like a tattoo or a body piercing. There was little room for anything else. Having sex with Carla, perhaps forty or fifty times, is my place in British political history, apparently. No one, thus far until the book is published next spring, knows anything of my true relationship with Leila, or about the beautiful child we have produced. No one knows what we did throughout the eighties in Iraq and Iran, although everybody is still living with the consequences. By my count it amounts to three wars in total in Iraq and a fourth in Afghanistan. That would add up to perhaps two million dead. Probably more. Perhaps I am glad that Wikipedia chooses to focus on Carla instead. My conscience squirms with guilt, but the book will be my expiation. The quotation my agent sent me from Orwell in *1984* will form part of the dedication to the fallen, to the innocent victims of our stupidity and malice and benighted self-interest. It seems most apt. Orwell's book is remembered for the idea that our political culture was doomed. Big Brother would, by 1984, lord it over us, and we would live in a dictatorship of the mind and the spirit.

Curiously – thankfully – wonderfully – as Zumrut kept telling me, our British democracy has proved resistant to totalitarianism. But my agent forced on me an overlooked passage about our newspapers and popular culture.

'*And the Records Department,*' Winston Smith says, '*after all, was itself only a single branch of the Ministry of Truth whose primary job was not to reconstruct the past but to supply the citizens of Oceania with newspapers, films, textbooks, telescreen programmes, plays, novels … Here we produced rubbishy newspapers containing almost nothing except sport, crime and astrology, sensational five cent novelettes, films oozing with sex, and sentimental songs which were composed entirely by mechanical means …*'

I read and re-read Orwell's words, and I laughed out loud – a bitter nasty, gut-wrenching laugh. It was the first time I had laughed since Harry and Zumrut died in the tunnel. I laughed because I realized that Orwell was wrong about the politics of the future. We have not completely defeated the totalitarian spirit, but in most countries it is on the run. It is yesterday's bad idea. Democracy – flawed and sometimes awful and corrupt – is the success story at the end of the twentieth century and the beginning of the twenty-first. But Orwell writing in 1948 was absolutely right about our popular culture in the twenty-first century. Our newspapers are full of sport, crime and astrology, nothing much more. Big Brother used to be a political bogeyman, now it is merely the name of a shitty television programme featuring people I would not wish to sit near in the Tube. I open my newspaper and I read reports about people I have never heard of, who have never achieved anything, except to behave badly and then to appear in the newspapers regretting their exploits. It seems very odd, or perhaps I am just very old.

I do, however, feel my strength returning. I do believe there are enough good people in this country who wish to turn things around and to get at the truth. I am going to make as big a fuss as possible with the book, and annoy as many people as possible. With luck I will make some people very uncomfortable indeed, including – no doubt – David Hickox. Hickox will forgive me. He understands that it is strictly business. Leila says there are no second acts in public life, but perhaps I may yet prove her wrong. We shall see.

I have decided to get back in the ring. I will work with my new friend Rajiv Khan to do something to better the lot of the asylum seekers and illegal immigrants, the new wretched of the earth.

The gunshot of August 1914 when Gavrilo Princip killed the Archduke Franz Ferdinand led to two World Wars and the Cold War. The mess did not end until 1989. It took three generations, and it ruined the lives of millions in the twentieth century. Our own mess started in 1979, and it could easily drag on for more than three generations, ruining the lives of millions more in the twenty first. For my part, I have decided that I am going to expose everything that we have done, every dirty trick, every double deal, every shady agreement, in the hope that truth and light will be the best disinfectants against the virus that we have helped create and which may yet destroy us.

I believe that the good within us will triumph, but then, I always was the optimist.

Of course I am angry. Angrier than I have ever been. I am angry that the biggest decisions in our lives are taken for us by people who never listen, angry that supposedly democratic power has become a game for a small club, an elite whose identities keep changing but whose interests never do, angry at the incompetence and arrogance of those who seek power – and I was one of them – by wanting to make a difference and then end up being hooked on the crack cocaine of ambition and self-interest.

So I am resolved that I will make big trouble. The real scandal would be to do nothing.

Harry would expect no less of me. I think I might yet make him proud. Harry told me once that he knew that I was not really there for him in the beginning. But I am there for him at the end.

The Whisperer

Word reaches The Whisperer that disgraced former Thatcher Minister Robin Burnett is planning a comeback – AS A SUPPORTER OF ILLEGAL ASYLUM SEEKERS! The Top Tory, aged 64, fell from grace after frolicking with lingerie lovely Carla Carter (PICTURED). Burnett, The Whisperer has learned, is planning to publish his kiss-n-tell memoirs with the title A Scandalous Man. Now he has taken up a job with a charity aimed at making it even easier for illegal foreigners to come to Britain! A friend says Burnett must be hard up to put pen to paper since he has always refused to talk about his cavortings with sexy Carla. The Whisperer reckons that few may care to read his warmed-over account of a sex scandal long, long ago. It all comes after the tragic loss of his son, Harry, in the London bombings in July following Harry Burnett's crazed attack on The Whisperer in April. As 66-year-old Robin Burnett lay in hospital recovering from his suicide attempt, The Whisperer understands he was comforted by his newest best friend top American newsreader Leila Rajar. (PICTURED). Strange but true. The Whisperer will be first with the latest. As per usual.

Author Note

The central characters in this book are all invented, but many of the events are real.

British and American dealings with Iran and Iraq since 1979 have demonstrated the kinds of activities I have outlined in *A Scandalous Man*, although my account is fiction. Many of the real incidents are already in the public domain.

Those interested in further reading will find *The Scott Report* on dealings with Iraq worth a look, and also the voluminous coverage of the Iran-Contra affair (sometimes called Irangate.) I can specifically recommend the report of the counsel Lawrence Walsh, plus extensive and entertaining accounts of the role of Colonel Oliver North. I was privileged to report on the Iran Contra scandal for the BBC, and to meet many of the key players. They told me they believed they were acting in the best interests of their country.

Children of Freedom

Marc Levy

Freedom knows no boundaries.

France 1943. Hundreds of thousands of people are left bereft of family and home by the German occupation. But Jeannot and his little brother Claude, along with their friends are different – they are young, their parents came to France from elsewhere, they are passionately committed to the fight for freedom.

The group become partisans, tackling the Germans and their French supporters in every way they can: their strong bond of friendship supports them in the face of terrible danger and fear and their growing up, their forbidden love, continues even under the dark shadows of betrayal, deportation and death.

Marc Levy's *Children of Freedom*, a bestseller all over Europe, is a remarkable book. Moving, dramatic, and based on true stories, it also celebrates the importance of standing up for your beliefs, as relevant now as then.

ISBN 978 000 7274956

Dreams of Water

Nada Awar Jarrar

'Twenty years ago, when civil war broke out in Lebanon, Nada Awar Jarrar was forced to flee with her family. Her novel *Dreams of Water* recasts this experience in a tale about a family whose son goes missing in war-ravaged Beirut' *Vogue*

As a young man disappears, his family is left fearing for what may have become of him. Aneesa, his sister, unable to live in the vacuum left by his disappearance, leaves her home and all she holds dear. She moves to London seeking a new life and there meets another exile who reminds her of home. Brought together by their shared feeling for their homeland, they form an unlikely friendship.

Meanwhile, back in Lebanon, Aneesa's mother is grieving for her son, her life devastated by his loss. Aneesa reluctantly returns home, determined to uncover the truth behind her brother's disappearance, and rekindle the sense of belonging that she left behind.

'A slow-burning, powerful story of loss and grief' *Good Housekeeping*

'The beauty of this novel lies in its images which are vivid and strange, sometimes even fantastical ... There is comfort in reading about characters, all of whom are withdrawn and inhibited, yet who are shown as capable of great tenderness.' *Times Literary Supplement*

ISBN 978 000 7221967

Souls of Angels

Thomas Eidson

Sister Ria made a promise on her mother's deathbed that she would care for her wayward father. And, when he is charged with the murder of a prostitute, she is called upon to act on her word. Reluctantly she returns to the town of her childhood, and to her father's home hoping to reconcile herself with her past and to prove his innocence.

But, with only eight days until his execution, she finds herself being hunted by a shadowy figure, a sinister person who has killed before and is capable of doing so again. She must draw on her faith and appeal to God to protect her and aid her in her quest for answers. Beautifully drawn and cleverly realised, *Souls of Angels* is a book to savour.

ISBN 978 000 7181759